Did I Mention I Need You?

Estelle Maskame started writing at the age of thirteen and completed her DIMILY trilogy when she was sixteen. She has already built an extensive and loyal fanbase for her writing around the world by sharing her work in instalments on the digital platform Wattpad. Book 3 in the DIMILY trilogy will be published soon.

Praise for *Did I Mention I Need You?*

"I loved every page of it."

– So Little Time For Books blog

"Definitely a 5/5 must-read. It is so addictive."

– TeenBookHoots

"Be prepared for the day to be a complete write-off when you pick up this book because you›re not going to put it down no matter what's on your to-do list. It is so much fun to read."

– The Mile Long Bookshelf

"I loved it even more than I loved DIMILY."

– Queen of Contemporary

"There is nothing like this series currently. It is truly addictive."

– Never Judge a Book By Its Cover

Did I Mention I Need You?

ESTELLE MASKAME

HARPER

First published in India in 2015 by Harper
An imprint of HarperCollins *Publishers*

4th Floor, Tower A, Building No. 10, Phase II,
DLF Cyber City, Gurugram, Haryana -122002
www.harpercollins.co.in

P-ISBN: 978-93-5177-712-0
E-ISBN: 978-93-5177-713-7

2 4 6 8 10 9 7 5 3 1

First published by Black & White Publishing Ltd, UK

Typeset in 11/14.75 Plantin MT Std by
Iolaire Typesetting, Newtonmore

Printed and bound at
Manipal Technologies Limited, Manipal

To those who told me I couldn't,
and to those who told me I could.

1

Three hundred and fifty-nine days.

That's how long I've been waiting for this.

That's how many days I've counted down.

It's been three hundred and fifty-nine days since I last saw him.

Gucci paws at my leg as I lean against my suitcase, fizzing with nervous excitement as I stare out the living room window. It's almost 6AM, and outside the sun has just risen. I watched it filter through the darkness twenty minutes ago, admiring how beautiful the avenue looked and the way the sunlight bounced from the cars lining the sidewalk. Dean should be pulling up any second.

I drop my eyes to the huge German Shepherd by my feet. Leaning down, I rub behind her ears until she turns and pads her way into the kitchen. All I can do is gaze out the window again, mentally running through a list of everything I packed, but it only stresses me out and I end up sliding off my suitcase and zipping it open instead. I rummage through the pile of shorts, the pairs of Converse, the collection of bracelets.

"Eden, trust me, you've got everything you need."

My hands stop shifting through my clothes and I look up.

Mom's standing in the kitchen in her robe, staring over the counter at me with her arms folded across her chest. She has the same expression she's been wearing for a week straight now. Half upset, half annoyed.

I sigh and shove everything tightly into the suitcase again as I close it back up and set it on its wheels. I get to my feet. "I'm just nervous."

I don't quite know how to describe the way I'm feeling. There are nerves, of course, because I have no idea what to expect. Three hundred and fifty-nine days is a long time for things to change. Everything could be different. So I am also terrified. I'm terrified that things won't be different. I'm scared that the second I see him, everything will come rushing back. That's the thing about distance: It either gives you time to move on from someone, or it makes you realize just how much you need them.

And right now, I have no idea if I simply miss my stepbrother or if I miss the person I was in love with. It's hard to tell the difference. They're the same person.

"Don't be," Mom says. "There's nothing to be nervous about." She walks over into the living room, Gucci bouncing behind her, and she squints out the window before sitting down on the arm of the couch. "When's Dean coming?"

"Now," I say quietly.

"Well, I hope you get stuck in traffic and that you miss your flight."

I grit my teeth and turn to the side. Mom's been against this whole idea since the moment I mentioned it to her. She doesn't want to waste a single day, and apparently leaving for six weeks is exactly that: wasted time. It's our last few months together before I move to Chicago in the fall. For her, this translates into the last time she'll see me. Ever. Which is totally not true. Once finals wrap up, I'll be home again next summer.

"Are you really that pessimistic?"

Mom finally cracks a smile. "Not pessimistic, just jealous and a little selfish."

Right then I hear the sound of a car engine. I know it's Dean before I even look, and the soft purr fades into silence as the car pulls up on the driveway. Jack, my mom's boyfriend, has parked his truck further up, so I crane my neck to get a better view.

Dean's pushing open the door of his car and stepping out, but his movements are slow and his face is blank, like he doesn't want to be here. This doesn't surprise me in the slightest. Last night his replies were blunt and he spent the evening mostly looking at his phone, and when I left his house he didn't walk me out to my car like he normally does. Just like Mom, he's a little pissed off with me.

A lump grows in my throat and I try to swallow it down as I pull out the handle of my suitcase. I wheel it toward the front door but then pause to fix Mom with an anxious frown. It's finally time to leave for the airport.

Dean doesn't knock before he enters the house. He never does; he doesn't have to. But the door swings open slower than usual before he steps into the house, looking tired. "Morning."

"Morning, Dean," Mom says. Her small smile becomes a much wider grin as she reaches out to gently squeeze his arm. "She's ready to go."

Dean's dark eyes flash over to meet mine. Normally he smiles when he sees me, but this morning his expression is neutral. He does, however, raise his eyebrows at me, as though to ask, "Well, are you?"

"Hey," I say, and I'm so nervous that it comes out sounding weak and pathetic. I glance down at my suitcase and then back up to Dean. "Thanks for doing this on your day off."

"Don't remind me," he says, but he's starting to smile and it puts me at ease. Stepping forward, he takes my suitcase from me. "I could be in bed right now, sleeping until noon."

"You're too good to me." I move closer to him and wrap my arms around his body, burying my face into his shirt while he laughs and squeezes me back. I tilt my face up to look at him from beneath my eyelashes. "Seriously."

"Aw," Mom coos from beside us, and it makes me realize that she's still in the room. "You two are so cute."

I shoot her a warning glance before looking back to Dean. "And that is our cue to leave."

"No, no, listen to me first." Mom stands and her brief smile quickly disappears, a disapproving frown taking its place. I fear that when I come home this frown of hers will have become permanent. "Don't go on the subway. Don't speak to strangers. Don't step foot in the Bronx. Also, please come home alive."

My eyes roll to the back of my head. I received a similar lecture exactly two years ago when I was leaving for California to reconnect with Dad, only then the warnings were mostly about him. "I know," I say. "Basically, just don't do anything stupid."

She looks at me hard. "Exactly."

I let go of Dean's arm and step toward her, wrapping my arms around her. Hugging her will shut her up. It always does. She squeezes me tightly and sighs against my neck. "I'll miss you," I murmur, but it's muffled.

"And you sure as hell know I'm going to miss you too,"

she says as she pulls away from me, her hands still on my shoulders. She glances at the clock on the kitchen wall before gently pushing me back toward Dean. "You better get going. You don't want to miss your flight."

"Yeah, we better head off," Dean says. He swings open the front door and rolls my suitcase over the threshold, pausing. Perhaps it's to see if my mom has any more unnecessary words of advice for me before I leave. Thankfully, she doesn't.

I grab my backpack from the couch and follow Dean outside, but not without turning back around to offer Mom one final wave. "I guess I'll see you in six weeks."

"Stop reminding me," she says, and with that, she promptly slams the front door. I roll my eyes and make my way across the lawn. She'll come around. Eventually.

"Well," Dean calls over his shoulder as I follow him to his car, "at least I'm not the only one who's being left behind."

I squeeze my eyes shut and run a hand through my hair, lingering by the passenger door as he throws my suitcase into the trunk. "Dean, please don't start."

"But it's not fair," he mutters. We slide into the vehicle at the exact same time, and the moment he gets his door shut, he lets out a groan. "Why the hell do you have to leave?"

"It's really not that big of a deal," I say, because I really don't see what the problem is. Both he and Mom have disapproved of New York since the second I mentioned it to them. It's as though they think I'll never come home again. "It's just a trip."

"A trip?" Dean scoffs. Despite his foul mood, he manages to start up the engine and get me on my way, backing out onto the street and heading southbound. "You're leaving for six weeks. You come home for a month and then you move to Chicago. All I'm getting is five weeks with you. It's not enough."

"Yeah, but we'll make the best of those five weeks." I know that anything I say won't help the situation in the slightest, because this moment has been building up for several months now, and finally Dean is putting everything out in the open. I've been waiting for this to happen for a while now.

"That's not the point, Eden," he snaps, and it momentarily silences me. Although I was expecting this, it's still odd seeing Dean aggravated. We rarely argue, because we've never disagreed on anything until now.

"Then what is?"

"The fact that you chose to spend six weeks over there instead of being with me," he says, but his voice has suddenly grown a lot quieter. "Is New York really that great? Who the hell needs six weeks in New York? Why not just one?"

"Because he invited me out for six," I admit. Maybe six weeks is a long time, but back when I agreed to it, it seemed like the best idea in the world.

"Why couldn't you compromise?" He's getting more riled up each second and he moves his hands in sync with his words, which results in some rough steering. "Why couldn't you just say, 'Hey, sure, I'll come, but only for two weeks,' huh?"

I fold my arms across my chest and turn away from him, glaring out the window. "Okay, chill out. Rachael hasn't complained once about me leaving. Why can't you be the same?"

"Okay, Rachael's your best friend, but I'm your *boyfriend.* And maybe also because she gets to meet up with you while you're there," he fires back, which, admittedly, is true. Rachael and our friend Meghan, who I've barely seen since she left for Utah State University, have had a trip to New York planned for months now. I'd have been invited along too, but Tyler beat them to it. Either way, I would have inevitably ended up in the city this summer, but I guess I can't blame Dean for feeling left out while me, Rachael, Meghan, and Tyler—nearly our whole group of friends—have a reunion in New York without him.

Dean sighs and remains quiet for a minute, neither of us saying anything until we come to a stop sign. "You're making me start this whole long-distance-relationship thing early," he says. "It sucks."

"Fine, turn the car around," I snap. I spin back around to look at him, throwing my hands up. "I won't go. Will that make you happy?"

"No," he says. "I'm taking you to the airport."

Silence ensues for the next half-hour. There's just nothing more to talk about. Dean is pissed off and I'm not sure what I can say to cheer him up, so we end up stuck in this strained quietness all the way to Terminal 7.

Dean cuts the engine the second he pulls up against the curb by the entrance to the departures level, and then he turns to look at me intensely. It's almost 7AM by now. "Can you at least call me, like, all the time?"

"Dean, you know I will." I let out a breath and give a small smile, hoping that he'll succumb to my widening eyes. "Just try not to think about me too much."

"You say that like it's easy," he says. Another sigh. But when he glances back at me, I think he might be lightening up. "Come here."

He reaches over to cup my face in his hands, gently drawing

me over the center console until his lips find mine, and soon it's as though our argument didn't even happen. He kisses me slowly until eventually I have to pull away.

"Are you trying to make me miss my flight?" I arch an eyebrow at him as I push open the car door, swinging my legs out.

Dean smirks. "Maybe."

I roll my eyes and step out, throwing my backpack over one shoulder and gently shutting the door behind me. I grab my suitcase from the trunk before heading around to his window, which he rolls down for me the second I near him.

"Yes, New York City gal?"

I reach into my pocket and pull out our five-dollar bill, the exact same one we've been tossing back and forth to each other ever since we met whenever we get a chance, like whenever we do each other a favor. But the bill is now unbelievably torn and tattered, and I'm surprised it hasn't disintegrated yet. "Five bucks for the ride."

Dean presses his lips together as he takes the bill from me, but it does little to hide the fact that he's smiling. "You owe me a lot more than five bucks for this."

"I know. I'm sorry." Leaning down through his window, I plant a sharp kiss on the corner of his lips and then finally turn to make my way inside the terminal. Behind me, I hear the sound of his engine starting up once more.

I haven't been to LAX in almost two years, so part of me wishes that Dean had come inside with me, but I decide that it's better I didn't drag all of this out longer than need be. He would have hated watching me disappear beyond check-in. Besides, I can manage on my own. I think.

As I predicted, the terminal is incredibly busy when I get

inside, even at this time. I weave my way through the flow of people until I find a clear spot to stop for a moment. Swinging my backpack off my shoulder, I rummage around inside and pull out my phone. I draw up my text messages, grab hold of my suitcase and, as I make my way toward check-in, I begin to type.

Looks like next summer is here. See you soon.

And then I send it to the person I've been waiting three hundred and fifty-nine days to see.

I send it to Tyler.

2

It's only when I land at Newark Liberty International Airport that I realize it's not even in New York. It's in New Jersey, and it's packed. Despite taking off ten minutes late, we land ten minutes early. My body is still telling me that it's 2PM and I'm craving lunch, but really, it's now 5:17PM here.

Which means that any second now, I'll be seeing him.

My heart skips a beat as my eyes scan the information signs above me. I'd take a moment to stop and figure out where I'm supposed to go, but I can't stop now. There's no way I can delay this any longer. I just want to see him already, so I sling my backpack over my shoulder and follow the people who have gotten off the same flight as me. But with each step, the more nauseous I feel. The more I realize I shouldn't have come here. The more I believe this is a bad idea.

Of course it's a bad idea, I think.

As if I'll get over him by spending time alone with him. If anything, this is going to make it worse, harder. It's easy for him. He's probably long over me and he's most likely dating some cute girl with a New York accent. And then there's me, the idiot who's spent an entire year still thinking about him. I know that when I see him, everything I ever felt will come rushing back at once. I can feel it already. I can feel that same nervous feeling in my stomach that I always did whenever he smiled at me, and I can feel my pulse racing at the same speed it always did whenever his eyes met mine.

I wonder if it's too late to turn around.

The group I've been following heads down an escalator, but I hesitate at the top and step to the side, lingering for a moment. Maybe this won't be so bad. I *am* excited to see him, despite the fact that my nerves are outweighing my excitement, and I've been waiting so long for this that it's stupid to be having second thoughts.

I'm just confused and my head's a mess, but I'm here now. It's time to see him for the first time in a year.

My grip tightens around the strap of my backpack as I step onto the escalator, and my heart is quite literally thumping against my ribcage. I wonder if the people around me can hear it. It feels like I'm having a heart attack, like I'll collapse any moment now from an anxiety overload. My legs feel stiff, but somehow I manage to keep moving, somehow manage to get off the escalator and advance across the arrivals level.

I'm half looking for the baggage carousels and half looking for a pair of green eyes. Around me, I can see people hesitating, looking. People in suits holding placards. Families searching the crowds flowing off the escalator. I study them in return twice as thoroughly. I know exactly who I'm looking for. For a moment, I think I see him. Black hair, tall. But just as my heart's about to stop, he draws a woman into his arms and I realise that it isn't him at all.

My eyes return to roaming the concourse as I make my way toward baggage claim, still forcing my feet to move, however numb my legs feel. I'm stealing glances at the line of placards as I pass, taking in the last names and wondering what all those people are coming to New York for. My thoughts don't last long, however, because suddenly one placard in particular catches my eye. It draws my attention, of course, because I see my name scrawled on it in black Sharpie, each letter slightly out of alignment with the next one.

And that's when I see him.

That's when I see Tyler.

He's holding this stupid placard of his just below his eyes, and the second mine meet his, they crinkle at the corners. He's grinning. Suddenly, everything calms. The tightness in my chest relaxes. My heart stops thumping against my ribcage. My pulse no longer throbs beneath my skin. And I just stand there, in the middle of the arrivals area, allowing myself to be nudged by my fellow travelers. But I don't care that I'm blocking the way. I don't care that I look like I'm lost. All I know is that Tyler's right here, that we're in front of each other again, and that everything immediately feels like it's back in place. It's like it hasn't been three hundred and fifty-nine days since he last smiled at me the way he is now.

He's slowly lowered the placard to reveal his face fully, and his grin and his jaw and the color of his eyes and the way one eyebrow slowly arches reminds me of some of the many things I used to adore about him. Perhaps I still do love these things, because now my feet are moving again. And fast. I make my way straight over to him, gaining speed with each step, my eyes locked on him and nothing else. My beeline forces the people around me to move out of my way, and by now I'm running. The moment I reach him, I throw myself into his arms.

I think it takes him by surprise. We stumble back a step, his placard fluttering to the ground as he grasps my body, and I'm vaguely aware of some people around us gushing "Aw!" as though we're some sort of long-distance online couple meeting for the very first time. It might look like that because in a way it's true. It has been a long-distance relationship. Stepsibling relationship, that is. Nonetheless, I don't pay attention to our small audience. I wrap my legs around him and bury my face into his shoulder.

"I think they're getting the wrong idea," Tyler murmurs by my cheek, laughing slightly as he stabilizes us. I might have heard his voice on the phone each week over the year, but it's entirely different hearing it in person. Almost like I can feel it.

"Maybe you should put me down," I whisper, and he does exactly that. With one final, firm squeeze, he gently sets me back on my feet. That's when I glance up to meet his eyes, up close this time. "Hi," I say.

"Hey," he says. He wiggles his eyebrows at me and there's just this sort of relaxed and positive vibe radiating from him. I find it impossible to stop grinning. "Welcome to New York."

"New Jersey," I correct, but my voice is a mere whisper as I stare at his face. He looks like he's aged four years in the space of one, but I think this is mostly due to the stubble that now decorates his jaw. I try not to think about how attractive it looks, so I shift my eyes to his arms instead, which only makes the whole thing worse. His biceps are bigger than I remember, so I swallow the lump in my throat and stare at his eyebrows instead. Eyebrows can't possibly turn me on.

Seriously, Eden, what the hell?

"New Jersey, whatever," Tyler says. "You're gonna love the city. Thank God you came."

"Hold up." I take a step back and stare at him curiously, tilting my head. I'm pretty sure he just placed emphasis on his vowels. "Is that a . . . Is that a New York accent I hear?"

He rubs at the back of his neck and shrugs. "A little. Kinda rubs off on you, you know? Doesn't help that Snake's from Boston. You're lucky I'm not walking around dropping my R's."

"Your roommate, right?" I try to recall all of our phone calls over the year, when Tyler would fill me in on which school he visited that day or tell me about something cool that happened, like when winter rolled around and he got to witness snow in real life for the first time, but I'm too distracted by the slight change in his voice. I don't know why I never noticed it whenever he called. "What did you say his real name was again?"

"Stephen," Tyler says with a quick roll of his eyes. "C'mon, we should get outta here."

He turns in the direction of the exit, but I quickly make him aware that I still have to grab my luggage, and he sheepishly directs us over to the baggage carousel instead. I've wasted five minutes by throwing myself at him, so thankfully it's not so crowded by now. I spot my suitcase after only a minute, and soon we're making our way out of Terminal C and into the parking lot, with Tyler pulling my suitcase effortlessly along behind him.

It's extremely hot out. Like, hotter than Santa Monica and hotter than Portland. I shrug off my hoodie and stuff it into my backpack just as we near his Audi, which, surprisingly, is still in pristine condition. Honestly, I assumed it would have been decorated in graffiti by now, or at least have had a window or two kicked out.

Tyler yanks open the trunk—which is actually at the front of the car—and places my suitcase inside, right before slamming it shut again. "How's your mom holding up?" he asks, but he's smirking.

I roll my eyes and slide into the passenger seat, waiting for him to join me inside before I answer. "Not that great. She's still acting like I'm moving here permanently or something." I run my fingers along the leather of the seat and inhale. Firewood. Febreze. Bentley cologne. Oh, how I've missed that damn cologne. "Dean's mad too."

Tyler's eyes flicker over to study me for a moment. He looks away, starts up the engine, and pulls on his seatbelt. "Are you guys still good?"

"Yeah," I lie. Honestly, I have no idea if we're still good or not after our argument this morning. I think we are. Knowing Dean, he'll most likely let it blow over. "We're alright." I stare at Tyler out of the corner of my eye and wait to see if he'll react, wait for something to happen, anything. His jaw to tighten. His eyes to narrow. But all he does is smile as he backs out of the spot.

"Good," he says, which immediately shreds any ounce of hope that I possibly had. Of course he's not mad that I'm still dating Dean, because he's totally over me. "How's he doing?"

I swallow and interlink my fingers, trying my best not to look disheartened. I shouldn't be, anyway. I shouldn't care. "He's okay."

A simple nod. His attention is now focused on the road as we peel toward the exit. "So how's my mom?" he asks, his voice soft. "I feel like every time she calls, she gets more and more frustrating. Like, 'Yeah, Mom, I'm doing my laundry. No, I haven't set the apartment on fire and no, I haven't gotten into any trouble.' " He gives a small laugh and then adds, "Yet."

"Except for that ticket you got when that cop pulled you

over for speeding," I point out. *Just act normal. Casual,* I tell myself.

As we pull out of the winding parking lot and onto the interstate, he throws me a small smirk. "What she doesn't know won't hurt her. But serious question: Is Jamie's girlfriend hot?"

I stare at him, and he shrugs innocently. "You're such a guy," I say. "But yeah, she's cute." I don't get to see Jen much, mostly because Jamie is adamant that I stay away from them after I supposedly embarrassed him the first time he brought her to the house. Apparently, informing your stepbrother's girlfriend that he recites "The Road Not Taken" in his sleep is against the sibling code of conduct. "Hey, guess what happened the other night?"

"What?"

"Chase was asking your mom if he could have some girl in his class over to study, but it's summer, so what the hell are they studying for?"

"Studying," Tyler scoffs. "That's smooth for an eighth-grader. He's finally switched video games for girls."

My lips curve into a teasing smirk, but he's not even looking at me. "Looks like they take after their brother when it comes to getting a girl."

"I'm gonna kill them both when we get back," he murmurs, but he's laughing. "Stealing my high school reputation. Totally unoriginal."

We're heading along the interstate, but it's rush hour, so the traffic is moving slowly. I reach for the sun visor and pull it down. The sun is starting to hurt my eyes and my shades are in my suitcase, which in retrospect was a stupid place to put them. "Do you think the year has passed fast?"

When the traffic rolls forward to another standstill, Tyler takes the opportunity to look at me. He thinks for a moment and then shrugs. He's not exactly smiling anymore. "No. Feels like each month lasted twice as long as it should have. It's been hell waiting for summer to come around."

"I thought it would have gone quickly for you," I say. "You know, with the touring and stuff. You were always busy." Whenever I spoke to Tyler, he always kept me up to date with the program. There was a lot of traveling around schools and other organisations, raising awareness of child abuse by sharing the story of the violence his dad inflicted on him when he was a kid. Sometimes he'd be in Maine. Other days he'd be in New Jersey. A lot of the time he was hardly in New York at all. Although he was often tired, I believed he'd enjoyed his time over here.

He shakes his head and looks back to the road, the traffic moving again. "Sure, on dates that we had an event, the days would go by fast, but the nights seemed to drag on forever. I'd get home and Stephen would be messing around on his computer trying to finish up assignments for class and so half the time I was bored as hell. You run out of things to do in New York after, like, a month when you barely know anyone."

Tyler never mentioned that he was ever bored. During our phone calls he was always telling me how much he loved the city, and how much better the coffee in New York tasted, and that he was having a kickass time. It didn't occur to me that he was lying. "If you're so bored, why are you choosing to stick around for another six weeks?"

For a second, I think he almost smiles. "Because you're here now."

"What's that supposed to—?"

"Hey, I love this song," he interjects, reaching over to crank up the volume of the radio, tapping quickly at the screen. I don't get the chance to finish my question, so I arch an eyebrow at him as he nods his head in sync with the track. I think it's Drake's new single. "Kanye West dropped his new album today."

"Uh-huh," I say, but I'm barely paying attention. Honestly, I really couldn't care. I don't even like Kanye West. Or Drake.

I'm not exactly sure what our conversation is even about after that point. It's mostly just Tyler commenting on something pointless and me agreeing. Like the amount of traffic there is, and the fact that the weather is great, and that soon we'll be leaving New Jersey and entering New York. That gets me a little stoked. Finally.

The car spirals around some sort of helix until we approach a line of tollbooths. Tyler merges into a cash-only lane and edges toward the barrier. "You know what I think is weird about the Lincoln Tunnel?" he muses as he pulls out his wallet.

"What?"

"You can head to New Jersey for free, but you gotta pay to head eastbound to New York." He shakes his head, cash in his hand, and then pulls up to the booth. "Kinda makes sense. No one really wants to go to New Jersey." I laugh as he rolls down his window, and the car is so low to the ground that he has to almost stretch out of the window just to reach up to the booth.

The guy manning it takes the money, murmurs, "Nice car," and then lifts the barrier for us, which Tyler promptly shoots through. And not without revving the engine, as though in reply to the guy's comment.

I fold my arms and angle my body to face him. "Some things never change," I remark playfully.

Tyler smirks, but it's a little sheepish. "Force of habit," he says with a small shrug.

Only a matter of seconds later, the sunlight that's been beating down on us disappears as we enter one of the three tunnels, leaving us in a warm orange glow. My eyes take a moment to adjust to the darkness. Once they do, I peer out the window despite there being not much to look at besides concrete walls. I lean forward and glance up at the roof of the tunnel.

"What are we under?"

"The Hudson River," Tyler tells me.

"That's so cool." I gnaw on my lip and settle back against the seat, suddenly reminded of the fact that I am actually in New York for six weeks. Over the past half-hour I seem to have forgotten where we've been heading, but the mere mention of the famous Hudson is enough to bring me back to reality.

"Now welcome to New York," Tyler says after a minute. He lifts his hand to point out the windshield, and I follow the direction of his outstretched fingers as he points to the wall of the tunnel.

There's a vertical line running down the wall. On one side of the line, it says "New Jersey." On the other, "New York." We're passing the state line, which means we're in New York, finally.

"We'll be in Manhattan in a couple minutes," Tyler adds. I think he can sense my excitement, because despite the fact that I'm too overwhelmed to say anything, he still smiles at me as he drives. "And I was thinking that if you aren't too exhausted, we could head to Times Square later. You know, since it's your first night in the city and all. You gotta spend your first week getting the tourist must-dos outta the way."

"Times Square sounds good," I say. I'm trying to act collected, like I'm not about to squeal any second. I've never left the West Coast until now, and not only am I over here in the East, I'm over here in New York City, of all places. Quite possibly, other than Los Angeles, the greatest city in the country. At least that's what people say.

Soon, I'll find out if they're right.

3

The light slowly begins to filter into the Lincoln Tunnel as we reach the end of it, and once we're back outside in the daylight, the sunlight almost blinds us. I squint through it, nonetheless, because I don't want to miss a second of the city. I want to see everything.

And at first, everything feels almost familiar.

The excessive amount of traffic on the roads. The constant flow of people making their way down sidewalks, running across streets. The height of the buildings, which for a moment almost makes me feel slightly claustrophobic. Santa Monica feels like a field in the middle of Arkansas in comparison. Everything feels so packed in, so tall. The buildings do, however, offer shade from the sun. There also seems to be this complete and utter sense of . . . busyness. Nothing seems calm, or relaxed, or slow. Everything just looks fast-paced, like everyone and everything is rushing to do something, and I think that's why it feels familiar. It's exactly what I expected, only without the steam emitting from the manholes. The movies must exaggerate that.

"Woah."

"I said the exact same thing," Tyler says with a laugh, but he's watching me from the corner of his eye as I take everything in, and at the same time he manages to slowly maneuver his way around pedestrians and cabs, heading along Forty-second Street. “Feels kind of crazy, right?”

“I mean, it’s New York,” I say. “New York freakin’ City.”

“This is the Garment District,” he tells me. “We’re heading toward Midtown.”

I’m vaguely paying attention to him, hearing his words but not exactly taking them in immediately. My eyes are being drawn to the towering buildings surrounding us, and the trees that line the sidewalks, and the fact that a lot of the streets are one-way. I lean forward so that I can get a better look out the windshield at everything above us. “Your apartment’s on the Upper East Side, right?”

I focus on Tyler again, so I notice his smug smirk. We come to a stop by some traffic lights. “Did you expect anything less from my mom?”

“No,” I admit. “There’s no way she would have put you somewhere like Harlem.”

He tuts and shakes his head at me playfully. “Oh c’mon, Eden, I thought you wouldn’t be so stereotypical. East Harlem isn’t actually that bad, but that’s probably because I can speak Spanish, so I totally fit in. It’s these Hispanic genes, seriously.”

“Tyler, you’re, like, 25 per cent Hispanic. You don’t even look it.” I try not to pay attention to the crowd of people gathered on the corner of the sidewalk waiting to cross the street who are snapping a quick picture of Tyler’s car as we wait, but it’s almost impossible not to see what they’re doing. Tyler ignores it.

“Still Hispanic genes,” he says defensively, “which is awesome, all thanks to Grandma Maria. And my dad, I guess.”

For a moment, I don't say anything. I'm a little surprised that Tyler even brought his dad up, and I'm waiting for his jaw to tighten or his mood to shift, but he just keeps on smiling as he points out the windshield. He must be okay with talking about his dad by now. He's been doing it for a year.

"In case you haven't noticed, Times Square is right there."

"What?"

The lights flash green just as my eyes are flickering over to the street ahead of us, and Tyler immediately floors the gas so that the car shoots off around the corner, leaving a plume of exhaust fumes behind us, which will no doubt impress our audience back on the curb. I snap my eyes back over to Tyler.

"We're taking a detour," he explains, grinning at my bemused expression. "I don't want you to see it yet. Not until tonight."

"Really? You're really going to tell me that Times Square is right in front of me and then drive off before I get to see it?" I fold my arms across my chest and turn to look away from him, dramatizing my irritation but smiling too.

"It looks better at night," Tyler says.

We're heading northbound along Eighth Avenue, passing hotels and stores and restaurants and, of course, hundreds of tourists. It's easy to differentiate between the locals and the tourists, mostly because the latter have this fascinated expression playing on their faces and seem to be taking pictures of almost everything. If I weren't hidden behind Tyler's tinted windows, I'd blend straight in with them.

"Crossing Broadway," Tyler murmurs almost immediately after turning off onto Fifty-seventh Street. "Central Park is two blocks to your left. Carnegie Hall is about to be on your right."

"Stop it!" I throw my hands up in exasperation as I try to fire my eyes around, hoping to catch everything at once. I glance to my left, hoping to see a flash of green, but there are still two blocks of leaning buildings in the way, so I focus back on the street we're crossing over: Broadway. It doesn't run parallel to the rest of the city streets but rather runs diagonally, which looks pretty cool. But other than that, it looks like every other street we've passed, so I shift my eyes to the road ahead and wait for Carnegie Hall to appear, although I'm not even sure what it looks like. I only know what it is: famous and prestigious.

"There," Tyler says, and nods to the building on our right as we pass it. I only get to look at it for a few seconds, but it's enough for me to realize that it pretty much just blends in with everything around it. Maybe if I were into classical music I'd find it more exciting.

"That's it?"

"Yeah."

We keep heading east along Fifty-seventh Street, stopping every few minutes at traffic lights. There are so many stores that I've never heard of before and soon I'm struggling to remember even half of them. It must take people forever to go shopping in Manhattan.

We're stopped at some lights again when I glance to my left and can finally see green: Central Park. Just the edge of it, but it's enough to get me feeling excited again. The initial rush of being here has worn off over the twenty-five minutes that we've been navigating through Manhattan, but it's coming back again. Central Park is the place I've been looking forward to most. It's supposed to be an amazing place to run.

"Fifth Avenue," Tyler informs me. He nudges my arm,

noticing that I'm not quite paying attention to the luxury stores that are within meters of us. I couldn't care less about them.

I finally avert my eyes from the trees to Tyler. "Is that Central Park?"

He grins. "Yeah."

And then the lights are green again, and we're off before I can even glance back one last time. The city feels huge and confusing, but Tyler seems to know his way around, and we turn north onto Third Avenue, which makes me think of Third Street and the promenade and Santa Monica. I wonder how Dean's spending his day off work.

"We're almost there, by the way," Tyler says. "About fifteen blocks. Just look for Seventy-fourth Street."

I glance out the window. Sixty-first Street. Ahead, the avenue looks gorgeous. The sky is clear and the buildings are all lit up by the sunlight so most of them look white. And then we come to Seventy-fourth Street, which I don't even notice until Tyler turns right onto a narrow one-way road. Almost immediately Tyler slows the car and maneuvers it into a spot by the sidewalk between a Honda and a truck, leaving barely a couple of inches between each.

I lean forward to peer through the windshield and frown. "Aren't you worried they'll hit your car when they try to get out?"

"No, they never move," Tyler says as he kills the engine. He pulls the keys from the ignition and pulls off his seatbelt, and I follow suit. "Truck belongs to some old guy in the building next door who doesn't drive anymore and the Civic is some girl's home. It's been parked here for as long as I can remember. She comes back every night and sleeps in it." His expression is neutral, so I can't figure out if he's joking or not, and I don't get the chance to ask because he's already saying, "C'mon, I'll grab your stuff."

I push open my door and step out, stretching my legs.

And it's like: *Woah.*

New York.

I'm standing in New York. Actually standing here on the streets of Manhattan. I glance down. There's a lot of gum. And some trash. But still. Manhattan.

"You okay?"

My eyes snap up from the ground. Tyler's hauling my suitcase out of the trunk, careful not to hit the Honda Civic with it, and he's arching an eyebrow at me. I offer him a sheepish smile and reach into the car to grab my backpack before stepping away and swinging the strap over my shoulder. "It's just that this . . . this is so surreal."

I feel like I can hear the busyness now. The sound of engines. Voices. Horns blasting. It feels loud yet somehow not loud at the exact same time. Like a constant buzz of noise that I think I'll grow accustomed to. Now I understand why New Yorkers talk so loud.

"I know," Tyler says. He slams the trunk shut and locks up. "You'll get used to all of this within a week." He walks around to meet me on the sidewalk and just when I'm about to ask where his apartment is, he nods at the building across the street. The tallest on the block. Right on the corner. It looks nice from the outside, with off-white bricking and huge brown-framed windows.

"Yeah, this was definitely your mom's doing." Of course Ella chose the nicest-looking apartment building. I wonder what the inside will be like. Tilting back my head, I quickly count the number of floors. Twenty. "Which floor are you?"

"Twelfth. Apartment 1203." He's still smiling at me. I don't think he's stopped since the airport. "Wanna head inside?"

I nod and follow him across the street toward a set of glass doors. He punches a code into the number pad and there's a sharp beep as the doors unlock. Wheeling my suitcase inside, I stay by his side and study the entrance as he leads me over to an elevator. There's a collection of mailboxes covering an entire wall, and some vending machines, but mostly it's bare. The elevator is huge, though. You could probably fit twenty people inside it, but there's only Tyler and me. He stands at one side and I stand at the other, and it feels like there's too much space between us, like we should be standing closer. Or perhaps it's just wishful thinking on my part.

"Snake should be back by now," he says after a moment. The elevator moves with a soft jolt. "He headed out with some guys from school, but I'm pretty sure he'll be here."

"Do I have to call him that?" I don't mind nicknames, but his just sounds ridiculous. Who would even want to be called that? "Can I just call him Stephen?"

"Yeah, sure, if you want him to hate you," Tyler deadpans. Slowly, he cracks a smile. "After a while, it stops sounding so stupid. Especially when you're yelling it across the street to him. You learn to ignore the weird looks you get."

There's a ding and the elevator door opens, revealing a lobby that's painted off-white, presumably to match the exterior bricks. Three doors down, Tyler draws my suitcase to a halt outside apartment 1203.

"I tidied up this morning for you, but if Snake's home then I can't make any promises that it'll look the way it did when

I left," Tyler admits as he reaches into the back pocket of his jeans and pulls out a set of keys. He looks a little nervous.

"I don't mind," I say. Now I'm smiling again. The thought of Tyler trying to clean up his apartment for my sake makes me feel like perhaps he's hoping to impress me. But the more I think about it, the more I doubt it.

There's a click and Tyler pushes open the door, stepping back to allow me to enter first. The first thing I think is: *Yep, Ella.*

I'm standing before an open-plan layout. Beige carpet, red plush couches, glossy black furniture, unbelievably large flat-screen TV mounted onto the wall between two huge windows that look out over the city. To my right there are two doors, which I assume lead to bedrooms, and on my left there's a kitchen. Everything follows a black, red and white color scheme. With the open-plan layout, the kitchen and living room are simply divided by one of the kitchen counters, enabling you to stand in the kitchen while staring into the living room. The cupboard doors and worktops are a glossy white. On one side of the kitchen, there's an open door leading to what seems to be the laundry room. On the opposite end, there's another door, but it's closed.

"Man, is that you?" a voice yells from the other side of it. " 'Cause something's wrong with the shower again. Water's mad cold. Won't heat up."

I arch my eyebrows at the sound of the thick Boston accent. It makes Tyler's odd mix sound totally normal again in comparison. The bathroom door is pulled open and a tall, blond-haired guy wanders out. He's pale-skinned and is evidently not paying too much attention, because as he makes his way across the kitchen his hand is inside his sweatpants, fumbling around, adjusting himself. "Do these assholes really think I wanna freeze my balls off—" He cuts off when he notices me. Stops walking. Slowly takes his hand out from his sweats. "Oh, shit." He fires his eyes at Tyler. "You could've warned me or something."

Tyler lets out a laugh and glances sideways down at me with a small shrug, almost apologetically. "Eden . . . this is Snake."

"Hey," I say, but I feel slightly awkward, like I've just walked into a total man cave. In a way, I feel like I'm kind of intruding. "Nice to, um, meet you." I can think of nicer ways to meet someone than with their hand on their crotch.

"Yeah, you too," he says as he joins us by the door. The first thing I notice is that his eyes are really, really dull. Blue, but so faded that they seem almost gray. He extends his arm and offers his hand, but I shake my head no. He smirks. "Don't you wanna shake my hand?"

"Not particularly," I say.

Tyler clears his throat and folds his arms across his chest, glancing between Stephen and I as he talks. "Right, first things first: ground rules."

"Ground rules?" Stephen—or Snake, whatever—echoes, almost like he's never heard the phrase before.

"We've got a girl living with us now, so shut the bathroom door when you're in there," Tyler explains. "Eden gets the bathroom last in the mornings since she'll take longer." I'm about to object to this, but then I see his point: If I'm last, neither of them will be banging on the door telling me to hurry up.

"Aren't you just the luckiest girl in the world? Getting to share an apartment with me. How much better can your life get?" Snake looks at me and cocks his head, an eyebrow raised. Tyler just rolls his eyes. "I mean, you're living with the coolest guy you'll ever meet."

I pull a face. "Are you always so . . . ?"

"Charming? Yes." He grins and reaches over to pat my head in a condescending manner—thankfully, not with the earlier, offending hand—and then turns for the couch. "TV's mine."

"Don't worry," Tyler murmurs quietly by my ear, "it's just his humor."

I'm not really paying attention to his words, though. I'm paying attention to the fact that I can feel his breath on my skin and I'm trying my best not to react to it. I bite my lip to stop myself from shivering and numbly reach over to touch my suitcase. "Um, where will I, uh, put my stuff?"

"My room," he says. He grabs my suitcase out from beneath my grip and drags it across the carpet to the first of the doors on the right of the apartment. Kneeing the door open, he lets me in first again and then places my suitcase down by the king-sized bed. It isn't as cluttered as his room back home used to be. The beige carpet continues into the room and his comforter is red, bedside drawers black. The walls are covered in NFL and MLB posters.

"Since when were you all that interested in baseball?" I ask.

"Since I moved to New York," he says with a slight grin. He nods to the bed. "You can have my room. I'll take the couch."

"Why don't we just bunk?" Oh my God. The words slip out of my mouth so fast I barely realize I've said them until I see Tyler's smile fade. He rubs at the back of his neck and shrugs. Sharing a bed is totally not a sensible suggestion.

"I think I'll just stick to the couch, Eden." He tries to smile gently at me, but it looks a little forced, and suddenly the atmosphere feels so suffocating that it's making me want to open up the window and climb out. I know the suggestion was stupid, but Tyler still rejected it, which means he totally is over me.

I force myself to act casual, to make it look like I am actually breathing. "Yeah, that was a dumb idea. Do you mind if I take a nap? I'm really tired." I glance at my watch. It's 6:30 by now, and although it's only 3:30 back home, my body still feels exhausted all of a sudden. The early-morning flight was a bad move.

"Yeah, sure, go ahead," he says, taking a step back toward the door, like he's getting ready to make his escape from his insane stepsister who's trying to drag him into bed with her. "Do you wanna cancel Times Square tonight? We could go tomorrow instead."

"No, no," I say quickly, a little too eagerly. "I still want to go to Times Square. Just give me an hour to sleep and then we can go."

"Just an hour?" Tyler looks at me suspiciously. If there's anything he's learned about me over the two years that he's known me, it's the fact that I will sleep endlessly. I think he doubts that I'll be able to wake up again once I doze off.

"An hour," I confirm. "Wake me up if you have to."

I hope Times Square can wait.

4

I flex my hands as I roll onto my side, grasping the sheets in search of my phone. The bed is too warm and I'm sticking to the sheets. I groan as I push back the comforter and sit up, not quite sure what time it is. Sunlight is still streaming into the room and the sound of the TV echoes faintly through Tyler's bedroom door. I slide my body out of the bed and push open the door only to discover Tyler and Snake slumped on the couch, watching some football game.

I clear my throat to catch Tyler's attention. He immediately cranes his neck to look at me, his face lighting up. Snake, however, doesn't even bat an eyelid. He only curses at the TV and takes a swig of the beer in his hand.

"How long was I asleep for?" I ask, my voice quiet and slightly raspy.

Tyler gets to his feet and makes his way over to me, which only makes my heart race yet again. I'm hoping that by tomorrow I'll be able to concentrate better and won't have palpitations every time he looks at me, speaks to me, or comes anywhere near me. "Twenty minutes," he tells me.

I squint at him. Twenty minutes? There's no way. But when I glance at my watch, I realize he's right. It's not even 7PM yet. "Oh. Are we still going to Times Square?"

"Yeah. I'm taking you to dinner, so I hope you're hungry." His smile falls for a moment and he arches a brow, perhaps waiting for me to object.

"Yeah, I'm hungry," I say. With the early flight and the traveling and the time difference, I have somehow managed to get to 7PM without having a single thing to eat all day. Unless my coffee this morning at the airport counts.

Back comes Tyler's smile. "Say a half-hour?"

"Yeah, I'll be ready." Snake's still not paying any attention to us, and my eyes drift past him and over to the bathroom door. I nod toward it. "Can I?"

"You don't have to ask, Eden," Tyler tells me with a laugh. "This place is all yours. Go ahead."

At that exact moment, we both turn for his bedroom. His clothes are in his closet and my clothes are in my suitcase on the floor, so I smile sideways at him as we both enter the room.

"Since this is your room and all now, it looks like you gotta get used to me coming in to grab stuff," he jokes while pulling open the door to his closet. "I'll knock first; don't worry."

I roll my eyes and haul my suitcase up from the floor, struggling to lift it before finally throwing it onto the bed. I'm not particularly sure what to wear, so as I'm unzipping my case I watch Tyler out of the corner of my eye to see if the clothes he's choosing are casual or smart. After a few minutes of shuffling clothes around in his closet and rummaging through his chest of drawers, he lays a pair of tan pants and a button-up dark-blue denim shirt onto the bed.

"You're taking the bathroom, right?"

"Um." I quickly drop my eyes back to my suitcase and swallow, feeling his eyes on me. "Yeah." He's standing by the window, waiting for me to leave so that he can change his outfit, so I sift through my pile of clothes as fast as I can so as not to keep him waiting. I grab some options and then make my way out of the room. "I'll be quick. I'm gonna shower."

"Towels are on the second shelf in the cabinet," he calls.

When I close the door behind me and enter the living room, Snake's no longer sprawled across the couch, though the football game is still playing. I make my way toward the kitchen and suddenly a head appears from behind the refrigerator. Snake holds up a bottle. "Do you want a beer?"

"A beer?" I repeat. His Boston accent isn't the clearest.

"Yeah, a beer. Do you or don't you?"

"Sure," I say. I extend my hand and wait, but I'm half expecting him to retract his offer. However, he yanks a bottle of Corona out of the pack and slides it into my hand. It's my first night in New York City, so a celebratory beer won't do any harm.

"Wait, let me get that for you." Grabbing the bottle opener from the counter, he spins back around and pops the cap off my drink. He fetches his own bottle from the counter and takes a sip. "I didn't take you as a beer kinda girl."

"And I didn't take you as a guy with much hospitality," I shoot back, but we're just playing. "Thanks for the drink."

He clinks his bottle against mine as though to say, "You're welcome," and then takes another swig as I make my way into the bathroom, my clothes in one hand and the beer in the other.

"Don't you wanna leave the door open so that I can get a good view?"

I turn back around and narrow my eyes at him. I'm not sure we share a similar sense of humor, but I'm sure I'll get used to him eventually. "Definitely not." I knee the door shut and lock it.

It doesn't take me long to get ready, mostly because I don't wash my hair, and once I've freshened up and washed off my makeup, it's really only a matter of pulling on my clothes. I leave my hair down and step into my pink skater skirt, slipping a denim jacket on top of a white tank top. I've consumed almost the entire bottle of beer in the time that it takes to get ready, so I take the remainder with me as I carry my belongings back through to Tyler's room. He's spraying cologne when I enter. The Bentley one.

"Did Snake give you that?" he asks, nodding to the bottle in my hand. For a second, I think he's about to frown, but he keeps his expression neutral.

"Yeah." I place the beer on top of the bedside table and throw my clothes into my suitcase, not bothering to fold them. I'll sort it all out later, but right now, all I need is my makeup bag, which I pull out from beneath a pile of sandals. I glance around the room quickly in search of a mirror and spy a small one above the chest of drawers that Tyler is standing by. "Can I get in there for a sec?"

"Sure," he says. Stepping to the side, he allows me to position myself in front of the mirror, watching me as I do so. "Did you do something different to your hair?" he asks after a moment.

"My hair?" I lift my head and look back at him in the mirror. "Just some highlights." He only gives me a single nod back, so I drop my eyes back to my makeup bag as I rummage through it. I don't want to keep Tyler waiting, so I only apply mascara to make my eyes pop a little more.

I don't know what it is about the two of us, but suddenly it feels awkward. It wasn't awkward at the airport and it wasn't awkward on the ride to Manhattan, but now something feels different. I'm starting to worry that perhaps it was my inappropriate suggestion earlier that's made Tyler feel uncomfortable. The suggestion about sleeping together. Or maybe it's just awkward because he no longer cares about me in that way, the way that he shouldn't.

"Ready," I say quietly, forcing a smile on my face as I spin around. I didn't notice it when I was looking at him in the mirror, but he's wearing his brown boots, which only makes me sigh. I wonder if he knows how much I love it when he wears them.

"What?" he asks.

"Nothing." I bite my lip in an effort to stop me from blushing and quickly grab my Converse from the floor, slipping them on and standing upright. "Let's go."

I follow him back into the living room, and Snake is by the refrigerator again, fetching himself another beer, which I think could possibly be his third. He tells me to enjoy Times Square, despite the fact that the whole thing is just "overrated bullshit," in his words, and then Tyler finally guides me out of the apartment building.

It's still extremely hot when we get outside onto Seventy-fourth Street, and I can hear that buzz of noise again. There are still a lot of cars honking, but I quite like it. It's almost relaxing, in a weird sort of way. Tyler doesn't say anything as I follow him across the street, and then I linger by the passenger door of his car. The truck and the Honda haven't moved.

"We're not driving there," Tyler informs me, laughing as

though I should have known we wouldn't be taking his car. He stares at me from a few feet away, smiling, which gives me some hope that the awkwardness in his room was only temporary. "We're taking the subway."

"The subway?" I vaguely remember Mom telling me not to go on it, yet I've only been in New York for three hours and it looks like I'll be breaking that rule already. Besides, I've always secretly wanted to use it at least once in my life, just for the experience.

"Yeah, we're catching the 6 train at Seventy-seventh Street," he says. I don't think he realizes that I have no idea what he's talking about. "We're heading downtown to Grand Central. You know what Grand Central Station is, right?"

"The really famous station?" I match my pace with his as I follow close by his side, though I'm paying more attention to my surroundings than I am to him.

"Yeah, that," he says. "We'll get you a MetroCard."

"A what?"

He looks at me as he attempts to bite back another laugh. "God, you really are a tourist."

We make a right onto Lexington Avenue, where the buildings seem dingier. They're all a murky brown or red, and there's the same amount of traffic as there is on Third Avenue, but it still manages to seem busier. We reach the station in five minutes, but I'm confused by which entrance to take, given there are eight of them: two on each corner. I turn to Tyler. "Why are there so many stairs?"

"These four are for uptown trains," he explains, pointing to the four entrances on the east side of the street. He then nods at the entrances on the opposite side. "Those four are for downtown trains, which is where we're going."

When there's a clearing in the traffic we almost jog across the street, and then Tyler nudges me toward the subway stairs. Looking down, it resembles nothing more than a crack den. I have a feeling that once we're a couple flights down the daylight from outside won't suffice, and the electric lighting seems minimal. I've watched enough horror movies to know that I'm more likely to die down there.

Pedestrians are nudging past us as they exit and enter the station, but I'm still apprehensive. Tyler's arms are folded across his chest and he's studying me.

"Do you do this a lot?" I ask.

"Pretty much every day," he says. "Trust me, it's safe."

I still don't move. I'd rather walk to Times Square, however many blocks away it is. I stare at Tyler's jaw. "Aren't there buses or something we can take instead?"

He rolls his eyes, turning up the sleeves of his denim shirt before he reaches for my hand. It's so out of nowhere that I think my body stops functioning, even when Tyler starts yanking me down the stairs. "Little kids go on the subway, Eden, so I'm taking you on it. End of discussion," he calls over his shoulder.

I don't even reply. I can't reply. It feels like I'm in middle school all over again and my eighth-grade crush has just held my hand for the first time. It's such a simple gesture, but it feels so significant. His skin is warm and our fingers interlock and fit each other almost perfectly. It feels exactly like the way I remember it, and it also feels like I can't breathe, and I can't tell if it's because he's touching me or if it's because I'm underground. I try to convince myself that it's the latter.

"See, it's not that bad, right?" Tyler's voice echoes in my

ear, and his hand quickly disappears from mine. My senses come rushing back and I glance around, wondering how many flights of stairs he's pulled me down and also wondering why there's lighting down here, until my eyes finally settle back on his.

"Right," I say, but my voice is almost a whisper. I'm such a kid. All he did was guide me down to a subway station. I glance down at his hands, which are now stuffed inside the front pockets of his pants, and he's looking at me with a curious glint in his eyes. "So what's a MetroCard?"

"The thing that's gonna let you get through those." He nods behind me to a row of turnstiles and it only occurs to me right then how loud everything is. I can hear a train arriving in the distance and it almost feels as though the ground is shaking, but it's not. I think I can also hear a busker out on the platforms somewhere. "Over here."

There are some machines lining a wall and I follow Tyler over to them, close behind, partly because I don't feel safe and partly because I'm hoping he'll grab my hand again. He doesn't.

"Are you still freaking out?" he asks. He steals a glance at me from the corner of his eye as he taps at the screen, selecting options so fast that I struggle to keep up with what he's doing.

"It's making me feel a little claustrophobic," I admit. My eyes drift around the station. I'm not sure how far down we are, but it feels like we're trapped in the middle of nowhere, yet nobody else seems to have a care in the world. They're definitely not tourists.

"You'll get used to it in a few days. You'll get used to New York as a whole by the end of the week." Taking out his wallet, he pulls out his credit card and slides it into the bottom of the machine, typing in his PIN and removing the card again. A yellow and black card shoots out from a slot higher up. "Unlimited for a month," he says, handing the card to me. "You're good to go."

I squint at it for a moment as he slides his credit card back into his wallet and takes out his own MetroCard. "How much did you pay for this?"

"Why does it matter?" He looks at me hard. Almost like he's offended that I'm asking.

"Because now I owe you."

He lets out a laugh in the middle of the station and rolls his eyes at me, twice. "Get outta here. You don't owe me anything. I'm under strict orders to look after you." Throwing his arm over my shoulder, he pulls me against him and squeezes my body before pushing me away. It's only playful, but his touch still exhilarates me for a few seconds.

And once the sensation fades away, I can focus on his words. "Under strict orders from who?"

"C'mon, there's a train about to come in." Completely ignoring my question, he places his hand on my shoulder blade and directs me over to the turnstiles, and I have to slide my MetroCard through the slot before forcing my body through the bars.

Tyler follows right behind me. The subway station, on a whole, isn't as busy as I expected it to be. We're two of around fifteen people standing on the platform, but it's most likely due to the fact that by now it's 7:45PM. Rush hour is long over.

"Here it comes," Tyler says, and he has to raise his voice in order for me to hear him clearly over the sound of the train as it approaches. The ground is definitely shaking now. I can feel it vibrating beneath me as the noise drills in my ears, and when the battered train pulls to a stop by the edge of the platform I'm scrunching my nose up.

Tyler pushes me onto the middle car of the train the second the doors slide open. There are several people seated and a few hovering by the doors. Tyler remains standing, so I shoot him a puzzled look.

"We're getting off in three minutes," he says. "Literally."

"Where at?" The car is awfully silent, so I keep my voice quiet in fear of disrupting the peace of the people around us. "Grand Central?"

"Yeah. And then we get the shuttle to Forty-second." He's holding on to a railing and I'm holding on to the one opposite, and we're both staring at each other. The corner of his lips pulls up into the smallest of smirks. "So, dinner first?"

5

My eyes glaze over the moment we step out onto Forty-second Street. In fact, I think they do everything they possibly can: glisten, squint, widen, stare. There's so much to take in, and as Tyler places his hands on my shoulders and guides me around the corner onto Broadway, the first thing I notice is how bright and vibrant everything seems. It may still be light out, but it all still looks incredible. At first, I'm not too sure what to do or say. I'm stunned into silence as my eyes drift from left to right and back again. It seems not all movies set in New York are misleading, because the sight before me is an exact replica of all those scenes set in Times Square that I've seen so many times before. And that's exactly what this all feels like: some sort of incredible movie, like none of this is actually real.

The huge neon illuminated advertisements are flickering around me and it makes me wonder how you can come here if you have epilepsy. There are people everywhere. It's mesmerizing, and I don't even care that I totally look like a tourist right now. I've been drunk on the image of Times Square for so long that I can barely contain myself now that I'm actually here.

For a second I must forget the fact that Tyler's still standing behind me with his hands on my shoulders, because I pull out my phone and immediately start taking pictures. They're not the best, my hands so shaky that half of them are blurry, but I'll send them to Mom and Dean later nonetheless. I snap some shots of the LED billboards, some of the bustling crowds, some of the sky, which only seems cool because it's the New York sky. Everything seems cooler over here.

Even the yellow cabs fit my perception of Times Square perfectly. They're skimming past each other dangerously, screeching to halts as the drivers slam on their brakes for potential passengers. The traffic lights are shifting between colors, pedestrians rushing to cross over to the other side of the road. There's a strange smell in the air, like a mixture of hot dogs and peanuts.

Times Square.

It's real. It's actually real.

With a grin on my face so wide that it's beginning to hurt, I spin around and pull Tyler toward me, ensuring the neon lights are behind us. I bury my body into his warmth and hold my phone up. I'm much smaller than him; my eyes are in line with his mouth. He tilts his head down, resting the side of his face against my own.

"Smile," I breathe, and as I do, I take the picture. The flash dazzles us for a few moments, but when my eyes return to normal, I glance down to admire the image.

Tyler's smile matches mine. It's just as wide, if not wider, and there's something so attractive about it that I could turn around and kiss him right now if I was brave enough to even attempt something like that. I think being here in New York with him has made me go insane already, and it's only been three hours. Three hours and already everything is coming back, ten times worse. If I thought I was attracted to him before, then I'm completely addicted to him now.

"I like that picture," Tyler says quietly, and I feel my eyes being drawn to his. He's been staring at the photo from over my shoulder, at the way we both look happy. His eyes are still sparkling.

"I like it too," I say, swallowing the lump that's growing in my throat. I wish he didn't have this effect on me. I wish it had worn off over the past year, but it hasn't. I glance back down to look at my phone, which is about to die any second, and quickly I set the image as my wallpaper. It replaces a photo of Dean. I almost feel guilty, like I've betrayed him, but before I can actually think through what I'm doing, Tyler is talking again.

"I'm taking you to Pietrasanta. It's an Italian restaurant over on Ninth Avenue."

"Italian?" Of all the restaurants Tyler could have chosen, he chooses the one that's most likely to remind me of Dean. I bite the inside of my mouth.

"You love Italian food, don't you?" He suddenly looks worried, but the truth is, suddenly I am too. And it's not because of his restaurant choice. "You told me a few months ago, right?"

"Yeah, I do." Every Wednesday I have dinner over at Dean's place, and his mom makes the best Italian dishes. Dean thinks his mom's tradition is just embarrassing, but I think it's cute. Her food tastes amazing. I told Tyler this a while ago, and the fact that he took note of it is the reason my frown is turning back into a smile. "Italian food sounds great right now."

"I've, uh, actually had a table booked for a couple weeks

now." He rubs nervously at the back of his neck and I don't think I remember him ever being this shy before. It almost feels like he's taking me on a date, which I kind of wish he was. "It's for 8PM, so we gotta get moving. You don't care about seeing the stores tonight, right?"

"Tyler, c'mon." I shake my head. He knows I'm not the biggest fan of shopping, and some bright lights and flashing signs aren't enough to make me enthusiastic about it. "You know me better than that."

He's not joking back with me, though; he's only shrugging and staring anxiously at the ground. "Sorry, I'm just . . . I just want you to enjoy New York. I want to make sure you have a good time."

"You're doing good so far," I tell him gently, but I'm confused. He seemed completely confident and comfortable around me right until we got back to the apartment. Since then, everything has felt different, and it's because Tyler's acting weird around me. "You're, like, my tour guide for the summer."

"Yeah, I guess you could say that." He rubs his temple. And then his eyebrow. And then he sighs. "The restaurant is five blocks north."

And so we head northbound on Broadway, with Tyler stepping proudly into his role of being my personal tour guide, pointing out each detail and briefing me on some common knowledge about Times Square. For starters, I shouldn't stop dead in my tracks to gawk and take pictures, which is exactly what I just did, because the locals apparently get frustrated with us tourists blocking the way. Also, on the off chance that I end up in Times Square without Tyler, looking at a map is the worst thing I can possibly do. But I doubt I'll be going anywhere without him, so I don't have to worry about making the pickpockets aware that I'm a clueless tourist.

We make a left off Broadway and onto Fifty-seventh Street after passing the famous red bleachers atop the TKTS booth, which I do stop to take a picture of, but Tyler doesn't let me block the way for long before moving me on.

It takes us fifteen minutes to get to Pietrasanta. It's right on the corner of Fifty-seventh and Ninth, with wooden doors that have been opened up to allow for an open-air setting. It looks adorable, and by the time Tyler leads me over to the door he's got a sheepish smile on his lips.

"I, uh, asked around my building for recommendations," he admits, "and a lot of people said this place is the best Italian restaurant around. I hope it lives up to the hype for you."

"I'll bet it's great," I say feebly, trying to reassure him. I can't figure out why he seems to have put so much effort into this. It's just a simple meal, yet it's as though he's trying to make everything perfect. He shouldn't care this much. He doesn't need to impress me. I'm just his stepsister.

We head inside, and although we're slightly late our waitress takes us over to our table without a problem. It's right at the back, by the collection of Italian wines. I sit myself down opposite Tyler and quickly study the restaurant. The tables are wooden, the lighting is dim, it's rather small, and there's a soft breeze finding its way inside through the open doors at the front. I prefer it back here, out of sight of those passing by on the sidewalk. I listen closely as I try to decide whether or not I can hear music playing, and after a moment I realize that there is none, only the voices of the people around us, mixed with some occasional laughter. The atmosphere feels intimate.

Tyler taps his fingers on the table in front of me to reel my attention back in. His eyes are smoldering when I glance up. "Good enough to stay or bad enough to walk out?"

"Good enough to stay," I say, with a nod of approval. "I like it."

"Hopefully the food doesn't suck." He picks up my menu, opens it, and then hands it to me. He reaches for his own. "Choose anything and everything you want. It's on me."

"You're being too nice." I study him suspiciously over the top of my menu, but he just shrugs, still smiling. I'm starting to wonder if he'll ever stop.

"What can I say? I'm the nicest guy around."

I press my lips together and lift the menu up higher to hide my face. "I think your roommate's egotism has rubbed off on you."

He laughs, but it's soft and gentle, and just as I think he's about to reply, our waitress approaches us to order our drinks. She's young, perhaps around our age, but she's sweet. She disappears for five minutes to get our drinks while we scan the menu.

Tyler ends up squinting at the endless list of Italian words, biting his lip repeatedly as he struggles to comprehend the language. I'd point out that the English translation is on the reverse side, but his confusion makes him look cute, so I keep quiet.

"This is so confusing," he says after a while, glancing up at me. My eyes are boring into his, but I don't bother to look away. "Why couldn't you love Spanish food?"

I lay my menu down, having decided what I'm going for, and then prop my arms up on the table, resting my chin in my hands. "Say something."

"What?"

"In Spanish," I say. "Say something in Spanish."

Tyler furrows his eyebrows at me. "Why?"

"I like it when you do."

For a long moment, he thinks. I can see the gears in his mind shifting as he considers what to say to me, almost like he needs a minute to string a sentence together. Maybe he's not so fluent after all. "*Me estoy muriendo por besarte,*" he murmurs quietly, almost rasping. Leaning forward, he folds his arms on the table and looks at me intensely, and I become aware that we're in such close proximity to one another that I can almost feel his breath as he speaks. It causes mine to catch in my throat. "I just told you that the waitress is coming."

I glance to my left and, of course, our waitress is approaching us with our drinks, and Tyler immediately leans back in his seat. I wish he hadn't moved.

Tyler orders the capellini primavera (without the chicken broth, of course, given he's a vegetarian), giving his best attempt at Italian pronunciation, while I expertly order the lasagna alla nonna. And when the waitress takes our menus and leaves, my eyes drift back to Tyler, only to find that he's arching an eyebrow at me.

"That accent was mad good," he says, impressed.

"And that New York slang is going to get annoying."

Slowly, his lips curl up into a grin, and he clears his throat to correct himself. "Sorry. That accent was hella good."

"Thanks. All I do is mimic Dean's mom's voice." I reach for my glass of water and Tyler follows suit by picking up his glass of Coke, and as we each take a long sip, we never cease our staring. My eyes mirror his over the rim of my glass.

Swallowing, I breathe a sigh of satisfaction and set my drink back down. "Can I ask you something?"

There's concern on Tyler's face for a split second, but he doesn't make it too noticeable, and soon he's giving me a go-ahead nod. "Sure."

I take a deep breath and interlock my hands together on the table. I still haven't looked away from him. "How is everything? You know, with you?"

"Really, Eden?" Tyler's taut expression relaxes as he shakes his head at me, losing all seriousness. "You've asked me this so many times."

"I know." I'm not smiling anymore. Instead, I'm worried. I have a bad habit of asking if he's definitely okay, but it's hard to tell over the phone whether or not he's telling me the truth. "I need you to answer me honestly, face to face. I'll be able to tell if you're lying or not."

He rolls his eyes, almost smirking at how relentless I must seem, but then he straightens up and leans forward again, his lips pressed into a firm line. He's even closer to me than he was before, and I think I might have stopped breathing again. Slowly, he parts his lips to speak. "I'm as fine as I can be, Eden. That's the truth. I'm not lying to you."

He widens his eyes dramatically, as though to prove that he's sincere, so I squint back at him as I search for anything in his features that'll tell me otherwise. He doesn't give me long, though. Only a few seconds, and then he retreats, settling back against his seat.

"C'mon," he says gently. He tilts his head down slightly, looking up at me from beneath his eyelashes. "You know I would have been kicked off the tour if I'd messed up."

I consider this for a moment before realizing that he has

a point. If he'd been caught drunk, high, in handcuffs, or involved in any trouble whatsoever, he would have been taken off the program. His job was to tell his story and set a positive example. The fact that he took part in every single event right until the end only proves that he didn't get into any trouble. Which means he is okay. But it's hard to forget the way things used to be a couple of years ago, and sometimes I can't help but wonder if he'll ever end up in that state again. But for now, he's doing good.

I'm not even sure why I had to ask him to clarify this for me again. I should have known he was telling me the truth, that New York would be the best thing for him. From the moment I saw him at the airport, there's been nothing but a positive vibe radiating from him. I think that's why I keep smiling.

When I draw my attention back to Tyler, he's waiting for me to say something, but I can't muster up a single word. I can't stop staring at him, at his eyes that are still wide, at the stubble that's making him look years older than he really is, at the corner of his lips as he holds back a smile. And then it finally occurs to me that it isn't any of these things that attract me to him so much. It's that positivity around him. It's the way he's managed to change his entire mindset and attitude within the space of two years. I can only imagine how hard it was for him to stop hating everything around him, for him to finally get over the shitty childhood he had, yet he managed. He did it.

That's why I'm even more attracted to him than I ever was before. That's why this sucks. It's been two years since our first summer together. By this point I'm supposed to be over him, but now it seems like I never will be. New York was a bad idea. I should never have come. I should be in Santa

Monica with Dean, not here, falling even harder for his best friend.

My stomach churns, and I can only hope that it's out of hunger and not guilt. Reaching for my water, I take another long sip and buy myself some more time to collect my thoughts, to think of something to say. After a moment, I think of Tyler's words back at the Seventy-seventh Street subway station. I place my glass back on the table and look at him, curious. "Who gave you strict orders to look after me? My mom?"

Tyler sighs at my change of subject before folding his arms across his chest, his posture still straight. He offers me the smallest of shrugs as he drops his eyes to the table. "Yeah. Your mom, my mom . . ." He glances back up. "And Dean."

"Oh," I say flatly. It's not surprising. It's such a Dean thing to do. Frowning, I stare at my glass and run my fingers around the rim, not quite sure what to think. "What did he say to you?"

"He said that I have to make your trip worth it. You know, since you chose this over him." Tyler shrugs again, and I can feel the tension growing around us. Or perhaps it's only me who can notice it, because I'm the guilty one. I'm the one who's gazing at Tyler in the middle of an Italian restaurant in New York City while my boyfriend is on the other side of the country, most likely still mad at my departure. "He'll be pissed off if you don't even have a good time."

"What did you tell him?"

"I told him that I'll guarantee it," Tyler says, and he smiles again, wide and sincere.

Silence ensues. It's mostly because I have no idea how to navigate the whole Dean situation, but partly because I'm desperate for Tyler to look uneasy. He looks too comfortable talking about Dean and I, like it doesn't bother him anymore, which is only more evidence that he's over me. Totally and completely over me.

My heart sinks, and I decide right then that I'm just going to go for it; I'm just going to blurt it out and ask. I just need to man up and get it over with, otherwise I'll spend my entire vacation wondering "What if?" I just need him to tell me straight up. I think hearing him admit it will kill me inside, but hopefully it'll help me to get over him too. I have to.

I swallow down the lump in my throat and take a deep breath, trying my best to keep calm, but Tyler still notices how panicked I must suddenly appear, because his smile slowly fades away.

"Are you okay?"

I force my eyes to find his, and when I finally do, I part my lips to speak. My voice is nothing more than a quavering whisper when I dare myself to ask, "Does it bother you?"

Tyler's eyebrows immediately furrow. "What?"

"Dean," I say. The group of people on the table next to us erupts with laughter, and both my and Tyler's attention is grasped for a split second before Tyler's eyes return to study me. I press a hand to my temple and lower my voice even more. "Does it bother you that I'm still with him?"

"Eden." There's no trace of a smile left. Now his lips are a bold line, his eyes sharply narrowed. "What are you doing?"

"I'm just wondering," I splutter quickly, and I'm so nervous that I can't even look at him, so I press my hand over my eyes and tilt my head down toward the table. "It still bothered you a year ago, before you left. I just want to know if it still does now."

"Eden," he says again, his voice coarse, firm. He pauses

for a long moment. I'm too scared to move my hand away. Eventually I hear him slowly exhale, and his words are even slower. "Are you asking me if I still . . . you know?"

"I'm trying to," I whisper.

"We're not talking about this here," he says abruptly, loudly. Loud enough for me to lift my head and remove my hand from over my eyes. His jaw is clenched, the muscle twitching.

My voice rises to match his, and I keep on pushing. "Are you over me?"

"Eden."

"Have you met anyone else? Are you single?" I'm so frustrated and terrified all at the same time that it ends up fueling some sort of adrenaline, and within a matter of seconds I'm brave enough to look him straight in the eye, and he must be even braver to stare back. "When did you get over me? I just need to know, so please just tell me."

"Eden," he says, more forcefully this time. "Please stop talking."

"So that's it?" I shake my head in disbelief, my temper quickly rising. All of this has been going on for far too long. I need to know whether I'm wasting my time. I need to know whether he and I are a lost cause. "You're not going to give me an answer? You're just going to leave me to go insane over this?"

"No," he says, and his voice is much calmer than mine, despite how hard his features have grown. He has definitely grown up. Two years ago, he would have lost his temper by now and he would have been muttering and cursing and glaring at me. Instead, I'm the one who's losing it. "I'm just not going to answer you here."

"Then where?"

"When we get back to the apartment," he answers, and he narrows his eyes into smaller slits as he fixes me with a firm look, as though to tell me to give up for now, which I do, but only because our waitress is arriving with our food.

She must think I'm rude, for I'm too busy glaring across the table at Tyler to even thank her when she places the dish in front of me, and I barely even blink. Once she disappears again, Tyler leans forward to grab his cutlery, and within a matter of seconds his smile has returned.

"There's something I still need to show you," he murmurs, swiftly twirling pasta around his fork, his eyes on his plate.

"What?"

He pauses and tilts his head up, a small smirk on the corner of his lips. "It's a surprise," he says. "But here's a hint: It has an amazing view, and we'll talk about all of this there."

6

Tyler remains nonchalant for the rest of the evening, acting so casual that it's almost as though he doesn't care that I desperately need an answer to where we stand with each other. He muses on irrelevant things during dinner, tells some jokes on the walk back through Times Square, and even attempts to cheer me up while we're on the subway by relentlessly wiggling his eyebrows at me until I eventually crack a smile. It's fake, of course, and the second I turn away from him I wipe it from my face.

"So where's this place with the amazing view? Empire State Building? Statue of Liberty?" I fold my arms across my chest and watch him, awaiting an answer.

But he only grips the railing even tighter and shrugs, and I swear he looks as though he's about to laugh. I'll bet he was being sarcastic back at the restaurant. I'll bet he's going to show me the ugliest spot in the city, the perfect place to shred my heart to pieces. "Not exactly," he finally says. "C'mon, our stop is next."

We linger by the doors for a few seconds, the train vibrating and the noise drilling into my ears. I'm starting to understand why the majority of the people around us have earphones in. But it's bearable for the few minutes that we're on here, and when the train screeches to a halt at the next station, Tyler promptly reaches for my wrist and yanks me onto the platform.

I immediately recognize the station. It's the Seventy-seventh Street one, which means that we're not venturing anywhere other than Tyler's apartment, it seems. This becomes even more obvious when we head out of the station and back the way we came from earlier. Tyler keeps on talking the entire time, but I've tuned out by now. I'm kicking at the sidewalk with my Chucks as I walk, slowly starting to feel sick the longer Tyler drags all of this out. I'm switching so fast between being frustrated and being nervous. One minute I'm mad at him for not getting this over with back at the restaurant, the next I'm wondering why I even brought it up in the first place.

We pass his car (and the truck and the Civic) and just as we're about to head inside the apartment building, I come to a halt on the sidewalk. I tilt my head back and squint up at the building, which is taller than those surrounding it.

Tyler lingers by the entrance as he swings open the door, leaning back and pressing his weight against it as he folds his arms across his chest. "What's up?"

I drop my eyes to his. "You said a nice view, didn't you?"

"Yeah." I think he knows what I'm about to ask next, because his mouth is forming another one of those smiles of his.

It's cooler now and the breeze has picked up only slightly, but it's enough to blow my hair across my face, so I tuck some strands behind my ears and ask, "Is it the roof?"

Tyler doesn't even reply to begin with. Only locks his eyes on mine as his smile grows into a grin. Eventually, he murmurs, "Maybe."

I'll bet the view from up there really is beautiful, but honestly, I want to tell him to just forget it. There's no need to take me all the way up there to simply say the words I'm expecting him to say. It's like he wants to be cruel.

"It's not much," he says as I follow him inside and toward the elevator. He pushes the button for the twentieth floor, the final one. "I mean, there are some chairs and some plants, but it's mostly just concrete. It's cool, though. You know, to go up there."

I stuff my hands into the pockets of my jacket and stare at the floor of the elevator, biting the inside of my cheek as I try to think about how much the next few minutes are going to hurt. I think I might cry when he admits it, but I'm praying I'll be able to hold up, at least until I get away from him. I'm worried that I'll look pathetic, but even more worried that this talk we're about to have will only make the rest of our summer together awkward.

The elevator door pings open, and this time Tyler doesn't stand back to let me out first. Instead, he clears his throat and makes his way into the lobby. He's trying to act casual, but I can tell he wants us to hurry up. Some guy squeezes past us, heading in the opposite direction, but we keep on walking until Tyler comes to a stop by the very last door on the left, one that looks different from the rest. It's because it's not an apartment but simply a door opening up to a flight of metallic stairs.

"Just up here," he calls over his shoulder as he makes his way up, three steps at a time.

It's dimly lit, but it's only one flight of stairs, and when I reach the top Tyler is waiting for me by the fire exit. He offers me a closed smile before shoving the door open. We step out onto the rooftop, and it's twilight by now, so at first all I can see are the tops of some of the other taller buildings in the area. As Tyler already told me, there are some wooden deckchairs dotted around, complemented by some matching tables, and some pots of plants that appear to have dried out in the heat.

Just as I'm glancing around, Tyler moves his body behind mine, and out of nowhere I feel his firm hands grasp my waist. My breath catches in my throat the second I feel his touch, and I lock my eyes on the tip of a building a few blocks away as I try not to focus on the fact that I can feel him breathing on the back of my neck. His lips creep closer to my ear, suddenly murmuring, "Come check this out," in a husky tone. It's enough to send a shiver surging down my spine. With his hands still on my waist, he directs my body toward the edge of the roof.

And the moment my eyes fall to the sight below, I totally forget the reason we're up here in the first place. I forget that Tyler's hands are on my body. I forget that he's about to tell me that he's over me. Because all I can think about at that second, all I can process, is how gorgeous the view really is.

I think it might be that the sky is a deepening blue splintered with streaks of pink, and I think it might be that everything below and around us now glows, but I can only imagine all of this appearing more stunning now, at night, than it would during daylight. The headlights from the traffic and the illumination from the street lights make everything look orange, and the fluorescent lighting emitting from windows of office buildings creates a map of scattered flecks of light. The further into the distance I look, the more it all becomes just an abundance of buildings, like they're all piled on top of each other, lights shining through. I'm quickly realizing why it's known as the city that never sleeps. Now the city seems even more alive than it did only hours ago.

I don't sense Tyler letting go of me until he's standing by my side. He leans forward, folding his arms on the wall and letting out a breath. "I like it up here," he says quietly. He doesn't have to raise his voice. The city might seem even louder at night down there, but up here it just sounds like faint background noise.

I want to tell him that I like it too, but I'm still marveling at the city surrounding us, too stunned to attempt to speak. It's almost terrifying how huge it all is and how insignificant we seem in comparison. How many other people are standing on rooftops around the city right now? How many other people believe, at this exact moment, that the city is theirs?

A gentle breeze whistles between us and my hair sways around my face. I lift my hand and press a finger to my lips, and slowly I shift my gaze from the city to Tyler. His eyes are carefully studying the skyline, but he must notice that my attention is now on him, because the muscle in his jaw tightens. Exhaling, he lowers his head and stares at the top of the wall for a moment.

"I guess you want to have that talk," he murmurs.

Part of me still wants to, but the other would rather do anything else. Up here is too perfect for this, but I've already got myself into this situation, and Tyler might not give me another opportunity to get this over with. I've been waiting an entire year to find out. Why wait longer? Why do that to myself?

I take a deep breath and swallow back the nerves. The adrenaline that built up back at the restaurant is long gone by now and I can only pray that it'll take over again. Maybe that way it'll block out how much this is about to hurt. I glance down at Third Avenue. "We've needed to talk about this for a while now."

There's a brief silence as Tyler shifts his footing. Then he unfolds his arms and interlinks his hands on the top of the wall instead. He stares at them. "Where do we start?"

"With you telling me that you're over me," I say, but despite how strong I'm trying to be, my voice still cracks on the final word. I squeeze my eyes shut and shake my head at the ground, taking a step back from the wall, away from the edge. "Just admit it. It's all I'm asking."

It's crazy how much things can change within a year. Before Tyler left last June, we still had something there, lingering in the atmosphere whenever we were around each other. We both knew it. We just never spoke about it. I'd already done what I'd believed to be the right thing. I'd already made it clear that none of this was ever going to work and that we were wasting our time, yet as the months went on it became apparent that getting over each other was a lot harder than I thought it would be. Whenever I dropped by Dad's place and Tyler was there, it always felt like we were forcing ourselves to act innocent to our parents. We weren't guilty, yet we always felt like we were. Even hanging out with Dean, Rachael, and Meghan would get hard. The five of us would be at the pier together and Tyler would glance between Pacific Park and me when no one was looking, and I always remembered the time he took me there, because it was our first and only date. None of our friends ever noticed Tyler's smirks. But I always did. Sometimes he would stare at me in the hallways at school. Sometimes I'd stare back. Then he'd smile and turn away, and I'd reel my attention back to Dean, who was often by my side. I used to worry about Dean to begin with. I thought Tyler would hate me for it, for breaking things off and dating his best friend instead. But he never commented on it. Ever. Only narrowed his eyes at me whenever Dean and I were together.

But all of that was before he left. All of that was a year ago.

It's all different now. I can tell. He's more distant already, more casual about Dean and me. I don't know why it's hitting me so hard. It's exactly what I expected. I mean, a year in New York City? I can't possibly think of a better city to live in while trying to get over someone. How many new girls has he met over the months? How many new people has he surrounded himself with while doing events? Maybe he's been dating. Maybe he's already seeing someone.

And yet here I am, standing on this rooftop by his side, still hopelessly in love with him.

"I'm not going to tell you that I'm over you," Tyler says eventually.

My eyes flicker open and I raise my head, studying his face as he continues to stare down at the avenue below. His jaw is still tightened, but he doesn't look mad. Just serious. Straightening up, he stands back from the wall and turns to face me. And the second his vibrant eyes lock with mine, only one thing runs through my mind: hope.

"I'm not going to tell you that," he says. "Because I'm not over you."

7

It takes a long moment to fully absorb Tyler's words, for them to actually hit me. At first I think he's kidding, or that I've only heard what I want to hear, but then he smiles at me and they crinkle at the corners. The sincerity within them only makes me realize that he's being totally honest.

"What?" I splutter, finally.

"It's gonna take me a lot longer than a year without you to get over you."

The atmosphere is so thick and suddenly everything feels deafeningly silent. So silent it almost hurts. But I can't even process my thoughts, much less get out any words, and so I stare back at him even more dumbfounded than I was ten seconds ago. I shake my head, fast. There's no way in hell this is really happening.

"But I thought—"

"You thought what?" He stuffs his hands into the front pockets of his pants and drops his eyes to the concrete. Weeds are growing through the cracks. "I'd come over to New York and move on just like that? You thought it would be that easy?"

I never prepared myself for this. I never even imagined Tyler would be standing in front of me saying these words. Yet he is. I'm so overwhelmed and stunned that I still don't entirely believe him. I bite my lower lip. "But you've been acting different. You've been treating me like your sister."

"Well," Tyler says with a smirk, "you are."

"Tyler." I press my lips together and look at him hard.

He heaves a sigh as his smirk falters, running a hand back through his hair and rubbing the back of his neck. "Honestly, Eden? I thought you were over me. I didn't want to be that asshole who messed with your head. I was gonna do the right thing. I was gonna keep my distance."

I think if I wasn't so numb, I would cry. But I just can't seem to stop staring back at him from three feet away, my lips parted in disbelief. It takes me a second or two to muster up a reply, and then all I can murmur is, "Does Dean still bother you? You know, him and me?"

"No," Tyler says.

"Why?"

He pauses to study me for a second. In the background, I can still hear New York City. It doesn't even feel like we're part of it anymore. The atmosphere is so tense that it feels as though we're the only two people around for miles, like we're on this rooftop in the middle of nowhere. My eyes are set on him and nothing else. "Because if you're not going to be with me," he says, "then I'm happy that you're at least with him. He's good for you."

The numbness stops, so quickly that I can almost feel my chest collapsing all at once. It feels heavy, like my ribcage might just shatter, and it only takes me a second to realize that it's all because I feel so guilty, so awful, and so, so confused. In that exact moment, my thoughts on everything seem distorted. Being with Dean seems wrong. Being with Tyler even more so.

"Look, Eden, we shouldn't be having this conversation," Tyler says after a while. He must realize that I'm not going to reply. My voice has disappeared. "Why does any of this matter? You've got Dean."

I grit my teeth, grinding them together as I try to relax the tightness in my stomach. I shouldn't be in this situation. It's unfair, and it's all because our parents had to randomly be in the same parking lot one day. Dad pulled into the spot Ella was about to maneuver into. She got out the car and argued. He bought her coffee to apologize. And so I blame that sought-after parking spot for causing all of this. Why did our parents have to meet? Why did I have to end up with a stepbrother like Tyler and, more importantly, why the hell did I have to end up falling for him? Sometimes, like right now, I hate the way the world works.

"It matters because I'm nowhere near over you yet, Tyler. That's why this matters, because I have no idea what I'm supposed to do."

"Don't fucking say that," he mutters, his voice coarse. Coarse, yet somehow attractive. Familiar, in a way.

"Why can't I? Why do you get to tell me you're not over me but I can't say the same back?"

"Because I'm not the one who's dating someone else," he snaps. His eyes narrow and his features harden. He takes a step toward me. Now we're only two feet apart. "I'm not the one who gave up two years ago. You were. And now you're suggesting that you're having second thoughts? Sure, it feels pretty damn amazing, but at the same time, you're getting my hopes up for fucking nothing. You said it yourself. None of this is ever going to work. Especially now. We had our chance and you threw it away. Now you have Dean, which pretty much translates to game over for me." By the time he finishes talking, his voice has lost its sharp edge. He just frowns and glances sideways, fixing his eyes on a spot near the fire door.

"I'm *sorry,*" I try, exasperated. "I was only sixteen. I had no idea what I was doing. Can you blame me, Tyler? Can you seriously blame me for being scared? Back then it seemed like we were never going to be able to make it work. It was impossible, okay? I wasn't going to waste my life sitting around in love with someone I couldn't be with. And then Dean was in the picture, and I liked him, and you were a lost cause, so why shouldn't I have started dating him? I love him." I stop to catch my breath, trying my hardest to gauge Tyler's reaction, but he's still staring at nothing in particular. His expression is hard, yet neutral. I move toward him. Only a foot between us. "We're not kids anymore, and I'm starting to realize that maybe now we could make it work, but it feels like it's too late. I'm stuck in the middle between you and Dean and I have absolutely no idea in hell which side I'm supposed to choose."

Silence ensues. It feels like it takes forever for Tyler to finally shift his eyes back to mine. His eyes are still narrowed, but the longer we look at each other the more he softens his gaze. He takes that final step closer to me and my breathing stops completely. His body is only inches from my own, and he stuffs one hand back into the front pocket of his pants before cautiously moving the other to my waist. He runs his gaze over my body. "*Me estoy muriendo por besarte.*"

I furrow my eyebrows. "The waitress is coming?"

"No," he says with a minute shake of his head. He smiles gently, his eyes resting on my collarbone. "That's not what it means," he murmurs. "I said that I'm dying to kiss you."

Right then, I forget about Dean. I forget, because the only

thought running through my mind is that I'm dying to kiss Tyler too. It's been two years since the last time and I've started to forget the way his lips felt against mine. I haven't quite forgotten the way his kisses would make me feel. I remember the goosebumps. The racing of my pulse. The weakness in my knees. That I doubt I'll forget.

I swallow and glance down at his grasp on my waist. I stare at his knuckles, and then his fingertips, and then back up to his eyes. "Why don't you?" I whisper.

"Because of Dean," he says sharply, and immediately he retreats. His touch disappears and the distance between us increases as he turns his back on me and walks off. "Wait here," he calls over his shoulder.

Thankfully my voice doesn't escape me despite the fact that my throat feels dry. "What?"

Tyler yanks open the fire door and pauses, then cranes his neck to look at me. "Just stay here," he tells me. "I'll be back in a couple minutes."

He disappears back inside the apartment, down the flight of stairs, leaving the door to softly click shut behind him. I stare at it for a short while. My thoughts take a minute to piece together and I struggle to even comprehend everything at first, but slowly it sinks it. I pull my jacket tighter around my body and turn back to the city.

I didn't notice the pink in the sky fading, but it's completely gone by now, replaced by deep blue streaks instead. The lights all appear even brighter, if that's possible. I can hear a siren a couple blocks away, but I mostly pay attention to the way the air feels much cooler now and the way the breeze is picking up. I edge back over to the wall and grip the edge.

Tyler has a point. We can't hurt Dean. Neither of us set out with the intention to do that, and if we take this further then Dean gets hurt by not only his girlfriend, but his best friend too, which makes it all the more complicated. None of this is fair on him. He shouldn't be with someone who's in love with someone else. All I know is that I'm an awful person, and I can already tell where all of this is heading. It's inevitable: Tyler or Dean.

"Pull yourself up and sit down."

I spin around to find Tyler approaching me again, a box in his hands. I arch an eyebrow and glance over my shoulder, down to the street below. We're twenty floors up. "Are you crazy?"

"C'mon, you're not gonna fall," he says, but it doesn't sound too reassuring. His expression has softened and he's smiling again, like the past fifteen minutes never happened. He joins me by my side and places the box on the wall in front of him. It's rectangular and wrapped in silver paper. "Sit on the wall or I'm not giving you this."

I frown back at him, yet I am curious. "What is it?"

"A gift," he says. He nods at the wall again and folds his arms across his chest, dramatically checking his watch. He clears his throat.

"Fine." I sigh and turn around, pressing my palms flat against the top of the wall. The concrete feels rough beneath my skin and I push myself up. The wall isn't narrow, but it's still terrifying. I try not to look down once I'm up, and so I turn to face Tyler, swinging my legs over the edge. The extra height makes me taller than him for once. "Happy?"

"Here," he says. He gently thrusts the box into my hands, his skin brushing mine for a split second, and then he moves his hands to either side of my body, pressing his palms down against the wall. And he remains there, never taking a step back. His close proximity is suffocating me again. "Open it."

I gaze back at him skeptically before finally moving my attention to the box I'm holding. The wrapping isn't the neatest, so it's easy to tear off. Accidentally, I drop the ripped paper over the side of the building, and Tyler sighs. But I barely even notice my carelessness, because I'm left holding a box that I recognize all too well: the familiar, standard Converse box. I stare down at it for a minute, and then glance up to Tyler.

"Why?"

"We lost your other pair. Remember?"

How could I forget? That was the first night—the *only* night—we spent together. And in the morning I couldn't find my Chucks.

"I told you I'd get you a new pair," he says, but then he shrugs nervously and bites down on his lower lip. "I'm sorry it took me two years."

The fact that he even remembered takes me by surprise. So surprised, in fact, that I don't even reply. I drop my eyes back to the box. Carefully, I run my hands over the cardboard before opening it up. Inside, there's a pair of new white low-tops. An exact replacement for the pair I lost that night, only without the lyrics I'd scrawled across the rubber.

"Tyler, you didn't have to—"

"I did." His smile widens and he takes the box from my hands, placing it down on the wall next to me. He nods to my feet. "Give me your old pair."

I tilt my head and squint at him. I'm not sure what he's thinking right now, but I do know that I'm too overwhelmed to question him, or even thank him, so I do as he orders.

I'm wearing my white high-tops, a pair I've had for a couple years now, and admittedly, they are a little battered and worn. I reach down, slipping them off. Tyler takes them from me immediately.

"You can't come to New York and not leave your mark somewhere," he says slowly, his attention focused on my shoes as he ties the two sets of laces together. And then, right in front of me, he leans out over the wall, stretching down to tie my Chucks to a wire that's running along the edge of the building. When he steps back, he offers me a smug grin. "Don't even attempt to reach for them."

"I can't believe you just did that." Carefully, I glance over my shoulder again and shake my head at my shoes that are now swaying in the breeze. It seems I'm never getting them back.

Tyler laughs as he picks up the box again. That positive vibe is back, and it's giving me no choice but to smile, despite how much of a mess my head is. "As for these," he says, "put them on."

Delicately, I reach into the box and pull out the sneakers. They're bright and fresh, and I slowly untangle the laces and then slip them on. They fit perfectly. I study them until Tyler catches my attention once more.

"Just one more thing," he says, his voice suddenly filled with enthusiasm. He reaches into the back pocket of his jeans, fumbling around for a second before pulling out a black Sharpie. He pops the lid. "No objections."

I chew at the inside of my cheek, mostly to stop myself from screaming, and I pull my feet up onto the wall. At first I think he's about to add some lyrics to recreate my old pair. He studies the new Converse closely, and he finally decides on a spot along the rubber. He concentrates on what he's writing, and when he's done, he takes a step back and watches me, waiting to see my reaction.

However, when I glance down, it's not lyrics that I see. It's three words, scrawled messily in his handwriting. Three words, and they're in Spanish: *No te rindas.*

Before I can even open my mouth, Tyler's already answering the question that's on my lips.

"It means 'Don't give up'," he says quietly, toying with the pen in his hand. "When it comes to you, it's simple: As long as you don't give up, I won't either."

"I don't know what to say," I admit. I can't meet his eyes, so I keep staring at the words instead. *Don't give up*. What does that even mean, exactly? He wants to give us another shot? He wants me to choose him?

"You don't have to say anything," he says. His voice is firm. "You just have to think about it."

Think about it? Does he really think I'll be doing anything else? Thinking about all of this is the only thing I can do. My entire summer is most likely going to be spent overthinking Tyler and Dean. In the end, I'm going to have to choose one of them.

"It's getting late," Tyler murmurs. "You should probably head back. I'm gonna stay up here for a little bit. Snake's probably passed out by now, so here." As he shoves the Sharpie back into his pocket he switches it for his keys, and he promptly tosses them to me without warning. Thankfully, I catch them before they fly over the edge of the building.

I analyze his expression, but it's nonchalant. He just stares out over the city once again, his eyes avoiding mine. I'm not sure why he's choosing to stay up here alone in the dark, but the more I consider it, the more I realize it's most likely because he wants space away from me.

Stressed out, worried, yet happy, I slide off the wall and land softly on my feet. "Thanks for the shoes," I say.

"No problem."

I linger for a moment or two to see if he'll say anything else before I head off, but he doesn't even flinch. His eyes are locked on something in the distance, so I turn and head back inside, looking down at my new Chucks as I walk. The building is quiet, and I silently slip into the elevator and press the button for the twelfth floor, alone with my thoughts. Right now, they suck. I'd rather be asleep, because at least when I'm sleeping I don't have to think about any of this.

The elevator door slides open and I trace my way along to Tyler's apartment, his keys still hooked over my index finger. I fumble with them as I try to fit them into the lock, but Snake clearly hasn't passed out yet, because the door swings open while I'm still attempting to get it unlocked.

He runs his blue-gray eyes over me, shaking his head at my pathetic attempt to get into the apartment. "Where's Tyler?"

"Roof," I say bluntly. I'm waiting for him to move to the side to let me in, but so far he doesn't seem to even notice that I'm still standing out here in the lobby.

"You look like you could do with another beer," he says.

I finally breathe then, exhaling for what feels like the first time in the past half-hour. "You bet I do."

8

I don't remember when I fell asleep. I don't even remember how I fell asleep. All I know is that when I wake up I'm wrapped up in Tyler's comforter and I can hear a voice murmuring my name. Yet I'm too tired to even attempt to open my eyes, so I roll over and bury my face into one of the pillows, groaning. It feels like it's the middle of the night.

"Eden," the voice says again, louder.

My head feels heavy and I'm starting to wonder how many beers Snake supplied me with last night. I don't recall Tyler coming back down from the roof, at least while I was still awake. I do, however, remember sharing a cold pizza with Snake in the kitchen. I can't even remember what kind it was. It could have been margherita or it could have been pepperoni. Either way, I don't remember it being good.

"I have coffee," the voice informs me, and immediately my attention picks up. It sounds like Tyler. "Vanilla latte, extra hot: just the way you like it."

I yawn before rolling back over, slowly peeling my eyelids open, forced to squint as the sunlight streams in from the open window. My eyes take a moment to adjust, and when they do, Tyler's the first thing I see. He's arching his eyebrows, a gentle smile on his lips. I feel a little hazy, but I still manage to stretch my arm out, flexing my fingers and reaching for the cup in his hand.

"No way," Tyler says immediately, drawing the coffee away from me and taking several steps back toward the door. "Not until you get up."

I let out another soft groan before pushing back the comforter, forcing my body upright into a seated position. I widen my eyes and offer him a hopeful smile, but he shakes his head, so I roll my eyes and swing my legs out of the bed. I stand.

"That wasn't so hard, was it?" Grinning, he slips the cup into my hand, and I sigh with satisfaction. It's burning-hot against my skin. "Nice pajamas."

I glance down only to discover that I'm still wearing my skirt and white tank top from last night. Out of the corner of my eye, I spot my jacket curled up in a heap on the floor. "I was tired," I say.

"Tired," Tyler says skeptically. "All those empty beer bottles in the kitchen suggest otherwise."

Color rises to my cheeks, so I press the cup of coffee to my lips in hope of blocking half my face. He still notices, though, because he laughs, and I'm surprised he's not frowning in disapproval at me the way he used to. Maybe he no longer minds. "I only had a couple," I say after taking a quick sip. It's only then that I realize it's a Starbucks cup I'm holding. Not quite the Refinery, my favourite coffee place back home, but it's good enough to appease my craving. "Why didn't you come back inside?"

Tyler shrugs, but he doesn't answer my question. Instead, he moves around the bed to adjust the curtains, despite the fact that they're already open. After a moment he turns back around, his eyes smoldering at me from across the room. "I know you really want to check out Central Park. So today, I was thinking, how about it?"

My face lights up. Central Park is what I've been most excited about. "No way! It looks amazing."

"It is," Tyler says. "How does an hour sound?"

"I'll be ready."

With a final nod of agreement, he spins around and turns to leave, but he comes to an abrupt halt by the door. He looks back to me. "I forgot to tell you: Monday night we're taking you to the Yankees game."

I can't help but pull a face. Tyler knows I'm not the biggest sports fan around. "A football game?"

With a slow sigh, he shakes his head. "Baseball, Eden, it's baseball. Yankees vs. Red Sox. Derek Jeter is finally gonna be playing again. He broke his ankle last fall."

"Who?"

"Oh my God." Tyler stares at me in disbelief, pressing both index fingers to his temples. He parts his lips. "Derek Jeter? You know, the legend?"

"Who?" I ask again.

He gapes at me. "Unbelievable."

"I don't even know how baseball works," I explain indignantly. I take another sip of my coffee. Still doesn't beat the Refinery. Never in a million years. "How do you expect me to know who the players are? And since when were you a fan of this Derek Jeter guy? I thought you were a 49ers fan."

"I am," Tyler says, very slowly. "It's just that the 49ers are a football team, Eden."

"What the hell?"

"Okay, okay, that's it," he says. Shaking his head, he fixes me with a playful gaze. "Central Park has ball fields, so we're gonna play baseball. You are not leaving this city until you love our national sport." Without waiting for me to object, which he must know I'm planning on doing, he swivels back around and immediately disappears out of the room. Over his shoulder he calls, "One hour!"

I roll my eyes and push the door shut. I may hate sports, but perhaps it won't be so bad. Tyler running around, all athletic and sweaty? Sounds good to me.

Laying my coffee down on the bedside table, I quickly make Tyler's bed before dropping to the floor to flip open my suitcase. I'll get around to unpacking eventually, once I figure out where I'm supposed to put everything. I grab an outfit, finish off my coffee and head through the apartment to the bathroom.

Tyler's hovering by the sink, pouring himself a glass of water. He watches me as I approach.

"Where's Stephen?" I ask. The apartment is quiet, nothing like it was last night. The only sound I can hear is the faucet.

Tyler nods to the closed door next to his room. "Sleeping. He probably won't get outta there until the afternoon." He switches off the faucet and presses the glass of water to his lips.

"He's in college, right?"

"Yeah." He takes a sip and licks his lips, leaning back against the counter. "Studies computer technology. Networks. Something like that. He graduates next summer."

"He doesn't seem like a college kinda guy," I murmur. Last night, I vaguely recall him shoveling two whole slices of pizza into his mouth at once with a beer in his other hand. And the longer I think about this, the more I realize he's exactly like a college student. I've got a lot to look forward to. "I'm taking a shower."

Tyler nods and steps to the side, allowing me to squeeze past, which I do as gracefully as I can manage. But I still end up nudging his glass of water, spilling a few drops over his shirt. He rolls his eyes and walks away.

I shower quickly, drying my hair with my towel, and then pull on my denim shorts and a blue vest. With no motivation to haul out my hairdryer from my suitcase, I simply throw my hair up into a damp, messy bun and decide to stay clear of makeup for the day. Rachael wouldn't approve, but thankfully she's not here to frown at my lack of effort.

I grab my things and make my way back through to Tyler's room. Snake still isn't awake. Tyler's watching the weather forecast on TV, so focused on it that he doesn't even notice me as I pass behind him, disappearing back into his room, which is now mine.

I ram my stuff back into my suitcase and then pat the pockets of my shorts. Empty. I don't recall the last time I had my phone. It could have been at Times Square last night, where I remember taking pictures. My eyes scan the room until they land on my jacket, still curled up in the corner. I reach down and check the pockets, breathing a sigh of relief when I pull my phone out. It's completely dead.

Right then, I realize I haven't spoken to Dean since I left. I was supposed to call him when I landed. And before I went to sleep. And when I woke up. In fact, I'm supposed to talk to him throughout the day, every day. That was the deal. Yet I haven't even sent him a single text.

"Are you ready?"

I jump at the sound of Tyler's voice behind me. I spin

around and he's staring back at me from the door, a baseball bat in one hand, a ball in the other. He tilts the bat up and smiles.

"Yeah," I say quickly. It's only taken me twenty minutes to get ready, not an hour, but there's no point in waiting around. With the time to spare, I know I could call Dean, but my phone is dead. And I know I could just borrow Tyler's, but after our conversation last night I don't think asking Tyler if I can borrow his phone to call my boyfriend is appropriate. It's kind of like slapping them both in the face at the exact same time.

God, I'm awful. So, so awful.

"One sec," I tell Tyler. I grab my backpack and rummage around inside, sifting through all the crap I've thrown into it until finally I yank out my charger. Finding a socket, I plug in my phone to allow it to charge while we're gone. I'll call Dean when we get back. Hopefully he won't be too mad at me.

"Now?" Tyler asks. He's leaning against the door frame, and I throw him a quick nod over my shoulder as I slip on my Converse. My new pair. The ones from him. The ones that tell me to not give up.

"Yep, good to go," I say. I straighten up and hook my index finger around the loop of my shorts, eyeing the baseball bat challengingly. I might not know how to play, but I know that I want to kick ass. "Are you sure you want to teach me?"

"Definitely," Tyler says. He steps back from the door and waits for me to join him in the living room. He reaches for my hand, his skin warm against mine, and slowly he places the baseball onto my palm. He wraps my hand around it, his fingers over mine. "Don't get your hopes up," he tells me. "I'm not gonna go easy on you."

"I don't need you to."

"Good." He squeezes my hand, then lets go. He walks over to the door casually, like he hasn't just touched me again and as though my breathing isn't hitching. I think he does these things on purpose, like brushing our hands together and grasping my waist. I'll bet he knows it's going to drive me crazy. I'll bet he knows how much I love it. "So, you coming?"

I look over at him and in that moment I decide that his hair looks slightly longer than I remember. More styled, less tousled. Somehow, I manage not to stare for too long. I grin instead. "Let's go."

Tyler checks the apartment before we leave—he's even cleared away the empty beer bottles while I've been getting ready, it seems—and then we head out to the elevator, leaving a sleeping Stephen behind. We're joined by a woman and her screaming toddler, so there's no room for conversation as we suffer through its relentless tantrum for the time it takes to descend twelve floors. I try not to make eye contact, so I stare at Tyler's boots instead. I'll bet he's staring at my Chucks. Neither of us smiles.

Awkward elevator ride over, we make our way back through the main lobby and over to the main doors, with me close behind Tyler. I can't move my eyes away from the back of his neck and he holds the door open for me using the baseball bat, earning him some hard looks from passers-by on the sidewalk.

"You might wanna give me that ball back so that it doesn't look like I'm about to commit a felony," he says, laughing. He waits for me to brush past him before letting the doors slap shut again.

"Hmm," I say, hesitating on the sidewalk. I tilt my head and narrow my eyes, playfully scrutinizing him. The bat is swinging from his left hand. "Yep, you definitely look like you're about to beat the hell outta someone. Maybe I'll just hold onto this ball for a little while longe—"

Before I can finish teasing him, he nudges his shoulder hard against mine and snatches the ball from my hand, somehow without our hands even touching. "Funny," he says dryly, but he's smirking as he tosses the ball up into the air and swiftly catches again. "So," he says, his voice deeper than it was a second ago, "baseball. Our nation's favorite sport."

He starts to head west along Seventy-fourth Street as I match my pace to his, crossing over Third Avenue and continuing straight along the narrow streets. The city is heaving again with traffic, both vehicles and pedestrians, and it makes me wonder what New York would be like if one day it was ever completely still. It's impossible to imagine these streets without the cars and the people and the noise. It's impossible to imagine this city without the buzz.

I weave my way around people as we walk, trying my best not to bump into anyone, though everyone seems determined to nudge shoulders with me. I drop back a little and focus my attention all on Tyler. "Isn't our favorite sport football?"

"I'm not even going to answer that question," Tyler shoots back. He holds up the baseball between his thumb and forefinger, studying it intensely, like he's never seen one before. "Okay, Eden, here's the deal. Baseball is simple."

"Hit the ball and run?"

"Yes, but no," he says. He shakes his head and lets out a sigh. "It's not that simple."

I expect to have to force myself to keep listening as he goes on to tell me the rules, but surprisingly I don't have to pretend that I'm finding it interesting. The more enthusiastically Tyler talks about baseball, the more I want to play. He informs me that there are nine innings, each played in two halves. There's no time limit. Each team has nine players. He tells me about the foul lines. The roles of the pitchers, the fielders, the batters. Something about a shortstop. He tells me what a walk is. What a strikeout is. He even tells me that there are three bases before the home plate, despite the fact that I already know this. And eventually, he talks about home runs. He talks about them as though they're easy.

And in the time it takes for Tyler to go over all of this, tossing the ball and swinging the bat in sync with his words, we end up on the perimeter of Central Park before I even realize it.

"Oh my God." Glancing to my right, the greenery seems to stretch on along Fifth Avenue endlessly. I try my left instead, searching for the end of it all, but it's the exact same at this side too. We've crossed over Fifth Avenue without me even noticing, and as I stand on the sidewalk in front of Central Park, I'm presented with trees. Lots of them. "I knew it was huge, but I didn't know it was this huge."

"I think it's like two and a half miles north to south. Maybe half a mile east to west." I shoot him a sideways glance, surprised at his accuracy. "I read that somewhere," he admits sheepishly, shrugging.

"Where are the ball fields?"

"There are some in the Great Lawn. Kind of in the center of the park, so we need to head this way." He tilts up the bat and points the barrel north along Fifth Avenue. "Now's probably a good time to tell you that I've only stepped foot in Central Park maybe, like, five times. So if we end up lost, it's totally on me."

"Five times? In a year? And you live right next to it?" I stare at him in disbelief, my lips parting as he laughs.

"It's not my kinda thing," he says, right before fishing out his phone from the pocket of his jeans and pulling up a map. He studies it for a while before saying, "Alright, this way."

We make our way along the side of the wall running along the outskirts of the park until we arrive at an opening to a footpath. There are some carts on the sidewalk selling hot dogs and pretzels, but we quickly shuffle past them and into the park.

The paths are winding and are surrounded by fencing that blocks access to the trees and shrubbery, which are quite literally everywhere. Everything is so green that it almost feels as though a filter has been added. Everywhere I look, I see green, green, green. It feels so relaxing. People are jogging and cycling and rollerblading past us as we stroll along. Tyler doesn't seem to mind that I'm walking at a leisurely pace in order to take in our surroundings, because he saunters along by my side while swinging the baseball bat gently.

"There's a track, right? A running track?" I don't look at him as I talk, simply because I can't tear my eyes away from everything. It's so calm and relaxing, nothing like Manhattan as a whole. It's like we've stepped into a completely different city.

"Yeah, around the reservoir," Tyler says knowledgably, even though he's admitted he doesn't know his way around. He keeps checking his phone every few seconds when he thinks I'm not looking, but I still see the way he scrunches his face up at the screen before telling me, "It's this way."

We cross under a bridge, keep following paths, cross over a road (which takes me by surprise, because I had no idea that it's possible to drive through the park) and keep heading north on the winding route that Tyler's leading us on. It doesn't even feel like we've been walking for twenty minutes when we stop for a short break by a pond. Several other people seem to have the same idea, and they stand and observe the water alongside us. We look at it for a while before discovering that it's named the Turtle Pond. When I ask Tyler if it's named that because turtles live in the pond, he laughs and says, "Duh."

We set off again and it's only a matter of minutes before the trees seem to disappear to create a clearing. And sure enough, it's the Great Lawn: open and huge, surrounded by a footpath running around the fenced perimeter. If I squint enough into the field, I can see the light dirt of several ball fields.

"There's one free over there," Tyler points out. I can hardly even see the ball fields, let alone tell if they're occupied or not. He clears his throat and starts walking again, heading along the fence. "Do you remember what you need to do?"

"Hit the ball," I say, "and make my way around the bases until I get a home run. Unless you're a jerk who purposely goes out of your way to catch the ball and put me out."

Tyler lets out a laugh and passes the ball back to me. His skin finally brushes mine. It's only for a split second, but it's enough. "I warned you already, I won't go easy on you."

"But I want that home run."

He doesn't reply for a moment. Instead, he stares ahead at some tourists taking group photos. They look European and he studies them for a long while before switching the baseball bat over to his opposite hand. "Aren't you a base kinda girl?"

"What do you mean?"

"You know," he says, smiling. "Bases. Don't you wanna stop at them?"

"Not unless I have to."

He shakes his head and laughs again, but it's under his breath. Out of the corner of my eye, I notice how he's ended up closer to me than he was only a minute ago. There are three inches between our bodies, max. He's biting his lower lip as we walk. "Don't you think bases are too slow? First base, second base, third base . . . Satisfying to get to, but slow. I'm more of a home run kinda guy."

And suddenly, the husky tone of his voice and the glint in his eyes and the way he's trying not to grin all suddenly click together.

I slow my pace down until he turns around to look back at me. His smoldering eyes meet mine and I almost feel too nervous to ask the question that's in my mind. A rose hue tinting my cheeks, I force myself to quietly ask, "Are you really talking about baseball here?"

A corner of his mouth pulls up into a smirk. He drops his eyes to the concrete path, his jaw tight as he tries his hardest to press his lips into a bold line. But I can still notice the way his eyes are crinkling at the corners, and when he parts his lips to speak, his voice is laced with both honesty and mischief. "If only."

9

I tilt my face up to the sky. It's a dull blue, almost gray, and I run my eyes over the tips of the trees, over the mass of greenery. Behind it, the buildings of Manhattan stand tall. It's so beautiful. So New York.

"Ready?"

I drop my eyes back down to Tyler. He's standing directly opposite me on the pitcher's mound, a playful smile on his face as he tosses the ball back and forth. I angle my body slightly to the side and raise the bat, preparing myself. I want to impress him. "Hell yeah."

"Eyes on me," he calls. It's the easiest part of all this. Eyes on Tyler? Ha. They hardly ever rest on anything else. "All you have to do is swing. Not too soon, not too late." His voice is husky despite the fact that he's talking loudly, and I try to keep my attention focused on the task at hand rather than how attractive his voice sounds. "You gotta swing at just the right moment."

I nod and hold my stance, narrowing my eyes as I lock them onto the baseball in Tyler's hand. *Please hit it,* I tell myself. *Please look cool.*

Smirking, Tyler kicks at the dirt before narrowing his eyes straight back at me. He firmly draws his arm back and, in a split second, hurls the ball at me. It comes whistling through the air and I panic, flinching as I swing the bat, almost dislocating my shoulder. I miss by a mile and the ball flies past my cheek, forcing me to jump to the left.

Tyler's laughter echoes across the field as I glare at nothing in particular. Baseball isn't as easy as I thought it would be. "C'mon, bring it back," he yells.

Huffing, I prop the bat under my arm and stalk off across the lawn to fetch the baseball, which has rolled to a stop. The first swing doesn't count. I'll get it this time for sure. I reach down and scoop up the baseball before jogging back over to the home plate, carefully tossing the ball across the field to Tyler, who's still laughing.

"Okay," he finally says, clearing his throat. He smirks. "You swung way too early. Don't panic this time. Just focus."

I press my lips into a firm line, concentrating hard on the ball in his hand as I take up my stance again. The bat hovers in the air by my shoulder and I say nothing, just wait.

Tyler nods once and pulls back his arm once again, snapping it forward and releasing the ball. It comes spiraling in my direction but this time I don't panic, only remain still until just the right moment. With as much strength as I can possibly muster up, I swing, and suddenly there's a thunderous crack.

It doesn't hit me at first what's happened until I see the ball curving back across the field, soaring over Tyler's head as he raises his eyebrows, surprised. I lose sight of where the ball lands, but I realize that I'm still standing on the home plate. I shouldn't be. I should be running.

I turn for first base at the exact same time as Tyler runs off to collect the ball. My heart pounds in my chest and my eyes almost feel blurred, but I keep going, passing first base within a few seconds. I head for second, but I can see Tyler turning around in the distance and making his way back over, perhaps running just as fast as I am. I try to speed up, almost sliding on the dirt as I round second base. *I want a home run,* I think. *I really, really want a home run.*

"Don't do it!" I yell as I set my eyes on third base, but Tyler keeps getting closer. He's right. He's not going easy on me. I start to panic as he approaches, willing myself to make it, my pulse racing.

But just as I'm within touching distance of third base, Tyler's body swings in front of mine and I collide with him before I even get the chance to stop. He grabs my waist and pulls me down with him, tackling me to the ground until we land in a heap on the dirt.

He starts laughing while I try to catch my breath, my breathing just as ragged and uneven as his. The ball has landed several feet away from us.

"That's so not fair," I mutter, but I don't mind that much. My body is touching his, and I quickly roll off him and onto my back. I rest my head on the ground by his side as we both stare up to the gray sky. It keeps growing darker. "I wanted that home run."

"Welcome to the world of baseball," Tyler says, but he's still chuckling. He eventually calms down and sighs, sitting up. His green eyes are smoldering. "How badly did you want that home run?"

"I wanted it more than anything," I say, folding my arms across my chest and turning my head away from him. I'm still out of breath. "I wanted to look totally badass."

"Get up," Tyler orders. I sense him getting to his feet, and his towering body casts a dark shadow over my body, despite the fact that there's not much sun. "C'mon."

Heaving a sigh, I push myself up from the ground and brush myself off. Standing straight, I arch my eyebrows at Tyler and wait for an explanation. He's smiling gently.

"I didn't touch base or tag you," he says slowly, his smile widening, "so you're still in. The home run is all yours." He must see my confusion, because he shakes his head. "Didn't you listen to anything I told you on the way over here? Didn't you listen to any of the rules?"

"I'm not out?"

He rolls his eyes and doesn't even bother to answer me. Instead, he reaches for my hand. I should be used to the feeling by now, but I'm not. We've gone so long without seeing each other that now even the slightest touch is overwhelming. I can't seem to figure out why our hands seem to fit more perfectly together than Dean's and mine. It could possibly feel this way because Tyler's hands are smoother, whereas Dean's are calloused from working at his dad's garage. It could even feel this way because Dean's hands are often cold and Tyler's are often warm. I don't know. It just feels different. My body never reacts to Dean the same way it reacts to Tyler, and I can't figure out if it's because I'm more in love with Tyler than I am with Dean, or if it's simply guilt that causes my heart rate to pick up. Tyler and I are wrong for so many reasons. We're wrong for not being over each other. We're wrong for flirting behind Dean's back. We're wrong because we're stepsiblings.

We'll always be wrong.

Tyler's pulling me along behind him, his skin smooth and warm. We leave third base and head across the dirt, but I'm not focused. I'm still thinking about our interlocked hands, and I'm thinking about Dean, and I'm thinking about how much of a mess everything is turning out to be. This summer is going to be hell and I highly doubt I'll be able to survive until the end of my six weeks here. Dean was right to be worried. I'm spending the summer almost three thousand miles away from my boyfriend with the person I'm in love with. Is there a difference between loving someone and being in love with someone? Because I think that's what separates Tyler and Dean.

I love Dean, but I'm in love with Tyler.

And to think I used to believe that nothing could ever be more confusing than AP Biology.

After only a few seconds, Tyler comes to a halt. He releases his grip on my hand and turns around to face me directly. His emerald eyes stare down at me as he moves one hand to my hip, and he nods to my feet.

I drop my gaze to the ground and only then do I realize where I'm standing. I'm back on the home plate, right back where I started. I kick at it with my Chucks before firing my eyes back up to meet Tyler's. I furrow my eyebrows at him.

He takes a moment to swallow before squeezing my hip and taking a step back. Quietly, and with a small smile on his lips, he says, "You got your home run, badass."

We keep playing until it rains. To begin with it's only drizzle, but gradually the sky darkens even more and the rain grows heavier, and soon it's pouring down over the city. Everyone else seems to have abandoned their ball fields by now and only Tyler and I are insane enough to stick around. Finally, after my hair is drenched and Tyler's shirt is soaked against his chest, we decide to give up.

We even run, and we laugh while we do so. It's not because we look ridiculous or because we're running a little awkwardly. It's because it's just so typically messy of us. Tyler keeps falling behind and I keep having to stop and wait for him because I don't know the route back. The rain keeps getting into my eyes and I drop the ball a couple of times on our way out of the park. Even my new Chucks are becoming squishy. I worry that Tyler's writing will wash off, but it doesn't even smudge.

"I'm so not used to rain!" I call over my shoulder as I leap out onto the sidewalk, pushing my wet hair out of my face. I blow out a breath and scan the avenue. I'm pretty sure we need to head right.

Tyler joins me by my side, out of breath, his hair flat. Drops of rain roll down his forehead, but he doesn't make the effort to wipe them away. "Looks like you're losing your Portland roots," he says, loud enough for me to hear him over the sound of the rain pelting against the concrete.

I roll my eyes and push his shoulder. He's right, though. How I survived rain like this for the majority of the year, I'll never know. After living in Santa Monica for two years, I'm now accustomed to the constant sun and heat.

"Trust me, I don't think I ever had any Portland roots to begin with," I say. He leads me right, just like I thought he would. I'm slowly getting my bearings. "I hate Portland. The only good thing about it was the coffee."

"Better coffee than the Refinery?"

"For sure."

Tyler doesn't reply until we've made a lucky dash across the avenue, back onto Seventy-fourth Street. The tourists are soaked to the bone and look disgruntled, but I can't blame them. We keep weaving our way around the damp flow of people still out on the sidewalks, and Tyler finally glances sideways at me, rain rolling off his eyelashes. "Do you still go there? The Refinery?"

"All the time." I don't think I've ever bought coffee from anywhere else the entire time I've been in Santa Monica. It would feel like betrayal if I did. "Best coffee in the city."

"Did we ever tell you how we found that place?"

"Is it because it just so happens to be on the main boulevard?"

"Ha. No." He smiles a little and runs his free hand through his hair, pushing it back. We've stopped running by now, despite the fact that the rain's just as heavy, and he swings the baseball bat loosely in his hand. "Back when we were all in freshman year, we skipped classes after lunch and headed downtown because we wanted everyone to see us. Don't ask. It was lame." He shakes his head and gives a small laugh. "Rachael needed to find a restroom and we were passing the Refinery, so she ran inside and begged them to let her use their toilet. They wouldn't let her because she wasn't a customer. So she bought a mocha." His mouth pulls up into a soft smile, like he's fond of the memory of Rachael's restroom dilemma. "She came running back out and told us that they served the best coffee. We ended up hanging out there for five hours, and we started going most days from then on."

I study the warmth in his expression and I try to picture it, try to imagine them all together. It's hard to think about it now. The moment they graduated, they all headed off to do different things. Tyler moved to New York. Jake's in Ohio. Tiffani's up in Santa Barbara. Meghan's in Utah. So much has changed in a year. "Do you still talk to them all?"

Tyler's smile quickly shifts, almost turning sad, and he gently shakes his head. "Mostly just Dean. Sometimes Rachael," he says. "I mean, Meghan's kind of disappeared off the face of the earth with that Jared guy, and Jake's still an asshole. Did you know he's dating three girls now?"

"Last I heard it was two," I murmur. Jake hardly ever stays in touch with any of us, but when he does decide to drop one of us a text, it's usually to Dean, informing us of the current total number of girls he's conquered over in Ohio. Dean never replies. "I knew the long-distance thing wouldn't work with Tiffani and him, but I at least thought they'd give it more than three weeks."

"Tiffani needs a guy by her side and Jake needs a girl by his. Of course it wasn't going to work."

I look away from him for a moment and stare at the traffic, all wiper blades on at the fastest possible speed. I swallow and squeeze the baseball in my hand even tighter. "Do you ever talk to her?"

"Tiffani?" I can feel Tyler's eyes latching onto me, but I'm too scared to look back. I focus on the sidewalk, on my sneakers, as we walk. He takes my silence as agreement. "That's a dumb question. Do you ever talk to her?"

"No," I answer immediately.

Tyler doesn't say anything back. He only gives a brief sigh, swinging the baseball bat even harder. His narrowed eyes glance away from me and I doubt he's planning on looking at me anytime soon. He hates it when I mention her. No one ever really likes to discuss their ex, especially when that ex is Tiffani. She put him through hell before, and once she discovered what was going on between Tyler and me, I swear she despised us both. "So when are Rachael and Meghan coming over here?"

I arch an eyebrow at his quick change in subject, but I don't mind. I don't particularly enjoy talking about Tiffani either. "The 16th. Meghan's still gonna be in Europe with Jared until then, so they're taking her birthday trip a little later than they planned."

"So I'm guessing you're gonna be hanging out with them rather than me for a while?"

I try to catch his gaze, but he's adamant on staring at the sidewalk. By this point I think we're both past caring how wet we get. Our pace is slow. "Hey," I say, "they're only gonna be here for a few days. I would have been coming with them if I wasn't already here."

Finally, Tyler glances sideways at me. There's a smile on his lips. "Thank God I called dibs."

We cross over on Third Avenue as we approach his apartment building, and just the sight of it and the thought of warmth is enough to make me break into a jog for the last few yards. Tyler follows suit and the two of us burst through the entrance, our bodies dripping, silence around us. We just stand there for a moment, attempting to recover, until finally Tyler laughs.

And finally, he runs his hand over his face and wipes away the drops of rain. "Maybe today was a bad day to play baseball."

"You can say that again," I murmur, but I'm grinning.

We don't hesitate for much longer and we shuffle into the elevator, leaving behind a wet trail that decorates the main lobby. We're a little giddy, and part of me wonders if perhaps it's simply the effect of the rain, but soon I realize that it's not the weather that's making us laugh; we're both genuinely in a good mood. I make an attempt at wringing out my T-shirt as I follow Tyler along the twelfth floor and into his apartment.

We're greeted by Snake, who's seated on the carpet with his back pressed against one of the couches. He's on his phone, texting. To begin with he doesn't even glance up from his device, but he eventually decides to acknowledge our presence.

When he does, his eyes widen and he studies us both for a long moment before asking, "What the hell happened to you guys? Did you jump into the fucking Hudson?"

"Did you realize it's raining?" Tyler smirks, then turns and heads through the kitchen, tossing the baseball bat onto the worktop and slipping into the bathroom. A few seconds later he reappears, two towels in his hands. "You know . . . raining like hell?"

"Since when?" Snake asks, oblivious. He cranes his neck, eyeing up the large windows, before murmuring, "Oh shit, you're right." He glances back over to Tyler. "I was too busy hanging out with the 1201 girls to notice."

"The what?" I pull a face at him as he fires his eyes to me.

"The apartment two doors down," Tyler murmurs before Snake has the chance to reply. He joins me again and passes me a towel, which I accept with a smile of gratitude. "Some college chicks. They're hella annoying." Bending over slightly, he ruffles his hair with his own towel.

"Huh," Snake says after a second. "You weren't calling them annoying when you were all doing body shots on each other last month."

"That was a dare," Tyler interjects, his body shooting upright. His hair's everywhere, and if I weren't so focused on Snake's words then perhaps I'd find it cute. "Your dare, actually."

Snake grins and it makes his nose seem a little crooked, like it's been broken before. "Yet you had no complaints when it came to doing it."

Tyler just shakes his head, yet I'm hoping he'll say something. Defend himself. Even, hopefully, tell me that Snake's just kidding. Who are these girls that live in apartment 1201? College girls? I'll bet they're gorgeous. I'll bet they're smart. I'll bet they all hang out often.

"I'm gonna call Dean," I blurt. I'm not sure why the thought even crosses my mind, but after I say it I realize that I really, really do need to call him. It's overdue and I can almost hear my phone yelling my name from Tyler's room. So I turn around, towel in hand, and float through into his bedroom. Or my bedroom. Whichever.

I catch Tyler furrowing his eyebrows at me as I shut the door and I'm tempted to throw him an apologetic smile, but then I remember the body shots. I look away quickly and click the door shut, my expression blank. It doesn't remain like that for much longer, though, because soon I'm gnawing on my lower lip as I reach for my phone and dial Dean's number.

The sound of the monotonous ring almost makes me feel sick. If I could, I'd avoid all contact with him for the next six weeks. Six weeks to get my thoughts in order, to decide if I want to stay with him or if I don't. Right now, I'm too busy trying to figure out how I feel about Tyler. It'd be better if I could figure out how I feel about Dean much later, but apparently I have to figure it all out now, at the exact same time. I'm juggling the two of them back and forth, trying not to hurt either of them, but already I'm struggling. I can't think of a way to resolve any of this.

"So you *are* alive," Dean's voice mutters into my ear, his abrupt greeting bringing my attention back to the call. His contemptuous tone makes me regret this already.

"Sorry," I say. I almost want to sigh, but for his sake I manage to suppress it. "I got so caught up in everything and then my phone died and—"

"And what? They don't have landlines in New York? They don't have phone booths?"

I draw my phone away from my ear and scrunch my face up at it. Damn. Part of me wants to hang up right there and then because of his bitter attitude, but the rest of me seems to have the common sense to know that that'll only make this worse. So I press the phone back to my ear. "I haven't even been here twenty-four hours. Just chill out. You're acting like I haven't called you in a week. I'm here. I'm in one piece." I grit my teeth and set myself down on the corner of Tyler's bed. The mattress is soft, but I'm far from comfortable. "And the city is great, thanks for asking."

Dean doesn't reply immediately. Instead, he remains silent and the only thing I can hear over the line is the sound of his breathing. Slow and deep. "I'm sorry," he mumbles after a while. "It's just that we're on completely different coasts and I'm not getting to see you every day. I need to be able to talk to you. You owe me that at least."

"I know." I glance around Tyler's room, nervously looking for something to focus on, but only end up staring back at the towel in my lap. I hadn't realized I was still holding the baseball, either. I squeeze it hard. It's cold and slightly wet. "I'll try to call you more."

"You better," Dean shoots back, but his tone is softer now. "Do you want to drive me crazy over here?"

"Just try not to think about me," I joke. After the words leave my lips, I realize I'm not even kidding. I don't want Dean to be thinking about me. I'm too busy thinking about Tyler to pay Dean the same amount of attention. "Really," I say, "don't think about me."

"It's not that easy."

I let out a sigh away from the phone so that he doesn't notice, and then I toss the baseball onto the floor and flop backward onto Tyler's bed, pulling the towel over my head. "Are you really still mad at me for coming here?"

"I've never been mad, Eden," Dean says gently, reassuringly. I wish he was, though. In the background I can hear the purring of engines and the faint echo of the radio. He must be at work. "Just disappointed that you'd rather spend your last summer with me . . . without me. We're hardly ever going to see each other after the fall, and you know that, yet you still chose to take up the whole New York idea."

"It's New York, Dean," I say quietly, squeezing my eyes shut. "New York." And Tyler. Tyler, Tyler, Tyler. Endlessly.

"Sorry, you're right. It's New York," Dean repeats. His tone is quickly growing sour again, his voice deepening. "I'm sorry I can't compete with Times Square or Central Park. I'm sorry that I must seem so shit in comparison."

"I didn't mean it like that—"

"I gotta get back to work." Dean's usually so soft-spoken, but right now his voice is rough. "Enjoy New York. You know, since it's so much better."

He hangs up before I can even reply.

I sit up and gape at my phone for a minute. As if Dean just

hung up on me like that. Pissed off at him, I grit my teeth and get to my feet, quickly wrapping the towel around my damp hair. All I want to do is hang out with Tyler again, away from Dean and his crappy attitude, so I swing open the bedroom door and enter the living room.

Snake's still texting, only now he's standing and leaning against the kitchen worktop. He glances up at me from beneath his eyelashes, not quite lifting his head. He looks at me a little strangely, like he wants to laugh at the towel wrapped around my head.

"Where's Tyler?"

"You're a minute and a half too late," Snake says. "He just left. He had to head out."

"Why?"

"Emily needs his help with something. Asked for a favor." He shrugs.

"Emily?" I echo. Something inside of me shifts, like I can quite literally feel my stomach dropping. *Emily?* I swallow. "Who's that?"

Now Snake looks up. "He's never mentioned her to you?"

10

For exactly forty minutes, I can't sit still. I gnaw on my lip, I bite at my cuticles, I pace the living room. Every so often I think I might throw up, but I hold my breath and force the feeling away. I'm so nervous. And so scared. And so furious. Who is Emily and why am I only hearing about her now?

"What's your problem?" Snake calls over his shoulder from the living room, craning his neck to stare across the room at me. He's been watching some documentary about an airplane crash for at least a half-hour now, and he even puts it on mute for a second as he shifts his attention to me.

"I don't have a problem," I lie. Standing in the kitchen, I grip the worktop even harder and try to meet his eyes, but I worry that he'll notice my panic, so I try to smile.

"She's nice," Snake says in an effort to reassure me. It does little to help, though. In fact, it only makes me feel worse. "She's British."

"British?" I echo. *Awesome,* I think. Cute accent. Something different. There's no way I can compete against a British girl. No way in hell.

"Yeah, from London." Snake laughs and turns back to the TV, putting the sound back on. "Every time I hear her talk it puts me in the mood to watch Harry Potter."

He must think I'm weird. He must wonder why I'm so uneasy. I mean, what's the big deal about my stepbrother hanging out with a girl? What's the big deal about this girl potentially being more than just his friend? That's the thing. It wouldn't be a big deal if he were nothing more than my stepbrother. It wouldn't bother me if I weren't so in love with him.

But the truth is, I don't know who this girl is. I don't know why Tyler's never brought her up before. What if they are dating? What if everything he said last night was just bullshit?

I feel nauseous yet again, and I try to push the thoughts out of my mind until my stomach settles once more. I'm just about to turn to the cupboard to fetch myself a glass when I hear the apartment door unlocking. My eyes fire over immediately and Tyler steps into the apartment, dragging a suitcase behind him. A bright-pink suitcase. He pauses and pushes the door open further.

Beside him, there's a girl.

I almost hurl my fist into the worktop at the mere sight of her.

She's taller than me, yet still smaller than Tyler, and her complexion is warm. Her hair is straight (and damp) and it ends just below her bust, gradually growing lighter at the tips. Anxiously, she interlocks her fingers as her eyes flit around the room. They're bright, yet they look swollen. And she's pretty. Really, really pretty. Pretty in a natural, simple way.

Snake doesn't mute the TV this time; he turns it off completely. He rotates his body around and folds his arms across the back of the couch, eyes curious. "Tyler," he says, "can I ask you why it's becoming a daily occurrence for you to bring home a girl with a suitcase?" He throws me a pointed glance.

"Hey, Snake," the girl murmurs with a sad smile, her voice apologetic. And her accent? Her accent is British. I'm in no doubt at all that I am now standing within a twelve-foot radius of Emily.

The only thing I can think is, *Why the hell is she here?*

"Hey," Snake shoots back. "So what's going on?"

Tyler knees the door shut behind him as he moves into the center of the room, but Emily remains by the doorway. He clears his throat and meets Snake's gaze. He's yet to look at me. "Emily's gonna be staying here for a little while," he says.

Staying here? *Staying here?* I almost want to scream the apartment down, but I'm frozen in place, my throat too dry to even attempt to make a sound. I dig my nails into the worktop.

"No questions asked," Tyler adds, giving Snake a firm warning glance before he can open his mouth.

"Honestly," Emily says, rushing to Tyler's side, "if it's too much of a hassle . . ."

"No, it's fine." His voice is firm.

"Are you sure?"

I want her to stop talking. I want that accent to disappear. I want her to walk out. But I know that none of these things are going to happen, so I try to control my breathing instead. It's ragged.

"Positive," he says. "We're just, uh, a little short when it comes to beds. Snake?"

"Sure, she can sleep with me," Snake agrees, a smirk on his lips. It soon fades when Tyler narrows his eyes at him. "Fine, fine," Snake huffs. "I'll take the couch like you. She can have my room."

"There you go," Tyler says. He smiles reassuringly down at Emily, right before he tilts his face in my direction. It's like he hasn't even realized I've been standing here the entire time, because he widens his eyes and then gestures for me to come over. I don't even flinch. "Emily," he says, giving me a clipped nod, "this is my stepsister, Eden."

Slowly, her lips form a warm smile. She's about to reply, about to ask me what's up or tell me how great it is to meet me or simply say hey, but I can't take it. I can't handle standing in the same room as her and I can't handle the idea of her dating Tyler.

And so before she can even speak, I storm through the living room, marching past both Tyler and Emily as fast as I can without meeting their eyes. I feel like I might just burst into tears any second, so the moment I get into Tyler's room and shut the door behind me, I let out a sigh of relief to be away from them.

My heart is pounding so hard that I can hear it vibrating in my ears and only then do I realize just how fast I'm breathing. I don't know why I'm getting so worked up. At first I think it's just anger. Anger at Tyler for never mentioning the fact that he's seeing another girl, anger at him for telling me everything he did last night and leaving me with false hope. But for some reason, I realise I don't feel that furious. Just disappointed and unable to cope. And then, slowly, it sinks in that I'm not angry at all. I'm jealous. So unbelievably jealous.

The door swings open, ending my fifteen seconds of privacy, and Tyler steps into the room, muttering, "What the hell?"

Even looking at him hurts, so while he clicks the door shut behind him, I fold my arms across my chest and turn my back to him. "Don't try to introduce me to your girlfriend after telling me last night that you're not over me," I spit, bubbling with contempt. Why does this girl have to stay here? Why does my summer have to be ruined already?

"Girlfriend?" Tyler echoes. "You think she's my girlfriend?"

I glance over my shoulder. I think my heart might have even paused for a second. "She's not?"

"God, Eden, no." He shakes his head and breathes a laugh, which puts me at ease. He even rolls his eyes. "Emily's just a friend. We toured together."

Relief is flooding through my body, but I try not to look too thrilled. I remain calm, staring back at Tyler. "How come you never mentioned her to me?"

"Honestly, I don't know," he murmurs. Brushing past me, he sits down on his bed and interlocks his hands between his knees. "I never mentioned any of the people I toured with. Well, I did. I just never really told you their names."

I can tell by his eyes that he's being truthful, so I sigh and sit down next to him. I make sure to leave a few inches between us. "Why is she staying here?"

"Because," he says, "she needs a place to crash. She's got some stuff going on right now. She's from the UK."

"I noticed," I murmur, slightly irritated. I don't mean to sound gruff, but I can't help it. Stealing a sideways glance at Tyler, I quickly go over his words. They're not dating. They're just friends. They toured together . . . Toured the East Coast, raising awareness . . . Raising awareness of abuse by sharing their own stories. I press a finger to my lips and stare at Tyler until he shifts his eyes to mine. "If she was on the tour, does that mean . . . ?"

I can see him swallow as he looks away again, his eyes

dropping to the ground. "Yeah. Not physically," he says after a moment of silence. His voice seems almost fragile. "Emotionally. She's really sensitive, so think about what you say to her before you say it."

I groan and press my hands to my face. Bending over, I hang my head between my knees, wishing I hadn't jumped to conclusions and dramatically stormed away from her. "She must think I'm a rude bitch."

"I can't argue with that one."

I quickly sit up and push his shoulder, rolling my eyes. I don't feel sick anymore. I feel relaxed and content. "I thought you were dating her. Can you blame me?"

"Did the thought of me with someone else piss you off? Did it totally get your temper going?" He's grinning as he gets to his feet, standing tall and smoldering his eyes down at me. Gently, he reaches for my hands and pulls me up. He doesn't let go of me once I'm up and standing, only moves his hands to my shoulders, firmly looping his arms around the back of my neck and pulling my body tight against his. "Are you that addicted to me, Eden Munro?"

I wrap my arms around him too, just above his waist. "You wish," I tease, but I'm lying. Hopefully he can't tell.

I tilt my head back a little to look up at him, and I almost knock my forehead against his chin as he smiles down at me, eyes sparkling and all. "So about Emily," he says. He moves his head forward and to begin with I think he might be attempting to kiss me, but he doesn't. He hugs me tight, his face lingering just above my left shoulder. "You've got nothing to be worried about," he whispers slowly, his breath hot against my cheek, "because, baby, I'm all yours."

11

It rains until Saturday. Relentless and annoying, it hardly ceases for three days straight. Sometimes it stops for an hour or so, and just when we believe the sun might return, it starts again. It alternates between light drizzle and heavy showers.

And so for three days, we watch the Harry Potter movies. Every single movie, all eight of them, twice. It's Snake's suggestion, of course, and it's all because Emily and her British accent decided to walk through the door. Eventually I did muster up the courage to apologize to her for being so rude, so there's no longer any tension between the two of us. It's quite nice lounging around inside, all four of us wrapped in blankets, surrounded by pizza boxes and beer bottles. Again, Snake's suggestion. None of us has the energy to suggest anything else, and quite frankly we're all content with the lifestyle we seem to suddenly be living. By night two we run out of beer, and by day three we start ordering Chinese takeout instead of pizza. Tyler isn't too impressed with the food choice and by this point I'm starting to feel guilty for eating so much crap, so we leave the Chinese food for Snake and Emily. When it's nearing midnight on the third day, we're on to the eighth movie for the second time, and I'm unable to keep my eyes open.

I end up falling asleep on the couch that night, my head resting on Tyler's shoulder, a huge blanket wrapped around us. Through half-closed eyes, I try to focus on Snake and Emily in the darkness, lit up only by the glow from the TV. They're on the couch opposite us, both already fast asleep. Snake's mouth is open, his head tilted back against the couch, and Emily's sprawled out across his body, her face buried into his chest. If I listen really closely, I can hear one of them quietly snoring.

"Are you still awake?" Tyler whispers, his voice raspy.

"Yeah," I murmur. My eyes are shut, though, and I pull the blanket a little closer around us, despite how warm we already are. We've been lying in the same spot for hours.

"You can head to bed if you want," he says, voice still quiet. "You don't have to stay here."

Half asleep, I still manage to slowly smile in the darkness. I angle my body into his, pressing a hand to his chest and burying my face into his shoulder. Against his shirt, I whisper, "I want to stay here."

And so I fall asleep to the feeling of Tyler's chest rising beneath me, to his soft breathing warming my cheek. I fall asleep as he plays with my hair, as he rests his chin on my forehead. I fall asleep in the arms of the person I'm in love with, with the sound of the rain gently pattering against the windows. Ultimately, I fall asleep that night without the smile ever fading from my lips.

It's early Saturday morning when I finally stir. I awake feeling far too warm, craving water, and, oddly enough, finding myself squinting at the sunlight that's streaming in through the windows. It takes me a moment to absorb the fact that there's finally some sun, and it takes me even longer to realize that the apartment is dead silent for the first time in days. Silent, because there's no rain. No hammering on the windows, no pitter-patter of raindrops.

Rubbing at my eyes, I yawn and push away the blanket, which is close to suffocating me. The heat is almost unbearable, and I toss the blanket as far across the room as I can. It lands next to Snake and Emily's couch, but they're too deep in slumber to notice. The TV has shut itself off and I can still smell the Chinese food from last night. Carefully, I lift my head, my neck stiff, and steal a glance to my left. I'm hoping to see Tyler still fast asleep, because the few times I've seen him sleeping, he's looked adorable. But he's not there. He's not next to me. All I'm faced with is the indentation my body has left in the leather of the couch.

I'm suddenly wide awake. I get to my feet immediately as my eyes flit around the apartment. They finally settle on the clock over on the kitchen wall by the refrigerator. It's almost 8AM.

I start to wonder if perhaps Tyler moved through to his room during the night, perhaps too uncomfortable on the couch and craving a comfy mattress, but just as I'm thinking about checking his room, the bathroom door creaks open.

Tyler wanders out into the kitchen, nothing but a towel around his hips. It's while he's running a hand back through his damp hair that he notices my stare. Instantly he freezes and a flash of panic crosses his face, but then it disappears just as quickly.

"I didn't know you were awake," he says. Nervously, his eyes glance everywhere but me, and he turns to throw open the refrigerator.

"I didn't know you were either," I murmur, but I'm not

entirely focused on my words. Instead, my attention is all on Tyler's body as he rummages around inside the refrigerator for something. My throat feels dry as I slowly run my eyes over him.

It's so obvious now that he's been working out a lot, because there's certainly been a huge progression from what I can remember. Everything is so much more defined. Like his arms, which are bulky but not too massive, and his abs, which are tight and visible. I even find myself wondering if he ever had V-lines before. They really stand out, unbelievably sharp, drawing my eyes straight to the edge of the towel around his waist. Suddenly feeling guilty, I gulp and try my best to look away, but it takes a lot of effort. By now I think my cheeks are tinted with red.

"Thank God the rain has stopped," I splutter.

"Yeah," Tyler says. He shuts the refrigerator door, a protein shake now in his hand. "If I had to watch all the Harry Potter movies again for the third time I think I'd go insane, so I was thinking that we can finally head out today. You've barely seen half of Manhattan yet."

"I'll go anywhere," I say. "I just need to get outside. I might even go for a run. You know, around the reservoir in Central Park."

Tyler looks doubtful and I can't figure out why he's looking at me the way he is, but then he rubs the back of his neck and shrugs. "Your mom said she'd kill me if I let you loose in the city on your own."

"I'm eighteen, Tyler," I remind him, sighing. I'm not surprised, though. My mom's always been overprotective, even more so now than she was before. "It's only a couple blocks away. She'll never know."

He laughs and rolls his eyes at me. "Just be back before lunch." Playfully, he nudges his bare body against my shoulder as he passes, and my body tingles. Any day now, I won't be able to stop myself from kissing him.

It's even more tempting when we both end up in his room: me to fetch my running gear, and him to get dressed. I grab my stuff as fast as I can and awkwardly scramble out of the room before I can suffer from anymore inappropriate thoughts, and I dart into the bathroom. I'm ready to go within five minutes, and once I've filled a bottle of water at the faucet, I set off, promising Tyler that I'll definitely return.

It's so nice to be able to step foot outside, feeling the fresh air against my face rather than the stuffy heat of the living room that we've grown accustomed to over the past few days. The city feels packed to the boundaries, more so than usual, and the sidewalks are heaving to the point where I can't walk two feet without being brushed against or barged into. It feels great to hear the noise of the city again and I find myself breaking out into a jog before I've even reached Central Park, weaving my way swiftly through the flow of people. I manage to pick up a map from a stall by the entrance to the park opposite Seventy-sixth Street and so I easily trace a route to the running loop around the reservoir.

It's busy when I get there, with people running and sprinting and jogging and speed-walking, and I slip onto the pathway and get going. I'm only planning on completing one full circuit, but it feels so relaxing and so amazing that I end up circling the full track two more times, racking up four and a half miles. It's the first time I've run since I've been in New York and I'm now entirely convinced that Central Park is one of the most beautiful places to run through. There's something so refreshing about being surrounded by the greenery and the water, something new and beautiful rather than the sight of the Santa Monica pier every morning. I'm getting bored of seeing the beach. I like seeing the trees instead.

In less than an hour, I'm already on my way back to the apartment, safe and alive. The heat doesn't help the fact that I'm sweating from the run, and by the time I reach the apartment I'm dying for a cold shower. However, it doesn't stop me from taking the stairs, just to finish off. I jog up all twelve flights of them and I'm most definitely out of breath when I knock rapidly on the door to Tyler's apartment.

Unfortunately, Emily opens it, her eyes running over my panting body. "Are you okay?"

"I'm fine," I say. I might look like I'm dying, but I'm not. I've just worked hard and I love the feeling of satisfaction that comes from that, even if it does involve the pain of having my chest contract and my legs stiffen.

"We're leaving in an hour," Emily tells me as I walk past her into the apartment, my hands on my hips as I bring my breathing under control. I shoot her a sideways glance as she shuts the door. "We're going to walk south to Union Square and back, so I hope you're not too worn out."

"How far is that?"

She shrugs and walks further into the room. "Maybe three miles? Just guessing."

"It's over fifty blocks," Tyler says from behind me, and when I spin around he's walking over to us while adjusting his flannel shirt, rolling the sleeves up to just below his elbows. "We'll head straight down Fifth Avenue."

When he talked earlier about heading out today, I hadn't assumed our plans would include Emily and most likely Snake, too. I was thinking more along the lines of hanging out just the two of us again, but it doesn't seem like that's the case at all. But perhaps the four of us spending the day together won't be that bad, so I smile and say, "Sounds cool. I'm gonna shower."

By just after 10AM all four of us are dressed and ready to go. Snake's not that enthusiastic about the three-mile walk, but he comes along anyway. We head four blocks west onto Fifth Avenue with the sun beating down on us and I think it might be the hottest day since I've been here. Admittedly, I haven't visited Fifth Avenue that much with Tyler. It's fascinating to walk down, but there's no way I'd ever step foot in the stores. The price tags are way too high. It reminds me of Santa Monica Place but ten times bigger and more luxurious, with stores like Gucci and Cartier and Rolex and Versace and Louis Vuitton and Prada all on one street. It's obvious why it's one of the most expensive shopping streets in the world.

It's not all flashy stores, though. We pass the New York Public Library and the *Saturday Night Live* exhibition and then, finally, the Empire State Building, which I haven't seen until now. It's absolutely huge, towering over every other surrounding building, and it looks beautiful even from the outside. Tyler, Snake and Emily don't complain when I spend a few minutes admiring the iconic landmark, snapping pictures next to all the other tourists before finally I'm whisked away. We come to Madison Square Park next and cross over, passing by the Flatiron Building. The architecture is amazing, and it looks so odd and incredible and, again, so iconic that I stop. I know Tyler, Snake and Emily have seen all of this before, but for me, it's another reminder that I'm here in New York City. I snap some photos here, too, before we head back on our way. We continue down Broadway until, finally, an hour and a half after leaving the apartment, we reach Union Square.

It's a gorgeous park, full of both locals and tourists. There's a farmers' market selling fresh organic produce and there are a couple of street performers, but mostly it just feels peaceful, like a breath of fresh air compared to how crazy the rest of the city is. We manage to find ourselves a free bench along one of the pathways and I immediately drop down onto it, my legs aching. By the time we get back to the apartment, I'll have covered over ten miles between this and my run. My legs feel like they're burning.

"Starbucks is on the corner," Tyler says. "We'll be back in a sec. Eden, latte?"

"Make it iced," I murmur, pressing the back of my hand to my forehead, feeling the heat. I wipe away a bead of sweat from my brow.

"No problem," Tyler says. He turns to Emily. "Strawberries and crème frap with a shot of vanilla?"

"You know it," she says, grinning. As Tyler and Snake head off, Emily sits down next to me and I can't help but feel irritated that Tyler remembers her order. "How lush is this weather?"

"Yeah, it's great," I say. I pull my bare legs up onto the bench, crossing them and leaning back despite how scorching-hot the wood is. "Hotter than Santa Monica, that's for sure."

"Really?"

"Yeah. We get the ocean breeze over there." I'm not looking at her as I talk, mostly because I'm focused on the people walking by us. I think parks like these are the best places to people-watch. The diversity of people here is really cool and, again, I find myself wondering what they're doing and why they're here and who they're with. I'm far too curious for my own good.

"I've always wanted to see California," Emily tells me with a sigh. "Tyler says I need to visit it one day."

Now my gaze finally shifts over to her. "Tyler said that?" He told her to visit? Why would he tell her that?

"Yeah, he said I'd love it over there," she says, voice overflowing with enthusiasm. "I've never been off the East Coast, but it's too late to head west now. London is calling my name."

I press my lips together. If London is waiting for her, then why is she still sticking around in New York? Why is she living in Tyler's apartment?

"You think you'll ever come back here? To the States?"

"I hope so," she admits, smiling. "A year isn't long enough. I'm on the lookout for opportunities that'll get me back over. I might apply for some of those summer camps."

"Oh, that's cool." I turn away from her again and study the park, my eyes resting on a squirrel that's darting between trees not too far ahead.

"Tyler says I should just move over here permanently."

I grit my teeth. I think if she mentions Tyler's name one more time, I'll combust. Why is he even telling her to move here in the first place?

"You really wanna do that? Isn't the UK cool enough?"

"I suppose," she says with a shrug. "It's just that there are so many more possibilities over here and you guys have so much spirit." She sounds almost sad as she talks, like the thought of going back home doesn't particularly make her happy. Maybe her life here is better. Maybe her life back there isn't the greatest, and the more I dwell on this thought, the more I realize this is most likely the case. Just like Tyler, she has suffered from abuse, and perhaps being over here allows her to escape from what has happened in her past, the same way it's allowing Tyler to. "I'll miss everyone too much if I never come back."

The squirrel disappears and I have no choice but to look back to Emily again. I decide just to go for it. I decide to just blurt out, "Would you miss Tyler?"

"Obviously," she says immediately with a small laugh. "He's such a great guy. We toured together and he helped me out a lot. I wish I had a brother like him."

"No, you don't," I murmur under my breath, sighing hopelessly. She wishes she had a brother like Tyler? Does she have any idea how difficult it is? Does she realize how easy it is to end up falling for him?

Thankfully, I spot Tyler and Snake in the distance and their approach cuts my conversation with Emily short, but I don't mind. I was growing sick of hearing her talk about Tyler anyway.

"Here you go, Eden with the runner legs," Snake says as he passes my iced latte into my hand. I arch an eyebrow at his words, but he's already diverted his attention away from me as he sits down on the other side of Emily.

Tyler's handing her the frappuccino, smiling down at her as he does, and I quickly get to my feet.

"Tyler, can I talk to you for a sec?" I say before he has the chance to sit down, fixing him with a hard look.

"Sure," he says, looking back at me a little unsurely. I think he can tell by the tone of my voice that I'm not exactly overjoyed.

Leaving Snake and Emily behind on the bench, I head around the pathway, walking far enough to be out of their view. Tyler drifts along behind me, drinking whatever drink he has.

"So I was talking to Emily," I start slowly, turning around to face him. I squeeze the cup in my hand. "She says you keep telling her to move here and to visit California. Why?"

"Because California's great and she loves it here," Tyler answers instantly, his tone unsure. I think he's confused as to what I'm getting at. "What's the big deal?"

I furrow my eyebrows at him. "So it's definitely not because you want her to come and visit you?"

I can see Tyler's eyes widening as he realizes what my problem is, his mouth curving into a small smile as he laughs. He takes a step forward and shakes his head down at me. "C'mon, Eden. Not again." He purses his lips. "Why is it so hard for you to understand that you're the one I'm into and no one else?"

I'm still convinced that there's something going on, but for now I just sigh while I gaze at his lips, the ones I haven't touched in a year. "How come you haven't kissed me yet since I've been here?"

My question takes him by surprise and it's enough to make his smile fade and for his eyes to narrow. "Because I can't bring myself to yet," he murmurs, slowly and softly, his voice suddenly solemn. His emerald eyes flash up to meet mine and his lips quirk into a sad smile. "You're still Dean's."

12

It's late Monday afternoon when Snake starts pacing the apartment, repeatedly punching at his palms. He's wearing a white and red jersey with the words "RED SOX" printed across the front. To complement it he's also wearing a matching navy cap, settled backward on his head. I study the letter "B" on it for a while.

"I thought we were going to the Yankees game," I say. I throw him a puzzled glance from the couch, and he dramatically draws himself to a halt to stare back at me from the kitchen, mouth wide.

"The Yankees disgust me. It's the Red Sox game, alright? *Red Sox*." He fixes me with a hard look when I laugh, so I quickly bite my lip to stop myself. Snake folds his arms across his chest. "*And* we're going to win."

"It's the Yankees game!" Tyler's voice calls from his room. A few seconds later, the door swings open. He comes striding out into the living room, shoulders broad, chest out. He's wearing a jersey, too, only his is white with navy pinstripes and the Yankees symbol is by the top left. There's also a navy snapback in his hand, the peak white. "The Yankees game," he says again, "where they kick your asses."

Snake shakes his head and staggers around the kitchen

worktop, edging his way over to Tyler. He looks menacing. "And who won last week's game?" he asks, eyes narrowed. "Oh yeah, that's right. The Red Sox. We're gonna do it again, so why don't you save yourself the shame and stay here?"

"Twenty-seven World Series championships," Tyler says, voice firm, confident. He takes a step toward Snake and raises an eyebrow. "What about the Red Sox? How many have they won? Wait a second . . . Isn't it only seven?" Tyler's competitive grin turns playful, and he pulls Snake's cap around to the front and pushes it down over his face.

"That was a cheap shot," Snake mutters, adjusting his cap once more and making his way over to the door. He's scowling, defeated.

Tyler turns his attention to me and I figure we're about to leave, so I get to my feet and walk over to him. "Hmm," he says. Studying my outfit, his expression tells me that he's not all that impressed. He lifts up the Yankees snapback in his hand and places it on my head, pulling it down until it fits snugly. He points the peak upward and smiles. "Better. Tonight you're a Yankees fan."

"God, Tyler, why do you have to put her through that embarrassment?" Snake comments from the doorway, smirking. "But seriously, guys, we gotta go. Gates open in thirty minutes."

Tyler nudges me forward as he reaches for the set of keys on the kitchen counter, swiftly scooping them up into his hand. There are no goodbyes to be said. Emily is already out, hanging with whoever the hell Emily hangs out with besides Tyler. The three of us head out into the lobby and Snake throws some more insults at Tyler regarding the Yankees as they lock up, but it's all just playful. By the time we get outside, they're both stoked. I'm even slightly hyped myself. I'm not entirely sure what to expect, but I'm looking forward to experiencing my first baseball game.

The weather is glorious, the same as it has been all weekend, and it seems that last week's rain is long gone. The sky is blue and the sun is hot, and instantly I regret leaving my hair down. I'll be sweating in no time.

"Hurry up!" Snake yells over the traffic as he crosses Third Avenue, so buzzed for the game that he can hardly slow down, and so Tyler and I speed-walk to catch up with him.

We make our way toward the Seventy-seventh Street station, and as soon as we near it, I can already tell that it's much busier than it was when Tyler first took me here. It's rush hour combined with a Yankees game, so I'm not that surprised. Snake shoves himself through the thick flow of people on the stairs, using his shoulders to barge them out of the way, and Tyler pushes me after him. It's loud and people are yelling and I can hear trains arriving and Snake is muttering under his breath and Tyler is following close behind me, and we're descending these stairs as best we can until finally we reach the ticket turnstiles.

"We're getting the 6 and the 4," Tyler says loudly as he heads through the turnstile next to mine. Once through, he places a hand on my shoulder, and I'm assuming it's so that we don't get separated amongst the crowd. "The 6 to 125th Street," he says while guiding me, "and the 4 to Yankee Stadium."

Snake has somehow managed to weave his way onto the platform, finding us a spot to stand in. Tyler and I join him a few seconds later, and with the station overflowing there are a lot of people to study while we wait. There's some lady struggling with a stroller. Many people in work attire. Even more in baseball jerseys, mostly Yankees.

"Are you excited for the game?" Tyler asks me, his voice slightly muffled under all the noise.

"Yeah." I angle my body around to face him fully, smiling. I watch as he raises his eyebrows.

"Really?"

"Yeah," I say again. I am excited, but I believe Tyler might think I'm lying. "I wanna see this Derek Jeter guy you speak about."

Just then, the train pulls up and the crowd immediately starts shifting. Everyone makes a beeline for the doors, carelessly tripping over one another, and Snake is no exception. He grabs my arm and starts to tug me along with him, so I reach back and grasp Tyler's wrist, the three of us holding onto each other as though we're back in elementary school. Embarrassing or not, we all manage to get into the rear car with only a few seconds to spare, squeezing in and reaching for rails just as the doors close.

"Fucking New York," Snake mutters under his breath, but everyone hears him anyway. He receives some pointed glares, either because of his comment or the fact that he's riding the New York City subway wearing the baseball jersey of a Boston team. The surrounding Yankees fans don't look too impressed.

Rivalry aside, the ride uptown is quick, and after gazing lustfully at the back of Tyler's neck for the journey, he finally turns around to direct me off the train, with Snake striding along beside us. The 125th Street station looks a little bigger than Seventy-seventh Street, but it also smells like something died in here. I scrunch my nose up as I follow Tyler and Snake across the uptown platform until we're approached by a guy trying to sell us loose cigarettes for a dollar. Snake buys two just to end the guy's pestering.

The 4 train arrives only minutes later, and again, it's just as packed as the 6. This time, though, there are fewer people waiting on the platform, so we edge our way onto the train with ease and even manage, somehow, to locate seats. Before I know it we're arriving into the 161st Street station for Yankee Stadium. It's an elevated station and it takes me a minute or so to adjust to the daylight. By this point Snake is so hyped up for the game that he quite literally leaps onto the platform the moment the doors open. Judging by the amount of people who get off at this stop, it seems half the train is heading to the Yankees game.

The stairs down to ground level are a nightmare, but Snake isn't afraid to yet again shove his way through the flow of people while Tyler and I tag along behind him. I roll my eyes as I walk, and it's not until we reach the bottom of the stairs that I realize we're here—we're outside Yankee Stadium.

It's absolutely huge, massive beyond comprehension. There are hundreds upon hundreds of fans lining the outside walls, their tickets in hands, kids fizzing with excitement around them. The structure is rounded, the gorgeous pale limestone walls giving it a clean and modern appearance. There are even narrow glassless windows near the top, and below there are ticket gates, the letters huge and colored a deep blue. The standout detail, however, are the words "YANKEE STADIUM" on the very top of the stadium wall, indented in gold in the limestone. It seems to glitter when the sun hits it at just the right angle.

I let out the breath I've been holding in. "Woah."

"Right?" Tyler agrees, grinning from my side as he places

both hands on my shoulders and directs me across the road toward Gate 6. Well, the line for it, at least.

Unsurprisingly, Snake's already there, keeping a spot for us as the line moves along quickly. He's impatiently tapping his foot on the ground when we reach him.

"Relax," Tyler tells him, his grin shifting into a playful smirk. He lets go of me. "It must be tough knowing you're gonna lose, but you need to chill out, man."

"Gimme the fucking tickets," Snake snaps. He shoves Tyler in front of him, snatching the three tickets that are sticking out of the back pocket of Tyler's jeans, while Tyler laughs. Snake studies the tickets for a moment, his eyebrows furrowing. "Where's Section 314?"

"Terrace level," Tyler replies.

Under the beating sun, the line continues to move along, and it only takes ten minutes for us to reach the gate. It's a relief to get inside, away from the heat, and the three of us scan our tickets and head through the turnstiles.

We enter a large concourse, with large banners of Yankees players along the walls. I hear Snake mutter under his breath, most likely something insulting, and Tyler throws his arm over my shoulders as we start to walk, leading us left.

"This is the Great Hall," he tells me.

We don't walk very far before we reach the elevators and stairs to the grandstand and terrace levels, and Snake makes for the elevators.

"No." I reach for Tyler's arm and pull him back, pointing to the stairs as Snake glowers at me. "Always take the stairs." Whether they'll follow or not, I don't care. I head off, making my way up the first flight, only slowing down when the two of them come rushing up after me.

"How come you never use this logic back at the apartment?" Tyler asks once he's by my side again. He matches his pace to mine while Snake groans from behind us.

"Always take the stairs unless it's twelve flights of them," I correct, smiling. Tyler nods in agreement, and I let him take the lead again, but only because I'm not sure where our seats are.

We wind our way up several flights of stairs, over and over again, through the mass of people milling around, all the way until Level 3. There are a lot of concession stands, selling beer and hot dogs and nachos and soda, and I can see Snake staring desperately at each one we pass. Echoing around us, the commentator is announcing safety information in between the sound of commercials, but I don't pay too much attention. I'm too focused on the final set of stairs Tyler seems to be directing us up.

It takes us outside to the terrace level, where we're greeted by tiered seating beneath the grandstand. It's louder out here as people find their seats, yelling and cheering, commercials and sound effects blaring around the stadium. It's hard to believe, but somehow it looks even bigger on the inside.

I follow Tyler and Snake to our seats, five rows back and three seats in, and they position themselves so that I end up in the middle. I sit down on the plastic seating and exhale. Overwhelmed, I try to take everything in.

The stands above are rumbling, the levels below are buzzing, and all the noise clashes together to create an energetic atmosphere filled with hyped-up excitement for the game, both teams' fans hopeful. We're not that close to the field, but our view is still great and unobstructed. We're situated to the right of the home plate and I run my eyes across the field. From what I can see of the bleachers the crowd appears pretty rowdy already, but there's a lot of security throughout each section of the stadium, so I doubt any brawls will be occurring. Behind the bleachers, the video board has switched from playing commercials to playing footage from previous games. Around us there's a mixture of Yankees and Sox fans, but I think there are slightly more Yankees jerseys and caps than there are Sox.

"This is amazing," I say. I'm not talking to anyone in particular, just stating a fact, but Tyler still smiles.

"So," Snake says. He leans forward, edging over me and raising an eyebrow. "Now that we've got our seats, I'm heading back for a beer. Eden?"

I shake my head, declining the offer. I don't think I can have another beer yet. We drank so much last week during our Harry Potter marathon that even the thought of it makes me feel nauseous. Snake, however, seems to survive on beer alone. He sighs at me before glancing at Tyler, who also decides to avoid booze for the night.

Snake shrugs. "More for me," he says, and heads off, shuffling his way back down the stairs.

Left alone, just the two of us, Tyler takes full advantage of it. He angles his body slightly to face me more and he smiles, eyes smoldering. I try to look back at him, but I can't. Seeing him look at me like that only makes me blush, so I bite my lip and stare at my Chucks instead. The pair he gave me.

My attention shifts, however, when my phone vibrates in my back pocket. I'm grateful for the distraction, and quickly I reach for my device and tilt the screen up. It's Dean calling. Of course it is, it *always* is. I can feel Tyler's eyes on the screen too, so I angle it away from him, declining the call and shoving my phone back into my pocket. Now isn't the time to talk to Dean. Not while Tyler's by my side.

"Why didn't you answer that?"

"Because I'm with you," I say.

Tyler nods once, turns to the field, stares at it for a few minutes in silence, and then out of nowhere he slips his arm over my shoulders and gently draws me closer to him. He lingers for a moment, and I wait, holding my breath while I try to figure out what he's playing at. And then slowly he breathes a laugh and moves his lips to my ear. "I want you more than that kid down there wants to catch a foul ball," he murmurs. His breath is hot, voice seductive. "I want you more than Snake wants the Red Sox to win." Carefully, he brushes his lower lip over the soft spot just below my ear, and my entire body shivers. I'm frozen in position, though, and my eyes are set on the field below as I listen to his words. "You know what Derek Jeter is great at?" I can feel him smiling against my skin as he pauses for a moment. "Home runs," he says. I sense him shift his free hand to my leg as he gently squeezes my thigh. "But I'm starting to wonder if tonight he wants a home run as much as I want you."

Everything inside of me, every single inch of my body, ignites.

My stomach flutters and backflips and plummets and twists. My pulse pumps erratically beneath my skin so fast I can feel it. My heart is either contracting or exploding. Either way, my chest hurts with how hard it's pounding. Goosebumps appear along my arms. My breathing slows until I think it's stopped, until I think I'm suffocating. I can even feel myself breaking out into a sweat, but I try to convince myself it's because of the heat and not the fact that I really, really want to kiss my stepbrother right now.

"How about we make a deal?" Tyler whispers, voice as lustful as ever. I grip the edge of my seat to stop myself from making a move toward him. Right now is most definitely not the time for me to be all over him.

"A deal?" I echo, but it sounds much more like a squeak than anything else. I'm still staring at the field, at the grass, at the home plate. Anything but Tyler. If I look at him right now, if I even so much as steal a glance at his smoldering green eyes, then there's no way in hell I'll be able to hold myself back.

"How about," Tyler murmurs quietly, softly, "we play baseball?" His grip on my thigh tightens.

My voice catches in my throat when I realize he's not talking about the sport. He's talking about something entirely different, something so terrifying yet exciting at the exact same time. A thousand and one thoughts are consuming me as I try to process his words, and I'm so taken aback that there's no way I can even attempt to reply. I feel sick with exhilaration and my chest rises and falls as I focus on my breathing.

Tyler doesn't wait for me to say anything. Instead, he starts to rub soft circles on my thigh with his thumb as he leans even closer to me. He buries his face into my hair, all while he presses his lips to the edge of my jaw. I feel him smile again. "If Jeter hits a home run tonight," he whispers against my skin, "how about we get our own too?"

He must feel my body shaking beneath him. He must surely feel the way I'm trembling at his touch. He must definitely notice, because when he pulls back slightly, out of the corner of my eye I can see him smirking at me. He knows the effect he has on me. He likes the effect he has on me. And admittedly, I like it, too. I like his proposition even more. I know I shouldn't agree to it, though. I shouldn't agree to it because of Dean, because I have a boyfriend back home, but it's so, so tempting. How can I say no to Tyler? How can I say no to the person I'm in love with?

Finally, I look at Tyler. He's smiling back at me, eyebrows raised and eyes sparkling, emerald as ever. "Deal," I whisper.

13

Snake returns shortly after with a plastic cup of beer in each hand and a wide grin on his face. He's so pleased that I don't think he even registers how on edge Tyler and I must seem. Tyler has scooted back over to the other side of his seat, as far away from me as he can possibly position himself, and I'm gnawing at my lip hoping that no one around us will somehow figure out that we're stepsiblings. It's impossible for them to know, but it still makes me paranoid knowing that they've most likely witnessed Tyler whispering in my ear and touching my body.

As I try to relax, I realize how much the stadium has filled up. Most of the sections seem to be full by now, and only a matter of minutes later, roll call comes into action. The noise within the stadium amplifies as each player is announced, the crowds cheering and whistling as they stride onto the field. Beneath their caps, each player has a competitive look in their eyes. However, none of these players are the slightest bit familiar to me. There's only one player whose name I recognize: Derek Jeter.

His name is announced and the stadium erupts into applause: applause which I don't hesitate to join in with. I'm on my feet alongside Tyler, chanting Jeter's name in unison with the thousands of other Yankees fans while a middle-aged guy saunters onto the field, smiling. It occurs to me while I'm cheering that I'm seriously rooting for Derek Jeter. I'm depending on him to hit a home run.

The game breaks into play at exactly 7:30. I'm not sure what I'm expecting, but the game starts off relatively slow and ends up being rather tedious. The first two innings are a total waste of time, with neither team gaining any runs. The most action I see is a Red Sox player get to third base. He's tagged before home plate. By the second half of the fourth inning, the Yankees have two runs, the Red Sox have three. No home runs yet.

Snake keeps slipping out for more beers every twenty minutes, and by the sixth inning, I'm considering him impaired. I'm not sure why the staff at the stadium keep on serving him. Drunk or not, he still manages to sit down in his seat without swaying too much.

"This game sucks," Tyler murmurs.

" 'Cause you're losing," Snake slurs, smirk lopsided. "Losing, losing, losing. Losing bad. Losing *so* bad."

"We're only down by one run," Tyler shoots back. He folds his arms across his chest and slumps further back into his seat, sighing. "We'll catch up, trust me."

The sixth inning drags on and I'm really starting to wonder why people find baseball entertaining. The Red Sox gain another win and Tyler keeps on groaning from my side. The other Yankees fans around us also seem to be growing impatient, and it's not until the break between the sixth and seventh innings that everyone seems to liven up.

Suddenly and out of nowhere, our section seems to go wild. People start yelling, and people start cheering, and people start whistling. Someone behind me grasps my shoulders and shakes me around carelessly, whooping in my ear. From my left, Snake is howling with laughter, chuckling so hard he ends up spilling his beer. He covers his face with his hand and points his beer over in the direction of the video board.

My eyes immediately follow. Up on the video board, in front of Yankee Stadium and in front of fifty thousand people, I see myself. I see myself and I see Tyler. I see us surrounded by a pink border with love hearts. I even see the word "KISS" flashing over us.

I shift my horrified stare to Tyler. He looks back at me, eyes wide, his forehead creasing. Snake's still laughing and our surrounding audience are still cheering, but all I can do is sit there, absolutely paralysed. Maybe I'd find it hilarious, too, if I did see Tyler as just my stepbrother. Maybe then we wouldn't look so panicked. I can't laugh about any of this, though, because I really do want to kiss him, but I just can't. I can't because Snake's here, because there are fifty thousand people around us, because this game is being televised.

Burying my head in my hands, I shake my head firmly. I feel so humiliated. The cheering turns to booing and I'm too afraid to even sit up again, so I steal a quick glance through my fingers instead. I'm so relieved to discover that Tyler and I are no longer on the screen. Instead, there are now two guys frantically locking lips.

I meet Tyler's eyes. He shrugs back at me, but his mouth is gradually forming a small smile. "Why us?" I groan as I run my hands back through my hair. "Out of everyone here, the camera had to land on us?"

"That was hilarious!" Snake yells, leaning forward to look at us both. He pats my back with his free hand, hard. "So awkward."

"Tell me about it," I mutter. I shrug him off me and he returns to drinking the remainder of his beer. I look back to Tyler again, but he's only staring at me intensely and smiling.

After a moment, he looks back to the field as the seventh inning comes into play. His smile never falters. I want to ask him why he seems to have enjoyed our embarrassing moment, but he's so focused on the game again that I doubt he'll answer me.

The Red Sox end up gaining their fifth run, putting them three runs ahead, and then there's the seventh-inning stretch, where the stadium sings "Take Me Out to the Ball Game" and "God Bless America" in unison. I don't join in, mostly because I'm not in the mood to, but Snake and Tyler have absolutely no apprehension whatsoever when it comes to getting on their feet and singing alongside everyone else.

The Yankees' performance in their half of the seventh inning is a pathetic excuse for baseball, but by the eighth, something clicks. They gain three runs while the Red Sox gain none, and when Derek Jeter is up to bat, my heart pounds faster than usual. Each time he swings, I get this strange sort of flipping sensation in my stomach that makes me feel like I might hurl. The nervous excitement that's consuming me is so overwhelming that I fear I might just pass out from it, my knuckles paling from how hard I'm gripping the edge of my seat. Tyler is calm the entire time, only ever groaning and shaking his head when Jeter's home run never seems to happen, and as the game draws nearer and nearer to a close my excitement turns to panic. By the ninth and final inning, it's 5–5. Derek Jeter still hasn't hit a homer.

The Red Sox have the top half of the inning again, but they totally blow it. I wonder if it's because they can feel the tension around the stadium or if they've just genuinely turned to crap as the game has progressed, but either way, they have three strikeouts before any of the players even get the chance to leave home plate. And when the Yankees move to offense for the bottom half of the inning, the Red Sox fans are definitely worried. Snake's cursing under his breath while he anxiously squeezes his cap in his hands.

The Yankees, however, aren't much better. They do progress at one point, only when Mark Teixeira makes it to second base, and he lingers there while Derek Jeter comes up to bat. That's when I start paying more attention. It seems as though it's his last turn at batting for the game, which means there's not much hope left for my deal with Tyler. Our deal only stands if Derek Jeter gets a home run, and so far all he's managed to achieve during this game is reaching third base.

He saunters over the dirt to take up his position at home plate and my heart starts to race. He's wearing an ankle support, but it doesn't seem to stop him from kicking at the plate as he adjusts his helmet. Everyone around us suddenly gets to their feet—all but the Red Sox fans, of course—and Tyler reaches for my arm and gently pulls me up. He flashes me a knowing grin, a hopeful one. We both turn back to the field, and I'm not sure about Tyler, but I'm definitely holding my breath. Jeter swings a couple times before nodding and raising the bat, hovering it just by his shoulder, his stance strong, eyes narrowed. The pitcher hurls the ball toward him, but he doesn't swing, only shakes his head. This happens again on the second pitch. In a last-ditch attempt at keeping the spirit up, the stadium starts to chant, the noise echoing all around me at once. Derek Jeter's name is called over and over again, with applause in between, and I join in with the rhythm. I can hear Tyler chanting too, and there's nothing to be heard except for the yelling of Derek Jeter's name. Everyone is focused on him and nothing else.

The Red Sox pitcher lines up once more. Raising his leg, he draws back the ball, and in one fast jerk of his arm, he propels the ball toward Jeter. I stop chanting. I stop chanting because I stop breathing, because I'm squeezing my hands into fists so tight I think my fingers might snap.

And then, in the space of a split second, there's a thunderous crack.

The entire stadium stops yelling. Even the Red Sox fans get to their feet, everyone's eyes wide as the ball soars across the field. I keep my eyes trained on it as it moves, backspinning toward left center field. It's almost in slow motion and I part my lips as Tyler presses his hands to his head. The ball flies over the Yankee Stadium letters, over the video board. It's out of the park.

More importantly, it's a home run.

The stadium erupts. The stands above me begin to rumble again and the thundering roars from all around deafen me. Teixeira strolls back to home plate while Jeter follows, jogging at a calm pace. There's no rush. The Yankees have just gained two more runs, and have inevitably won the game. Somewhere in the excitement and mayhem of it all, I find myself jumping and cheering in celebration. Beside me, Tyler is grinning as he whistles, and when he catches me looking at him, he throws an arm around me and pulls me in close. I can't stop smiling, either. The atmosphere is electric and I don't think I've ever experienced something so energetic. It feels so incredible to be here at Yankee Stadium in New York City celebrating a Yankees win over the Red Sox, with the crowds so thrilled and with Tyler right by my side. Derek Jeter got his home run. My deal with Tyler still stands, and in this exact moment I don't think my summer can get better.

I steal a glance to my left. Snake's on his feet, too, but he's not celebrating. He's arguing with the Yankees fan sitting directly behind him, his words slurred. Tyler's still cheering next to me despite the fact that I've stopped, and I quickly throw Snake a warning glance, but he doesn't take notice. Instead, he jabs his finger into the chest of the Yankees fan. And that's it. That's all it takes.

The Yankees fan retaliates by throwing his beer at Snake, and Snake immediately throws a punch. Before I even get the chance to move out of the way, the Yankees fan throws himself over the row and tackles Snake to the ground, knocking me sideways. I fall into Tyler, who promptly catches me by my waist. I glance up at him, but he's not looking at me. He's glaring at the fight that's broken out right next to us, his jaw tight, eyes narrowing. Hands still on my waist, he moves me over to the right.

Snake and the Yankees fan are on the ground, fists spiraling through the air, all while everyone else around us switches from cheering to oohing. The girls in the row in front of us let out screams as they try to get out of the way, but everyone else seems to encourage the fight. When I fire my eyes back down to Snake, I realize he's on top of the Yankees fan, repeatedly hitting the guy's jaw before catching his nose. Tyler jumps in at that point. He grabs at the back of Snake's jersey, attempting to pull him away, but before he even gets the chance to, another Sox fan jumps over the row of chairs and punches Tyler square in the face out of absolutely nowhere.

"Hey!" I yell. I reach out for Tyler, but he jerks away from me and throws a punch back. It doesn't make sense at first why some random guy has decided to hit Tyler, but once I notice all four jerseys, it becomes clear.

Snake's a Sox fan fighting with a Yankees fan. Tyler's a Yankees fan, too, and I highly doubt anyone would believe he was trying to help Snake. It's not surprising why another Sox fan would get involved. He's backing up Snake, a fellow fan, while believing that Tyler is backing up the other Yankees fan. It's messy, with punches being thrown all over the place, and Tyler gets clipped on the corner of his eye.

My temper heats up at the mere sight of seeing Tyler get hit, so I do my best to intervene. I reach for his jersey and try to tug him away from the Sox fan's punching range, but someone tosses their drink into the brawl and it hits my shoulder, soaking my shirt. I gasp, releasing my grip on Tyler as I'm knocked backward. I land on the ground with a painful thud and I hit my head against the seats. For a moment, I sit there, slightly dazed and unable to get back up. All I can think is that Snake's an asshole when he's drunk.

When I glance up, there seems to be a lot of yelling, and I realize security are breaking up the fighting. There are around four security guards and two cops, and it takes four of them alone to split up Snake and the Yankees fan. Tyler and the Sox fan break it up themselves, but they're still grabbed and dragged out onto the stairs, nonetheless. One of the security guards even reaches for me, yanking me up from the ground by my elbow without much consideration for the fact that I'm in pain. He almost dislocates my shoulder as he pulls me along the row, twisting my arm in ways unimaginable.

The five of us are escorted away: me, Tyler, and Snake, plus the Yankees fan and the Sox fan, lips busted and eyes swollen. Section 314 starts to chant "BOSTON SUCKS!" as we're led away, and they're all cheering. Public fights are always entertaining unless you're part of it.

We're guided back down the stairs until we're inside again, and the security guard holding on to me seems to trust me enough to finally let go. Snake's yelling and muttering as we all walk, and I'm mentally daring him to shut up before he makes the situation worse. My stomach twists at the realization that we're most likely going to be arrested for assault or battery, and I'm starting to wonder if perhaps I should take the opportunity I have right now to inform the security guard by my side that, in fact, I didn't do anything wrong.

For some reason, however, none of us ends up in cuffs and in the back of a cop car. None of the security guards or the two cops says a word as they take us down all the flights of stairs, straight back down to the Great Hall. All they do is promptly shove us outside, turning their backs on us and heading away.

It's growing dark by now and as we take a moment to realize what's happened, the Yankees fan calls Snake an asshole and I think they might just break into a fight again, but they don't. Snake only shakes his head and walks over to join me as both the Yankees fan and the Sox fan head off, their heads hung low.

Tyler stuffs his hands into the pockets of his jeans and saunters over. "Nice one, moron," he mutters. His eye is slightly swollen and red, and Snake's cheek is cut open.

"Yeah, yeah, whatever," Snake says. He shrugs, attempts to gently nudge Tyler, and then sighs. "Game was over, anyway. You won. I get it. Whatever, whatever. Shut up. Don't mention it. Let's go home. I wanna sleep for, like, two days. Two days or two months." He turns around and starts to make his way across the road toward the subway station. He's not all that well balanced, and he sways as he walks.

I shoot Tyler a sideways glance. He appears almost apologetic, but he also looks worn out and defeated. He manages to offer me a smile. "Did we really just get kicked out of Yankee Stadium?" I ask. "Did we really just get kicked out of my first ever baseball game?"

"Well," he says, "at least you'll never forget it."

We follow Snake over to the station, and I quickly discover that there's a benefit to being kicked out of the game before the end—the subway is quiet and there are plenty of empty seats on the downtown 4 train. Snake's too lethargic and drunk to even talk to us, so he spends the entire journey back to Manhattan with a scowl on his face. Even when we step off the 6 train at the Seventy-seventh Street station he doesn't wait for us, and I realize he's a total sore loser. He marches his way down Lexington Avenue and turns the corner onto Seventy-fourth Street, and we lose sight of him after that, but it looks like he'll get back to the apartment long before we do. Tyler and I are strolling along at a much slower pace, despite the fact that we're not talking. It still feels comfortable, though.

It's after eleven by the time we reach the apartment building and the sky is a deep blue. The streetlights are casting a warm glow over the sidewalks, and Tyler comes to a halt by his car. The Honda Civic has disappeared, leaving an empty spot in front of the Audi, allowing Tyler to reach back for my wrist and gently pull me in front of the hood. He doesn't say anything as he does this, though, only smiles at me in the dark, his teeth bright. Carefully, he pushes me against the car.

He's grinning now, his emerald eyes sparkling. Pressing his palms down on the hood either side of me, he traps my body between his and the car. His gaze meets mine. "So Derek Jeter got that home run, huh?"

He looks at me so sincerely that I can't help but blush, because, as always, we're not really talking about Derek Jeter or baseball or home runs. We're talking about us and we're talking about the deal we made: the deal that just so happens to now be in play. Now we're getting our home run. "I guess so," I whisper. I can't raise my voice any louder.

Tyler nods and drops his eyes to the ground, still smiling. It's as though he's nervous too. While I wait for him to say something, I study the veins in his neck and his arms, noticing how they stand out right now more than they usually do. I only look away when I sense Tyler glance back up to me, and when he does, he furrows his eyebrows and asks, "Why didn't you kiss me?"

"Tyler . . ." I sigh as I struggle to form words, surprised by his question. Shouldn't the answer be obvious? Swallowing, I shift my gaze to his hands either side of my body, and I place mine on top of his. I don't look back up. "You know we couldn't," I say, finally. "Everyone was watching."

There's a silence. He pulls his right hand out from beneath mine and runs his fingers up my thigh and then my arm, slowly. The sensation of his skin, warm against mine, seems to set my body alight. His hand reaches my shoulder, and delicately he reaches up to cup my jaw. It's at that point that my eyes flicker back up to meet his, gazing anxiously back at him from beneath my eyelashes. With a lustful expression pooling in his eyes, he dares to breathe the words, "No one's watching right now."

Pushing his body against mine, he lifts his other hand and pushes his fingers through my hair, and in that split second, his hot breath brushes my face. He crashes his lips to mine, eager yet gentle, and he kisses me deeply straight from the get-go. It's so sudden yet so familiar, and I can't stop myself from sinking into him. It's the first time he's kissed me in almost two years, but it feels like it's only been a couple of days. Everything is exactly like how I remember. The movements of his mouth against mine, my body trembling beneath his touch, both our hearts pounding against our chests. Throwing my arms around his neck, I pull him closer to me, pressing my lips even harder into his, my fingers tangling into his hair. His hands drop from my face to my thighs, and he grips them tightly as he lifts me onto the hood of his car, pushing my body back as he does so, knocking the Yankees cap off my head. His touch is electrifying, his lips even more so, and the power surging through my veins right now makes me feel euphoric. Tyler groans softly just before he bites down on my lower lip, kissing me carefully once before I feel him smile against the corner of my mouth.

Before he captures my lips with his again, he whispers against my skin, "I hope Dean'll forgive us."

14

On Saturday, I'm perched on the kitchen worktop, my legs crossed and a frown on my lips. My eyes follow Tyler across the living room as he slips back into the apartment and makes his way to the kitchen for the third time now. He's carrying another crate of beer, and he flashes me a small smile as he slides it onto the worktop beside me, right next to all the others.

"Is all of this necessary?" I throw a pointed glance down at the worktop. Covering every inch of it, except for my reserved spot, there's alcohol. Endless amounts of it, from crates of Corona to bottles of Cazadores to vodka, it's all there, waiting.

"Did she just ask if this was necessary?" Snake gasps, slightly dramatically as he slides through the door. He kicks it shut behind him as he carries over the final crate of beer, dumping it atop the rest. He turns to me then and shakes his head in disapproval. "Oh, little Eden from the forests of Portland, welcome to the real world."

"I live in California, *Stephen,*" I shoot back. I place emphasis on his real name, drawing out the syllables slowly as I raise my eyebrows at him. "I'm well aware of the real world."

Snake's smirk falters and he looks to Tyler for backup, but he's standing there watching us with his arms folded across his chest and a smile on his lips. He shrugs, and Snake quickly fires his eyes back to me. "Don't call me that."

"Don't call me 'little Eden from the forests of Portland' and don't assume that I'm not game for a party." I smile, victorious, and hold out my hand, which Snake hesitates to shake. He eventually does, though, and he rolls his eyes at the same time. Agreement made, I place my hands back in my lap and glance at the alcohol once more. "What I meant was," I say, clearing my throat, "is all of this necessary for ten people?"

Snake fixes me with a hard look, his gray eyes narrowed. "Of course it's necessary. No one likes a party that runs out of booze after the first hour." Slowly, his mouth alters from a bold line to a small smirk. "Except small girls from the forests of Portland, apparently."

Tyler lets out a laugh just as I raise my fist in a threatening manner, and even though I'm only being playful, he reaches out and clasps my wrist. Just in case. "Alright, alright," Tyler says, wiggling his eyebrows at me. I snatch my hand back and flip Snake off instead. "As great as it would be to watch you kick his ass, we've got a party starting in three hours."

Snake scoffs and grabs a crate of beer, yanking out a bottle and popping the cap on the edge of the worktop by my thigh. He shakes his head at me again, but he's smiling as he tilts the bottle to his lips. It's right then that the bathroom door creaks open, and Emily steps into the kitchen with her hair damply thrown up into a ponytail.

"Ah, the Briton has finally decided to join us," Snake remarks. He points his beer to the collection of alcohol next to me. "Impressed or nah?"

Emily runs her eyes over all the bottles and breathes a small laugh. It's light and giggly and it makes me want to sigh out loud, but I refrain from making my irritation known, so I close my eyes instead. I'm trying my best to like her, but it's getting more difficult each day.

"Dude, I thought you said we had limes?" Tyler says from the refrigerator as he glances over his shoulder, his lips parted and his eyebrows furrowed.

Snake's eyes widen. "We don't?"

Groaning, Tyler gently elbows the refrigerator door shut and reaches for his car keys on the counter. "I'll head back out."

"I'll come with you," Emily offers.

Immediately, I push myself off the worktop and get to my feet, blurting, "I'll come too." *No,* I think. *No way in hell is she spending any time alone with him.*

Tyler glances between the two of us for a second before shrugging at me apologetically. "Only got two seats, Eden," he says. Shifting his eyes to Emily, he smiles at her right before the two of them make for the door. I stare after them in disbelief, and just before they disappear, Tyler calls over his shoulder, "Don't kill each other."

There's a moment of silence after they leave and the only sound I can hear is Snake gulping more beer. He sighs in satisfaction, yet he doesn't say anything.

"Did he really just do that?" I ask, finally. He chose her over me?

"What's the big deal? You really wanna go get limes?" Snake laughs as though he's mocking how pathetic I must sound and he turns for the speakers, resting his elbows on the worktop as he starts to play around with the settings, attempting to connect his phone. "You're better off here, where you can get a head start." He gives the pile of alcohol a sideways glance.

I'm just about to roll my eyes, but suddenly his words give me an idea. A head start. Exactly. A head start is beneficial to me, only it's not the kind that Snake's thinking of.

"I'm gonna go get ready." Grinning, I spin around and make my way out of the kitchen and through the living room, barely giving Snake a second glance as I slip into Tyler's room.

"Already?" he yells, but I don't reply. I've already shut the door.

I'm still smiling to myself, and I'm feeling pleased because I already know exactly what I'm going to wear. It's the one thing every girl owns and it's the one thing I made sure to pack—a little black dress. A necessity. Ella helped me pick it out a few months back while telling me that it would be sure to impress Dean. Ironically, I'm now wearing it to impress her son.

Slipping the dress over my arm, I grab some more of my things and make my way back into the living room, weaving my way around Snake as I claim the shower before he can. If I've learned anything over the past two weeks, it's that it takes forever for four people to get ready when there's only one shower available. Sometimes Snake even gives up entirely.

"Are you sure you don't want anything?" he asks as I pass.

"Totally sure," I say.

I dart into the bathroom and ensure the door is locked behind me—I even double-check, just to be sure—and get myself freshened up. I go all out, using my most lavish body wash and my most expensive perfume, all in a pathetic attempt at outdoing Emily. I know I shouldn't stoop to this, but I can't think of anything better. Emily has that accent. Her hair looks softer than mine. She's shy in a way that makes her seem nicer than me. She's intelligent. And, more importantly, she seems to have Tyler's attention more often than I do. The only thing I can do is resort to my little black dress.

I only spend fifteen minutes in the bathroom once I decide not to wash my hair, making my way back into the kitchen only once I smell like vanilla and my legs are smooth. I'm wrapped in nothing but a towel, but it doesn't even bother me as I brush past Snake once more, my dress over my arm again. I'm too afraid to let it out of my sight.

"They're not back yet?" I call over my shoulder just before I reach Tyler's room.

"Nope." Snake pops his lips on the "p" and shrugs. Still drinking that Bud Light. Still listening to that same music that I've never heard before.

I click Tyler's bedroom door shut behind me and carefully lay the dress down on his bed, worried I might crease it. I'm glad that Tyler and Emily aren't back yet. The more time I have, the better. If Tyler saw me right now then my pathetic attempt at grabbing his attention would be ruined. Unless, of course, I dropped my towel a little lower.

God, Eden. I shake my head at myself and turn for my makeup bag, perched safely on Tyler's bedside table. I drop down to the floor, crossing my legs and edging close to his mirrored closet doors, and I start. I can hear Snake increasing the volume of the music from the kitchen and it soon becomes loud and clear enough for me to hear it through Tyler's closed bedroom door. I might not have heard the music before, but it's not half bad. Slightly indie, but mainly rockish. I nod my head in sync with the guitars, which results in some uneven applying of my makeup. I go for dramatic but not too heavy.

I spend most of my time working on my eyes, concentrating carefully on creating the perfect smokey eye, but it doesn't quite end up the way I hoped it would. It's enough, though, and once I've convinced myself that I look nice, I turn my attention to my hair.

That's another task altogether. It's been thrown up into an extremely messy bun all day, and when I try to take it down I discover it's matted and horrifically tangled. I have no option but to sheepishly video call Rachael. Thankfully, she answers, but I'm pretty sure she wishes she hadn't once she sees the mess I've gotten my hair into. She gasps for a while, but eventually talks me through the steps necessary to convert my hair into a subtle, sexy updo.

"So how's life in the city?" she asks. She's observing me through the screen as I follow her instructions, carefully attempting to pin back the specific strands of hair she's told me to.

"Everything is so different," I murmur, my voice slightly muffled through the hairpins that I'm holding between my lips. I'm looking at my mirror, concentrating on my hair, but my phone is perched up against the glass, angled toward me to allow Rachael to see my progress. "I seriously love it here. How's this?" I turn my head to one side and show her the braid I've been working on, the one I've added to the updo without her guidance.

"Cute, but loosen it up a little," Rachael says. I turn back around, dropping my eyes to my phone, looking at her. She's laying in her bed, propped up against her pillows, a bagel in one hand and her phone held up in the other. For once, her hair is tangled up in a messy bun atop her head and she's not wearing any makeup. I can hear her TV in the background. "So this party is in the apartment?"

"Yeah." I start to finger the braid, loosening it up and making it seem a little messier. "What about you? Are you doing anything tonight?"

"Sounds awesome. I'm jealous." Rachael takes a bite of her bagel and glances at her TV as she swallows. She sighs as she looks back at her phone. "Do you know Gregg Stone? He was in the grade above me, so you probably don't, but anyway. He's throwing a party at his place tonight. Tiffani and Dean are going, but I might just stay home. Got cramps." She takes another bite of her bagel. Actually, she takes two.

"Dean's going?" I ask, pausing what I'm doing, dropping my hands from my hair. "He never mentioned it."

"Yeah," she says, mouth full. "He wasn't going to at first, but Tiffani convinced him that he won't miss you so much if he's drunk. So yeah. Now he's going."

"Why couldn't she just stay in Santa Barbara for the summer?" I mutter under my breath, but Rachael hears me anyway, because she throws me a stern glance. Peacemaker. That's Rachael. If there's one thing she hates, it's when her friends don't get along, which is ironic, given that she still can't bring herself to get along with Tyler. I raise my voice and say, "Seriously, why is she telling him to get drunk? Where did that logic come from?" Dean's never been all that into drinking.

"It's not a bad idea," Rachael says quietly. She shrugs, lays the remainder of her bagel down on her bedside table, and sits up. "He's been kinda down ever since you left. He needs to live a little."

"Oh." Swallowing hard, I reach for the hairspray and quickly spray some over my hair, setting the updo in place, but not without feeling guilty. Here I am, trying my best to look pretty for Tyler and not Dean. Dean, who's on the other side of the country, being persuaded by my dear friend Tiffani to get wasted. I wish Dean didn't miss me so much.

"What about you? How are you coping without him?"

My eyes drop back down to my phone. "What?"

"Dean," she says. "Do you miss him?"

I think about this for a second. Do I? Do I really miss him? I'm not entirely sure. I like to believe that I do, that I think about him every second of each day, but the truth is, I don't. I'm too preoccupied with being with Tyler again after such a long time that I don't have much time to spend missing Dean. Yet Rachael is waiting, so I say, "I miss him more than anything," and once the words leave my lips, I feel like the most awful person in the world. "But hey, thanks for your help," I say, forcing a smile as I motion toward my hair. It's finished now, and I like it. "It's almost seven here. I should finish getting ready. Take care of Dean for me."

"You can count on it," Rachael says.

We say our goodbyes and shut off the video call, and I focus my attention back on getting ready for the party later, rather than on Dean. I can't bring myself to think about him right now.

In the end it takes me around forty minutes to perfect my makeup and my hair, and once I have, I'm extremely satisfied. Satisfied enough to finally put my dress on.

It fits just the way I remember: tight but not clingy, sexy but modest. I like the way it seems to enhance my figure, and I end up staring at my reflection in the mirror for a short while. It's the first time in months that I've gotten so dressed up. The last was back in March for Rachael's birthday.

I'm still staring at myself in the mirror when I hear voices for the first time in the past hour, voices that don't belong to Snake. Voices, in fact, that sound exactly like Tyler and Emily's.

Instantly spinning around, I almost trip over my makeup bag as I make a dash across the room. My suitcase is still kicking around on the floor, containing nothing but shoes by now, and I flip it open and grab the only pair of heels I decided to pack. They're black to match, and in fear of Tyler walking in any second, I slip them on as fast as I can and take a minute to balance myself.

And before I can doubt myself, I head straight for the door without even stealing a glance in the mirrors as I walk by. I still feel rather shameful for trying to coerce Tyler with my little black dress, but I try not to think about it too much as I reach for the door handle. All I can think as I swing open the door is, *God, jealousy sucks.*

I topple into the living room, suddenly nervous, and immediately my eyes drop straight to the carpet beneath my heels. I can feel the three of them looking at me, sense their gazes. From beneath my eyelashes, I see Snake sitting on the worktop where I was sitting earlier, and I can just about see Tyler widen his eyes beside him. Emily is at the other side of Snake and, surprisingly, she's the first to speak.

"Wow!" she says, her accent strong. "You look amazing, Eden!"

I glance up then, because I wonder if she's being sarcastic. I study her so intensely that again I must appear rude. I never seem to reply to her. Or smile at her. Or even acknowledge her half the time, for that matter. But her expression seems honest, and I realize that she's not kidding at all. She's genuinely complimenting me. It's always been something I've loved—girls complimenting other girls. And now, suddenly, I feel so awful for gaining satisfaction at the thought of her appearing less than me simply because she's still wearing jeans and a hoodie while I'm in a dress and heels.

"Thanks," I murmur. I can't look straight at her, mostly because I feel a little ashamed, and so I turn to Tyler and Snake instead. Tyler doesn't look like he's head over heels in love with me yet, whereas Snake's nodding.

"Little Eden from the forests of Portland brushes up alright in the end," he comments. There's a mischievous smirk on his lips once again and I believe he's waiting for me to mutter something back at him, but I'm no longer in the mood to have another playful argument.

Tonight, I'm in the mood for Tyler.

"You look nice," he finally murmurs.

I shift my gaze to his. He's looking at me, his eyes running my body up and down, and as Snake turns around to change the song and Emily fixes herself a drink, he smiles. Just a small one.

It's not enough for me, so I breathe a sigh and head for the couch. Admittedly, I strut my way across the living room, kind of hoping that he's still looking, but I doubt he is. I sit down on the couch closest to the windows, the couch that sort of belongs to Tyler, the one he's been sleeping on. I'm not quite sure what to do with myself now that I'm ready too early, so I simply stare out the windows instead. The evening sun is shining in, and down below the traffic is forever endless, but that's nothing new. I start to focus on the people on the sidewalks, who look tiny from up here. I wonder if they live here in Manhattan. If they're here on vacation. Business trips. Visiting family. Runaways. I wonder about them all so thoughtfully that I barely register Tyler sitting down by my side.

I glance sideways at him. "Hello," I say. The second the word leaves my lips, I mentally roll my eyes at myself. *Hello?*

It's like he doesn't even hear me, because instead of saying anything in reply, he slowly moves his body closer against mine so that we're touching. It takes me by surprise, especially with Snake and Emily only a few feet away from us, and he even goes so far as to place his hand on my knee as he leans in close, right by my shoulder. "You look better than nice," he whispers. His voice has adapted that edgy, husky tone once again. I stare at the veins in his hand on my knee as he breathes against my ear. "But I know you understand that I couldn't say out loud that you look hot as hell."

He squeezes my knee gently as he draws away from me, expression nonchalant, as though he isn't flirting. Innocently, he raises his eyebrows. I'm now completely content, not only because my little black dress seems to have worked well, but also because Tyler's by my side again.

Unable to reply, I blush and bite down on my lower lip. That's when I catch a glimpse of Emily again out of the corner of my eye, and I focus back on Tyler. "What took you guys so long? You were gone for an hour."

All Tyler can do is shrug. "Uh, yeah, we got talking and—"

Talking? He and Emily got talking? What's that supposed to mean? What was there to even talk about? All they were doing was buying some freakin' limes. "Okay, that's it," I say, pushing his hand off my knee as I press myself up to my feet, "now I definitely need a drink."

I can hear Tyler sigh as I walk away from him, and as I make my way back into the kitchen, Emily heads off to get ready. It's a good thing that she does, because if she stuck around here with me the only type of acknowledgment she'd get is a glare every five minutes. Once she brushes past me, I lean back against the worktop and smile rather widely at Snake. It's my best attempt at hinting that I'm now ready to start drinking.

"Boston bartender at your service," he says in a thick accent. He even offers me the smallest of bows.

"Vodka and Coke," I murmur.

I hear Emily say something from the living room, and when I glance over my shoulder I find her talking to Tyler. His eyes are trained on her as they head over to the bedroom doors, and just before Emily disappears into Snake's room and Tyler disappears into his, they laugh at something.

I shift my eyes back to Snake. "Make it a double."

Everyone's here by nine. The girls from apartment 1201 are the first to arrive and they're not as wild as I expected them to be. They're slightly apprehensive and I think it might be because Emily and I are here. They do introduce themselves, though, after five minutes. Natalie is the tallest of the three, with silky black hair that reaches her hips, and then there's Zoe, who wears huge round-framed glasses that totally suit her. Ashley is the shortest of the three and definitely the loudest of them all. The first thing she asks Snake is if there are going to be body shots later.

Two guys turn up from an apartment three floors below, and it takes me a good hour before I finally figure out what their names are. The blond is Brendon. The auburn is Alex. Tyler talks to them more than he talks to the girls from apartment 1201, so I eventually decide that I like them both.

Emily ends up inviting a friend of hers last-minute, and so some quiet girl named Skye appears at the door by herself, and I quickly realize that I'm glad she's here. She keeps Emily occupied, which in my eyes means keeping her away from Tyler.

The last to arrive is Zoe's boyfriend, some guy with blue hair who's already wasted before he even steps foot over the threshold.

I'm in no position to pass judgment, however, as I'm way over the tipsy borderline. I think as the night is going on Snake seems to be making my drinks a lot stronger than I'm requesting, but I'm too busy watching Tyler to argue about it, so I drink them anyway. It's most likely the reason why, only an hour into the party, I'm already dancing with the 1201 girls. There's a lot of jumping and some occasional screams, and I'm not quite sure what kind of dancing I've been thrown into, but with the lights dimmed I feel relaxed, like no one can even see me. I'm so relaxed that I keep on drinking, keep on asking Snake for more, keep on tossing empty cups onto the worktops. I might be used to all of this by now, given Rachael's guidance over the past couple years, but when it comes to my body handling such excessive consumption there's still no improvement. I'm as much a lightweight as she is.

It's after eleven when my head starts to pound. I try to convince myself that it's the excessive music volume causing it, but I know I'm lying to myself, so I take a timeout. I drop down on the coach, slump against the back of it, and close my eyes for ten minutes. I think in retrospect it's quite possibly the worst thing I can do, for when I stand again, everything hits me at once. I immediately topple to one side and the only thing that stops me from falling straight into the TV is Emily's friend Skye, who grabs me, steadies me, and rolls her eyes at me. I find it worrying how distorted my vision seems to have gotten, because even quiet Skye looks odd as I stare back at her.

"Are you okay?" she asks. She looks as sober as a stick in comparison.

"Yeah! Yeah!" I know I'm not, but I don't particularly want to talk to her, so I draw her into a brief hug for some unknown reason before swiveling around rather shakily and stalking off.

I spot Tyler in the kitchen, mixing drinks. He seems to have taken over Snake's mixed role of bartender/DJ for a minute, so I decide to join him. He doesn't look too drunk, if at all, and he's biting his lip as he studies the drink he's making.

"Hey," I say. It could be slurred, but I'm not quite sure. Messily, I clear a spot on the worktop and push myself up. It's a lot harder than usual, like my wrists are broken, but I finally get up after a moment of struggling. Once I'm perched, I cross one leg over the other and gently swing my feet. "Hey," I say again.

"I think you should stop drinking now," he murmurs, but he doesn't even glance up. He reaches for an almost-empty bottle of vodka and tips the remainder of it into the drink. I'm not sure if it's for him or someone else, but he definitely seems more interested in it than he is in me.

"Tyler," I say. Again, possibly slurred, possibly unintelligible. My blurred gaze is resting on the side of his face. I like the way his stubble perfectly traces his jaw, shaved and smoothed just right, and the way the white shirt he's wearing fits tightly against his body. I try to flutter my eyelashes at him, but he's not even looking at me, so I do the only thing I can do. I slowly slide my body a few inches along the worktop until my legs are touching his waist. That's when he stops focusing on the drink.

I see him swallow as he moves his eyes to my thighs. I rub my leg against his hip and I find myself pursing my lips as a rather guilty expression crosses his face. He swallows again and glances up. "What are you doing?"

"What am I doing?" I echo. Smiling as seductively as I possibly can right now, I raise my eyebrows innocently, as though I'm unaware of just what exactly I'm playing at. All the vodka seems to have boosted my confidence. Like, a lot. I have so much confidence that I'm hardly taking into consideration the fact that we're in the middle of his apartment, in the middle of the party, in the middle of people.

"Eden." Tyler says my name firmly, with a slight edge to his voice, as though he's holding back from losing his temper. He takes a step to the left, away from me, breaking our touch. Quickly stealing a glance over his shoulder, he checks to ensure no one has seen. "Not here."

"But Tyler," I whisper. Throwing an arm over his shoulders, I reach forward with my free hand and steal the drink from him. If I were sober, there's no way I'd drink it, given the fact that the color looks slightly off and I have no idea what's in it, but I'm past that point. I press the cup to my lips and tilt it back, taking a long sip as I stare at Tyler over the rim. There's definitely some vodka, maybe some rum. Cranberry juice? Whatever it is, it tastes alright, and when Tyler attempts to grab it from me, I press a hand to his chest and push him back. "No, no."

"Eden, you're drunk." Tyler frowns at me for a long

while. I'm not sure if he's disappointed or pissed off, but I'm assuming it's the latter, because he closes his eyes for a moment while he exhales.

It gives me the perfect opportunity to lean in and kiss him, so that's exactly what I do. I loop my arms around his neck and press my lips to the stubble right on the edge of his jaw, but it doesn't last long. He pulls away immediately and fixes me with a sharp glare.

"Eden," he hisses, "I'm being totally fucking serious right now when I'm telling you to cut it out."

I slide off the worktop and land a little awkwardly, but once I regain my balance I close the distance between us once more. He tries to step away from me, but he only ends up hitting his back against the door to the laundry room. I can see him panicking, his eyes flitting around the apartment through the low lighting as he tries to figure out if anyone is watching us, but I'm so drunk and so fuzzy and so desperate for him that I don't think I care if anyone is.

"Eden," he tries once more. His harsh tone has softened and his voice becomes a whisper. It's difficult to hear over the sound of the music. "Start thinking straight. Do you wanna get caught? Because that's what's gonna happen if you don't drop this."

Perhaps I'd be more concerned if I were in a state to take in what he's saying, but right now his words just don't sink in. Right now, I'm nothing but desperate. I'm desperate to kiss him, I'm desperate to be with him, I'm desperate to finally make all of this work, and I desperately, desperately need him.

Tyler presses his lips into a firm line and reaches for my wrist, turning around and pushing open the laundry room door. He not so gently pulls me into the small room and slams the door behind us, but it's barely audible over the sound of the party. He stands in front of me for a second or two while I watch him, waiting. For a moment, I think he might just turn and walk out, but he doesn't. Instead, he starts to edge closer to me. He's breathing deeply, his eyes narrowed, and he only stops moving once our bodies are touching again.

"Why are you making it so hard for me to resist?" he whispers, right before he crashes his lips into mine, his hands grasping my jaw as he pushes me back against the dryer.

He kisses me a lot differently from the way he did on Monday, back on the hood of his car. That was slow, deep. This isn't slow. It's fast, and eager. More fueled by some sort of sexual adrenaline as he runs his hands down my body, all over my little black dress. My knees weaken, and I'm pretty sure it's a mixture of both the exhilaration of his lips and the alcohol. He can probably taste it on my tongue, just like I can taste the beer on his, and I eagerly kiss him back as hard and as best as I possibly can in my drunken state. My hands numbly find their way to his belt, but I've barely even attempted to undo it when Tyler pauses. His hands immediately latch on to mine, moving them away and pinning my wrists to the dryer behind me. I stand there, my lips parted as my breath rushes back to me, and Tyler stares at me in disbelief.

"But Derek Jeter got that home run," I pant in defense. I may be drunk, but I'm still perfectly aware of the deal we made.

With his hands still pinning my wrists down, he moves his lips to my neck, trailing soft kisses from my jaw straight down to my collarbone. It makes me shiver and I want nothing more than to run my fingers through his hair, but when I make an attempt to move my hands, he only tightens his grip on them even more. I can feel him breathing against my skin as he leaves one final lingering kiss right below my ear. "But, Eden," he murmurs, his voice raspy, "no one gets a home run at the start of the game."

15

As I attempt to peel my eyes open the very next morning, I stretch out my stiff arms. I grab the leg of the coffee table, and only then do I get my bearings, realizing that I'm sprawled across the floor. The living room carpet feels sticky with spilled drinks, and as I finally force my eyes open fully, the room becomes clearer. There's a faint stream of sunlight illuminating the apartment, but it's neither bright nor amber enough to pass as dawn. It could be any time of the day. It could be the middle of the afternoon. Who knows? I don't even know how or when the party ended. The only thing I can remember is kissing Tyler in the laundry room. After that . . . Nothing. Blank.

From the corner of my eye, I catch sight of my heels a few feet away from me. I don't remember taking them off. The apartment reeks of booze and cigarettes, and I don't think I've ever felt so gross. Awkwardly and slightly shamefully, I push myself up from the ground, where I clearly must have collapsed into a drunken slumber at whatever hour in the morning. I'm on my feet for barely a split second when a sudden shooting pain fires its way up the left side of my head, and I breathe as deeply as I can in a poor attempt to make it stop. It does little to help. In fact, it seems to only make it worse. The shooting pain develops into a heavier, throbbing kind of pain. I rub at my temples as I scan the apartment, but it's just littered with crap. Half-empty bottles of beer and crushed plastic cups and shot glasses are scattered over the kitchen worktops, and when I glance around the living room I'm slightly relieved to discover that I'm not the only one here. There are two others.

Snake's on one couch, his blond hair ruffled, and he's on his stomach with his face pressed into the black cushions. He's snoring quietly and it doesn't seem like he'll be stirring anytime soon, so I reach for his arm, which is dangling over the edge of the couch, and place it back next to him.

Opposite him, one of the guys from the apartment three floors down is spread out upside down across the other couch. It's the auburn-haired one, Alex. His jaw is hanging open so wide that I think it might just have become unhinged.

I rub at my temples in a second attempt at soothing away my headache as I head to the kitchen, my eyes set on the coffee machine and nothing else. I could go with a cup or five. Part of me even considers waking up Snake and Alex to offer them coffee, but just as I'm debating this with myself, I drift past the mirror on the living room wall.

I pause. I edge back in front of it. I part my lips, horrified.

My dress is no longer modest. It seems to have crept its way up my thighs a lot more than it should have and I'm just thankful no one is awake yet to witness it. I adjust the dress as quickly as possible and can do nothing but sigh at my appearance. The makeup that I slaved over hasn't survived the night. My eyes are completely smudged, and smears of black and silver seem to decorate my face. My mascara feels clumped and my eyes look swollen, sort of like they're bloodshot, and half my hair has fallen out of my updo. There are strands flying around all over the place, and once again, I sigh. Sigh, sigh, sigh. Why did I drink so much?

I know the answer. It's obvious. It was because of Tyler. It was because of Tyler and Emily and the fact that it took them over an hour to buy limes from a damn convenience store. Why did they end up talking? I don't know what they talked about. I don't know where they went. All I know is that I didn't want to think about it, and Snake was manning the alcohol supply, which suddenly appeared much more appealing at that point. Last night, drinking a lot didn't seem like such a bad idea. Now? I see it was the worst idea.

I feel so groggy and my stomach feels unsettled, and as I turn away from the mirror a new thought occurs to me that doesn't revolve around coffee. Right now, I realize I can't see Tyler. He usually sleeps on the couch that Alex is sprawled across. My eyes immediately flicker over to his bedroom door. It's closed and I can't blame him for reclaiming his bed for the night, given that I'd passed out on the floor and definitely didn't need it. I can't help but wonder if he tried to help me up or if he decided to just leave me here. Maybe he fell asleep before I did. Maybe he didn't even notice I was down here. Either way, my body now feels stiff after spending the night on the floor.

Tyler's usually awake before me, but not today, so I decide to reverse the roles for once. Today I'll wake him up. Today I'll bring him coffee.

I weave my way back through the couches, past Snake and Alex, and I reach for the handle of Tyler's door. There's a soft clicking noise as I open it, and softly I swing the door open. The room is in complete darkness, with only the sunlight from the living room allowing me to actually see anything, and it's extremely warm and stuffy.

"Tyler?" My voice is quiet, gentle. I squint down at the bed as my swollen eyes adjust to the lighting. I can make out his outline. He's not moving. "Tyler," I say again, a little louder. "Wake up."

He shifts slightly, rolling gently onto his other side, now facing me. He buries his face into the pillows and murmurs, "What time is it?"

"I have no idea," I say. I keep my voice quiet. "Coffee?" Without thinking, I flick on the lights, and it's so bright that Tyler immediately groans and pulls the sheets over his head.

"Damn, Eden," he mutters.

"Crap. Sorry." I'm just about to switch the lights back off, but then I hear a faint, breathy "Mmm," and I pause. I must have imagined it. It's far too high for Tyler's voice.

The sheets move. But Tyler's not moving. My eyebrows shoot up, and as I'm gradually piecing together the obvious, my hungover mind processing at an extremely slow rate, Emily pushes herself up from beneath the sheets. Her eyes meet mine and suddenly she seems wide awake. We both freeze. I'm not sure why I'm so surprised at finding her here, next to Tyler, staring back at me wearing nothing but a black lace bra. She gasps and grabs the sheets, hugging them to her body and glancing sideways at Tyler. He's shot upright too.

My entire body seems numb, and all I can do is shake my head as I take a step back to the door. I knew it.

"Eden," Tyler says. He pushes the sheets away from him and gets to his feet. He's still wearing his jeans, but they're dropped low and several inches of his black boxers are on display, the elastic tight against his V-lines. If this were under any other circumstances, I'd be staring and my eyes would most probably be glazed over. But right now, I'm too hurt to care.

"Just don't," I whisper. I push him away from me as he approaches and I spin around quickly and storm out of the room. I sense him behind me, which does nothing but make me angry. Halting in the middle of the living room, I swivel back around and fire my eyes at him, furious. "Just friends?"

"You're getting this all wrong," he says. Placing his hands on my shoulders, he looks at me hard. His eyes are wide.

"No, Tyler." I try to shrug off his grip, but he refuses to let go. "I knew it. I knew there was something more and now I feel stupid for believing you when you told me there wasn't." My voice cracks and I can't figure out if I'm disappointed or if I'm mad or if I'm both. I think it's both. I'm disappointed that there's another girl and I'm mad that he lied about it. "What did you guys really do yesterday? Hook up in your car?"

"Eden," he says, jaw tightening. He takes a deep breath and narrows his eyes down at me. "We. Are. Just. Friends." He exhales while finally letting go of my shoulders. "We just fell asleep. It's nothing."

Part of me could laugh. Does he really think I'm that gullible? That stupid? I take another step away from him. "And she ended up half naked?" My tone is contemptuous and my voice is seething with venom, and if I wasn't so livid then maybe I'd cry. "Real nice, Tyler."

"It was hot as hell, alright?" he snaps, eyes fierce for the first time in forever. He's been doing pretty good lately when it comes to keeping his temper in check. Until now.

"I don't believe you," I whisper.

Out of nowhere, I hear Snake groan, "What the hell, guys?" His voice is raspy, and both Tyler and I glance sideways at the exact same time. Snake glowers back at us from the couch, propped upright, his eyes heavy.

I look back to Tyler. He's shaking his head, either at Snake or me or both of us, and with his expression still hard, he turns and makes for the door. He doesn't even bother to go back and pull on a shirt.

"Where the hell do you think you're going?" I yell, exasperated. How dare he walk away? If anything, it's only making him look guilty. Nothing is resolved and I feel even more upset than I did a second ago.

"The roof!" Tyler snaps back, slamming the door behind him. I stare at it in disbelief.

"Jesus Christ," Snake says. "The fuck is wrong with you guys?" He gets to his feet, glaring at me as though it's all my fault as he drags himself over to the kitchen. He's not all that well balanced and there's a slight possibility that he might still be drunk. Through all the commotion, however, Alex doesn't appear to have even flinched. He's still asleep.

"Tyler's a liar, that's what's wrong," I mutter. Snake's eyes never leave mine as he lingers by the coffee machine. He squints back at me curiously, as though he's expecting me to update him on what's happened. It's an explanation he's not going to get. "Snake," I say, "please, please make me some coffee before I die."

"Eden?"

I flash my eyes in the direction of Emily's voice. She's hovering by the door of Tyler's room, only now she's pulled on some clothes. Tyler's clothes. The shirt he was wearing last night. It only pisses me off even more.

"What?" I fold my arms across my chest, over my creased little black dress that no longer looks appealing.

Emily touches the tips of her hair, twirling strands around her fingers. "Can I talk to you?" Admittedly, she does look mortified and her voice is trembling a little. It doesn't make me feel any sympathy. In fact, it only makes her appear guilty, too.

"I don't think there's anything you can say that's gonna justify you," I state, loud and firm, just to ensure she gets the memo that I'm far from happy. I can hear the coffee machine churning in the background and I'm aware of Snake's eyes on us, so I make the decision right then that I'd rather he didn't get involved. Pressing my lips together into a firm line, I add, "But fine."

With my arms still folded, I march back across the living room and into Tyler's room, brushing against Emily as I squeeze past her. Thankfully, she has the common sense to shut the door to give us some privacy, and she flicks on the lights. This time, no one is complaining.

"Eden," she starts, "I know what it looked like and I know why you're mad. Like, he's your brother, so it's weird for you, isn't it?" Her hands move as she talks and her eyes are wide and it seems like she's trying to trick me into believing she's innocent, but I stand my ground, only blinking back at her. "We didn't sleep together," she says quietly. "Honestly, we didn't. We're just mates."

I think I could stand here and argue with her all day, but her words start to sink in and I take a moment to collect my thoughts. *He's your brother, so it's weird for you.* That's what it seems like to her. I must come across as the crazy stepsibling who's way too overprotective, and I realize then that for the past ten minutes I've totally forgotten that none of them know. Alex from the couch doesn't know. Snake doesn't know. Emily doesn't know. None of them know that I'm in love with Tyler. None of them have any idea.

And now, I just seem insane.

I know I need to chill out, whether they did or didn't hook up, otherwise my anger will seem uncalled for. Guilty or not, I need to let them off the hook. I can't tell yet if they're telling the truth or if they're lying through their teeth, but I sigh, anyway. "Whatever," I say. It's hard to force myself to seem nonchalant, to look as though it doesn't bother me, but I do it. I do it because keeping my secret with Tyler is more important. "I know it's not really any of my business. You know, it's just weird with this being my room while I'm here."

"Honestly, Eden, I'd never go there," she says.

Part of me wonders if she's lying, but a stepsister wouldn't question it, so I keep quiet. It seems like every day it gets harder and harder to keep pretending that there's nothing going on. I forget to remind myself that to everyone else we're just stepsiblings. To Tyler and me, we're so much more.

There's the tapping of knuckles against Tyler's door and Snake swings it open without waiting for us to give him the all-clear. He wanders in with three mugs of steaming coffee and passes one to Emily and one to me, keeping the third for himself.

"Seems like you guys needed it," he says with a nod. He's still wearing his clothes from last night too, only the buttons on his shirt are undone. There's a tattoo of a sun on his chest and he notices both Emily and me staring at it. "It's 'cause I'm just as hot," he answers before we can even ask. I can't tell if he's kidding or not.

Anyway, my head is still pounding and I wrap my hands tightly around the mug of coffee as I steal my way back into the living room without so much as a glance back in Emily's direction. There's still that awful waft of booze that seems to be clinging to the air throughout the apartment, and as I perch myself down on the couch, I stare across the coffee table at Alex for a while. He still hasn't moved an inch.

As Snake stumbles across the room to sit down next to me, I shoot him a sideways glance and then nod to the guy who's spent the night here. "Can you wake him?"

"Nah," Snake says with the shake of his head. "I'll get Brendon to come get him." He takes a loud gulp of coffee, sighing as he swallows. "Shit, I feel like hell. How about you?"

"Not that great," I admit. It draws my attention back to the fact that my head is throbbing and suddenly it seems much worse than it originally was. I'm grateful, however, that I don't feel like I'm going to throw up. "Do you guys have painkillers?"

"Second cupboard along from the left, top shelf," Snake informs me, pointing his mug to the kitchen.

I get to my feet, taking a long swig of my coffee before laying it down on the coffee table, and shuffle my way over to the kitchen. It takes effort to even walk. My back hurts from sleeping on the floor and I could do with some rest, but I'm way too riled up to sleep. I open up the cupboard and stretch up on my tiptoes, rummaging around. My hands only seem to be grasping at lighters.

"Do you smoke or something?" I call over my shoulder to Snake.

"Huh?" he says, perplexed. I hold up a lighter as I continue to search with my free hand, never turning around. "Oh, those," he says. "Nah, I don't. You find those painkillers yet? Red box?"

"Got them," I say. I fetch myself a glass of water and take a couple of the pills, hoping to feel much better, and head back to the living room to grab my coffee. I don't sit down, only fix Snake with a defeated look. "I'm gonna go freshen up." I frown at Alex once again. I'm starting to wonder if he's even alive anymore. "Make sure he goes home."

Snake nods in agreement as he slumps further into the couch. Behind him, Emily darts from Tyler's room to Snake's, which is technically her own. Just like Tyler's is kind of mine for the summer. She's still wearing Tyler's shirt, but she's carrying her dress and her heels, looking rather shameful. At least the walk home is only two feet across the room.

I'm thankful she's left Tyler's room, though, because now I can actually go grab some fresh clothes. With my coffee in hand, I head over, and when I enter the room, I'm surprised to find that Emily has tidied the place up. The curtains are drawn back and the windows are pushed wide open to allow the sun and some fresh air to come in. The bed's been perfectly made, the pillows fluffed up. Even my own crap that's been lying around seems to look neater.

Quickly, I grab some sweats and a hoodie and dash to the bathroom before Emily can beat me to it. Hot showers are the best when it comes to soothing away a hangover, so I increase the temperature and stand under the water, my back against the shower wall and my eyes closed. I stand there for a while, motionless, just breathing. I try my hardest to relax, but I don't think I can. I'm still mad at Tyler. Emily? Not so much. It's not like she knew about Tyler and me, and at least she was brave enough to stay in the apartment, unlike Tyler, who ran away at the first chance he got.

Dithering in the bathroom for thirty minutes, washing my hair and pulling on my clothes, I pull the hood of my hoodie up over my head and float back into the apartment. I'm holding my little black dress. The one that I think I'll never wear again. I swoop down and grab my heels from the living room floor as I pass by, and I also notice that Alex is gone. Emily and Snake seem to come out of nowhere, both diving for the bathroom, but Emily gets there first, shutting the door on him as he groans.

"Seriously?" he yells through the door. "You girls take forever. I only take five minutes. C'mon. Let me in first."

"You can help me clean up," I suggest from the other side of the room. Snake cranes his neck and looks at me hard. "What?" I say. "We're gonna have to do it at some point anyway."

I drift into Tyler's room to toss my dress and heels onto my suitcase, not bothering to pack either away, and then join Snake again. Surprisingly, it doesn't take much to convince him to help me. In the twenty minutes that Emily takes in the bathroom, the two of us make a start on cleaning up the apartment. We start in the kitchen, ramming the leftover booze into the refrigerator and piling the empty bottles and cans into trash bags. The worktops are sticky with spilled drinks, so while I wash them down, Snake gathers all the shot glasses, cups and straws from throughout the apartment, groaning as he does so.

He makes a beeline for the bathroom the second Emily opens the door, and they switch roles. It's Emily's turn to help with the cleaning, although neither of us talks while we get on with what we need to do. The silence starts to feel too tense, so I turn on the TV as background noise. I open up every window possible and spray air freshener around the place. Emily trails the vacuum cleaner out from the laundry room and vacuums the whole apartment, even the bedrooms. I leave her to finish everything off while I shut myself in Tyler's room to dry my hair, and the longer time ticks by, the more I start to wonder what's taking him so long.

He's been up on the roof for over an hour now. He never used to take this long to calm down before. When Snake gets out of the shower, I send him to check what Tyler's doing. He rolls his eyes at my request, but he does it anyway. Five minutes later, he returns.

"He's not there," he says with a shrug.

I look up from the TV, eyeing him with a skeptical frown. I'm not sure if he's messing with me or not. "What?"

"He's not on the roof."

"Then where is he?" I'm not sure where else he could have possibly gone. There's no way he'd leave the building. He's wearing nothing but jeans.

"No idea," Snake says. He shrugs again and leans against the kitchen worktop, and then it's his turn to look at me with a skeptical expression on his face. "What were you guys all arguing about, anyway?"

"Nothing," I say immediately. He'll probably find out eventually, but right now I don't want to talk about it.

Snake scowls at me and I'm expecting him to press the matter further, but he doesn't bother to waste his time. He heads around to the refrigerator instead, rummaging around inside for something to eat.

I look back to the TV, but I'm not entirely focused on it. I'm thinking about Tyler. Despite the fact that I don't particularly want to talk to him right now, I decide to try calling his phone, but it's no use. I hear his phone ringing from his room. I hang up and let out a long breath that sounds something between a sigh and a groan. Where the hell is he?

It's not all bad, though. *Lady and the Tramp* is on TV. Snake mocks me from the kitchen for fifteen minutes straight as he rams sandwiches into his mouth, but I ignore him, increasing the volume each time he opens his mouth to speak. Disney movies aren't childish, as he believes. They aren't dumb, either, and once he stops laughing at me for choosing to watch them, he decides to visit the girls from apartment 1201 to see if they're as hungover as him.

It's nice to get some peace once he leaves. Emily, on the other hand, hasn't come out of Snake's room in over forty minutes, and I think she might have fallen asleep. I have the comfort of the living room to myself, with no one left to complain about my choice of movie, and I take advantage of this by spreading out on the couch and getting comfortable, snuggling into the cushions.

I finish watching the entire movie before Snake comes back and before Emily wakes up, and it's now been almost three hours since Tyler stormed out. I can't think of where he could have gone. He could be hiding out at 1201 or Alex and Brendon's apartment three floors down. He could have locked himself in his car as a way to avoid me. He could be anywhere in the building. Sooner or later, he's gonna have to come back and face me.

Right then, I hear the apartment door unlocking and I assume that it's Snake. Pausing the TV, I push myself up from the couch and look to the door. My eyes meet Tyler's.

"It's about time," I say. Looking anxious, he shuts the door behind him and drops his eyes to the carpet. He's somehow managed to change into a pair of black shorts and a gray T-shirt. "Where'd you get the clothes from?"

"My gym bag was in my car," he says quietly. He chews on his lower lip for a second before bracing himself and walking over to me. "Where is everyone?"

"Snake's with the girls from the other apartment and I think Emily is asleep, so right now is the perfect time for you to be honest with me." I get to my feet as I turn off the TV completely, silence forming around us as I walk around the couch. I don't stop until I'm in front of him. "Please just tell me what's going on."

"Nothing is going on, Eden," Tyler says. His voice is soft and sincere, much calmer than it was before. His eyes are gentle and faded again, although a little bloodshot. "I don't get why you won't believe me. What have I ever done to make you doubt me? How many times do you need me to tell you that Emily and I are just friends?" His voice grows firm. "Nothing happened last night," he states slowly. "Nothing ever has and nothing ever will."

"Nice to know you cuddled up close with her in bed and left me on the floor," I mutter, because it's the only thing I can think of to say right now. It feels like Emily has priority over me. Like Tyler had the choice of who to take care of last night, and he clearly chose her, which doesn't exactly back up what he's saying right now.

"You slept on the floor? I didn't know that."

All I can do is stare back at him. He seems honest, but Tyler's great at acting. Years ago, he had everyone fooled. No one ever suspected he was broken inside and not the tough, badass guy he made them believe he was. Keeping secrets is what Tyler is best at. He could be lying to me right now. "I just don't know what to think, Tyler," I murmur eventually.

"Do you see me looking at her the way I look at you?" he asks. Taking a step closer to me, he looks down at me from beneath his eyelashes, his eyes crinkling at the corners.

"No."

"Exactly, Eden," he says, frustrated. "It's stressing me out that you keep doubting me, and I thought for a while about how I can prove to you that you're the one I want." He stops for a second and shakes his head, heaving a sigh. "You know what? Fuck it. I don't want you. I need you."

"Need?" I echo.

"Need," he confirms, nodding once. "I need you because you're one of the few people I trust. I need you because you saw me the way I used to be and you still stuck around. I need you because I'm in love with you, Eden, and I have no idea how I'll ever get over you." His words hit me so hard that I don't think I even blink in response. I stand there, listening to him, and it becomes clear that he's definitely not putting on an act. His voice even sounds on the verge of pleading. "I got something to prove it," he says.

Slowly, he rolls up the left sleeve of his T-shirt to reveal his bicep, huge as ever, wrapped tightly in Saran Wrap. Underneath, glossy black ink stares back at me. Biting his lip, Tyler carefully unwraps the plastic and tilts his arm for me to see. Inked in small lettering, black and bold, is my name. Nothing else. Just four letters. So simple, yet so stupid. At first I'm taken aback by it, but then I quickly become irritated.

"You've got to be kidding me." Why would he even think about doing something so insane? I squint at the tattoo for a moment longer as I attempt to figure out if it's only henna. I'm hoping that it is, but his skin is red and raised and there are some traces of blood, and I feel my chest sink in dismay.

"It's real," Tyler says, stating the freaking obvious. "Permanent."

"You're so irrational." I take a step back from him without my eyes ever leaving his arm. My name. Doesn't he have any idea that people can be temporary? Isn't he aware that things can change? Right now, it feels like whatever is between us is real and endless, but the truth is, neither of us knows what could happen in the months and years to come. Still stunned, I manage to tear my eyes away from the tattoo and back to his. "What if I choose Dean, Tyler?" I whisper.

"I know you're not choosing Dean," he says with a shake of his head.

"Why do you think that?"

"Because if you were really planning on staying with Dean, you wouldn't have made that deal with me," he says, and he's right. "You wouldn't have cheered your ass off for Derek Jeter."

"I still haven't chosen yet," I blurt. I think I have, though. I think I know already that in the end, it's going to be Tyler. If I knew there were any hope for Dean at all, I wouldn't be doing what I'm doing. I wouldn't be avoiding him at all costs. "This is still so stupid, Tyler," I murmur, nodding to the tattoo on his arm.

Tyler glances down and analyzes it for a moment. "I like it."

"And what are you gonna do when we go home and our parents see it?" I fold my arms across my chest. I'm starting to feel panicked at the mere thought of it. Maybe we could stay in New York. Maybe we could hide here and never go back to Santa Monica. I wouldn't mind. "How are you gonna explain the reason for it? What then?"

Tyler's gaze meets mine again, his eyes vibrant and wide. He shrugs. "Then I guess we'll have to tell them the truth," he says.

And to my complete surprise, he smiles as though people knowing our secret no longer seems like the end of the world.

16

"Hmm," I say late Wednesday morning as I study the plate Tyler's just handed me. Considerately, he's decided to treat me to a late morning snack of toast. Unfortunately, it's burnt black. "I mean, it's . . . edible?" I pick up a slice and tap it against the edge of the plate. Rock-hard. I offer Tyler a small smile. "It's the thought that counts, right?"

Tyler laughs from the other side of the worktop, shaking his head as he presses his hands over his face. "My mom would not be impressed right now," he mumbles, chuckling at his attempt. He straightens up and takes the plate back from me, promptly tipping the toast straight into the trash. "I'm gonna try again," he says as he swivels back around. He grips the edge of the worktop and smolders his eyes at me. "Actually, I might need your expertise."

I roll my eyes and make my way around the worktop from the living room to join him in the kitchen, nudging him to the side as I reach for the loaf of bread. I place four slices into the toaster and pop down the lever, leaning back against the worktop and folding my arms across my chest. "You're nineteen and you can't make toast without burning it?"

"In my defense," Tyler says slowly, smirking, "I was too busy staring at you."

I whack his arm, careful not to touch the new tattoo on his bicep, which has started scabbing, and then purse my lips at him. "Can you say something in Spanish again?"

Tyler raises his eyebrows at me suspiciously, his body mirroring mine as he crosses his arms. "Is this all you're gonna do for the rest of my life? Ask me to speak Spanish?"

"Well," I say with a nonchalant shrug, "it's kinda hot."

He laughs again, and for a moment, I just watch him. Study the expression in his eyes. Listen. Two years ago, he never laughed like this. He never laughed like he meant it. It was always so sarcastic and so harsh back then, but now it's so gentle and so soft and so happy. I can feel that positive aura surrounding him again, the same way it does each day, the way it never did before. I think seeing him genuinely happy is the most attractive thing about him. From the way he was before to the way he is now, I couldn't be prouder. I'm grinning, but he doesn't even seem to notice the way I'm looking at him.

"*Me estoy muriendo por besarte,*" he says, smirking.

The words somehow sound familiar and I think for a second while I try to figure out where I've heard them before. It doesn't take long for me to realize. "Doesn't that mean that—?"

"I'm dying to kiss you?" he finishes. Arching a brow, he steps toward me. "Yeah. Yeah, it does." Before I can even laugh or blush or react in any way whatsoever, he plants a kiss on my lips. Just one. Just quick. And then another, softly, as he places his hands on my waist. "Tell me something in French."

I glance up at him from beneath my eyelashes. I think his good mood is brushing off on me. Courageously, I decide to murmur, "How about: *Je t'aime?*"

Tyler doesn't even flinch. However, the expression in his eyes shifts. "Only if *te amo* works for you," he says softly. He's still smiling, as am I, and I think we both know that neither of us are ready to say it in English yet. Once more, he presses his lips to mine, and just when I think it's about to develop into a deeper, French kiss, I hear the toast pop up.

Tyler's pulling away from me and laughing before I've even glanced over to the toaster, and when I do, I let out a sigh. The toast is burnt again.

"I think we should just give up on the whole toast idea," I say. I can't help but chuckle too. We're both ridiculous.

"For sure," Tyler says. "I'll take you out for lunch to make up for it. Wherever you wanna go, I'm down."

Just as I'm about to take him up on the offer, my phone starts ringing from the coffee table in the living room. I brush past him and head over. It's not my usual ringtone, and as I grasp my phone in my hand and peer at the screen, I realize it's because I'm getting a video call. And it's from Dean.

Automatically, I go to decline it, but I stop myself short just before I tap the screen. It's still ringing and Tyler's eyeing me suspiciously from the kitchen. I haven't spoken to Dean in a few days, not since Sunday. I know I need to answer, so I throw Tyler an apologetic shrug and accept the call.

"Hiiiii," I say, as cheerful as I can possibly sound right now without sounding too fake.

It takes a moment for Dean's face to appear and he stares through the screen at me, perplexed. I don't think he's heard me, so I wave to let him know I'm definitely here. Immediately, his face lights up. "Hey, you answered!"

"Sure did," I say. "What's up?"

"Just about to head off for work," he tells me, but I already know. He's wearing his signature blue jumpsuit, grease stains and all, hair ruffled. "Thought I'd check up on my favorite girl first. How you doing?"

"It's almost eight there, right? It's eleven here." I sink down into the couch, crossing my legs as I hold my phone in front of me, trying to focus all of my attention on my boyfriend. It's hard to ignore the fact that I can sense Tyler's eyes boring into me from across the room. "I'm great. Just hanging out."

Dean arches an eyebrow. "Got anything you wanna fill me in on?"

"Nope." I can't look at his eyes, so I stare at his shoulder instead. It's not like he can tell. I feel too guilty to meet his gaze.

"Nothing new since Sunday?"

"Just chilling out, I guess." I shrug and slump further back into the couch. Out of the corner of my eye, Tyler's tossing the new burnt slices of toast into the trash. "How's everything over there?"

Dean rolls his eyes and takes a deep breath. "Rachael's having a mental breakdown because her hair stylist cut off too much of her hair or something like that and so now she's refusing to leave her house, Meghan gets back from Europe next week, Tiffani's pretty much living on the beach because she's convinced herself that the sand here is better than it is in Santa Barbara, some new kid has started at my dad's garage and he has no idea what a wrench is, my mom says she misses having you over for dinner, and my dad says hey. I think that's pretty much it." He exhales, laughing. It sounds odd hearing his laugh rather than Tyler's for once. It feels even weirder seeing his dark eyes when I'm so used to the emerald of Tyler's. "Hey, what are you doing for the Fourth of July tomorrow?"

I throw Tyler a glance. His arms are folded across the kitchen worktop as he leans forward, a knowing smirk on his lips. July Fourth will always bring back memories. Tomorrow, it'll be exactly two years since I realized I liked Tyler in the one way I shouldn't. Tomorrow, it'll be two years since we got arrested for trespassing. I don't even remember celebrating our nation's freedom that night. I just remember feeling the most confused I've ever been in my entire life.

Swallowing the lump in my throat, I shift my eyes back to Dean. He's smiling at me. "We haven't decided yet," I say, my throat dry. "Tyler wants us to stay in New York, but his roommate wants us to go to Boston. Either way, it's gonna end up being fireworks over a river. They'll probably have to flip a coin or something. You?"

"I think we're gonna check out the display at Marina del Rey."

I'd reply to him, but I'm suddenly distracted as the video quality adjusts, becoming sharper and much less pixelated. I squint at his jaw. "Is that . . . Is that stubble I'm seeing?"

"Maybe." Sheepishly, he rubs at his chin and dramatically smolders his eyes at me through the screen. "I thought I'd quit shaving for the summer. I know you don't like it, but you're not here, so what the hell?"

My eyes are drawn to Tyler again. He's raising his eyebrows at me as he touches his own jaw, pointing out his own stubble. His smirk has yet to leave his lips.

I fire him a look that makes it clear I don't appreciate his distractions right now, especially while I'm trying to talk to Dean. I mute the call for a sec, tell him, "I like it on you," and then move my gaze back to my boyfriend.

"Hey, I think you cut off for a sec," Dean says, furrowing his eyebrows back at me from three thousand miles away. "What'd you say?"

"Nothing, I was talking to Tyler," I fire back. The moment I say it, I'm regretting my words. I shouldn't have mentioned that Tyler's here. Over in the kitchen, Tyler has shot upright as he glares at me.

"He's there?" Dean asks. His face seems to light up again. I knew I shouldn't have told him. He raises his voice louder and says, "Hey, man, come over." He's not talking to me. He's talking to Tyler, who's shaking his head in refusal from the opposite side of the apartment.

"Uhh, one sec," I blurt. This time, I pause both the camera and the microphone and spin around to face Tyler, desperate. "Okay, I know I shouldn't have said that you were here, but please just come talk to him for a second."

"No," Tyler says firmly, using hand movements for emphasis. "No way in hell. No, no, no."

"Pleeeeeease," I beg. My eyes crinkle at the corners and I purse my lips at him. "If you don't, he's gonna wonder why you're being such a jackass. You're his best friend, remember? Act normal."

"Eden, in case you forgot, I'm the guy his girlfriend is cheating on him with," Tyler murmurs as he rubs at his temples. With a sharp look, he adds, "I'm not talking to him."

Groaning, I turn back to my phone and resume the video call. Dean's waiting patiently. "He can't talk right now," I lie. "He's naked."

"Naked?" Dean looks at me with an odd expression, and Tyler throws his hands up in exasperation.

"I mean," I splutter, "he's getting changed. In the other room. Not here."

My awkward babbling must be worse to Tyler than the idea of talking to Dean, because he comes striding over from the kitchen and grabs my phone straight out of my hand. He holds it up in front of him, a smile plastered upon his lips. "Hey, bro. Sorry, was pulling on a shirt. What's up?"

I stare up at Tyler in surprise from the couch as I hear Dean say, "Man! Haven't seen you in forever! I'm great. Missing Eden a hell of a lot, though."

"I'll bet you are," Tyler remarks dryly. "She's having a good time, though."

I can tell he's annoyed at me for making him talk to Dean, but we have no choice. Dean can't find out yet, especially while we're on opposite coasts, and I know I need to handle this face to face. In a way, it feels like we're lying to him right now, but the only option we have is to make everything seem okay, even when it's not. It would tear Dean apart if he were to find out like this, through a video call while we're three thousand miles away, so we're forced into being deceptive, and although it's unbelievably difficult, it's for Dean's sake. I don't know how we'll tell him. I don't know what we're supposed to say, but I do know that we still have three weeks to figure it out. We'll fix this. We'll be honest and sincere, we'll explain ourselves, and we'll do it right. Dean deserves that at least.

Tyler settles down next to me on the couch, his body close against mine as he holds my phone up high in front of us, attempting to squeeze us both into the frame. For ten minutes, we tell Dean all about New York and how amazing the Italian food tastes over here, and he fills us in on all the latest drama back in Santa Monica. Some girl who was in my grade is engaged to a guy a decade older than her. Some guy who was in Dean's US History class is now in jail for sexual assault. Thankfully, Dean ends up having to leave for work and by the time we've ended the video call, Tyler's collapsing back against the couch in a heap.

"We are officially going to hell," he groans. All I can do is sigh next to him, feeling nothing but guilt and shame. Dean doesn't deserve any of this. After a second, Tyler sits up and leans forward to glance sideways at me. "This is gonna kill him. There's no way around it. We just have to be straight-up with him and accept the fact we've really messed up. When are we gonna tell him?"

"As soon as we get home. We can't wait any longer," I say. I can't look at him. I'm resting my elbows on my knees, hunched over slightly as I hold my face in my hands. "It's unfair on him."

Tyler's voice is solemn and quiet. "You think he'll ever forgive us?"

"I think he will eventually," I murmur. I won't blame him if he doesn't, but I like to hope that one day he will. It's Dean. Our Dean. He's never held a grudge against anyone in his entire life.

"God, I'm a shit excuse for a best friend," Tyler mutters.

"And I'm an even shittier excuse for a girlfriend," I add. It's gonna be hard to tell him. It's like he's losing both his girlfriend and his best friend at the exact same time. Betrayed by both.

Out of nowhere, Tyler moves his hand to my thigh. "Eden," he says, "does this mean you're really choosing me?"

The suddenness of his question doesn't take me by surprise.

Instead, his words sink in slowly as I breathe. Feeling calm, I finally look back at him only to discover that he's staring at me with wide, dull green eyes. He looks almost worried, as though I'm going to say no. "I was always going to choose you," I whisper.

I can see the relief in his eyes, despite the fact that his features don't shift in the slightest. His gaze only grows more intense. "And what does choosing me mean?"

"You know what it means, Tyler." I reach for his hand on my thigh, lifting it and interlocking it with my own, our fingers intertwining. Perfectly. The way it should be. The way it always has been. "It means I want to be with you." My voice is strong. I'm not nervous. I'm not doubtful. I'm content with knowing that I'm saying nothing but the truth. "Like, seriously."

Tyler's holding back a smile as he tries to remain serious, but it doesn't stop me from seeing the way his eyes are lighting up at my words. "You know we're gonna have to tell our parents, right?"

"I know," I say. Once more, I sigh. A long sigh. A sigh I've been holding in for two years. Telling our parents is the most terrifying thing about all of this, and it seems like the time for it is growing closer and closer. It'll be a relief to get it over with. "I'm ready to."

"And you're definitely not gonna give up again?" Tyler asks immediately, squeezing my hand in his, expression shifting. His words are fast and enthusiastic as he speaks. "You're not gonna change your mind when the time comes?"

"Tyler," I say firmly. "I'm going through with this if you are." My lips pulling up into a smile, I say, "*No te rindas.*" Tyler's words from the roof on my first night in the city. The words he scribbled along the Chucks he bought me. The words that have such a simple yet significant meaning: Don't give up.

In that moment, Tyler gives a wide grin, his eyes smoldering, teeth sparkling, jaw sharp, positive vibe radiating from him. "Thank God you didn't."

17

". . . and that's not even mentioning La Breve Vita. I think they're Italian. She loves 'em. She always closes her eyes when she listens to music, 'cause she's a little weird like that. I kinda like it, though. Every time I walked into her room, she'd be sitting there, earphones in, eyes closed. Half the time I don't think she even knew I was even there. She never looked up, but she looked cute as hell. Still weird, though."

I don't remember the exact moment I wake up. It feels gradual, and I slowly become aware of words facing in from somewhere around me. I'm wrapped up in Tyler's comforter and I lay there for a minute or two as I adjust. I don't even fully absorb what's going on until I hear Tyler's voice softly say, "Hey, you're finally awake."

My eyes flicker open slowly, taking in the brightness of the room, and I glance to my right. Tyler's by my side and he's smiling down at me, wide awake, with a camcorder in his hand. He's pointing it at me.

"What are you doing?" I murmur suspiciously. The red light is flashing.

"Just messing around," he says. However, he doesn't turn the camera off. He keeps recording me. "Happy Fourth of July, baby."

I sit up a little and rub at my eyes, but I'm still aware that I'm being recorded. My eyes drift to the camcorder and I smile at the lens. "Happy July Fourth."

"The Fourth of July is my favorite event of the year," Tyler tells the camera as he turns it on himself. He flashes me a dazzling grin. "I think Eden knows why." Stretching over me, he places the camera on the bedside table.

The curtains are drawn open, so there's a warm morning glow to the room. The warmth is perfect and calming as Tyler silently runs his hand down my arm, taking my hands in his. He nuzzles his face into my neck as he breathes against my skin, and I let out a small sigh of satisfaction. I could get used to waking up to him every morning. Reaching up, I loop my arms loosely around the back of his neck, my hands resting in his hair, and I pull him toward me. My lips find his, and for once, Tyler relaxes and lets me take control, but it feels so odd that I only end up laughing against his mouth. Smiling back at me, he grips my waist and pulls my body onto his. I sit up on his lap, strands of hair falling out of my messy bun and into my eyes, so I tuck them behind my ears and lean forward again, planting a series of kisses on Tyler's lips.

"Mmm," he murmurs.

"I think you better switch that off," I whisper. Throwing a glance at the camcorder on the bedside table, I kiss the edge of his jaw.

Tyler smirks, expression full of mischief. "How about we keep it on?"

"Hmm." Playfully, I lean back and sit up. "Never mind then." I swing my body off his and slide out the bed, getting to my feet.

"Okay, okay, I'll turn it off," Tyler says, leaning over to grab the camera. He shuts it off within a split second.

"Too late now," I say with a shrug, teasingly. It feels slightly odd looking at him in his own bed rather than the couch for once, and I decide right then and there that I'm going to let him sleep next to me every night from now on. I want to wake up like this each and every day. "Coffee?"

"You know it."

Late afternoon, thunder and scattered rainstorms began to torment the city. Dark skies and rain have hung over Manhattan ever since, and just as Tyler and I are deciding whether or not we're still going to head out to view the celebrations, the power suddenly cuts out.

The apartment plunges into darkness and there's no noise besides the sound of the rain rolling down the windows. Outside, the usual lights of New York City are just as they should be. It's only Tyler's building that's lost all power.

"You've got to be kidding me," I mutter in disbelief. I edge my body closer to Tyler's and reach out to touch his arm through the limited lighting.

"What a mess," he says, taking a few steps back. "July Fourth and it's raining like hell and now we don't have power?" I feel him grasping at our surroundings as he begins to edge his way through the living room. My fingers tighten around the hem of his tee and I follow slowly at his heels. "I think there are candles in the laundry room somewhere. Never thought we'd ever use them."

It's only a matter of seconds before Tyler clashes into the kitchen worktop, the noise of his hip hitting the edge enough to make even me flinch. He groans but doesn't stop for long, and leads me into the laundry room. I'm only wearing underwear and an oversized T-shirt, so I stretch my hand under my shirt to retrieve my phone from my bra. Although the light given off by my phone is limited, it helps Tyler to locate a collection of wax candles on one of the shelves above the dryer.

"Here," he says, handing me a couple of them. "Set them up in the living room for me?"

I do as he asks, and I squirm my way back through the darkness and set the candles down on the coffee table. My eyes are slowly adjusting to the lack of light and I'm beginning to make out the outlines of the furniture and even Tyler's body as he walks over to join me. "Over here," I say. Extending both my arms, I reach for his wrist and pull him over.

Setting down a few more candles, he stuffs his hands into the pockets of his jeans and there's a jingling noise of keys and loose change as he pulls out a lighter. He runs his thumb over the spark wheel and a burning flame flickers to life, illuminating a tiny proportion of the room. Lighting the candles we've brought through, he puts the lighter back in his pocket and picks up two of the six candles, carrying them back over to the kitchen. He positions one on each worktop, and as he approaches me again, I can see his entire face. There's an orange glow cast over the room, and despite the fact that it's raining outside the apartment feels warm and cozy.

"How about we just stay here?" he asks, arching an eyebrow. "I mean, you're not even dressed yet. We're gonna get soaked. Who knows, they might even cancel the display."

Snake and Emily headed out earlier to claim a decent viewing spot for the display over the Hudson River, and we're supposed to be meeting them within the next half-hour.

I'm not sure they'd be too impressed if we didn't show up, especially when it was Tyler who was adamant we stayed in Manhattan.

"Are we making it a tradition to skip the fireworks?" I ask teasingly.

"I've got an idea," he says quietly, ignoring my question, setting the two candles down on the table and making his way back toward me. He picks up another two, firing his eyes in the direction of his room. So I head over there, carrying a third candle with me.

"What's your idea?" I ask, placing the candle down onto one of the bedside tables. The room is dark and the weather outside is thunderous, yet the three small candles we've brought through provide us with some light, enough to see each other.

Only one half of Tyler's face is lit up, and as he moves toward his bed, I watch his shadow dance across the walls. "Baby, come here," he murmurs, and a lump rises in my throat as I follow his order. "I want to play a game."

"A game?" I echo. I try my hardest to appear calm and confident and cool, but it seems impossible. My voice is almost a squeak. However, it doesn't stop me from softly gripping the sheets as I crawl onto the bed next to him and sit on my knees.

Tyler licks his lips as he studies me, as if wondering if I'm too delicate, too fragile for what he has in mind. I'm not. Just slightly nervous. "Turn around," he says quietly but firmly.

"Turn around?" I repeat, swallowing. I analyze his features as I try to figure out what he's thinking, but he isn't giving anything away. He's just looking at me, expression nonchalant.

"Eden," he says again.

I loosen up, relaxing as I take a deep breath. In the candlelight, I twist my body around so that my back is to him and my legs are crossed, and I say nothing more. I just wait.

"Take your shirt off," he orders gently, and even against the rain, his voice seems like the most powerful thing around me right now.

It takes me by surprise, but I don't panic. Everything feels so comfortable and just right. Closing my eyes, I exhale slowly as I reach down for the hem of my T-shirt. My heart is beating fast, but it's not pounding against my chest and my pulse isn't racing, so I pull it off with ease and drop it to the floor. I'm not sure what Tyler's doing.

I suddenly shiver and I'm not sure if it's because I'm almost completely bare and slightly cold or if it's because I'm almost completely bare in front Tyler. Either way, I don't feel uncomfortable.

"And this," Tyler murmurs, the mattress beneath us shifting as he moves his body closer to mine. Carefully, he gathers my hair, moving it to one side and pressing his cool lips to the back of my shoulder, breathing heavily against my skin. His opposite hand runs along the clasp of my bra.

"What?" I whisper.

"Take it off," he urges, his lips running across the back of my neck.

Reaching behind me, I feebly fumble around with the clasp and release it. My chest relaxes and my breath finally hitches. Now I'm anxious. It's been so long. Two years, specifically. I don't know what to expect, but I do know that I don't want to say no. The sexual tension between us has been building up ever since the Yankees game, from the moment Tyler mentioned Derek Jeter and home runs. And I think, *Maybe this is it.* Maybe our home run is here. Maybe it's time. I have been waiting, always too awkward to bring it up, having assumed that Tyler had forgotten about the deal we made, and now that the moment has arrived I'm suddenly terrified. It feels like our first time all over again. And so I might be terrified and I might be nauseous, but I don't think I've ever wanted anything more than I want this.

Numbly, I push my bra onto the floor and close my eyes. I'm so glad I'm not facing him. I don't think I'd be able to meet his gaze right now. He doesn't say anything, though. We just sit in silence for a moment, and then I feel the tips of his fingers against my skin. Softly, he traces patterns on my back.

I say nothing either, mostly because I don't think I'm capable of stringing a decent sentence together right now, and I sit still, my eyes resting on the candle in front of me. Tyler moves for a second but quickly falls back into his position behind me, and I hear the clicking of a pen lid as he pops it off. I want to turn around or at least glance back at him to see what he's doing, but I get the feeling that he doesn't want me to look.

Suddenly, he presses the tip of the pen to my back and the ink feels strange against my skin. For a moment or two, I almost feel like giggling at the feeling. I avoid the temptation to move and I allow Tyler to write whatever it is he's writing. The pen tip swirls against my skin and the sensation of curves and dots forming is fascinating as he marks words on my body, an entire string of them.

"Done," Tyler announces, sounding satisfied. "Eden."

"Tyler?"

"Turn around," he orders again. His voice is completely hushed and I can feel the intensity of his eyes on me.

Now I'm shaking a little. Not because I'm nervous, but because I know it's wrong to turn around. I know it's unfaithful to Dean. I *know*. That's the worst part about this. I know this is wrong and I know it's unfaithful, yet I do it anyway. Squeezing my eyes shut, I turn my body around to face Tyler directly, and by the time I stop moving my pulse really is racing and my heart really is pounding like hell. Slowly, I open my eyes.

Tyler's gazing at me, his glowing eyes analyzing my body. They rest on my breasts for several long seconds, and then they drift back up to meet mine. " 'The nakedness of thy sister, the daughter of thy father, or daughter of thy mother, whether she be born at home, or born abroad, even their nakedness thou shalt not uncover,' " Tyler murmurs, his eyes never leaving mine, forever smoldering. "Leviticus, chapter eighteen, verse nine."

I'm surprised at myself for remaining there, unflinching and without feeling the natural reflex to cover my chest. Instead, I just play with my fingers in my lap as I raise my eyebrows at him.

His lips quirk up into a devious grin, revealing the tips of his teeth. His entire face is still glowing. "In other words," he says, "I am most definitely going to hell."

"Did you go to church or something?" I ask, holding back laughter. I never in my entire life believed that one day Tyler would be quoting the Bible. Even if it is with sarcasm.

"Googled it," Tyler deadpans. "I was making sure that I can't end up in jail for any of this and the good news is that I can't."

I do let out a laugh now, grinning back at him as he chuckles along with me, and I realize that I don't even mind that we're missing the fireworks. We missed them two years ago and we're missing them again now, but it's okay. Having intimate moments with Tyler is always much better, and as I think about this, a shiver shoots down my spine. Never do I think I'll be able to get over any of these moments. I'm not sure I'll be able to get over Tyler, either. Thankfully, I no longer have to.

It's only then, while I'm laughing, that I catch sight of the pen Tyler has used lying on the sheets. Reaching for it, I grasp it between my fingers and I hold it up to the light. It's permanent marker.

"Tyler!" I exclaim, immediately pushing myself up and hurling my bare body toward the door. Of all things, he had to use permanent marker? He's probably scrawled profanities across my skin and I'm having terrible visions of the ink taking weeks to fade. "Get this off me!" Running across the apartment with Tyler close behind me, I grab a candle from the kitchen as I pass and throw myself into the bathroom. I dump the candle on the floor and reach for a hand towel, covering it completely in soap. Desperately, I attempt to reach around for my back.

"Calm down," Tyler says, but he's still laughing and he's not even attempting to hide it. He takes the towel from my hand as he steps behind me. "I'll get it.

He starts to rub at my skin as softly as he possibly can and out of the corner of my eye, I see our reflections in the mirror. I tilt my head slightly to get a better look at my back, at the writing before Tyler wipes it all away. The words look foreign to begin with and I think he might have written in Spanish, but I realize that the mirror is reflecting them backward. I concentrate hard on each letter until it hits me all at once what's he's done. There's only one word. One word, but written over and over again, covering every single inch of my back from the tips of my shoulders straight down to the small of my back.

All it says is this: MINE.

Each letter capitalized. Each letter bold and sharp. Each letter significant.

I part my lips as I release the smallest of gasps. I feel satisfaction rippling through my entire body as I realise it's true. I'm his. I've always been his, never quite Dean's, and Tyler's always been mine, too.

As Tyler applies more pressure to my skin, he also sighs. "I hate to break it you," he eventually says, "but it's not exactly working. How about this?"

Suddenly his firm hands are grasping at my body, pushing me backward into the shower. Within a split second, he's flicked on the water. It pounds against my back, pouring over my face, drenching me. Tyler's laughing at my expression, but as I glare up at him through the water, I find myself shaking my head. I really can't bear this any longer.

"Screw it," I murmur. Slapping my hand against his chest, I grab a fistful of his shirt and pull his body into mine beneath the water. I stretch up on my tiptoes, crashing my lips hard against his. This time, I definitely take advantage of being in control, and with my new power, I push him against the back of the shower wall and press my breasts against his chest, my mouth moving in sync with the flow of the water.

His polo tee clings to his body as his clothes begin to soak straight through, but he doesn't appear to care in the slightest.

His hands are in my hair; his lips are against mine. The water keeps sparkling down over us in an endless burst, powerful and heavy, and it reminds me of what it's like to kiss in the rain. Heavy, fast rain. Eager, I drop one hand to the hem of his tee as I make a messy attempt to tug it upward, and I shift the other to his belt.

"Stop," Tyler groans against my mouth. It takes him a while to tear his lips away from mine, but when he does, he pants against my ear. I'm studying him through the stream of water, perplexed and irritated, wondering why the hell he keeps shutting me down, until I realize exactly why he's come to a standstill.

Somewhere in the apartment, I can hear Snake's voice.

"Wait here," Tyler whispers, breathing heavily, chest rising and sinking. Within a heartbeat, the water is shut off and Tyler is already by the bathroom door. He runs a hand through his dripping hair as he swings it open, peering around the frame. "Guys, guys, we're here. Shower went weird again. Was trying to fix it for Eden. Water kinda burst everywhere."

"Who cares about the shower?" I hear Snake mutter back. "The real question is this: Did you guys forget about something? You know, like the fucking fireworks?"

Sighing, I slide down against the shower wall. I'm absolutely drenched and my euphoric rush has quickly faded away. Hugging my knees to my chest, I throw my head back against the wall. All I can think about is the Bible verse Tyler quoted, and the more I repeat it in my head, the more my lips curve into a smile.

Sinners, indeed.

18

I tilt my face up to the sky, squeezing my eyes shut as the sun beats down on my forehead. We've been outside in the heat all day and I'm starting to feel nauseous, burning up and sweating. If there's anything I've learned about New York, it's that the weather can switch between scorching sunlight and rainstorms whenever it wants to. Today, it's ninety out. I tighten my hand around the plastic cup of iced tea I've been drinking for a while and exhale deeply. It's times like these that I miss being in Santa Monica, where there's always a pool to dive into no more than fifty feet away from my room. I've been taking that luxury for granted until now. There's no space for pools in back yards here. Hell, I think half the people in the city might not even have back yards. I'm not sure how to cool down. My skin feels like it's burning, and on the ride back from our day trip to Queens and Brooklyn, I stole a glance at my face in the sun-visor mirror, only to discover that my forehead is burnt. I even have pale circles around my eye sockets from where I was wearing my sunglasses.

"Hot, huh?" Tyler says. He squints up at the sky too, clear blue with not a single cloud in sight, and then glances back down to his car. I don't know why, but he gingerly presses his hand to the hood. Immediately, he flinches and steps back. He shakes his hand, trying to ease the burn. "Shit."

Rolling my eyes, I drop to the ground and sit down on the curb of the sidewalk. The concrete is burning hot against my thighs, but after a few seconds it becomes bearable. I set my drink down by my side—it's too warm and gross now to drink the rest of it anyway—and study Tyler's car as the sunlight bounces off the glossy white bodywork. A thought arises that's just too tempting to ignore. "Can I drive your car?"

Tyler stops soothing his hand. Frozen, he looks down at me and then, with a wary expression, he glances back at his Audi. "You? My car? This car?" He bites down on his lower lip and rubs at the back of his neck, uneasy. "Don't get me wrong, Eden, but . . . you know."

I place my hands down flat on the sidewalk behind me, leaning back as I squint up at him through the bright sunlight, an eyebrow arched. "You don't trust me?"

"For starters," he says quickly, "you drive automatic. My car's a stick shift."

"And you think I can't drive a stick?"

Both Tyler's eyebrows shoot up, and he stares down at me intensely. "You can?"

"Automatic is the easy way out," I say, pushing myself up from the ground and straightening up. Challengingly, I narrow my eyes at him and smile. "Stick shift is way better. Keys?"

He gives me a beaming smile and laughs, hooking his arm around my neck and drawing me toward him. "No way in hell," he says, and promptly plants a kiss on my cheek. Playfully, he pushes me away again.

I knew there was absolutely zero chance of him letting

me get behind the wheel of his car, but it was worth a shot. Shrugging, I grab my drink from the ground and head across the street to the apartment building. Tyler follows behind me, stepping into position by my side, interlocking my free hand with his. I think, for the first time, I don't react. It just feels normal, and Tyler doesn't make a big deal out of it either, because he simply leads me into the building and toward the elevator, never letting go.

It's not something we usually ever do—holding hands. That's what couples do, not what two people keeping a secret do. Today, however, we don't have to be so cautious. Snake left for Boston this morning to visit his family and won't be back until tomorrow. Emily is hanging out with some of her friends, the ones she's made while living in the city. Right now, Tyler and I are in the clear.

We head up to the apartment and I've only just stepped foot over the threshold when I decide that I'm going to take a cold shower in an attempt to cool myself down. The moment I tell Tyler this, however, my cheeks flush with color. Thoughts of Thursday night flood my mind, of Tyler and the shower and the rain and the writing and the Bible, and part of me wonders where that night might have taken us if Snake and Emily hadn't came home so early.

It's blatantly obvious that Tyler's thinking the exact same thoughts as I am, because he bites back a smirk. "No problem," he says.

It's so unbelievably tempting to slip him some remark about how he should join me, but I know I wouldn't be able to pull it off. I smile instead, as innocently as I can, turning for the bathroom and tossing my cup of iced tea into the trash as I pass.

Burning up, I strip off my clothes and steal a glance at myself in the mirror. I think I have slight tan lines and my face appears even redder than it did back in the car. Slipping into the shower, I lower the temperature. Freezing is too unbearable, so I keep the water lukewarm and stand under it for a short while. I don't bother washing my hair, so the second my skin feels like it's no longer on the verge of bursting into flames, I step out and wrap a towel around my body, holding it close to me as I make my way back into the living room.

At first, it doesn't occur to me that I'm alone. It's not until I've pulled on a pair of running shorts and a tank top that I realize that the apartment is not only silent, but also empty.

"Tyler?" I call out. I'm standing right in the center of the living room, my hands on my hips and my eyebrows furrowed. I wait a few seconds, but I get no reply. "Tyler?" I yell louder.

I sigh. He wouldn't have headed out anywhere without telling me. Maybe he left something in his car. Maybe he's on the roof. It wouldn't surprise me. He always disappears up there whenever he feels like it.

Even though I'm out of the sun now, my skin feels like it's burning up even more than it was before. My face feels so hot that it hurts and I'm regretting ignoring Mom when she pointed out that I should pack some aftersun lotion. Back then, I didn't think New York could be this hot. Walking around Queens was definitely a bad idea. I think the only time we got shade was when we stopped for drinks. The rest of the time? The rest of the time gave me sunburn.

I try to blow some air back on my face as I make a beeline for the kitchen, straight for the second cupboard along from the left. It's where the guys keep all the medicine and a first-aid kit, and if there's any hope at all of me finding some aloe vera, it'll be in here. I stretch up to the top shelf, unable to see as I rummage around for bottles. I find painkillers, the ones that soothed my headache last weekend, and I find Band-Aids, which are definitely no use, and I continue to find just about everything that I don't need. No aloe vera. Sighing, I pull myself up onto the worktop, getting on my knees and peering into the cupboard for a better look. Even my shoulders are starting to burn like hell, so I keep fumbling around, stretching my hand straight to the back of the cupboard. I pause when I touch a glass jar.

When I squint at it, I think my breathing stops. It's a Mason jar. Sealed and airtight. Inside, there are several clear, tiny Ziploc bags. The thing that takes me aback, however, is that inside them, there's weed.

To begin with, I'm too stunned to even process it. I take the jar in my hand, staring down at its contents in disbelief, my lips parted. I don't know why there's weed in the apartment. There shouldn't be. Tyler stopped smoking this stuff almost two years ago and Snake told me he doesn't smoke, but knowing him, that could be a lie. It's not mine, and I doubt it belongs to Emily.

My stomach tightens as I numbly glance back into the cupboard. There's still that stack of lighters, the ones I discovered on Sunday morning as I searched for those painkillers. *Why is this here?* I think. *Who's smoking this shit?*

I grasp a couple lighters in my hand, glancing between them and the jar for a few seconds. Eventually, I lay the lighters down on the worktop and focus all of my attention on the Mason jar. I don't know what brings me to do it, but I screw off the lid, and the smell is so overwhelming and all-consuming that I almost fall off the worktop.

It's so pungent that I almost feel sick. It's so much different to the stench of weed as it's being smoked and released into the air. Stronger, more musky. I slam the lid back on as fast as I can, almost gagging at the strength of the odor, and then glance back at the lighters. I stare at them for a while, trying to figure out whether or not I should just put everything back and pretend I never found it, but just as I'm deciding this, something clicks.

The lighters. On Thursday, Tyler and I lit candles. Tyler, who just so happened to have lighters on him. I understand there being lighters in the apartment. That's okay. But in his pocket? Who the hell carries lighters for no reason? No one does unless they . . . unless they smoke.

My jaw almost falls open as the realization hits me. No way. No fucking way. Tyler stopped all of this years ago. He made it clear on my first night in New York that he was okay, that he didn't need any of this stuff anymore. He wouldn't have lied to me about it. It has to be Snake's. The lighters have to be a coincidence. After everything, Tyler can't be doing this again.

Fury overcomes me, and without another second of hesitation, I open up the jar and grab one of the tiny bags, holding my breath as I screw the lid back on once more. Somehow, I feel both numb and angry, and I swing my body off the worktop, stuffing the bag into the pocket of my shorts. I fling open the apartment door and head out into the lobby, gritting my teeth to stop myself from screaming in exasperation. I know Tyler's on the roof. I know that's where he has disappeared to. It always is, and as I slip into elevator, I realize I've never wondered why he always goes up there. Always alone, sometimes for hours at a time. Why is that? The answer seems more and more obvious, but I don't want to believe it. There's still no way in hell that this is really happening, that this is really true.

I take the elevator straight up to the top floor, and with my hands balled into fists, I make my way up the set of stairs to the roof. As silently as I can, I edge my body through the door, closing it behind me with an inaudible click. When I spin around, the rooftop is empty, besides one person. It appears I'm right about Tyler being on the roof.

His back is turned to me and his elbows rest on the wall as he leans slightly over the edge of the building, staring down at the avenue below. He's not doing anything but that. Just standing there.

Taking a deep breath, I approach him and stop a few feet away. "Hey," I say. Calm. Nonchalant. Inside, I'm burning up.

Tyler swivels around, startled by the sound of my voice and a little surprised at my presence. He smiles, though. It's a warm one. "Hey," he says. "Sorry I didn't let you know I was up here. I thought you'd take longer in the shower so I don't know, I just thought I'd head up. It's too hot out to stay inside anyway, you know? Goddamn, it really is hot out here, though. Hey, your face looks kinda bur—"

"Tyler," I say quietly but firmly as I cut him off. My eyes meet his and he raises an eyebrow, waiting for me to talk. I feel nauseous as I reach into my pocket for the bag of weed. Grasping it between my thumb and forefinger, I hold it up right in front of his face, and I glare at him as sharply and as fiercely as I possibly can. "What's this?"

His eyes widen as he studies the bag and almost immediately his expression shifts from relaxed to panicked. I can see it in his eyes. He's speechless, and as I watch him wordlessly part his lips, I feel my chest collapsing.

"You're gonna tell me it's Snake's, right?" I ask quietly, my tone pleading. That's what I want to hear. It's what I need to hear, otherwise I'm not going to be okay. My voice cracks and all I can whisper is, "Please tell me it's Snake's."

"Eden . . ." Tyler says slowly, and the guilt pooling in his eyes gives me the answer I didn't want. He's not even trying to hide it. He's not even going to attempt to deny it.

Suddenly, I explode. It's a mixture of fury and disappointment, consuming me all at once and fueling my words. "You lied to me!" I yell, livid. "You lied straight to my face when I asked you if you were fine! You're not fine! You're a liar!"

"Eden, I am fine," Tyler protests, voice quiet. He looks ashamed, and so he should be. I'm so, so unbelievably letdown. "It's just—"

"Are you back on coke, too?" My voice is like acid.

"God, no."

"When did you start this shit?" I demand, waving the bag in the air. Part of me wants to throw it over the edge of the building. "When did you start all of this again?"

Tyler bites at his lower lip as he looks back at me, guilt still dripping from his face, his eyes softly crinkling at the corners. "A couple weeks after I moved here," he admits.

"Are you fucking kidding me right now, Tyler? That quick?" I explode, shaking my head in disbelief. This can't be real. "You could have gotten kicked off the tour!"

"I'm not stupid enough to get caught."

"You just did, moron," I snap. I throw the bag at his chest and it drops to the ground as I turn around, too furious to even look at him any longer.

"Eden, please, just chill," Tyler says from behind me, never raising his voice. I don't blame him. He's been caught. Of course he's quiet. "It's just weed."

"That's not the point!" Growing more pissed off each second, I spin back around and throw my hands up in exasperation. He doesn't get it at all. "You're supposed to be fine! Is that why you're up here all the time? To get high?"

"I can stop right now," he says, not quite answering my question, and he doesn't sound convincing at all. "Watch me." Bending down, he grabs the bag from the ground and closes his fist tightly around it, then lurches forward to latch on to my wrist.

"Don't touch me," I hiss, but it's no use. He's already pulling me across the terrace, straight for the door. He doesn't say anything as he drags me along with him. He's too focused, breathing heavily. I don't particularly want to talk to him now either, so we head down the stairs and into the elevator in complete silence.

I'm so mad. So furious. So livid. So angered. So confused. Why? Why would Tyler do this again? I don't get it. Folding my arms across my chest, I glance sideways and step further away from him as the elevator takes us back down to the twelfth floor. I don't want to be anywhere near him. He's totally blown it. Big time.

Nonetheless, he clasps my arm again and pulls me out of the elevator, walking so fast along the lobby to his apartment that I end up almost jogging. Because I forgot to lock the door, he leads me inside without hesitation, and the moment he glances over to the kitchen, I notice the way his eyes harden even more as he spots the jar of weed lying on the worktop. As for the apartment itself, it reeks of the stuff, and I'm now regretting ever opening it.

Releasing his grip on me, Tyler strides straight across the living room and into the kitchen, unscrewing the jar and reaching in to grasp the two remaining bags. With all three in his hand, he pushes open the bathroom door and glances over his shoulder at me.

"Look," he says, frustration in his voice. Unwillingly, I force myself to walk over to join him, and I fold my arms across my chest and glare at him from the bathroom door. "Fucking watch," he mutters.

He opens up the first bag and promptly tips its contents into the toilet bowl, shaking the bag vigorously before tossing it to the ground. He does the exact same with the other two while I watch with wide eyes, and once he's flushed it all away, still breathing heavily, he turns to me with a rather deflated look in his eyes.

"You wanna know why I wasn't fine, huh?" he snaps suddenly. "I wasn't fine because I wasn't with you, alright? That's why. It was because of you."

Perplexed, I stare at him as I try to absorb his words, but they don't sink in at all. "What?"

"Look, I thought when I moved here I'd be able to get over you, but I didn't," he admits, voice soft again. He sounds almost broken. Running a hand through his hair, he closes the toilet lid and sits down, hanging his head low. "I couldn't get you out of my fucking head and I had to distract myself."

I blink, overcome by disbelief again. Why are we having this conversation again? Why are we talking about distractions again? This was supposed to have ended years ago. "You're blaming me?" I ask, incredulous.

"Yeah, I'm blaming you," he says sharply as his head jerks up. He looks at me hard and indignantly. "I'm blaming you for making me believe that I had no chance with you."

"Are you ever going to let that go? Are you forever going to make me feel guilty for what I did?" I yell, stepping forward and bending down in front of him so that I can look up into his eyes as sincerely as I can. "I've already told you I'm *sorry*," I say slowly. "I never said I didn't want to be with you. I told you that I couldn't. There's a difference."

When Tyler doesn't reply, it all becomes too much for me. My fury fizzles out and all I'm left with is disappointment and confusion. It's not just the weed and us fighting, it's everything. All at once, I'm hit with the way we're betraying Dean, the reality that we've spent the last three weeks sneaking around because it seems to be the only thing we're good at, the realization that soon we have to tell Dean and our parents the truth, the fact that Tyler's been lying to me about being okay. It's all been building up since the moment I arrived in New York and now it's surfacing all at once. I can't deal with it.

Tears well in my eyes and break free only moments later, and I sink against the floor as I press my hands to my face, trying my best to hold back my sniffling. My attempt is useless, however, and soon I'm sobbing on the floor by Tyler's feet. I hear him breathing as I weep, but other than that, there's silence.

After a while, Tyler gently calls my name. I don't look up, though, I only cry harder at the sound of his voice, feeble and weak. Seconds after, I feel his hands on my body. Carefully, he wraps his arms around me and pulls me up with him as he gets to his feet. He doesn't let go. He pulls my body close against his, squeezing me tight as I bury my face into his flannel shirt. He just stands there holding me, and that's enough.

"I'm sorry," he whispers, resting his chin on the top of my head. "I should have told you."

I don't reply. I feel too hurt to even attempt to. I don't know what more I can say to him. I can only hope that he sincerely is sorry for doing this again, for resorting to the one thing we were all convinced he would never go back to.

Tyler suddenly moves his hand to my face, tilting my chin up with his thumb as he looks down into my swollen eyes, his expression utterly sincere. He even looks pained as he whispers more firmly, "I'm sorry."

He holds my face there, tilted up to his, and I can see the way his eyes rest on my lips. I don't move. I wait. He does, too. He's trying to sense whether I'm going to pull away or not, but when I don't, he closes his eyes and brushes his lips against mine.

It's so soft and so gentle at first, just the mere touch of our lips, but it quickly deepens. I cup his face in my hands as he kisses me faster, both of us fueled by all of our emotions combined. It changes from soft and slow to fast and furious every few seconds, a mixture of our anger and our sadness, and soon I'm sinking into him again, forgetting everything that has just happened.

With his lips never leaving mine, Tyler bends down slightly, sliding his hands under my thighs and lifting me up off the ground. I immediately wrap my legs tightly around his waist and loop my arms loosely around his neck, kissing him back just as hard and just as deep. He starts to walk, squeezing my ass as he carries me out of the bathroom, through the kitchen, across the living room. Roughly, I grab his hair and tilt his head to one side, and I move my lips to his neck, leaving a row of soft but deep kisses along his skin. He groans my name in response.

We inevitably end up in his room. Of course we do. Tearing his lips away from mine, he kicks the door shut behind us and places me down on the soft mattress of his bed. He looks down at me, eyes smoldering, and I blink back up at him with an anxious smile on my lips. And this time when I reach up for the belt of his jeans, he doesn't stop me, because this time I'm not drunk. This time there are no interruptions. This time we're ready.

I push him back a step and drop to my knees in front of him, pulling off my tank top and throwing it to the side. As I glance up at him again from beneath my eyelashes, I can see him swallowing as his glossy eyes encourage me to continue. So I do. My hands tremble only slightly as I unbutton his jeans, hooking my index fingers around the belt loops and pulling them down alongside his boxers. My eyes widen.

I don't remember much from two years ago, from that night of the beach party, the night he told me the truth. I remember it wasn't the greatest, but I expected that. Being my first time, I doubt I was impressive. Now, though, it's been two years, and one can gain a lot of experience in that time.

And so I get to work, showing Tyler just exactly what I've picked up over the past couple years. From one technique to another, the variation takes him aback, and I feel extremely satisfied each time he groans. His eyes are closed and he's got one hand pressed to the wall, the other holding my hair. I feel so dominant, but before I know it he's reaching for my hands and pulling me up from the ground, crashing his lips straight back to mine without hesitation.

It's rather messy, the two of us. We always are. Messy situations are all we ever get ourselves into, and this is no exception. Tyler's so focused on kissing me that he spends a good while fumbling with the clasp of my bra, struggling so much that I end up laughing as I momentarily pull away from him and do it myself. He looks a little sheepish as he steps out of his jeans at the same time, and once I've tossed my bra over his shoulder, he places both hands on my waist and pulls my body back against his. He runs his hands over me, his thumbs softly skimming the skin just below my breasts as he trails his lips down my neck to my shoulder and to my collarbone. I bite back a sigh of pleasure and focus on kicking off my Chucks and stepping out of my shorts.

His lips capture mine once more as he drops one hand to my ass and I move my hands to the buttons of his flannel shirt, trying my best to undo them as fast as I can all while kissing him. In the end, I'm just as useless as he is with clasps, so he undoes his shirt himself. The moment he slips it off his back and drops it to the floor, I run both my hands down his chest. His skin is hot and I can feel his heart pounding hard against his ribcage. Mine is too, and where Tyler's hand is on my body right now, I'm pretty sure he can feel it.

Gently, but with a sense of eagerness, Tyler pushes me onto the bed and I allow myself to fall back, landing softly on the mattress. He doesn't join me at first, though. He turns back around, grabbing his jeans and fishing around inside the pockets for his wallet, growing more panicked the longer he searches. I know what he's searching for, but I call him back over with a nervous laugh, and I inform him that he's got nothing to worry about. I've got that side of things under control. Mom insisted.

I can see the relief on Tyler's face as he throws his jeans and his wallet back onto the floor, biting his lip as he comes over to join me. My skin feels like it's on fire and I can't tell if it's the sunburn or his touch, but either way, I don't mind. I grab Tyler's hair, tightening my grip as he runs both his hands down my body without leaving a single inch of my skin untouched. He moves his lips to the edge of my jaw as he slips his hand inside my panties, and I close my eyes and focus on my breathing. I can't help but tug on his hair as I throw my head back into the pillows, my back arching.

He stops after a while, glancing up at me with wide eyes as though to ask if I'm ready, and so I nod.

I couldn't remember the way he moved and the way he felt until now. I couldn't remember the way our hips rolled together. I couldn't remember the way our breathing was never in sync, but rapid and uneven. I couldn't remember any of those things until right now, now that it's happening again. Only this time, Tyler's not afraid to be rougher than I recall him being the first time. Alternating between rhythms, one hand squeezing mine and the other gripping my hip, his body sweats against mine. It takes my breath away and it's so sensational that I think I might smile the entire time, even when I'm letting out soft moans. I can't help it. It's all just so . . . so Tyler. That's the best part about it.

It feels so scandalous, so wrong, which only makes it all the more exhilarating. It's a complete adrenaline rush. The worst thing is that I know it shouldn't be happening. Not yet. Not while I'm still with Dean. Tyler, on the other hand, has accepted the fact that Dean's going to get hurt at the end of this. He's accepted the fact that we're going to tell our parents the truth when we get home. I, however, haven't quite. I like to believe that I have. I try to convince myself that I'm ready to tackle it all, to deal with everything straight on, but there's still that panic and apprehension inside of me somewhere. I still feel guilty for loving Tyler. I still feel ashamed. It doesn't feel fair.

I think we'll forever be each other's biggest secret.

19

I don't call Dean at all the next week. I can't bring myself to hear his voice. Every time he tries to call, I let it go to voicemail as I stare at the screen, gnawing at my lip and feeling like the worst human being to ever walk this earth. It's not solely because of Saturday night, either. It's also because of Sunday afternoon, and Tuesday morning, and last night.

Tyler and I had to a lot to catch up on. Two years' worth. Each time both Snake and Emily were out of the apartment, we might have taken advantage of the privacy. So much advantage, in fact, that Tyler's been making jokes about whether or not we should tell the two of them to avoid the couch on the left of the coffee table. He receives nothing but a glare from me each time he brings it up.

It's not that we plan it or anything. It just keeps happening. I'm not complaining about it, either.

It's the middle of the night when Tyler wakes me up. I'm completely bare, wrapped up in his comforter and feeling completely exhausted from the workout we shared only a few hours ago. I'm perfectly happy basking in the warmth of his sheets, but I force my eyes open anyway. Tyler's standing by the side of the bed, hovering over me in the darkness, and I'm a little surprised to discover that he's pulled on clothes, a pair of jeans and a navy hoodie.

"What time is it?" I groan, squeezing my eyes shut again and burying my face into the pillows. I can hear sirens outside, but that's nothing unusual. New York never shuts the hell up. Ever.

"Three," Tyler says quietly. I sense him shift away from me and I wonder if he might possibly be sleepwalking or something, but the second he starts tossing my clothes at me, I realize he's not. "Get dressed."

I roll back over and prop my body up on my elbows, squinting down at the clothes Tyler's thrown at me. The exact same as his, jeans and a hoodie. He even tosses my bra over, and it promptly hits me in the face.

"Shit, sorry," he says, but he's holding back a laugh as he approaches me again. I only roll my eyes. "I've got a surprise for you."

"A surprise?" I murmur wearily. Something about his tone makes me feel rather alarmed. Surprises are never good. It could be anything. And at 3AM? That's even more worrying. Rubbing at my eyes, I sit up even further, and I don't even bother to cover myself with the comforter. By now, it feels like Tyler sees me naked more often than he sees me in clothes.

He leans over to flick on one of the bedside lamps and as it lights up his face, I see that he's smiling smugly. Bending down by the edge of the bed, his eyes are level with mine as his lips pull up into a wide grin, and he reaches into his pocket for something before holding it up in front of my face. It's the keys to his car. "All yours."

I part my lips, blinking in surprise. Being offered the chance to drive an Audi R8 in the middle of the night was the last thing I expected. I study the car keys and the Audi keyring shines in the light. Gently, I reach out to grasp them, a small smile growing on my lips. "Even though you don't trust me?"

"I must be crazy, right?" he says quietly, smirking. He gets to his feet, reaches for my free hand and pulls me out of the bed. He steadies me on my feet and looks down at me. "But it's New York. We don't do anything less than crazy in this city."

Now wide awake, excitement rushes over me. The thought of driving Tyler's car, the possibilities of what that engine can do, fills me with euphoria. I've never been all that into cars, but Tyler's is an exception. Quickly, I reach for my clothes and pull them on, rummaging around the room for my Chucks afterward. The same Chucks I've worn for four weeks straight now. They seem to be the only shoes I ever wear now, and they're not as white as they were to begin with.

"One scratch on my baby and you're gonna get it," Tyler says once I'm dressed, but he's smiling. He throws an arm over my shoulder and leads me over to the door, opening it without a single sound and walking me through the living room.

Through the darkness, I can make out Snake's outline on the couch. His couch, thankfully. He's fast asleep and snoring softly, so Tyler and I creep our way over to the apartment door as silently as we can. We make it out into the lobby without waking him, and Tyler lets go of me while he locks up.

The building is silent and neither of us talk in fear of waking people up as we pass their apartments and head into the elevator. I jingle the keys in my hand and I sense Tyler watching me from the corner of his eye. I hope I don't get arrested for this.

Once we leave the building and step outside onto Seventy-fourth Street, I realize New York is still busy. Admittedly, the traffic and flow of people on the sidewalks is substantially less hectic than during the day, but for 3AM there are still a lot of cars on the roads. Cabs, mostly. It's hardly warm out, but it's not cold.

Parked against the curb on the other side of the street, Tyler's car awaits me. I eye it with excitement building up inside of me again and swiftly unlock it. To my surprise, however, Tyler snatches the keys from my hand and darts across the road. He throws open the driver's door and looks back at me with a glint his eyes. My eyebrows are raised, demanding an explanation.

"What, you thought I was gonna let you drive around Manhattan?" Tyler laughs into the night air as he slides into the vehicle, and just before he shuts the door behind him, he adds, "No way in hell."

Folding my arms across my chest in irritation, I force myself over to the car and slip into the passenger seat. I glare at him, disgruntled. "Where can I drive it then?"

"Jersey City," Tyler shoots back as he starts up the engine. It purrs smoothly to life and a chill runs down my spine.

"Jersey City?"

"Yeah," he says. "The Target parking lot."

The dashboard glows orange in the darkness, the numbers on the speedometer lighting up. The music and climate controls ahead of the center console also light up, and I lean forward to adjust the heating before sinking back into my seat, and as Tyler edges out of his confined parking spot, I pull on my seatbelt.

It's a good thing I do, because the moment we pull around

the corner onto Second Avenue, he floors it straight until we hit a set of traffic lights. I listen as he revs up the engine, waiting. Glancing sideways at me, he smiles, clenching his jaw before narrowing his eyes on the road ahead. We're the first at the lights. In front of us, the road is clear. Tyler's fingers tighten around the gearshift, his other hand firmly gripping the steering wheel. The red flashes to amber, and as he slams his foot down on the gas, there's a tremendous screeching of tires as the car catapults down the avenue. The speed is so forceful that it throws my body back against the seat. The engine roars behind us, the exhaust pipe sputtering fumes in our wake. Usually I would rebuke reckless driving, but right now, at 3AM in the middle of Manhattan, I'm loving it.

As Tyler shoves the gearshift toward sixth, his eyes flicker at me and there's a mischievous smirk playing on his lips. His eyes zero back in on the road, and as the car continues to increase in speed, I find myself gripping onto the seat with one hand and my seatbelt with the other. I glance over at the speedometer and find that we're flying along at double the speed limit, and Tyler only slows down when we reach the end of the traffic flow ahead of us, caught up in more traffic lights.

No more opportunities open up for reckless driving after that, only because the streets aren't clear enough for it. We're stuck trailing along behind a truck, and we only get away from it when we turn right onto Houston Street. We continue to head west across Manhattan until we enter a tunnel, just like the Lincoln Tunnel I crossed the first day I arrived in the city, only this time Tyler tells me this is the Holland Tunnel.

We're out of it within a couple of minutes though, and only moments after entering Jersey City, Tyler's pulling into the

Target parking lot. The store is closed, and not only is the lot huge, it's also empty. It's perfect.

Cutting off the engine right in the center of the parking lot, Tyler exhales into the sudden silence, his eyes scouring the area through the windshield. It seems to meet with his approval and he turns to face me. "Knock yourself out."

We both push open our doors and step outside the car at the same time. Nervously, I glance down at the asphalt as I walk around it, my body brushing against Tyler's as we pass each other. Now that the time is here to actually drive his car, I feel a little anxious. I'm worried I'll wreck it, but at the same time I'm eager to show Tyler what I've got.

I slide into the driver's side as Tyler slips into the passenger seat, and I swallow as I adjust the seat, pulling myself closer to the steering wheel so that my feet can actually reach the pedals. As Tyler watches me contentedly, I start up the engine again. I study the lot quickly once more, getting my bearings and figuring out how much room I have as we pull on our seatbelts.

I haven't driven stick shift in a while, and I'm so used to driving automatic that to begin with it takes me a short while to get back into the habit of not only using my left foot to operate the clutch pedal but also working with gears. The car jolts forward and stalls on my first attempt at starting it up.

"You're right," Tyler says, laughing from my side. "You're amazing at driving manual."

"Shut up," I mutter, but I don't even glance at him. I'm so focused on starting up the engine again that I totally tune out the sound of his laughter. He can mock my driving skills all he wants. I'll prove him wrong.

This time, I ensure I'm in my manual mindset. I put the

car into first, my foot pressed down on the clutch pedal as I slowly begin to rev up the engine, and once I'm satisfied with how loud it's roaring I slam my foot on the gas. The vehicle bursts forward, hurtling down the asphalt across the lot. It's so powerful that it momentarily scares the crap out of me, but I only grip the steering wheel tighter and step on the gas even more. Within a matter of seconds the car's already flying at sixty, and from the corner of my eye, I see Tyler's eyebrows rising as he glances between me and the road. Braking and changing down a couple gears as we approach the edge of the lot, I spin the wheel around to the right and the car swerves, tires screeching.

I race back across the lot again, even faster this time as I work my way back up to sixth gear, and there's something so enthralling about driving stick shift that I end up grinning the entire time. It gives me so much more control.

"How fast does this thing go?" I yell over the noise of the engine. My eyes never leave the road, and I promptly fly around the corner of the store, forgetting to change gear. The car almost spins straight across the sidewalk, but thankfully it holds its grip, as do both Tyler and I inside the car. Tyler grabs onto the handle above the door and I can do nothing but squeeze the steering wheel even tighter until my knuckles turn white.

"Don't push it!" he warns me. "You don't have enough space to build up to anything faster than ninety!"

"Ninety it is then." I flash him a smirk before setting my eyes back ahead, and I come to a halt by the far edge of the lot once I've turned the car back around to face the opposite direction. There's quite a bit a distance between here and the other end of the lot. I'll be able to make it.

"Fuck," Tyler murmurs as he listens to me rev up the engine once again. He knows exactly what I'm doing. "Baby, if it's the last thing you do, don't fucking forget to brake."

"If you don't trust me," I fire back, smirking, "you can get outta the car." I nod to the door and rev the engine even more, so loud that it vibrates in my ears.

Tyler's eyebrows quirk up, but he doesn't even flinch, doesn't even think about getting out. Instead, he tightens one hand around his seatbelt, places the other on my thigh, and in his husky voice, he demands, "Floor it."

So I do. I slam on the accelerator and the car takes off so fast that both our bodies fly back against the seats, and Tyler starts laughing again as the speed continues to increase. He squeezes my thigh and it's so distracting that I have to quite literally force myself to ignore him as I glance rapidly between the parking lot and the speedometer. Sixty. I press the gas straight down until my foot's touching the floor. Seventy. Eighty. Ninety.

But I don't stop. That's what Tyler's expecting me to do. Stopping is the easy way out. I like the risks, so I do the opposite of what I should do. I keep my foot on the gas. A hundred.

"Eden," Tyler says warily, firmly. His grip on his seatbelt tightens. A hundred and ten. "*Eden.*"

The second I hit that mark, I move my foot to the brake pedal, depressing it as fast and as hard as I can as the tires tear across the asphalt. I lock my arms tight against the wheel as my body flies forward, and I suddenly start to panic as I realize how little room there is left between here and the edge of the lot, so I squeeze my eyes shut. It feels like it takes forever for the car to finally skid to a halt. I'm breathing heavily by the time it does, and once I establish that we've stopped, I slowly open my eyes and glance out the windshield. We're only inches from the sidewalk.

When I glance to my right, Tyler's staring at me in disbelief. His eyes are wide and his lips are parted, and the only thing he can bring himself to say is, "Damn, Eden."

"I'm not finished yet," I point out with a smile, and now he really does look panicked. Letting go of my thigh, he sinks back against the seat and heaves a sigh of relief that he's still alive.

I pull off the hair tie on my wrist and gather my hair up into a high ponytail, out of my way. And, feeling fueled by adrenaline, I pull off my hoodie and my shirt. The car's heated up by now, anyway. I toss them onto Tyler's lap and I roll my eyes as he smirks back at me. It's like he's never seen me in my bra before.

I reach back for the wheel and, calmly and slowly, I drive back to the center of the lot and come to a complete stop. Breathing deeply, I concentrate hard. I've only successfully done this once before. I'm adamant I'm going to do it again, to impress Tyler, but I know there's a high risk that it'll go pathetically wrong and I'll end up looking like a fool. But it's worth a shot.

Tyler's focusing on me hard as he tries to figure out what I'm doing, and as I slowly rev up the engine for the final time, I turn the wheel completely around to full lock, and I hold it there.

"No way," he says once he realizes what my next move is. "You're gonna owe me new tires after this."

And he's right. I *will* owe him new tires after this, because I'm about to burn the hell out of them.

The engine revved enough, I hit the accelerator and floor it. The car spirals to the right, the tires burning against the ground, screeching. I laugh as the car continues to swerve, and when I glance in the rearview mirror, I smile proudly as clouds of smoke engulf the vehicle. As swirling loops appear on the ground, I decide to quit burning anymore rubber, and I hit the brakes.

We sit in silence for a few seconds, my heart beating rapidly from excitement, and we wait for the smoke to clear. "Okay, I'm done," I announce. I can't wipe the smirk off my lips.

"Where the hell did you learn how to do that?"

"Dean's dad showed me," I admit. It was back in March, and we spent hours on it until I finally got it right.

Tyler furrows his eyebrows at me as though he doesn't believe a single word I'm saying. "Hugh taught you how to spin donuts?"

"Yeah," I say with a shrug. I still feel rather smug about my impressive skills, however. Tyler most definitely wasn't expecting it. "He was about to replace the tires on his truck so he let Dean and me wreck the old ones first."

"Hmm," he says. "Alright, switch."

As he steps out of the car and walks around the hood to the driver's side, I climb over the center console and nestle myself into the passenger seat. I don't bother to pull my shirt or my hoodie back on, but I do tug on my seatbelt. We've got the half-hour ride home now.

But in Tyler's mind, the stunt show isn't over quite yet. He shuts the car door behind him, pulling on his seatbelt and glancing in the rearview mirror as he intensely studies the area behind us. He doesn't give me any warning whatsoever, and just as I'm narrowing my eyes at him suspiciously, he puts the car in reverse and steps on the gas. He cranes his neck to look back over his shoulder, his eyes zeroed in on the road behind us as he stares out the rear windshield. The car begins to pick up speed as we fly backward in a straight line, and as Tyler quickly turns back around to face the front, he murmurs, "Hold on."

The second he says this, he slams on the brakes, spinning the wheel in a full circle. The car spins around 180 degrees to the right, and the instant we're facing the direction we just reversed in, Tyler slams the gearshift up into first. The momentum from reversing at such a speed is transferred quickly, and we're suddenly driving along the same straight line, only now we're no longer backward. Tyler brakes just as we reach the exit of the parking lot.

I blink at him and reach up to switch on the overhead light. It makes the emerald in his eyes seem even brighter. "Since when could you do J-turns?"

"Since when did you know what J-turns are?" Tyler shoots back, right before he grasps my face in his hands and presses his lips to mine again.

It doesn't feel like the middle of the night and it doesn't feel like we just did all of this a few hours ago. I'm kissing him back and it all feels so familiar now that I can't help but smile against his lips. I like that none of this feels foreign anymore. I like that it just feels normal. Not wrong. Normal. Gripping onto Tyler's hoodie, I sit up on my knees and pull him toward me, pressing my chest to his. The space available is limited, but we persevere, and although cramped, it doesn't prevent Tyler from brushing his hands over my skin, grabbing my hips.

"I'm starting to wish my car had a backseat," he murmurs against my jaw with a slight laugh.

With the roll of my eyes and a seductive smile, I whisper, "We can improvise."

The engine's still running, but neither of us seem to pay any attention. I reach back up to turn off the overheard light again while Tyler's hand rests on the clasp of my bra. He's getting better, a lot less fumbling, and just as he's about to unclasp it, my phone rings.

It vibrates in the back pocket of my jeans and I freeze. I share a rather perplexed glance with Tyler as I pull back from him, reaching for the device. I'm taken aback when I see Rachael's name flashing across the screen.

Tyler slumps back in his seat in defeat as he runs a hand through his hair, resting the other on the steering wheel. "Goddamn, Eden."

"It's not my fault!" I apologize. I don't know what Rachael could possibly be calling for at this hour and, slightly irritated by the interruption, I answer the call sounding a lot more grouchy than I'd like. "What?"

"Woah, Eden, you sound like such a moody-ass New Yorker," Rachael's voice chirps back. "I haven't spoken to you in forever and you answer my call like that?"

"Rachael," I say slowly. "You realize it's almost four here, right? As in, the middle of the night?"

"Oh my God, no way!" she explodes, letting out a small gasp. Rachael often forgets the time difference. The first week I got here, she almost always called me when it was after midnight in New York. No matter how many times I remind her of the three-hour difference, she never seems to remember. "I totally forgot. It's barely one here yet. Did I wake you up?"

"No, I'm awake." Tyler fixes me with an impatient glare and I shrug back at him. I can't just hang up on her.

"Okay, so I have to talk to you about Tuesday."

"Hurry up," he mouths.

I wave him away with my hand, crossing my legs on the seat and pressing my phone harder against my ear. "What do you need to talk to me about?" Tuesday is when Rachael and Meghan arrive in New York for Meg's belated birthday trip. They'll be here for five days, and I can't wait to see them. Right now, however, my thoughts aren't exactly focused on my friends coming to the city. They're focused on Tyler and the fact that he's glowering at me. It's rather distracting.

"We're staying at the Lowell Hotel," Rachael informs me, voice clear and confident. I never expect anything less of her. "I'm looking at the map right now and it's on the intersection of Sixty-third Street and Madison Avenue. You got any idea where that is?"

I try to picture the grid layout of the borough. Madison Avenue, I'm pretty sure, is only three blocks west from Tyler's apartment. Sixty-third Street is eleven blocks south. "Tyler's apartment's on Seventy-fourth Street. North of your hotel."

"So we're close?" she asks.

"I guess?"

"Great. Here's what I need you to do." Pausing, she takes a deep breath while I sigh away from the phone. Knowing Rachael, I shouldn't be too surprised by any requests she makes. They're often unrealistic. This one, however, isn't. "On Tuesday night, can you come by our hotel? Tyler too. I'll text you the room number when we check in and whatever. We really wanna see you guys."

"Sure, we'll come by." Out of the corner of my eye, Tyler sits upright and arches his eyebrows, questioning my plural use. He wants to know what I'm dragging him into. I'll explain later. "Rachael, it's really late."

"Oh God, yeah. Sorry, Eden," she apologies, and for once she sounds genuinely sincere. Usually her apologies have to be forced out of her. "Night, babe."

I hang up the call and sigh, but then I begin to smile. I make a point of shutting my phone off completely, throwing it to the floor and stretching over the center console to run my fingertips along the edge of Tyler's jaw. He doesn't look impressed to start with, but the second I glance up at him as innocently as I can from beneath my eyelashes, he seems to forgive me for interrupting our moment, because he reaches for me and picks up exactly where we left off.

He doesn't bother to ask what we're doing on Tuesday.

20

It's just after eight on Tuesday evening when Tyler and I make our way to the Lowell on Sixty-third and Madison. The sun is slowly starting to dip behind the buildings of Manhattan as Tyler drives south along Park Avenue. He's wearing a pair of black shades as he drives, with one hand on the wheel and the other toying at his hair, his elbow propped up against the door.

"I think they're punking us," he murmurs after a while. "The Lowell? Give me a break."

I glance over at him. "What?"

"C'mon." He scoffs, and despite the fact that I can't see behind his shades, I can tell he's rolling his eyes. "Rachael and Meghan are college students. You think they can afford that place? I mean, Meghan just got back from Europe. She's probably only got ten bucks to her name."

"Tyler, you were a sixteen-year-old high school student when you bought this car with that big old trust fund of yours," I remind him, and then, to prove my point, I add, "You really think sixteen-year-olds can afford cars like these?"

"I'm just saying," he says, ignoring my comment.

It only takes us ten minutes to reach Sixty-third Street, and Tyler reverses into a free spot in one swift maneuver, right in front of the Santa Fe Opera. My parking skills aren't on a par with his—I'm still getting used to his ability to park in less than six seconds.

While I step out of the car, Tyler throws his sunglasses onto the dashboard right before slamming the car door behind him, and I can't help but arch my eyebrows as I follow him along Sixty-third Street. I'm not sure what his problem is.

The Lowell is only a few buildings down, just off the corner of Madison Avenue. With red bricking and gold-plated doors and a gorgeous white canopy, I stare at it from outside for a while before Tyler groans and pulls me inside by my wrist. A doorman greets us and holds open the door, welcoming us to the hotel and wishing us a great evening. I get the impression that Tyler doesn't particularly want to be here when he sighs. Right now, he's either anti-luxury-hotels or anti-Rachael-and-Meghan.

The lobby is small but inviting, with plenty of seating, and Tyler and I briskly whisk past the front desk and head for the elevator. Rachael and Meghan's suite is on the tenth floor, so that's exactly where we head. Tyler folds his arms across his chest and leans back against the hand railing.

"What's your problem?" I ask, finally.

"Why am I here?" he replies without missing a beat.

I furrow my eyebrows, perplexed at his question. "They're your friends."

"Eden," he says, "I don't think I've spoken to Rachael more than six times in the space of a year and I haven't spoken to Meghan at all. Neither have you. Admit it."

I shrug. He's right in a way. Meghan doesn't particularly make much effort to talk to any of us anymore. It's almost like she was glad to leave LA. The only time I really got the chance to talk to her was when she occasionally came home.

Even I don't feel as close to her as I used to be. "Okay, sure, Meghan's a little more difficult to stay in touch with," I admit.

"C'mon," Tyler says with a harsh laugh, "she clearly doesn't wanna deal with any of us anymore. She's all about Utah and that Jared guy. Are they married yet? Because they sure as hell act like they are."

"Jesus, Tyler."

"Look," he says quietly. "I just think it's awkward. I'm not friends with them anymore. It's just what happens."

The elevator comes to a smooth stop and the door pings open, cutting our conversation short. I'm not sure I would have mustered up a reply, anyway. Tyler still looks moody as hell and he doesn't even attempt to hide it as we head along the tenth floor. I pull out my phone again as we walk, double-checking Rachael's texts to ensure I've got the details right, and then draw Tyler to a halt outside the correct door. I rap my knuckles against it.

As we wait, my eyes drift to Tyler. He's staring at the door, expression now nonchalant, and I can't help but study every inch of his face. His tanned complexion and his dark, tousled hair that he blames on his Hispanic genes, his vibrant emerald eyes that alternate between dull and bright, his perfectly defined jaw with just the right amount of stubble . . .

All of that . . . All of that is mine.

"What?" he says, catching my stare. Those green eyes gaze into mine.

I can't even begin to hide my smile, and as my lips curve further up into a sheepish grin, I just shrug. "Nothing."

The door unlocks then. It swings open so fast it creates a breeze, and before I've even had the chance to look up I'm being yanked over the threshold and into someone's arms.

I recognize the perfume and the shampoo scent in a heartbeat. It's Rachael's, and it has been for as long as I can remember. Her long hair gets in my face as she hugs me tight all while squealing, and I can do nothing but laugh against her shoulder. It really is good to see her. It reminds me of my life back in Santa Monica. The past four weeks, I'd almost forgotten about it entirely.

"God, Rachael," I murmur, "are you trying to break my arm?" Still laughing, I manage to wrangle my way out of her firm hold and then take a step back so that I can study her.

Her hair's a few shades darker than I remember and has clearly had several inches trimmed off, but I don't mention it. I remember Dean said she wasn't all that impressed with it. Other than that, she's my same old best friend who's wearing a huge grin. "I've missed you!"

"I've missed you, too," I say. I hadn't realized that I had until now. I've just been so distracted by everything else going on, and now I'm starting to feel guilty.

"Tyler!" Rachael's eyes widen as she stares at him for a moment, and I honestly can't blame her. He looks like he's aged half a decade in the time that he's been gone. He's lingering awkwardly at the door, but Rachael steps around me to pull him into a hug, too. It's only brief, and once she draws away from him she pulls him into the suite by his arm and clicks the door shut. "I can't believe it's been a year!"

"Yeah, it's crazy," Tyler says. There's a small smile on his lips now, and I can't figure out if it's genuine or fake. Either way, he no longer looks uncomfortable.

While they talk, I take a minute or so to check out the suite. It's huge, and it looks like there are separate bedrooms, a bathroom and a kitchenette. It's all hardwood flooring with oriental rugs, and it all feels rather elegant and vintage, yet somehow modern at the same time. There's some impressive artwork on the walls, but I don't stare at it for long before I walk back over to Tyler's side.

"So is the subway safe?" Rachael asks him, eyes wide. "We won't get shot or anything?"

"Don't worry about the subway," Tyler says. I can tell he wants to roll his eyes at her, but he refrains. "Just don't look like a tourist and you'll be fine."

I glance around the suite again. Something's missing. It takes me a second to realize, and when I do, I flash my eyes over to Rachael and interrupt their conversation. "Where's Meghan?"

Slowly, Rachael glances over. She almost smiles, but she bites it back and shrugs rather nonchalantly instead. "She brought back some virus with her from Europe. She literally couldn't stop throwing up so she didn't come."

"So you came all the way over here on your own?"

The words have barely left my lips when someone throws their arms over my shoulders and Tyler's, grabbing us tightly. I flinch at the abruptness of it, and before I even get the chance to turn around a voice is murmuring, "Hey, New Yorkers."

My heart stops. Not because of the momentary scare, but because of the voice. It's one I recognize all too well.

It's Dean's.

Shrugging his arm off me, I spin around at the exact same time Tyler does, and I'm exactly right.

Dean's standing in front of me. There's a huge grin plastered on his face and his dark eyes are sparkling as he steps toward me, wrapping his arms around me and hugging me tightly against his chest. I feel so numb that I can't even hug him back. I just stand there, my lips parted in disbelief and my eyes wide. Over Dean's shoulder, Tyler's staring back at me, his face as pale as mine. We're both thinking the exact same thing: *I wish this wasn't happening right now.*

"Surprise," Dean whispers. His voice sends a chill down my spine as he buries his face into my hair, and it all feels so foreign now. I'm not used to Dean. I'm used to Tyler.

Dean shouldn't be here. He shouldn't be in New York with Tyler and me. He's supposed to be in Santa Monica. I'm supposed to have two more weeks to figure out what I'm going to do about him. I'm not ready to deal with this now. Dean being here could ruin *everything.*

When he finally lets go, he stares down at me in awe, shaking his head as he smiles. Wide and sincere. It hurts to see it. "God, I've missed you so much," he says, and he presses his lips against mine.

I'm taken aback at first, so surprised that I can't even bring myself to pull away. I used to feel something when I kissed Dean, but now I feel nothing. I don't experience any sort of rush. Dean kisses me softly but frantically, like he's trying to remind himself of what he's been missing, but I can't return his energy. I don't want to. To me, the kiss feels lifeless.

I try to shoot Tyler an apologetic glance. His body has stiffened and his eyes have hardened, and he's staring fiercely at us with a cold expression on his face. Out of nowhere he grabs Dean's shoulder and pulls him back a step, breaking our kiss. I'm thankful.

"Hey, man, are you forgetting about your best friend?" Tyler asks, and by the time Dean turns around to face him, he's got a smile on his lips. I can see straight through it, though. I can still the furious glint in his eyes. I can still see the way the muscle in his jaw has tightened.

Dean, however, can't see anything but the smile on his best friend's face. "Geez, what happened to your voice?"

"New York City. Roommate from Boston," Tyler says dryly. "Tends to mess up your accent."

Laughing, Dean draws him into a half-hug while they thump each other's back, and when Dean steps back Tyler asks, "So why are you here?" He doesn't bother to hide the harsh tone of his voice. Just folds his arms across his chest and raises his eyebrows at him, awaiting an answer.

"Filling in for Meghan," Dean says. He's wearing a pale-blue shirt and dark jeans, and he stuffs his hands into the front pockets. "It was really last-minute. I thought my dad wouldn't let me take the time off work, but he told me to go for it. Rachael's idea."

Both Tyler and I fire our eyes at Rachael at the exact same moment. She's watching the scene unfold with a beaming grin spread across her face. Right now, neither Tyler nor I are impressed. Inviting Dean to New York? That's quite literally the worst thing she could have done.

"Tyler, I brought you your best friend. Eden, I brought you your boyfriend," she states, grin stretching even wider. "Am I the greatest best friend in the world or what?"

I can't even bring myself to reply to her. I know her intentions were good, but she has absolutely no idea what she's just done. She's made everything so much more complicated. I doubt either Rachael or Dean notice it, but to Tyler and me the tension in the room is starting to feel unbearable.

I shoot him a panicked glance and he closes his eyes, running a hand back through his hair. I don't know what to think. I don't know what to do. And as Dean joins me by my side again, throwing his arm around me and pressing a soft kiss to my cheek, I begin to feel even worse.

Are we supposed to tell him the truth now that he's here in New York? Or do we wait like we'd planned? That's the hard part. Knowing when to hurt Dean. It's inevitable that we will: It's just a matter of when and where. Not here, that's for sure. Not right now. But soon, perhaps.

And if I thought it couldn't get any worse than this, then God, I'm so wrong.

The bathroom door swings open, drawing the attention of all four of us, and as I furrow my eyebrows in confusion, I hear a voice gush, "Guys, the tub is *amazing*."

It's another voice I recognize. A voice I never thought I'd have to hear again. A voice that belongs to someone I haven't spoken to in two years. And just as the color in my face begins to drain once again, she steps out of the bathroom with her hair thrown up into a messy bun and nothing but a white towel wrapped around her tiny body. She stops when she spots us and her eyes flicker between Tyler and me for a moment, and then, so slowly that it becomes almost painful, Tiffani smiles. "Why didn't anyone tell me that my favorite pair of stepsiblings had arrived?"

21

I'm convinced that none of this is really happening. It can't possibly be happening. Dean can't be in New York. Tiffani can't be standing opposite me, wearing a seemingly innocent smile. Only I know her better than that, and I know that behind that innocence there is deviousness. That's all Tiffani is and it's all she ever has been. Manipulative, controling and willing to defy everyone and everything in order to get what she wants. In her mind, her way is the only way. And she's standing in the same room as both Tyler and me. She's standing across from the two people she knows she can get the better of, the two people who are desperately trying their best to hide a secret only she knows about.

"Are you kidding me?" Tyler hisses, his voice slicing through the thick atmosphere. He's shifted his glare from Dean to Tiffani and he shakes his head in disbelief.

Rachael heaves a sigh as she folds her arms and leans back against the arm of one of the vintage chairs. She kicks at the rug and fixes Tyler with a hard look. "Can't you guys grow up already? You broke up, whatever. That was two years ago. Get over it."

"Are you being serious right now, Rachael?" Tyler blinks back at her, his eyes widening. He laughs, so stunned by the situation that I think laughing is the only thing he *can* do. "Fuck this. I'm out." Throwing his arms up in defeat, he turns around and strides straight for the door, pulling it open so forcefully that the hinges squeak. "I'll wait for you in the car, Eden," he throws over his shoulder, and promptly slams the suite door shut. There's a tremendous echo.

"So moving to New York clearly hasn't fixed his anger issues," Rachael says after a moment of silence. She's making a joke, of course, but I don't find it funny. In fact, I find it totally disrespectful. So rude that I can't help but glare at her.

"Why's he always such an asshole?" Tiffani adds, voice sweet and soft, as though she's deeply offended. "He's got serious issues. So aggressive. He clearly gets it from his dad."

I'm about to say something, about to open my mouth to call Tiffani out for saying what she just said, but surprisingly, Dean beats me to it.

"Guys, really?" he asks, dropping his arm from around my shoulders to around my waist. "Give him a break."

"He's a bit dramatic, though," Rachael murmurs. "Don't you think so? Storming out like that. Same old Tyler, I guess."

"I can't blame him," I say as I throw a pointed glance at Tiffani. I'm not even going to attempt to hide my contempt for her. Rachael is slowly aggravating me too. Same old Tyler? They're only seeing him right now. Of course he's going to get mad when Tiffani turns up out of absolutely nowhere. Neither Rachael nor Tiffani have *really* seen him, the Tyler who's always laughing those hearty laughs and smiling at random moments throughout the day. They haven't seen the new Tyler yet. Sure, he's still a work in progress, but he's getting there. He's a lot happier than he ever was before, and their insults are pissing me off. I'm always going to defend him.

"Not you too," Rachael groans, tilting her head back and closing her eyes.

"God, Eden," Tiffani says, "I thought maybe now that you've graduated you'd have matured." She flutters her eyelashes at me from the bathroom door and holds on to her towel, pursing her lips.

"What's your problem with me, Tiffani?" I demand, losing my temper as I shrug Dean's grip off me and make a move for her. "Why have you always been so—?"

Dean grabs me from behind again, pulling me back against his body as he stops me from lunging toward her. "Tiffani," he says. "Don't be a bitch."

"Shut the hell up, Dean," she orders. Her voice has lost its gentleness and now it sounds sharp. Fixing the two of us with a fierce glare, she storms into one of the bedrooms and slams the door behind her.

I glance back at Dean as his hold on me loosens, and he just shrugs at me as though it's no big deal. He's defended both Tyler and me, and it only makes me feel even guiltier than I already did. Dean's just like that. Always there for people. Soon I'll be throwing it all back in his face. It's difficult to think about, so I focus my attention elsewhere.

"She's a bit dramatic, though, don't you think so?" I throw at Rachael, quoting her earlier words about Tyler. I step away from Dean and fold my arms across my chest, raising my eyebrows at her. "What the hell is she even doing here?"

Rachael stands up from the chair, sighing as she walks over. She brings with her a waft of her perfume again. "She was always going to be coming, Eden. I just didn't mention it to you because I didn't want you complaining about it for months. Can't you guys just let all of this go?"

"Let it go?" I echo. "Seriously?"

"Look, I get it," she says. "You hate her because of what she did to Tyler and she hates you because you took his side. But that was years ago. Don't you think you're being a little childish? Can't you just forgive and forget? Tiffani has. She's ready to be friends with you again. Both of you."

I want to laugh, just like Tyler did, in disbelief. Rachael has no idea what really went down two summers ago. Sometimes I wish she knew. But she doesn't, so I can only grit my teeth to stop myself from telling her the truth. "I'm never going to be her friend, Rachael. Never."

"Don't worry about it," Dean says from behind me, and I flinch. I'm not used to hearing his voice. The fact that he's here is still taking me by surprise. He puts a hand on my shoulder and steps by my side, offering me a smile of reassurance. "You don't have to be friends with her."

"C'mon Dean," Rachael murmurs, "you have to admit that it makes it awkward for the rest of us."

"I don't find anything awkward," Dean states, expression calm as he shifts his gaze back to her. I can sense that he's lying, but I know he's only trying to fight my corner, so I remain still beneath his touch. "Nothing's awkward unless you make it awkward, which is exactly what you're doing right now."

Rachael presses her lips together. "All I'm trying to do is bring everyone back together," she says, but she sounds a little sad. She says nothing more, though, and turns and heads for the same bedroom as Tiffani, leaving Dean and I alone.

He turns to face me, looking a little deflated. I don't think any of this has turned out the way they'd planned. "Maybe it was a bad idea asking you and Tyler to come over here," he mumbles. "We wanted to surprise you guys, and I just had to see you tonight. I couldn't wait until tomorrow."

"Well, here I am," I say half-heartedly. I laugh, but it's not genuine. I'm starting to feel sick. I can't handle both Dean and Tiffani being in New York. It's too much to cope with all at once.

"And people say the skyline is the most beautiful thing in New York," he says, lips curving into a smile as he raises his eyebrows at me. That's when I notice he's shaved that awful stubble he'd been growing.

I roll my eyes and push his shoulder. "God, Dean, really?"

"I just had to," he says. His wide grin reaches his eyes as he places his hands on my shoulders, his gaze mirroring mine. "In the month that you've been gone I've thought of so many corny phrases I can throw at you." He kisses me then, and because we're alone this time he runs his hands down my body, from my shoulders to my waist. He kisses me like it's the first time.

I find it hard to kiss him back with enthusiasm. How can I? I try, though, because I'm not ready to raise any suspicions yet. I'm trying to act normal. I'm trying to act as though I'm not in love with his best friend and I'm trying to act as though I'm not going to be telling him the truth very, very soon.

I'm the one to pull away, when kissing him becomes unbearable. Shrugging, I frown and glance over to the door. "Dean, I should go," I say quietly. "Tyler's waiting in the car."

"Yeah, that's okay," he says. Finally, he releases his grip on my body and steps back. He's still smiling. "Us three are gonna head out for something to eat, anyway. See the city, I guess. But tomorrow, we're hanging out, okay?"

I don't think that'll go down well with Tyler and I find myself stammering that I have plans already tomorrow, but Dean just looks confused. I don't know what to do: Am I supposed to continue to act normal around him or am I supposed to give him the cold shoulder so that he knows something's up? I can't tell which will hurt him less, so I end up agreeing to a date tomorrow night instead.

All of this is too much to take in, and as I'm sharing a goodbye with Dean and yelling bye to Rachael through the bedroom door, I realize that my hands are shaking. I get the hell out of the hotel suite as fast as I can without looking like I'm desperate to leave, and I don't wait for the elevator. I'm in too much of a rush to get as far away as I can from both Dean and Tiffani, so I take the stairs, jogging down all ten flights of them at an uneven pace before striding through the main lobby. I burst through the main doors before the doorman even has a chance to open them for me, and he arches an eyebrow at me as I jog by him.

Thankfully, Tyler's car is still parked against the sidewalk, still outside the Santa Fe Opera. The engine is running, and I promptly throw open the passenger door and slip inside, yanking the door shut behind me.

Breathing heavily, I immediately glance at Tyler. His body is stiff against the seat, both hands gripping the steering wheel so tight his knuckles have paled, his arms rigid. He doesn't even look back at me, only clenches his jaw as he continues to stare out the windshield.

As he parts his lips to speak, all he can say is, "What the fuck do we do now?"

"I don't know," I say. Groaning, I throw my head down against the dashboard and run my hands through my hair. I squeeze my eyes shut as I try to process everything that has just occurred, but it all just feels like a messy blur. I can't piece anything together. Slowly, I lift my head back up and turn to face him. "Tyler, should we tell him? I mean, it's the right thing to do, isn't it?"

"We have to tell him," he says, but he's talking more slowly now and his voice is much calmer. He shifts his stare to mine, worry within our eyes. "I know we were going to wait until we got home to tell him, but he's here now and we've got to do the right thing for *once*."

"When?"

"What?"

I swallow the lump that's rising in my throat. "When will we tell him?"

Tyler shrugs. "We can tell him tomorrow. Hell, we can walk back in there and tell him right now, but that means we're going to ruin his trip to New York, because he'll be going through hell. Or," he says, "we can wait until their last day. Tell him the night before they leave. At least that way he'll be able to enjoy New York, *and* he won't have to be around us for long before he can hop on a plane and get the hell away from us. Get it?"

"You want me to pretend everything is fine for five days?" Nervously, I interlock my hands in my lap. I love Dean. That's why this is so hard. I'm not going to break up with him because I don't want to be with him. I'm going to break up with him because I've found my way back to Tyler, because it's unfair on Dean to have a girlfriend who's in love with someone else.

"Just act a little different so that he knows something's up," Tyler tells me, but he's frowning as he starts up the engine. "God, he's really gonna hate us, isn't he? Could you see the way he was looking at you?"

"Looking at us," I correct. I reach for my seatbelt and click it on, letting out a sigh I didn't know I was holding in. "He looked so happy to see us."

"Actually, forget Dean for a sec," Tyler says as he pulls out of the spot and heads onto Madison Avenue. His tone turns bitter once more. "Why is Tiffani here? 'Favorite pair of stepsiblings'? The fuck is that all about? She knows she hates us."

"It's just me she hates, actually," I say with the smallest of laughs as I settle back against the seat, watching Tyler as he drives. "You know, 'cause I totally stole her boyfriend and all."

Tyler glances sideways at me as he laughs, too, his expression softening up. One hand on the wheel, he reaches over the center console with the other, taking my hand in his. He intertwines his fingers with mine, his skin soft and warm, just like it always is. "I can't even begin to tell you how thankful I am that you did."

22

The next day, both Tyler and I are on edge. We can't help it. It's so nerve-wracking knowing that Dean's within such close proximity. We have to be extra cautious again, monitoring what we say and ensuring we never look at each other for too long. We're back to being nothing more than stepsiblings again.

And although we're trying to act as normal and as innocent as we can, Tyler's finding it difficult to hide his aggravation at the fact that Dean's about to pick me up any second. He's been brewing himself some coffee over in the kitchen as I pace the living room, awaiting the sound of a knock against the door, and eventually Emily picks up on the tension.

She pauses the TV, much to Snake's annoyance, and cranes her neck to look at us, her eyes flickering back and forth between Tyler and me. "What's the matter?"

"Eden's got a date," Tyler says. His eyes are zeroed in on me, and he stirs his coffee without even glancing down. His jaw is tight. "Her boyfriend surprised her last night by turning up in the city. Did I mention my psycho ex is here, too? Because she is."

"Tiffani?" Emily asks.

I stop pacing the living room to throw Tyler a curious glance, an eyebrow raised. He must have told Emily about Tiffani. In fact, I think he must have told her just about everything about his life. She always seems to know the smallest of details.

"Yeah," Tyler says stiffly. He turns away from us and focuses on his coffee, and it gives Emily the chance to turn her attention back to me.

"Eden, I didn't know you had a boyfriend," she says, eyes studying me intensely. It makes me uncomfortable.

"Yeah, yeah, who cares?" Snake mutters. He tries to lean over her to grab the remote for the TV, but she presses a hand to his chest and holds him back, her eyes never leaving mine.

"We've been together for over a year and a half," I say quietly. A year and a half. That's how much of Dean's life I've wasted. "His name's Dean."

As if right on cue, there's a knock at the door. All of us glance over at once, but Tyler and I are quick to flash our eyes back to each other. He stops dithering with the coffee, his hands pausing mid-air, and I gnaw at the inside of my cheek. I don't particularly want to see Dean tonight, but if I don't he'll know immediately that something's wrong. I'm not ready to tell him yet.

I can sense everyone's eyes on me as I turn for the door, smoothing out my skater skirt on my way over. Slowly, I fiddle with the locks and swing open the door. And, of course, I'm greeted by Dean.

He breathes a sigh of relief the moment he runs his eyes over me, a smile on his lips. "Oh, thank God we got the right apartment."

"We?"

Right then, Rachael and Tiffani appear at the door behind him, slightly out of breath, as though they've climbed up all twelve flights of stairs. My grip on the door tightens as Tiffani smiles at me, eyes wide.

"What are you guys doing here?" Tyler calls from the kitchen, and when I glance over my shoulder I see he's abandoned his coffee on the worktop and is making his way over. He's stuffed his hands into his pockets, but it doesn't stop me from noticing the way they're balled into fists.

"We wanted to see your apartment!" Rachael tells him, voice cheerful. However, it quickly falters and she shrugs a little sheepishly. "And also because last night sucked. We wanna talk to you."

Tyler glances between Rachael and Tiffani for a long moment. His eyes rest on Tiffani longer than they do on Rachael, and I can quite literally see the way he's fighting the urge to refuse them entry. He eventually takes a step back from the door. "Fine, come on in," he mutters.

Rachael leads the way into the center of the apartment, Tiffani close behind her. As Tyler shrugs at me, I frown back and turn to reach for Dean's shirt, pulling him over the threshold and kicking the door shut behind us all. Both Snake and Emily get to their feet, awkwardly studying our fellow West Coast guests. Snake's gaze never leaves Rachael, and Emily's never leaves Tiffani.

"Alright," Tyler says. He briefly runs over the introductions, stating everyone's names and summarising everyone as briefly as possible. Snake's the roommate from Boston. Emily's the Brit he toured with. Rachael's a friend. Tiffani's just Tiffani. Dean is nothing more than the guy I'm dating. Tyler doesn't mention that once upon a time they were best friends. There's no point. That friendship is going to end within the next four days.

Snake makes a beeline across the room for Rachael once the awkward greetings are over with, and I try to shoot him a warning glance, but either he doesn't catch it or he chooses to blatantly ignore it. His gray eyes are set on her, and as he holds out his hand he reintroduces himself. This time, surprisingly, as Stephen.

Rolling my eyes, I glance over to Tiffani. She's studying Emily intensely from a few feet away and I watch anxiously as Emily closes the gap between them, her expression nonchalant.

"So *you're* Tiffani?"

"What's that supposed to mean?" Tiffani narrows her eyes, taken aback by the tone of Emily's voice.

If only Emily lived in Santa Monica, she'd know not to mess with Tiffani Parkinson. But unfortunately she doesn't, so she's not aware of this basic rule of survival. She keeps on going. "Oh, nothing," she says with a curt shrug. "I've just heard a lot about you, that's all."

"Really?" Tiffani's face lights up at the thought of it, like she thrives on the idea of her name being tossed around in everyone else's conversations. Most of the time, the words that follow after her name are not flattering.

Emily smiles, but it's not genuine. For the first time, she seems like she's got her guard up. She's usually more vulnerable, more soft-spoken and quiet. Not today. "Sure have. Don't worry, though, I'm certain everything I've heard is entirely accurate."

I don't get to hear what kind of bullshit Tiffani musters up next, because my attention is drawn to Tyler as he steps closer to Dean and me. He's smiling. Sincere? I don't think so.

"So, Dean, how about I give you the grand tour?" he suggests.

Dean shakes his head at the offer as he says, "I think we're just gonna head out. I don't want to waste anymore time."

"Nah, man, c'mon, let me show you around." Tyler throws his arm around him, pulling him away from me as he tightens his grip on his shoulder. I don't think Dean would be able to get away from him even if he tried. "Come check out the view first. We're facing Third Avenue." He leads Dean across the room and gently pushes him in front of the windows, holding him there. As Dean looks out to the street below, Tyler throws me a cunning smile, and I can only roll my eyes in return.

Out of the corner of my eye, I spot Tiffani heading over to join them. She barges her body in between theirs, throwing an arm over their shoulders. Tyler promptly shrugs her off. "So what are we looking at?" she asks.

On the opposite side of the living room, Snake's still talking to Rachael. She's twirling strands of her hair around her fingertips, her lips parted slightly as she listens to whatever the hell it is that Snake talks to girls about.

The entire thing just confuses me. I don't know why, but my life in Santa Monica has felt completely separate to my summer in New York. The two were never meant to collide. Now that they have, I'm endlessly feeling nauseous. For the past month, New York has felt like a safe haven. It's like I've been able to completely shut off my life back home. Forget about our parents, forget about our friends, forget about Dean. The best part of it all is that New York has made me forget that Tyler's my stepbrother, right up until now. Reality has hit us at full force. And, God, it hurts.

"Bloody hell," Emily murmurs under her breath as she pads across the carpet to me, folding her arms across her chest. She stands by my side and nods to Tiffani. "She's exactly how I pictured her. Walking in here like she's all this and all that."

"You shot her down pretty quickly," I say. I glance sideways at Emily, studying the way she's glaring at Tiffani from afar. I keep my voice low. "What was all of that about?"

Emily shrugs and shifts her stare to me, her eyes softening a little. "Tyler told me all about her," she says. By the windows, Tyler's pointing out stores and cafés on Third Avenue, all the while continuing to ignore Tiffani's persistence as she pushes herself closer against him. "What she did was awful," Emily adds. "I can't stand girls like her. Besides, I stick up for my mates."

"Watch yourself," I murmur quietly, my eyes never leaving Tiffani. She's got one hand on the back of Tyler's shoulder blade, the other on her hip. "Her wrath isn't something you wanna suffer."

Emily steps forward and turns around slightly so that she's directly facing me. She laughs and asks, "Speaking from experience?"

"Indeed." Dealing with Tiffani was hell. It's hard to be around her now because of it all. She carries with her a sense of power, both in the way that she smiles and in the way that she talks. It's terrifying.

Speaking of Tiffani, she must have decided to give up her efforts at trying to weasel her way into Tyler and Dean's conversation, because she spins around and waltzes toward Emily and me instead. She sighs as she approaches, her eyes set solely on me. She smiles and, as always, it's fake and bitter. "Eden. Outside. Right now."

I don't even flinch, only remain where I am. "No, I'm good."

Tiffani doesn't take no for an answer, because she promptly grasps my wrist and roughly yanks me toward the door. I throw Emily a glance over my shoulder and she shrugs back at me with wide eyes. I'm unwillingly pulled out into the lobby, and as Tiffani clicks the door shut behind us, she finally lets go.

"What do you want?" I fold my arms across my chest, taking a step back as she spins around to face me.

Further along the lobby, a guy is leaving his apartment. Tiffani waits in silence as he brushes past us, heading for the elevator. Once he's gone, her smile turns devious and her eyes grow narrower. "The short answer? I'm starting to miss Tyler."

It's so ridiculous that I laugh. I can't suppress it, and before I even realize it, I'm smiling at how unbelievable she sounds. Maybe it wouldn't sound so hilarious if their relationship had been honest and real. It wasn't. She can't miss someone she never loved. Still laughing, I ask, "And what's the long answer?"

"I'm starting to miss Tyler and you're gonna help me get him back," she shoots back at me without missing a beat. Folding her arms across her chest, her smile turns into a thin line.

I stop laughing. Now it's just pitiful. She really is deluded. "You know that's never going to happen, right?"

"Why won't it? He's coming back to California, we're both single, and is it just me or has your brother gotten *so* much hotter?" She blows out a breath and dramatically fans her face, cheeks tinted with a rose hue.

"Go to hell, Tiffani."

"God, why are you so snappy?" She gasps and moves her hand to her heart, as though I've wounded her, but I only roll my eyes. She's always so dramatic. "Wait," she says. For a second, she seems to drop the act she's putting on, because she looks at me with a perplexed expression that is nothing but sincere. I can see the expression in her eyes shifting as she studies me, and the moment she's done thinking, she parts her lips and exhales. "You're not still hooking up with him, are you?"

I'm so taken by surprise by the question that I don't reply. Even if I tried to deny it, she'd see straight through me. She always does. Blinking at her, I swallow the lump in my throat and then drop my eyes to the floor. Tiffani makes it sound so casual. We've never just been "hooking up." It's always been more than that.

"Oh my God," Tiffani says quietly. The shock is evident in her tone. For once, she's neither taunting nor sneering. "You are?"

I glance back up at her, but I quickly squeeze my eyes shut and press my hand to my face. My cheeks feel rather flushed and all I can murmur through my hand is, "It's not that big of a deal." I know I'm lying to myself. I know it's a big deal. It always will be.

"Not that big of a deal?" Tiffani echoes. She seems to get over the surprise of finding out Tyler and I are still into each other pretty quickly, because now her voice is laced with the glee that she's trying so, so hard to hide. "But, Eden . . . you're dating Dean."

Shaking my head, I turn around and start to walk back to the apartment door. I'm biting down hard on my lower lip and breathing slowly to stop myself from crying. It hurts knowing that the one person who's aware of my relationship with Tyler is the one person who's cruel enough to tell everyone. I can tell she wants to, and the fact that she has yet to do so is the most nerve-wracking thing in the world. She's keeping our secret safe for a reason, and knowing Tiffani, it's definitely not because she's trying to be a good friend.

"Wait," Tiffani calls. I stop walking, but I don't turn around. I just keep my eyes shut and I listen. "Enjoy your date with Dean. Are you gonna mention that you're cheating on him?"

I grind my teeth together. I don't have to look at her to know that she's smiling right now. She's loving every second of this. I don't give her the satisfaction, however, of knowing that her words are infuriating me, because I keep my mouth shut and start walking again.

"Eden," she calls again once I reach the door to the apartment. I pause with my fingers tightened around the handle. I know I shouldn't listen to what she has to say, but I can't stop myself. "Have you gained a couple pounds since I last saw you?"

Her words immediately hit me right where it hurts. It's a phrase I haven't heard in years, the type of phrase I used to hear back in Portland and the type of phrase I used to fear more than anything else. I thought I was finally over worrying about my weight, but a split second after the words leave Tiffani's mouth every single ounce of self-esteem I've built up over the past few years disappears and my pulse races as I fight back the tears that press at the corners of my eyes. Even if I wanted to say something to Tiffani, I couldn't. Even if I wanted to look back at her, I couldn't possibly bring myself to. Not anymore.

I throw open the apartment door and get myself inside as fast as I can, slamming the door behind me and utilizing every lock possible. There's no way she's coming back in this apartment. Not after that.

Breathing heavily, I notice how silent the apartment is, and when I slowly turn around, everyone is staring at me. Rachael and Snake have stopped talking. Emily's standing alone exactly where I left her, her eyebrows raised. Tyler and Dean are in the kitchen, Tyler with his coffee in hand and Dean with a defeated sort of expression on his face. It's Rachael I look at for the longest time. Tiffani didn't throw that remark at me by chance. It was intentional, and the only people in this room who could have possibly told her are Tyler, Dean, and Rachael. It's not hard to figure out who to blame.

I don't intend to draw attention to myself, but I fear I might just burst into tears any second now in front of them all, so I call Rachael's name as I head straight for the bathroom. I push past Dean and Tyler and shut the door behind me, only opening it again a few seconds later when Rachael taps her knuckles against the wood. I reach out and pull her inside, and this time I lock the door.

"What?" she asks immediately, confused.

"Did you tell Tiffani?"

"Tell Tiffani what?"

"About . . ." I take a deep breath and walk around her, leaning back against the sink before glancing up again. If I could see myself right now, I'm pretty sure I'd look devastated, because that's exactly how I feel. "About me," I finish. "About why I work out."

The creases of worry in Rachael's forehead deepen as she frowns. "I mean, I may have told her like forever ago," she admits quietly. "She asked me why you were such a running freak."

"Rachael!" I groan and throw my head back, throwing my hands into my hair and staring at the ceiling. I'm starting to regret ever confiding in her. I'm starting to wish I hadn't told anyone at all. "Now she knows the best way to insult me," I murmur as I tilt my head back down to face Rachael. She guiltily runs her thumb over her lips and keeps quiet, unsure of what to say. "She just asked me if I'd gained a couple pounds. Have I?"

I glance down at myself, scouring every inch of my body. Lately, I'd been happy. I'd finally found the perfect balance between eating healthy and working out, without being too extreme about it all, without monitoring every single thing I ate. I no longer skipped meals. I no longer felt guilty for missing a run. Not a single thought has occurred to me in months regarding my weight, but now it's like everything hits me at once. I start trying to figure out how many slices of pizza I've eaten while I've been in New York. I try to count how many extra shots of caramel I've been adding to my lattes over the past year. I wonder if, perhaps, allowing myself to take it easier was a bad idea from the get-go.

"Eden, you look absolutely fine," Rachael says. Her hands gently cup my jaw as she tilts my face back up away from my body, fixing me with a pleading stare. "Stop it," she says firmly. Taking a step back and dropping her hands to her sides, she sighs. "Look, I'm gonna talk to Tiffani. She knows making comments like that isn't cool. But please don't get upset about it. Just go enjoy your date with Dean."

I don't know how I'm supposed to do that now. I don't even want to leave the bathroom anymore, let alone go out in public with the guy I'm going to be breaking up with pretty soon. In a mood like this, I don't think I'll be able to keep up the act.

There's a knock at the door and both Rachael and I glance

over. Dean's voice vibrates through the wood. "Are you guys okay?"

There's another knock, this time much gentler, and the voice that follows isn't Dean's but Tyler's. "Eden?"

"She'll be out in a sec!" Rachael calls back. When she turns to face me again there's already a tear rolling its way down my cheek, and she rushes to wipe it away with her thumb. "Hey, it's okay," she tells me softly. She wraps her arms around me then, pulling me into a warm, tight hug. "I'm sorry," she says into my hair. "You don't have to be friends with Tiffani. I won't mind."

"I sure hope you won't," I murmur, "because it's never going to happen."

Dean takes me out for dinner, to a restaurant named Bella Blu, four blocks south on Lexington Avenue. It's small and Italian, which doesn't surprise me in the slightest. Dean's always been proud of his Italian roots, the same way Tyler's always been proud of his Hispanic genes, despite the fact that he gets them from his dad.

We end up being late for our reservation by twenty minutes, partly due to Tyler purposely holding Dean up and partly because I locked myself in the bathroom with Rachael. Before I walked back out again, I dried my eyes and let Rachael redo my eye makeup, much better than I'd originally done it. No one asked what had happened and no one asked why Tiffani was locked out in the lobby. No one dared to.

Rachael had returned to her conversation with Snake as I left with Dean. Tyler had scowled at me. Emily had kept staring at me intensely, her gaze not only curious but also suspicious. Out in the lobby, Tiffani was leaning against the wall with her arms folded across her chest and a smile on her lips as she told us to enjoy the evening. Dean had said thanks, apparently unaware of the scheming undertone to her voice, and I didn't so much as glare at her as she took the opportunity to enter the apartment again. I didn't have that confidence anymore to stand up to her. I just wanted to hide.

At Bella Blu, however, the night is starting to get worse. I feel too guilty being here. On my first night in New York I was in a situation exactly like this, seated at a table in the middle of a cozy Italian restaurant. Only then the restaurant was Pietrasanta, not Bella Blu, and I wasn't facing Dean, I was facing Tyler.

"So I swear," Dean says as he swallows another bite of his lobster ravioli, "I'm definitely going to college next fall. I know I said I was gonna apply *this* year, but it's actually kinda nice working with my dad. No classes, no studying. Just cool cars."

I pick at my Caesar salad with my fork, not entirely focused, my stare blank. I've been moving the croutons around for the past ten minutes, barely eating any of it. I don't want to. "Uh-huh."

"And I know I was set on Berkeley, but I've been looking at the business programs in Illinois and—"

"What?" My eyes flash up from my salad to meet Dean's gaze, as warm and as bright as ever.

"Illinois," he says again with a smile. "So that we're closer."

My stomach twists and I try my best to keep my apprehension hidden. We've both always been aware that I'm moving halfway across the country in two months, but we don't often bring it up in conversation. Neither of us wanted to. It was always hard to talk about, us being separated for four years.

We'd have summers together. Spring break. Winter break. Thanksgiving. We'd see each other, but it would be different and it would be difficult. Now I'm not worried about moving away from Dean. In fact, I think by the time he leaves New York, he'll be glad I'm moving out of state. I don't think he'll ever want to see me again.

"But you've always wanted to get into Berkeley," I say quietly.

"I know," he says, "but we'll be two thousand miles apart if I choose to stay in California." He forks up another bite of his ravioli and takes a minute to swallow, reaching for his drink and taking a quick swig. Slowly, he leans forward. "I've been looking into Northwestern," he tells me. "The economics major there is meant to be great, and you wanna know what the best part is?" He pauses, not because he's expecting an answer but because he wants to grin at me. "It's in Evanston. Only twenty miles away from the University of Chicago."

I rest my eyes on the flower in the center of the table, taking in its brightness as I try to process what Dean's saying. He's willing to give up his dream college so that we don't have to be apart. That's just Dean. He's always been selfless, always been so considerate and willing to make sacrifices for the people he cares about. He could have started college last year, but he didn't because his dad always wanted him to work at the garage. I know he likes the cars, but I also know how badly he wants to build a career in business. Yet he's putting it on hold for another year, because he's living the Carter family tradition first. He's willing to apply for different schools because he doesn't want us to be thousands of miles apart. "I think you should keep Berkeley on the cards," I say, but I'm not looking at him. I'm still looking at the flower, still thinking.

"What's the point?" Dean asks.

"It's an amazing school."

"So is Northwestern," he points out, "*and* it's right next to you."

I glance up at him again now. Pushing my plate away from me, barely touched, I interlock my hands together on the table in front of me. "But you've always said you didn't want to leave California." I think Dean expected me to be thrilled at the idea of him potentially moving to Illinois next year, because his smile has slowly begun to fade. He frowns.

"Eden," he says firmly, eyes crinkling at the corners as he locks his gaze with mine, "I already have to go a year without you. It's almost a thirty-hour drive, but I could take trips over to Chicago every month, and you'll be coming home for the holidays, and I could even get a second job so that I could come see you more often. But that's for a year. I don't think I can cope with that for four."

"Dean."

"That's why when I go to college next year, I want to be near you," he continues, ignoring me. He leans back in his seat, folding his arms across his chest as he grins again. "Hey, imagine that. You'll be a sophomore and I'll be a freshman. Talk about role reversal."

If I was planning on staying with Dean, I think maybe I *would* be thrilled at the idea. However, it's so hard to hear him talk about our future plans together when I know that there is no future for us, and I don't think there's anything I can possibly say right now to change his mind regarding college. When Tyler and I tell him the truth, I think that'll change his mind. Then, I'm sure he'll be keen on Berkeley again. He definitely won't want to be anywhere near me.

"Dean," I murmur. It hurts to look back at him, to see the way he looks at me with eyes bright and full of nothing but honesty and love. I wish I could look at him in the same way. He deserves that, and so much more. I do love him. Since we got together, there's never been a time when I haven't. It's just that my heart belongs to Tyler. Letting Dean go is the right thing to do. "I love you," I say. My eyes never leave his. In fact, I'm not sure if I'm even blinking. "You know that, right?"

Reaching across the table, he takes my hand in his, and as his smile reaches his eyes, he says, "Of course I do."

And in that moment, I can do nothing but hope that he truly does.

23

By the time I return from my run the following day, the decision is made that the girls and the guys are to hang out separately. I'm not sure who exactly made this decision, all I know is that I'm against it. Tyler, Snake, and Dean head off to some vintage car show just outside of the city, while the rest of us head out to Times Square. Again, I have no say in the matter, and when I try to object to the plans that have been arranged for me, I get absolutely nowhere. Even Emily is hesitant about spending the afternoon with Rachael and Tiffani.

And so, for the several hours that we spend making our way around Times Square, Emily and I linger at the back. I can't even look at Tiffani, let alone talk to her, so I keep my distance at all times. Sometimes when she and Rachael dart into stores, Emily and I don't even join them. We stand outside, musing to each other, hoping that neither of them will notice our absence. Besides, I've visited Times Square a lot over the past four weeks, so the novelty has worn off by now, and it has for Emily, too. After all, she's lived in New York for over a year. For Rachael and Tiffani, however, Times Square is as fascinating and as mesmerizing to them as it was to me the very first time Tyler took me here. For that sole reason, I don't mind when they stop every so often to take pictures.

"Does she seriously walk like that or do you think she does it on purpose?" Emily asks under her breath as we follow our two companions along Forty-third Street. The gap between us and them is slowly increasing, and Emily tilts her head to one side as she studies the way Tiffani walks. She struts like she's on a mission.

"On purpose. She never used to walk like that," I murmur back, careful not to be heard. I don't think it's possible that they could hear our conversation even if they tried to, because Times Square is as loud and as buzzing as ever. "You know, she was actually nice when I first met her, and then it all went to hell."

"What happened?"

"Long story," I say. I don't think I could explain it even I tried to. *So, Emily, Tyler broke up with her for me!* Yeah, right. As if I could say that. "And don't say you have time, because I really don't want to talk about it."

"I wasn't going to push it anyway," Emily says, and when I glance sideways at her, it suddenly occurs to me that I'm choosing to be with her instead of Rachael, my best friend. I feel guilty for disliking Emily to begin with, but that was before I knew there was nothing going on between her and Tyler. Now I'm starting to consider her a friend, and our mutual dislike of Tiffani is a surprisingly great way to bond.

Only minutes later, Tiffani disappears into the Brooklyn Diner while Rachael lingers at the door, waiting for us. It's almost three now and we haven't had lunch yet, so we don't mind stopping. It gives us a break from dashing between stores.

We're given a booth over in the far corner, right by the windows, but Tiffani's shopping bags take up half the space on their side. I sit by Emily, of course, and I ensure that I'm opposite Rachael. Tiffani's diagonal to me, which helps because the only way I can see her is if I look out the corner of my eye, which I don't. I set my eyes on the table and nothing else, fumbling anxiously with my hands in my lap.

All three of them take a while to study the menu, yet I don't bother to pick one up. Rachael notices after a couple minutes, and her eyes narrow at me over the rim of the menu in her hands and she nudges me under the table with her foot. I promptly ignore it, shifting my gaze to the window to watch the flow of Times Square instead. The locals weave their way through the slow-paced tourists. The tourists don't even seem to notice that they're blocking the sidewalks as they come to a halt to study maps, to take pictures, to most likely ask their partners which direction they should head in next. Even from inside, I can feel the locals' frustration.

"So you're from England?" I hear Tiffani ask Emily. I prop my elbow up on the table and rest my chin in my hand, still staring out onto Forty-third Street. I do, however, keep listening.

"Yeah," Emily says, voice wary. "Just outside of London."

"Were you living here before or did you move over just to take part in the awareness tour thing?"

"I came over for it," Emily says quietly, keeping her replies as short as possible. I don't think she's particularly in the mood for a conversation with Tiffani. I can't blame her.

"So you were abused?"

My jaw falls open the moment the words leave Tiffani's lips. I'm so shocked that it's enough to make me spin my head around to look at her in disbelief. She's blinking at Emily, lips pressed firmly together as she awaits an answer.

"Tiffani!" Rachael gasps, horrified. "That's so insensitive."

"It was just a question," Tiffani says as she throws Rachael a sideways glance. Her eyes settle back on Emily, and she shrugs. "So? Were you?"

"She doesn't have to answer that," I say stiffly, narrowing my eyes across the table straight at Tiffani. I don't want to draw her attention, but she's crossing the line.

Tiffani's gaze flashes to mine. "Shouldn't you be choosing everything you're gonna eat instead of butting into conversations?"

"Tiffani," Rachael murmurs, biting her lip awkwardly as she offers me an apologetic glance. Tiffani just shrugs again as though she doesn't see what the problem is.

My stomach twists again as I try to let her remark go over the top of my head, but it's difficult to ignore. It's hard to pretend that it doesn't hurt, that it doesn't make me feel even sicker than I already do. I don't want to sit around here and wait for our waitress to arrive, because that way I'll receive a frown from Rachael and most likely a smile from Tiffani when I don't end up ordering anything, and I'd much rather avoid it completely.

"Excuse me," I murmur, and Emily immediately gets to her feet to allow me to slip out of the booth. Rachael furrows her eyebrows at me suspiciously, questioning my departure, so I quickly say, "Restroom," and head off in search of them.

They're over by the opposite side of the diner, and as I quickly slip through the door I realize they're rather small. Only a couple stalls, couple sinks. Thankfully, there's no one else here, so I lean back against the wall by the hand dryers, heaving a long sigh.

I don't want to go back out there. I don't want to face

Tiffani again. I just want to get out of here, get back to the apartment, and find solace in Tyler. For a minute, I try to picture the layout of the diner, trying to work out if it's possible for me to get from the restrooms to the main exit without Rachael or Tiffani or Emily even noticing. But then I think more carefully about Emily, about the fact that she's sitting out there with two complete strangers, one of whom she already dislikes. Tiffani's picked up on that, and I'm now convinced that she's adamant on ridiculing Emily the same way she's trying to ridicule me. I'm wishing I asked Emily to come to the restroom with me. I'm wishing I hadn't left her. For Emily's sake alone, I know I'll eventually have to force myself to rejoin the group. Just not yet. In the meantime, I can only hope that Rachael will have her back if Tiffani makes anymore inappropriate remarks.

My peace in the restrooms doesn't last for long, though, because after five minutes the door swings open. The person who walks through it is the one person I'm trying to get away from.

"What's taking you so long?" Tiffani asks, folding her arms across her chest as she steps nearer to me. I don't even look her in the eye. I just barge past her, my body brushing against hers as I make for the door. "Wait," she says.

"What, Tiffani?" I snap, spinning around on the balls of my feet. I will never be able to tolerate her. "*What?*"

"I was up late last night," she says calmly. "Thinking." She begins to pace the restroom, walking back and forth between me and the hand dryers on the farthest wall, her hands on her hips. She's purposely trying to be dramatic, as always. I don't buy it, though. I just fold my arms across my chest and sigh as I wait for her to continue. "So last night while you were out with Dean, I spoke to Tyler. Apologized for what's happened in the past. He was totally cool with it," she says. I'm not entirely sure if she's lying or not, because Tyler certainly didn't mention any of that last night when I got back from my dinner with Dean. He never mentioned an apology, or that he was cool with it. "I think I could have another shot with him," she says as she comes to a halt in front of me, her eyes meeting mine. "Of course, that's if *you* weren't in the way."

I get what she's hinting at almost immediately, and I can only laugh. "You really think he'll break things off with me so that he can be with you?" I roll my eyes at how pathetic it all sounds. That's the only thing that isn't terrifying about Tiffani—her ridiculous schemes. I think they're getting worse the older she gets. "God, you really are deluded."

"Of course I don't," she says. Almost so slowly that it's agonizing, her lips curl up into a tight smile. "I know he won't do that: that's why I need you to do it."

"Wait," I say. Her words no longer seem humorous. "What?"

"End whatever is between you and him," she orders sharply. Her eyes narrow as she taps her foot impatiently against the tiled flooring.

I shake my head quickly. She must seriously be crazy if she thinks I'd ever do such a thing. "That's not happening," I state, my voice firm despite how weak I feel in comparison with her.

"I guess I'll give Dean a call then." Reaching into her purse, she fishes out her phone. She takes a few seconds to tap around on the screen, and when she glances back up, she smiles at my horrified stare. She holds her phone up for me to see, and Dean's name is on the screen, his number already dialing.

"Don't!" I scramble forward as I attempt to snatch the device from her hand. My heart has dropped into my stomach and I feel like I can't breathe. The blood throughout my body has thinned, the color has drained from my face.

Tiffani smiles in such a way that she appears sinister as she stretches out her hand, holding me back. With her other hand, she holds her phone up in the air, as far out of my reach as she can keep it. She puts it on speaker, allowing the monotonous dial tone to echo around the restroom. "Cut it off with Tyler and I won't tell Dean. Deal?"

"Fine!" I yell. I have no other choice. Even my hands are trembling now, and my chest is heavy.

Immediately, Tiffani pushes me back a step, and she ends the call before Dean has the chance to answer. I'm so numb that I can't even feel relieved about it. "So here's what's gonna happen," she says with a wide grin, so malicious that it's hard to keep my eyes trained on her. Now I really do feel sick. Now I really do wish I'd escaped the diner when I had the chance to. "I need you to do it tonight. Say whatever you want to Tyler, as long as you make it clear that your gross fling is off. After that, I need you to come stay at our hotel."

"What?" My voice is a feeble whisper now, not firm and strong like I wish it would be. It's just weak. Defeated.

"You know, for dramatic effect." Tiffani's grin stretches even wider, and I'm not sure how it's even possible for her to smile back at me, for her to enjoy how stunned and how petrified and how numb I really am. It's sadistic, really. "And besides," she says with a nonchalant shrug, "I'm not stupid. You could tell Tyler all about this conversation, so I think it'd be best if you came and stayed with Dean. I've thought all of this through, so when it eventually occurs to you—and it will, if it hasn't already—that you could just tell Dean the truth yourself before I can, don't waste your time. I'll call your parents instead and let them know what's up, and I know you won't beat me to that, because there's no way in hell you'll tell them the truth over a phone call."

She suddenly seems a lot smarter than I've ever given her credit for. This scheme doesn't seem as comical as it did a few minutes ago. I'm being forced to decide who to hurt between Tyler, Dean, and my parents. She's got me cornered exactly the way she wants, with no other option but to do as she asks. "You're blackmailing me?"

"No," Tiffani says. Her grin finally turns into a smaller smile as she steps closer to me, her voice threatening. "I'm just ensuring you know what'll happen if you don't do me this favor."

"If you think it's going to work, it won't," I murmur, swallowing. "He'll never go back to you."

"Oh, but Eden," she says, her features relaxing as she takes a step back and lets out the smallest of laughs, "we both know how Tyler is with distractions, and ever so conveniently, I'll be there to distract him from you."

I part my lips to argue back, but the door to the restrooms swings open once again, and this time it's Emily. She peers around the frame, her eyebrows arched. She glances between Tiffani and me rather suspiciously before asking, "What are you two doing?"

"Just making a pact," Tiffani answers, stepping even closer to me and throwing her arm around my shoulders, squeezing my body tight against hers. I can sense her smiling again as her cheek brushes against mine, but I'm still too paralyzed to react. I can't force a smile for Emily's sake. I can't frown. I can only attempt to breathe, totally zoned out as I stare at the sinks to my right.

Tonight, I've got to hurt Tyler for the greater good, and I have never, ever felt so terrified.

24

Tyler's been wandering around the apartment for a while. He carries some of his clothes from his bedroom to the laundry room. He helps Snake replace the hinges on one of the cupboard doors in the kitchen. He cleans the coffee machine in silence, licking his lips in concentration, humming to himself every once in a while. The entire time, I've been watching him from the couch, my stomach in knots as I figure out the best way to do what I need to do. Emily's been sitting beside me, flicking between TV channels and occasionally asking me if I'm okay. I keep telling her I'm absolutely fine, but the truth is I'm nowhere near it.

It's not until Snake decides to head out on a late grocery shopping spree that I decide to just take a deep breath and get it all over with. Pushing myself up from the couch, Emily watches me curiously as I head across the living room, stopping at the kitchen counter. Tyler glances up from the coffee machine, smiling warmly at me.

"What's up?"

"Come to the roof with me," I say quietly, not quite answering him the way he expects me to. His eyes light up and he immediately stops cleaning the coffee machine. I swallow hard when he smirks.

"How come I've never thought of that before?" he whispers, leaning closer to me across the worktop so that Emily can't hear a single word we're saying.

"Tyler, this is serious."

His expression shifts from flirtatious to worried in a heartbeat, and I turn for the door, trying not to let him see that I'm on the verge of crying already. I try my best to stay strong, despite how ready I am to break down over all of this. If I open my mouth I might just scream, so I lead Tyler out of the apartment and up to the roof in silence. Thankfully, he doesn't attempt to ask any questions on the way up, even when we're standing in the elevator, several feet apart.

It's long after sunset by now, almost nearing 10PM, and the sky is a darkening shade of blue as I push open the door to the roof and step out onto the terrace. I scour the area to check there's no one else here, and when I'm sure there isn't, I slowly make my way across the concrete.

From behind me, Tyler suddenly places his hands on my waist and nuzzles his nose into my cheek, murmuring against my ear, "Baby, is everything okay?"

His voice only gives me chest pains, and a shiver runs down my spine, twice. I turn my body around in his arms, my eyes crinkling with a mixture of both pain and confusion as I face him. I still can't believe I'm in this awful situation and I don't know exactly what I'm going to say yet, but I do know that as I push Tyler's hands off my waist, the look in his eyes begins to mirror mine.

"Tyler, I need you to listen to me really carefully."

Nodding, he inhales a sharp breath. "I'm listening."

It takes me a while to build up the courage to say what I'm planning on saying. It's the only logical excuse I can think of that would even begin to make sense to Tyler. The only excuse that could justify something like this. Even though my words aren't the truth, they have to be believable. Unable to look at Tyler any longer, I drop my eyes to the concrete, to his brown boots, and my heart tightly clenches as I dare myself to finally tell him, "I want to stay with Dean."

"What?" I don't have to look at him to hear the shock in his voice, to hear the way it cracks at the end. It pains me to hear it. It hurts to know my words are the reason.

"I don't want to do this anymore," I say. "I love Dean."

Tyler's lips part as he registers my words. The moment he really absorbs them, his eyes immediately dilate with panic. Taking a step toward me, he gently reaches for my wrist. I even catch him glance down at his bicep, at the tattoo of my name. He swallows hard and looks back up. "You said you wouldn't do this. You said you wouldn't change your mind."

Closing my eyes, I pull my wrist away from him and take a step back, forcing myself to keep mustering up words however much I don't want to. "Seeing Dean again has made me realize that . . . that I want to stay with him. Not you."

He jerks his head to one side, exhaling a long breath as he walks away from me. Running his hands back through his hair, gripping tightly onto the ends, he tilts his face up to the sky and circles the terrace. When he looks back down again, he balls his hand into a fist and swings a punch through the air. "You can't do this to me *again.*"

Right then, my heart shatters. The pieces slice through my chest as my body trembles with guilt. I wouldn't dare to give up on us again, but it's out of my control. I have faith, however, that the moment Tiffani leaves New York, I'll be able to explain to him what's really going on. I have faith that he'll understand why I'm doing what I'm doing. "I'm sorry."

Tears suddenly press at my waterlines, and when I meet Tyler's eyes, the emerald in his has faded so much that it makes my stomach tighten. He's shaking his head at me, and I realize I can't stay up here with him any longer. Turning away from him, I try to blink back the tears as I head for the door.

"Eden, wait," Tyler calls softly after me, his voice raspy. I hear his feet hitting the concrete as he rushes after me, and by the time I'm inside the building he's right behind me, his voice pleading. "Please. This isn't fair."

"I'm sorry," I splutter again, refusing to turn around as I keep on walking as fast as I can. I don't want to take the elevator, because I don't want to be forced to talk to him in such a confined space, so I take the stairs. I end up jogging down them, two steps at a time, while Tyler runs behind me.

It's as I'm turning the corner onto the fourth flight of stairs that he shoves his body in front of mine, grabbing my shoulders and stopping me from going any further. "Why?" he asks, voice still cracked, still raspy, still pained. "I thought everything was fine between us. What's happened? Did I do something wrong? Tell me!"

I can't even begin to muster up a reply. The truth is, everything *was* fine. Everything was fine until Tiffani arrived. Tyler hasn't done anything wrong, and there's no way I can lie and tell him that he has, so I slam my shoulder against his chest and barge him out of the way. I break into an even faster jog this time, my Chucks pounding against the stairs as I try to tune out the sound of Tyler's voice as he relentlessly yells my name. His voice isn't coarse, though, nor is it firm and deep. It's because he's not angry. He's not furious. He's just . . . hurt. That's all he is. Completely and entirely hurt.

By the time I reach the twelfth floor, I really am crying. The tears are flowing down my cheeks and I don't even have the energy to wipe them away. My throat has tightened so much that it feels like I'm struggling to breathe. Tyler's breathing heavily and rapidly behind me, and as I reach the apartment door I pray that it's still unlocked. I throw it open and it completely startles Emily on the couch, because she jumps and spins her head around to stare at us in shock, her eyes wide and her lips parted.

However, neither Tyler nor I pay her any attention, because I head straight into his room. I keep my face down in an attempt to hide the fact that I'm crying, but I think Emily notices anyway. I even try to slam Tyler's door behind me, but he presses his hands against it just in time, pushing it back open.

"Eden," he whispers as he follows me into the room. He clicks the door shut behind him, keeping his voice low. When I glance at him through my blurred vision, I notice the corners of his eyes are slightly swollen. "What made you change your mind? Why Dean? Why not me? Just answer me that. Please."

"Because Dean isn't my stepbrother." I've stopped looking at him now. My heart is racing instead, my chest constricting as I move around the room, sliding open the closet doors and reaching up to grab my backpack from the top shelf. I start rummaging around inside the closest, yanking a few of my clothes off hangers and stuffing them inside the bag before moving past Tyler to the chest of drawers.

"What are you doing?" Tyler whispers, his shoulders dropping as he stares at me, his forehead creasing. For the first time in years, his eyes appear almost lifeless again, just like the way they always used to be.

"I'm going to stay at Dean's hotel." My voice sounds so pathetic. My words are more like a sob and I'm not entirely sure if they're even intelligible. Either way, I continue to grab some more of my things, fumbling around by the wall socket as I fetch my phone charger. I pile everything into my backpack and zip it shut, swinging it over one shoulder. I straighten up.

"What can I do to stop you from doing this?" Tyler asks, but it sounds like begging more than anything else. He steps toward me again, one hand cupping my jaw and the other grabbing my hand. He squeezes his fingers around mine so tightly that it momentarily hurts, and the heat from his skin is burning hot against my jaw. "Is there anything I can do that'll change your fucking mind?"

With all my might, I pull my hand free from his. "No."

That's when I leave. I grip the strap of my backpack as I run my opposite hand through my hair, wondering if there could have been a way to get around Tiffani. She was right—I could have told Dean the truth before she did, and that way she wouldn't have had anything to threaten me with. I was planning on telling Dean anyway, just not this soon. That would have been the only way to completely avoid doing what I've just done, but Tiffani already thought that through, and if I'd told Dean, she'd have moved on to our parents. I'm not ready for that.

Tyler doesn't try to follow me as I make my way out of his room and across the apartment. Even Emily doesn't question me as I pull open the door, stepping out into the lobby. I don't even care now that she can see me crying. She looks worried, and all I can do is offer her a sad smile as I close the door behind me. I don't know what Tyler will tell her, but I do know that right now, I honestly couldn't care less if he told her the truth about what's happened, the truth about us. I just want to get away.

I take the elevator this time, my lips quivering as I sob the entire way down, and even when I'm dragging myself outside the building and onto Seventy-fourth Street I still don't care. I don't care that I'm crying late at night on the streets of New York. All I know is that the night air feels relaxing as I breathe it in, and I squeeze my eyes shut for a few seconds as I slowly walk around the corner onto Third Avenue. My chest begins to relax and even my trembling begins to calm.

It's a twenty-minute walk to the Lowell, straight down Third Avenue and across Sixty-third Street. I don't mind it, though. I like the space and the privacy, despite the fact that there's still a flow of pedestrians on the sidewalks and a trail of traffic on the roads. It feels nice to just be alone for once. No Tyler. No Tiffani. No Dean and no Rachael and no Snake and no Emily. Just me. I do receive some curious glances from people as they pass me, and I wonder if I look like some runaway misfit. Again, I don't care. What the general public of Manhattan think of me isn't my biggest concern right now.

The night is colder than I remember it being up on the roof, so I stuff my hands into the front pocket of my hoodie when I reach Sixty-third Street, sighing with relief as I pass the Santa Fe Opera again. I've run out of tears by the time I reach the hotel, and they've already dried into my cheeks. Now my eyes just feel swollen and red, so I rub at them in an attempt to hide the fact that I've been crying, but I think I only end up making it worse, because they begin to sting.

There's a different doorman this time, a middle-aged man with graying hair who opens the door and wishes me a good night's sleep. I don't tell him I'm not even a guest here and I certainly don't mention that tonight I doubt I'll be sleeping at all, let alone sleeping well. I just say thanks.

I shuffle past the front desk and across the main lobby, tracing my way to the elevator as I try to remind myself of the route we took to get to the suite. I know it's on the tenth floor, so I push the button and wait as the elevator smoothly heads up. It's mirrored, so I stare at my reflection. My eyes look awful and it's obvious that I've just been sobbing for what felt like fifteen minutes straight. I know there's nothing I can do to hide this fact, and I'm pretty sure Tiffani will be thrilled when she sees me. In a last-ditch attempt to sooth away the swollenness, I dab at my eyes with the sleeves of my hoodie, right before giving up entirely.

I head out of the elevator, focusing on keeping my breathing steady as I make my way along the tenth-floor lobby to the correct suite. When I come across it, I stand outside of the door for a long while. I really don't want to go inside. I don't want to face Tiffani's satisfied smirks and I don't want to face Dean. I think Rachael is the only one I'm not worried about seeing, but it does make me wonder how I'm supposed to explain myself to her and Dean. How do I explain why I've been crying? What reason do I give them for staying in their suite? I doubt Tiffani has filled them in on our arrangement.

Once I've taken a few deep breaths, I finally knock on the door. It's after ten by now, but I can still hear their TV. It doesn't take long for someone to answer, and as I listen to the locks being released I brace myself for who it'll be. I'm seriously praying that it'll be Rachael, but it's not. It's Tiffani. It doesn't surprise me.

"Eden!" she exclaims in surprise, but at the exact same time a glorious smile spreads across her face. She's draped in a silk dressing gown, which she holds closed with one hand as she holds the door open with the other. "What are you doing here?"

I grit my teeth together and abruptly push past her. I can't deal with her act right now, of all times, and as I force myself into the center of the living area I hear her close the door behind me. Dean jumps to his feet from one of the ugly vintage chairs, his eyebrows shooting up as he wonders why I'm here. He's wearing a pair of black sweats and a white T-shirt and he immediately walks over to me. It doesn't take long for the concern to show on his face.

"What are you doing here?" he asks, ducking down slightly so that he's smaller than me, allowing him to look up at me intensely from beneath his eyelashes. "Eden, what's wrong?"

I reach for his hand, interlocking our fingers. I find comfort in his presence. Dean's always been able to put me at ease, even just with the sound of his voice. Always so caring, always so gentle. I step forward and bury my face into his chest, his shirt sticking to my damp eyes. "I had an argument with Tyler," I whisper, even though it's far from the truth. I'm also aware that Tiffani is watching us from a few feet away, but I ignore her by squeezing my eyes shut. "I thought I'd come stay with you." It's not true. It's just an act. My grip on Dean, however, isn't. I really do keep hugging him, not to keep Tiffani happy but because I need to. I need Dean right now. I need my boyfriend.

He squeezes me even tighter, pressing his forehead to my temple as he breathes softly against my ear. "I'm glad you came here," he says gently. "You're more than welcome to stay with us. Right, Tiffani?" He steps back, but he keeps his arm around me, holding me close.

"Of course!" Tiffani agrees, her voice sympathetic and laced with pity, as though she isn't behind all of this. "I can't believe you guys had a fight. You're usually *so* close."

If I weren't so damaged inside, perhaps I'd have the energy to cuss at her. All I can do for now, though, is press my body closer again to Dean's again. I wrap my arms around his back and inhale his scent. Usually he smells like grease and exhaust fumes, but now that he's three thousand miles away from the garage he just smells like plain soap.

"Please don't get upset," he tells me as he rubs his hand up and down my arm. "Whatever happened will blow over."

"I just want to sleep," I murmur, still sensing Tiffani's watchful eyes. The TV is still echoing in the background, too, and in all honesty I really do want to go to sleep. I want to fall asleep and then I want to wake up and realize that none of this has really happened. I'll feel better in the morning. Less broken.

Dean drops his hand and loosely interlinks it with mine again as he carefully leads me across the suite. He pushes open the door to one of the bedrooms, and when I throw a glance over my shoulder Tiffani's mouth has twisted into another one of her infamous smiles. She mouths something, but I don't quite catch it, and I don't quite care to either. I squeeze Dean's hand harder as I turn back around, following him into the bedroom and clicking the door shut behind us.

The room is large, with a huge king-sized bed right in the center, and there's more complex artwork decorating the walls. His luggage is lying across the floor and he quickly kicks it all to the side, letting go of my hand.

"Rachael and Tiff share the other room," he says. "This is mine."

I nod. Swinging my backpack off my shoulder, I place it

onto the bed and start to fumble with the zips. "Where *is* Rachael?"

"Already asleep." Shrugging, Dean moves around to one side of the bed and begins to adjust the pillows, throwing some to the side and pulling back the comforter. Everything is beige. He reaches for the hem of his T-shirt and swiftly pulls it off, folding it up carelessly and tossing it onto the single chair in the corner of the room. He looks worried again, his forehead creased with concern as he walks back over to me. "Are you sure you're okay?"

I press my hand to his bare chest, attempting to offer him a small smile. "Yeah. I'll be better in the morning. I just need to get some sleep."

I can tell by the way he frowns that he knows I'm lying, but he doesn't push it any further, and I'm glad, because I'd much rather not talk about it. I couldn't even if I wanted to. I couldn't tell him that the only reason I'm here is because Tiffani has ever so smoothly worked out the perfect way to blackmail me, and I can't bring myself to keep mustering up lies either. If Dean does ask, perhaps I'll tell him my argument with Tyler was about our parents. That'd work.

I strip off my clothes and stuff them into my backpack, and I realize I haven't even packed half the stuff I should have. Sighing, I zip up my backpack and toss it onto the floor as I make my way around the bed wearing nothing but my underwear. As Dean turns off the lights, I slip into the bed and pull the comforter around me. The room dips into darkness and I can hear Dean shuffling around the floor, joining me seconds later.

"Like I said, don't worry about it too much," he murmurs as he presses his body against mine, his skin slightly cold as his chest brushes against my back. He wraps an arm around my stomach, and I breathe in as I place my hand on top of his. "It'll blow over," he reminds me once more, and I really, really hope he's right.

By 2AM, I'm still awake. I'm lying still, staring at the ceiling and trying to force the image of Tyler's face out of my mind. I can't stop hearing his voice. I can't stop thinking about him. I think of the way his eyes looked when I told him I wanted to stay with Dean and I think of the way he pleaded with me to rethink my decision.

And by 3AM, I can't cope.

Dean's rolled over onto the other side of the bed by this point, his body several inches away from mine, so I easily push the comforter away and get to my feet without him stirring. My eyes have long adjusted to the darkness, so I follow the outlines of the furniture as I search for my backpack, grabbing it when I find it and rummaging through it until I find my phone. I dial Tyler's number straightaway. It's on speed dial.

The first time, it goes to voicemail, but that doesn't surprise me. It's 3AM. He's most likely asleep, but I'm desperate to talk to him, so I dial his number once more, hoping that if I'm persistent enough it'll wake him up.

"Eden," a voice says down the line as the call is picked up. It's not Tyler's, though. It's Emily's.

"Emily?" I keep my voice low, glancing over at Dean's sleeping figure. "Where's Tyler?"

"Eden, he's really drunk," Emily tells me without hesitation, her voice croaky and quiet, as though she's half asleep. "Like *really* drunk."

"What?"

She exhales. "Um, well, he woke me and Stephen up about half an hour ago. He was smashing bottles in the kitchen and he can barely stand." She pauses for a while and I press my phone harder against my ear, listening to the sound of male voices somewhere else in the apartment. I can't make out what they're saying, but I do recognize Snake's thick accent. "What happened between you two?" Emily asks, and she sighs across the line. I hear her moving across the room as the voices grow louder, and she raises her voice in order for me to hear her over them. "He's been super pissed off ever since you left and now Stephen's pretty much babysitting him in the bathroom because he can't stop throwing up." She draws Tyler's phone away from her ear for a moment as she murmurs, "Bloody hell, Snake, you're supposed to keep his head up. Here. Talk to Eden."

There's some fumbling as the phone is passed between them, and in the background I can hear Tyler retching in between groans. Emily continues to sigh and Snake continues to cuss. That's when I start to feel even guiltier, even worse than I did before. I know I'm the reason. I know I caused this.

"I'm coming over," I say, my voice no longer quiet. I reach for my bag with my free hand and begin to haul out some of my clothes.

"I don't think that's a good idea," Snake says immediately, his voice so firm that I stop what I'm doing. I pause with one leg half slipped into my jeans. "He kinda hates you right now. We don't need you over here making it worse. We've got it. Don't worry." Right after he says this, I hear Tyler throwing up. Emily sighs again, and on my side of the phone I can do nothing but run a hand through my hair, a frown upon my lips. "Fuck, man," Snake groans, promptly hanging up the call immediately after.

For a minute or so, I stare at the brightness of my device in disbelief as I step back out of my jeans, kicking them to one side. Now I really am dripping with guilt, and if the lights were on right now I'm pretty sure I'd look pale. Grinding my teeth together, I throw my phone across the floor in a fit of rage at myself, not even caring that it makes a loud thud. Dean doesn't even flinch, however, and as I start to break down again, I crawl back into bed next to him. I find comfort once again in his being, so I press my body against his back and reach for his hand. I play with his fingers for a while, twisting them around mine, before I squeeze his hand tight and bury my face into the back of his shoulder. In just three days' time, I'll be letting him go. I'll be telling him the truth, and I can do nothing but hope that both he *and* Tyler will forgive me for the decisions I've been forced to make.

25

By the time I fall asleep, it's almost 6AM. I don't end up waking again until after noon, so when I do finally wake I'm slightly disorientated. My head feels heavy, the way it always does if I've cried too much, and Dean is no longer by my side. I prop myself up onto my elbows and glance around the room through half-closed eyes. My phone is laying face down on the floor and half my clothes are still spilling out of my backpack. I sigh. Yesterday was a mess.

The suite is silent. No voices. No TV. I can't blame Dean for leaving. He's in New York City—he can't afford to waste time lounging around in the hotel. There are so many things to see and so little time. This doesn't stop me from calling out his name, however, just to check.

I'm surprised when I get an answer back. Dean's voice echoes through from the living area, and seconds later he pops his head around the door, smiling warmly at me as he says, "Finally."

Rolling my eyes, I sit up further and hug the comforter to my chest. "Where are Rachael and Tiffani?"

"Rachael went out for lunch with the lizard guy."

I arch an eyebrow. "You mean Snake?"

"Yeah, yeah, him," Dean says. Pushing the door open

further, he steps into the bedroom and closes it behind him. He's still only wearing those navy sweats from last night and it seems like he's been having a pretty laid-back morning. "Isn't he like twenty-five?"

"Twenty-one," I say quietly. If I wasn't still so in disbelief over what happened last night, then perhaps I'd wonder why the hell Rachael is going out for lunch with him. Ever since Trevor broke up with her during spring break, she's drilled the idea of being independent into herself. That mindset clearly hasn't lasted long. "Where's Tiffani?"

"I don't know," Dean says as he climbs onto the bed next to me, lying on his side and propping himself up on his elbow, "and I don't care." He reaches for my waist, placing a cool hand on my hip as he pulls my body closer to his. His lips immediately find their way to my neck as he trails slow, soft kisses along my skin. "I've missed you," he murmurs, voice low. He shifts his body across the mattress, pressing his chest to mine as he delicately runs his hand up and down the side of my ribs and moves his lips to the corner of my mouth.

He kisses me gently, just as I remember, but I can't kiss him back with the same tenderness. I can't bring myself to kiss him at all, because out of the corner of my eye I can see my Chucks lying on the floor. They remind me of Tyler. Of course they do. He gave them to me. He wrote on them. He told me not to give up, yet that's exactly what he now thinks I've done. I'm not sure how I'm supposed to make it clear to Tyler that I haven't given up, that this is all only temporary, just until Tiffani leaves New York. I'm not sure how I can fix any of this.

Frowning against Dean's lips, I run my hand through his hair and gently push him away from me. "Not today."

Dean glances up at me with wide eyes, confused. "What?"

My eyes find their way back to my sneakers. The faded white material, Tyler's scrawled handwriting along the rubber. It's entirely irrational, but an idea springs to my mind. It's an idea that only Tyler will understand. "There's something I gotta do," I tell Dean. Without even a split second of hesitation, I shove the comforter off me and swing my legs out of the bed, reaching straight for my backpack on the floor.

"What?" Dean says again, sitting up on the bed as he stares at me, as though he can't believe I've just turned him down. For starters, I just woke up. Second, I've been sleeping with his best friend. Third, I'm telling him the truth soon, and I think sticking around here and making him believe that everything is fine is quite literally the worst I thing I could do. "What do you need to do right at this moment that's so important?"

Still wandering around in my underwear, I scoop all of my belongings up from the floor, my bag and my phone and my Converse, and make for the bedroom door. "I can't tell you," I call over my shoulder. I head into the living area, darting straight into the bathroom. I hear Dean follow behind me. I lock the bathroom door before he can catch up.

"Eden," he says through the wood, knocking once. "What's going on? Is this about what happened last night?"

Ignoring him, I rush to pull my clothes out of my bag again, this time not in the darkness of the middle of the night, and I scatter them all over the bathroom as I try to piece together an outfit from the random items of clothing I managed to grab when I was leaving. I don't want to hang around, so I don't even shower, just freshen up. I spend five minutes in total pulling myself together, and once I've slipped on my shoes I zip my bag back up and swing the strap over my shoulder.

When I open the bathroom door, Dean's leaning against the frame. He instantly jumps back, his eyes full of panic as he takes in the expression on my face. Ever so quietly, he asks, "Have I done something wrong?"

"You haven't done *anything* wrong, Dean, and that's the problem!" I groan, shaking my head at him as I squeeze sideways past his body. I'm so angry at myself right now, so furious that I seem to be taking my rage out on him. I feel my heart shattering at the worry in his eyes. It's so hard to know that I have to hurt him soon, because he's the one person I never, ever want to hurt. He deserves way better than me.

I'm waiting for him to reply, but he doesn't. It's like he doesn't know where to even begin when it comes to figuring out what I'm thinking right now, and I can't bring myself to look back at him as I leave the suite. I just pull the door shut behind me and keep walking, and the further along the lobby and the further away from the suite I get, the more my attention shifts from Dean to something else. My current motive and mission. My irrational idea.

As I head down to the main lobby in the elevator, I double-check my backpack to ensure I threw my wallet in there last night, and breathe a sigh of relief that I did. I pull out my phone and weave my way around a group of tourists gathered around the front desk, careful not to bump into any of their luggage, and then thank the doorman again for opening the door for me.

I walk away from him as fast as I can, making my way along the street as I stare down at my phone. I draw up the subway map at the same time as I search for potential studios. With no idea yet which direction I'm going to be heading in, I pause on the corner as I figure it out. The streets are heaving, just the way they usually are, so I step back against the wall of the building nearest to me, adamant that I won't block the flow of pedestrians.

It takes me no more than ten minutes to decide on the studio and to map out the subway route, and even though I have to head two miles across Manhattan on my own, I feel pretty confident about it.

I expertly slip between fascinated tourists as though I've lived in Manhattan for years. The grid layout of the city has become easier and easier to navigate, especially after walking these streets for a month now, so I've got my way around Upper East Side memorized. I reach the station in just over five minutes, and luckily I've got my MetroCard with me.

Four weeks ago, the subway terrified me. Tyler had to drag me into the station back then, yet now I'm navigating a new station without a worry in the world. That is, of course, until I reach the right platform. There's a God-awful stench. The station is sweltering hot, made worse by the flocks of people, and I can't even try to hide my distaste for it all. Before I came to Manhattan, I never expected the subway to be luxurious or even clean, but at least the other stations haven't made me want to throw up. I hold my breath and come to a stop, jammed between a woman with a stroller and a group of young Asian tourists. If my mom knew I was down here alone, she'd kill me.

The train arrives after a few minutes, but there are so many people gathered on the platform that I don't even make it on. I'm not bold enough to elbow my way through the crowd, so I hang back as it fills up and leaves, and then I edge my way closer to the platform edge, silently wondering to myself how long I'm supposed to be able to survive down here before the toxic fumes kill me. I'm scared to breathe, so I close my eyes and hold onto my backpack as tightly as possible as I wait for the next train.

It turns up around five minutes later, and this time I do fight for my space. There's no way I'm sticking around in the black hole that is the Fifty-ninth Street station for a second longer. It's packed, so I stand, but I don't mind. I'm only on it for a couple minutes, just until Grand Central, so it's not long before I'm off the train.

I've been to Grand Central Station numerous times over the summer so far, so I transfer straight to the Forty-second Street shuttle with ease. The entire time nerves are building up inside of me, but I tell myself I won't back out. I might be acting upon a split-second decision and it might be crazy and it might be stupid, but it just makes sense. It just feels right, for some odd reason, and for that reason alone I keep pursuing my plans, taking the shuttle over to Times Square.

Quickly, I head out of the station when I arrive and follow the map I'm looking at on my phone, glancing between the streets of Manhattan and my screen as I check to ensure I'm still on the right route. I make a left onto the avenue and head two blocks south, just past Fortieth Street and the New York Times Building, and that's when I find what I've been looking for.

It's nestled above a store selling New York souvenirs and next to Subway, and I don't even take the time to study the studio from the outside before I head inside. I just want to get it over with quickly, rather than allowing myself to overthink what I'm doing. I do stop on the stairs, however, to glance down at my Chucks.

Tilting my foot onto its side, I run my eyes over Tyler's

handwriting. It's been four weeks since he told me not to give up. All I can do now is let him know that I haven't, in the rawest possible way I can think of, and by the time I'm pushing open the door to the tattoo studio, I'm smiling.

I'm just making my way down Lexington Avenue when Emily calls. It's almost five by now and rush hour is upon the city, with the traffic jammed and the sidewalks bustling. I didn't intend to stay out all afternoon, but after traveling around, suffering through a two-hour wait at the studio and stopping for coffee and lunch for almost an hour, I've ended up returning to the apartment only now. So when my phone vibrates in the back pocket of my jeans, I answer Emily's call as I continue to walk.

"Hey, what's up?"

"I'm sort of locked out of the apartment," Emily says sheepishly.

"What?" I accidentally brush shoulders with a guy as I pass him, and he fires me an indignant glare. I can only shrug in return, and then I scuttle away from him, desperate not to piss off anyone else. "How'd you do that?"

"I've been over at my own apartment boxing up some of my stuff and I didn't think to take keys with me because I thought Tyler would be here. Like, he's been in bed all day so I didn't think he'd go anywhere, but I've been knocking for ten minutes straight and no one's answering," Emily explains, sighing across the line.

"Where's Snake?"

"I'm pretty sure he took your friend out on a date," she says, and she's right. Dean's already filled me in on that, about Rachael and Snake heading out for lunch together. It's kinda weird. "At least I think that's what he said," Emily continues. "I have no idea; I was still half asleep at the time because Tyler kept us up all night."

"How is he?" Last night was the worst night of the entire summer and Tiffani was the reason behind it all. If she'd never arrived in New York, if she'd let go of her deluded vision of being with Tyler years ago, then none of this would have happened. I wouldn't have told Tyler those lies and he wouldn't have reverted to his old mindset, where being reckless is the best distraction anyone could ever ask for. "Tyler, I mean."

"Hungover, but he was starting to feel a little better by the time I left," Emily answers with a laugh, like she's rolling her eyes. "You don't happen to have a spare set of keys on you, do you?"

"You're in luck," I say. "I've carried the spare with me for the past two weeks. Never used it yet, though." Tyler finally trusted me enough to give me the spare, just in case I ever did need to get into the apartment when I was alone, and I've had it stored in the zipped compartment of my wallet ever since.

"If it's not too much of a hassle," Emily says, "do you think you could bring it over?"

"Sure." My voice is loud over the buzz of the city. Like a true New Yorker. "I'm on my way back just now, anyway. I'm only a couple blocks away."

"Perfect," she says. "Thanks, Eden. See you in a few."

Ending the call, I slip my phone back into my jeans. As I head along to Tyler's apartment I can see the building towering over on the corner of the block, just across the street, but my eyes don't rest on it for long. They end up drifting back to my wrist and I feel the same disbelief I've been experiencing the entire way over here. Even on the subway I stared endlessly, twisting my left arm in every position possible as I tried to get the light to hit my wrist at just the right angle. Even as I climbed up flights of stairs and weaved my way back through the stations, I couldn't tear my eyes away from my arm, occasionally running the tips of my fingers over the Saran Wrap just to remind myself that I'm completely and entirely insane. My dad will quite literally kill me when he sees me. That's if my mom doesn't kill me first for traveling around New York on my own.

When I reach the apartment building, I sweep past the mailboxes and head straight for the elevator. In the ten seconds that it takes for me to reach the twelfth floor, I quickly grab a hoodie from my bag and pull it on, ensuring that my wrist is covered. I don't want Emily to question me about it and I really don't know how Tyler will react when he sees it. I just hope he'll understand what I'm trying to tell him, without the need for me to even say a single word. Tiffani said I couldn't tell Tyler what was really going on, but that doesn't mean I can't attempt to *show* him the truth.

Emily's sitting crossed-legged by the apartment door when I reach her, looking slightly worn out. She gets to her feet immediately, pushing herself up and smiling.

"Hey," I say, quickly adjusting the drawstrings of my hoodie as I think about our phone call five minutes ago. I didn't really pay attention to her words then, but now that she's in front of me it's like I suddenly remember everything she said. "I didn't know you had your own apartment."

"Yeah, over in Queens," she says with a shrug.

"So why've you been staying here? Tyler's never told me the reason."

"I was sharing an apartment with this guy, and it was great

for a while, but recently it wasn't working out. We got into a huge fight and he pretty much kicked me out," she admits, not quite meeting my eyes. Her voice has grown softer and she sighs, frowning. "Honestly, he was just a prick, and I didn't know where else to go, so I called Tyler."

I swing my backpack off my shoulder and unzip it, raising my leg and balancing it on my knee as I rummage around for my wallet. I keep talking to Emily, but I'm too focused to look at her. "Why were you boxing up your stuff?"

"Because I'm about to ship everything home," she says. "I'm heading back to London next week."

I stop fumbling and glance up. "What?"

"I mean, it's about time I leave. The tour ended over a month ago." She smiles in such a way that it becomes clear she doesn't really want to leave, like the thought of heading back to England doesn't fill her with excitement. I can't blame her. Part of me doesn't particularly ever want to go back to Santa Monica. "So do you have those keys?" she asks, the tone of her voice altering as she changes the subject.

"Yeah. Here." I reach for my wallet, unzipping the tiny compartment inside it and pulling out the single key. I pass it to Emily as I close everything back up, and then follow her into the apartment.

She stops immediately after stepping over the threshold and I promptly walk into the back of her, my body bumping hers. When I glance over her shoulder, I'm greeted by the last thing I ever expected to see. Never, ever in a million years would I have believed that such a familiar sight would unfold in front of me. In fact, it takes at least ten seconds for my eyes to fully take in the scene, and at least twelve for Tyler to pull away from Tiffani.

He has her pressed against the kitchen worktop and her

hands are cupped around his jaw as he kisses her shoulder, the same way he kisses mine. He's got one hand on the small of her back and the other on her waist, and it doesn't take me any longer than a single second to notice the way the lacing on her blouse has already been undone. I'm having flashbacks of the very first time I ever met Tiffani, that day they were fooling around in the fitting rooms at American Apparel, and I can't bring myself to take in the fact that it's happening *again*. I can't accept that she's getting her way *again*. I can't even begin to fathom the fact that this entire thing, this whole game of manipulation, has worked completely in her favor. Even more so, I can't believe Tyler. I can't believe he's made it so easy for her to get exactly what she wanted.

When he finally notices Emily and me out of the corner of his eye, he immediately draws his lips away from Tiffani's skin, taking a large step back. He stares at only me, his eyes widening, right before he glances down at the bulge in his jeans. "Eden."

Tiffani dramatically gasps, stepping forward and wrapping her arms tightly around his bicep, the one with my name on it. "Oh my God! This is *so* awkward."

"Eden," Tyler says again. He doesn't nudge Tiffani's grip off him. He doesn't even flinch, in fact. He just stands there, looking at me with no shame whatsoever. Admittedly, he does look awful. His hair is all over the place and his eyes are heavy, like he's exhausted.

I'm not upset. I'm livid. Furious. Pivoting around Emily, who's blinking in shock and doesn't know how to react, I take a bold step across the room. "*Don't* try to explain yourself, Tyler," I hiss through gritted teeth, my hands balled into fists by my side. "I can't even believe that you would—"

"Eden," he cuts in, saying my name for the third time, his voice edgy yet firm. "I wasn't gonna explain myself," he says. "I was gonna ask if you could get the fuck out of my apartment."

My shoulders immediately sink and I falter as I blink at him, stunned. "What?"

"You heard him," Tiffani says. Unsurprisingly, there's a glorious smile spreading across her face. She looks vicious. "Can both of you leave and give us some space? Don't you guys have gyms and therapists to visit?"

My jaw falls open. Her words, thrown at us so casually, hit me so hard that I can't even find the energy to build up anger. I exchange glances with Emily. Her lips are parted, eyes wide, completely and entirely shocked at the remark. In that exact moment, I pity Tiffani. I pity her, because she gains satisfaction from hitting people where it hurts. I pity her, because she uses others' weaknesses to her advantage. For that, I'll never forgive her. Not now, not ever.

When I glance at Tyler, I realize he's no longer glaring at me. His eyes have shifted to Tiffani and he stares at her, disgusted. He reaches for her hands, pulling her grip off his arm as he takes a large step away from her, shaking his head. "You didn't just say that," he says slowly.

Tiffani rolls her eyes at him, but the entire time, something other than fury is building up inside of me. It's seeing her and Tyler together that's making me so uncomfortable. None of this was ever supposed to happen. Tyler was never meant to turn to her again for a goddamn distraction, no matter how upset and pissed off he is at me, and I realize that the feeling within me that keeps growing more intense with each passing second is nothing but desperation. I'm desperate to fix all of this, desperate to show Tyler that I'm still here, still endlessly in love with him.

Screw Tiffani. Forget her games. Right now, I can't keep any of this going for a second longer. I can't watch Tyler look at me with that expression of rebuke in his eyes, like he doesn't want to be around me.

I don't even care that Emily's in the room. I don't care that Tiffani will tell Dean the truth. I don't care, because Emily and Dean finding out the truth is a lot less terrifying than having Tyler never forgive me for the things I said last night.

Before I even realize it I'm walking across the room, edging my way toward Tyler, and the words begin to spill out of my mouth before I can rethink what I'm doing. "What I told you last night was bullshit," I splutter, my eyes focused on Tyler and only Tyler. "I don't choose Dean. I choose you. It's always been you." I flash my eyes to Tiffani, now furious and brave enough to lock my glare on hers. "She made me end things with you last night, because she's a *bitch*."

Tiffani still keeps smiling, but I can see the cracks appearing as she tries to hide her anger. Trying to maintain her calm, innocent persona, she stiffly says, "Why would I do that, Eden?"

"Because you want Tyler back," Emily cuts in sharply from behind me, and when I twist my neck around to face her, she's walking over to join me. I'm taken aback by the fact that she's not surprised, not gasping in disbelief in the background. I just made it clear that Tyler is a lot more than just my stepbrother, yet she hasn't even blinked. She just looks defensive as she folds her arms across her chest, her eyes on Tiffani. "You threatened her. I heard you at the diner." Her voice grows softer as she diverts her eyes to Tyler's, and she glances between him and me for a moment. "Eden's telling you the truth, Tyler."

"Please. If you're going to lie, at least make it sound logical," Tiffani scoffs, but I can see the panic in her eyes as she adjusts her blouse, well aware that the moment of winning Tyler back is now slipping through her fingers. She knows she's losing. "I'd never do such a thing."

Tyler's eyes are still fierce, but this time it's not because of me. It's because of Tiffani. He takes another step away from her, not to the side, but in front of her, joining Emily and me. It's the three of us against her. "Get out," he orders.

"What?"

"Get the fuck out," he repeats, his temper snapping as he points his thumb over his shoulder toward the door. His voice is sharp and his posture is firm, and he's definitely not backing down. "Right now."

Furious, Tiffani scrunches up her face and barges straight through us all, purposely shoving her palm into Tyler's chest as she pushes him to one side. She rams her shoulder into Emily's, unable to control her growing contempt for us all, and then promptly stops and turns to me. She only shakes her head and, unbelievably, she smirks. "You've really done it this time," she hisses, and I know that I have. I know she'll tell Dean now. Of course she will.

"The door's that way," I say calmly, despite however much I could yell and scream at her right now, and I step to the side. I nod to the door, and she finally storms out, slamming it behind her.

Silence ensues. None of us know what to say or how to react. No one wants to be the first to speak. Emily mostly just looks at me with raised eyebrows, and Tyler mostly just stands there, his back turned to us and his head tilted down to the floor. I can hear him breathing heavily, and it's like I can almost hear him thinking everything through, and I eventually realize that I need to be the first to say something.

Numb from what's just occurred, I have to force myself across the room, slowly approaching Tyler from behind. I reach for his arm, gently touching him with just my fingertips. "Tyler . . ."

Softly, he shakes his head. "I gotta . . . I gotta clear my head," he says quietly. Turning away from me, he makes his way across the living room and into his own room. A few seconds later, he returns while pulling on a pair of shoes. His car keys are looped around his index finger.

"You shouldn't be driving yet," Emily points out, concerned. I glance over to her, still wondering why she has yet to question what I said about Tyler. Maybe she didn't understand. I don't know. It's just odd. For the past two years I've always expected that people would be outraged and disgusted and confused when and if they found out. Emily's the first person I've indirectly told, and she hasn't even reacted to it. I just keep waiting for it. I keep waiting to hear her ask, "What the hell is going on between you guys?" I'm just waiting for *something*. Anything.

"Whatever," Tyler says. He grabs his keys for the apartment from the kitchen counter and brushes past both Emily and me, careful not to touch us, and then disappears through the door. He doesn't slam it like Tiffani did. Just quietly pulls it shut behind him.

I want nothing more right now than to go after him, to explain everything more fully, but I know he needs his space. He needs to get his head around the basic facts first, and *then*

I can talk to him about it. Later, when he gets back, whenever that ends up being. Right now, though, I'm still dumbfounded over Emily. Telling the truth wasn't supposed to be so easy. It was supposed to be terrifying.

"Emily . . ." I say slowly, feeling uneasy. She might not be asking any questions, but she must surely be thinking them. I can't let it go without clearing things up, without her knowing what's really going on, so I build up the courage to face my biggest fear: having to explain myself. "About Tyler and me. . ."

"You don't need to explain it," Emily says with a shrug, making her way past me as she heads for the kitchen. I blink at her from the living room as she grabs herself a bottle of water from the refrigerator. Casually, she unscrews the cap and leans against the worktop. To my utmost surprise, she looks back at me with a warm gaze and does nothing but smile in the gentlest and most comforting of ways. "I'd already figured it out."

26

At first, Emily's words don't make sense. Figured it out? Impossible. Tyler and I have been so careful, so cautious . . . It scares me that even though we've tried our hardest to keep our relationship a secret, Emily has still noticed. It momentarily terrifies me that she might not be the only one. How many other people over the years have had suspicions? How many other people have wondered if there's always been something more between us? All I can hope is that the answer is none. Emily, on the other hand, doesn't seem fazed by the fact that Tyler is my stepbrother. Not uncomfortable or judgmental, not disgusted or confused. All I can ask her is, "How did you know?"

She takes a sip of her water, still smiling. I'm glad that she's smiling. I was worried Tiffani's remark about therapy would upset her, but she seems to have let it go over the top of her head, the same way the remark about the gym has gone over mine. It was a cheap shot at trying to hurt us. Now, however, there are other matters at hand. Slowly, Emily twists the cap back on the bottle in her hand and shrugs. "It just became obvious."

"How? It wasn't supposed to be," I admit quietly, struggling to grasp the fact that I'm actually discussing the subject with someone other than Tyler. It feels foreign. I'm not used to it.

"Yeah, I figured that too," Emily says with a small laugh. A warm, friendly one. "Honestly, it was a number of things."

I make my way across the living room toward the kitchen counter. When I get there, I lean down and rest my arms on the worktop as I look across at Emily, both curious and confused. "Like what? What gave us away?"

"Well," she says, "Tyler went from sleeping on the couch to sleeping next to you. I mean, sure, siblings share beds all the time, but it just seemed like something more than that. When you guys went to sleep early the other night I was looking for you both when I got back here, and when I checked Tyler's room you were both asleep, but totally wrapped up in each other. All I could think was that I would never be caught dead like that with my brother."

I raise my eyebrows. "You figured us out just from that?"

"No," she says. "There was Tyler's tattoo, too. I noticed it one morning when you were in the shower, and when I asked him why he chose to get your name, he just shrugged and said it was because you're his sister. I thought that was weird, because what about his brothers? Why wouldn't he get their names too? Especially considering they're actually his real brothers. No offense."

"None taken. I knew that tattoo was a bad idea," I say, almost laughing. It's also rather ironic given what I've just done, and I quickly glance down at my wrist to ensure it's still hidden under my sleeve. I'll show Tyler later. Right now, however, I'm focused on Emily. And of all the times I had imagined this conversation with someone, about Tyler and me, I never once imaged it to be like this. So casual. So easy. "What else gave us away?"

Emily thinks for a moment as she brushes her fingertips over her lips, her eyes squinting at nothing in particular for a short while before she meets my waiting gaze. "Did Tyler ever let you read his speech from the tour?" she asks. It takes me aback for a second as I try to think about the answer, blinking at her.

Tyler and I shared countless phone calls over the year that he was gone, but I don't quite recall him ever reading his full speech to me. When he first moved over here to New York he was still in the process of writing it, and back then he did sometimes ask for my thoughts on the words he'd pieced together. I always told him everything sounded just fine, raw and honest and so him. I never heard the finished version. I never asked. "No," I finally admit. "Why?"

Emily's smile grows wider again and she leans back on the balls of her feet, passing the bottle of water back and forth in her hands. "Toward the end of our speeches, we had to talk about the after-effects of abuse. The psychological damage," she says, and I wonder if she's uncomfortable, but she's not. She's talked about this endlessly for an entire year, just like Tyler has. She's used to it. "And so Tyler would talk about the drugs and the booze and everything else," she continues, "and he always spoke about a girl. He never once mentioned her name, but he would talk about the fact that she was the first person in years to care about what he was going through. The first person to actually want to help, and that that was exactly what she did without her even realizing it. He told everyone that she was the reason things started changing and getting better. He spoke about her as though he was in love with her, and we always wondered why he never said her name." She pauses for a minute, not quite smiling but not quite frowning either. Exhaling slowly, she parts her lips and says, "I've realized it was because that girl is you."

Her words take a while to sink in. I can do nothing but stare at her as I try to process them. Tyler never mentioned that he spoke about me in his speech. He never once told me that he talked about me in such a way. I'm not sure how to feel about it. Uncomfortable? Not quite. Surprised? Yes. All I can think about is that I am so, so in love with him, yet he's not even here. I desperately want to reach out for him right now. Touch him, tell him I love him. And not in French this time.

When Emily realizes I don't have the ability to muster up a reply right now, she continues, walking around the kitchen counter as she does so. "So I thought there was something going on between the two of you," she says, "but I didn't want to ask, and then your boyfriend turned up so I thought I must have been imagining that there was something between you and Tyler. But then last night I found out that I *was* right and that I wasn't just imagining the entire thing."

"When I walked out on him?" I guess, pushing myself away from the counter as I turn to face her.

"No," she says. "After that." Moving away from me, she heads across the living room and my eyes follow her. She talks over her shoulder as she walks, raising her voice as she disappears into Tyler's room. "Tyler took a bunch of videos of the tour, so I was emailing them over to myself," I hear her say, reappearing at his bedroom door with a laptop in her hands, "and I found something that I think you should see. I'm not sure if you know about it or not."

My curiosity peaks and I rush over to join her on the couch as she places the laptop down on the coffee table, tilting open the screen. I interlock my hands anxiously in my lap as she starts it up. Neither of us relaxes back into the couch. We both sit right on the edge, leaning forward, staring at the screen. Emily doesn't take long to log in to Tyler's account, to pull up his files. She scrolls straight to the most recent video to be transferred onto the laptop, and she opens it. It's nothing but a dark screen. She quickly pauses it before the video can even start, and she turns to look at me.

"So I opened this video by accident and I swear I only watched the first ten minutes or so and . . ." Her words taper off as she glances back at the laptop. She reaches for it, picking it up and gently placing it on my lap. "Well, I just think you should watch it. You might want some space, and you might want to get comfy."

I furrow my eyebrows at her as she gets to her feet, feeling curious yet slightly suspicious at the exact same time. My eyes follow her as she heads back over to the kitchen to fetch her water, her loose ponytail swinging around her shoulders. She's always been so nice to me. Always.

"Emily?" Anxiously, I bite down on my lower lip as I wait for her to turn around. When she does, she raises her eyebrows at me and listens. "I'm sorry," I tell her.

She tilts her head slightly to one side. "What?"

"For the way I treated you at first," I say, and then I shrug rather sheepishly as I admit, "I thought you and Tyler had a thing." Embarrassed, I throw my head into my hands and groan.

Now Emily laughs. Really, really laughs, and I join in with her. "Don't worry about it," she reassures me. "I can't blame you."

It feels nice to be laughing after everything that's just happened. Despite the fact that Tiffani is most likely storming her way back to her hotel suite to tell Dean the truth and despite the fact that Tyler's disappeared to God knows where, I'm still smiling. I'm smiling because our secret no longer seems so wrong or so scandalous or so terrifying.

I stand up, the laptop resting on my arm as I look back to Emily once more. "And thanks," I add.

"What for?"

"For not judging us," I say softly. She doesn't reply, only nods. She's the second person to know yet she's the first to accept it, and for that I'll forever be grateful. Acceptance feels nice.

With one final exchange of smiles, I turn and head over to Tyler's room, scooping up my backpack from the floor with my free hand and then closing the door behind me as I lay the laptop down on his bed. The curtains are closed, like they haven't been opened all day, and Tyler's bed isn't quite made. I can't blame him. He must have been so hungover earlier. Sighing, I carefully pull off my hoodie and throw it to the side along with my bag. That's when I remember the new addition to my wrist.

I flick on the lights, holding my arm up as I study my skin up close. The Saran Wrap feels damp and clingy, and the letters are bold and dark underneath it. As delicately and as carefully as I can, I remove the plastic. My skin is slightly raised and a little inflamed, but looking good. It's exactly what I wanted, just the way I imagined it.

Along my left wrist, the words *No te rindas* stare back at me. It's in Tyler's handwriting, exactly as he wrote it on the Converse he gave me. His words. His writing. His one simple request. He's the only one who'll understand it, and for that reason alone, I adore it.

Tossing the plastic wrapping into the trash can in the corner of the room, I turn the lights back off and grab my earphones from the bedside table. Getting comfortable, I adjust the pillows and place them up against the headboard, climbing into the bed and leaning back. I pull the comforter over me and reach for the laptop. Without wasting another second, I plug in my earphones and stare at the dark screen. I hit the play button.

At first, nothing seems to be happening. The video does shift slightly, but it's too dark to make out what exactly I'm supposed to be looking at. I increase the volume, and to my surprise I hear Tyler's voice. Low and hushed, nothing but a gentle whisper.

I close my eyes and listen, feeling my stomach twist as I hear his voice. He tells the camcorder my name. He tells it my birthday. My favorite color. My birthplace. The color of my hair and the color of my eyes. Slowly, he keeps going. It takes him a minute to describe my eyes alone, and that's when I decide to pause the video. I wave the cursor over the screen to bring up the timeline, and the moment I see it, I blink and check it again.

The video lasts for four hours and twenty-seven minutes.

It has to be a glitch. There's no way.

For four and a half hours, I listen to Tyler's voice, endlessly whispering and quietly laughing. He tells the camcorder about the first time we met. He talks about all the things he loves about me, some of which are habits and mannerisms that even I've never noticed before. He talks and talks and talks, hardly ever pausing and without a single second of hesitation at all as he reflects on the moments we've shared together. Of conversations and kisses, trespassing and parties.

As the video goes on, as the hours go by, the darkness gradually lessens. It continues to brighten over time, and outlines begin to become clearer. After the second hour I can see Tyler's entire face, his bright eyes. He's in his room, right in the spot I'm in now. By the third hour, he turns the camera away from himself and points it at me. Me. Right there, right next to him, sleeping the entire time.

By the time the video wraps up, it's daylight on the screen. Tyler doesn't even look tired as he mentions La Breve Vita, and that's when it all begins to sound familiar. His words after the point . . . I've heard those words before.

It's at that exact moment that Tyler turns the camera on me again, his soft voice murmuring, *"Hey, you're finally awake."*

"What are you doing?" I sound half asleep as my tired eyes stare straight into the lens. I stare back at myself through the screen.

"Just messing around." His voice echoes through my earphones, and I shake my head in complete disbelief. Just messing around? He's been talking about me for over four hours. It's almost as though he never wanted me to see this, never wanted me to know about it.

I listen to us briefly talk about the Fourth of July, just like I remember we did, and then he moves the camera to the bedside table. That's when I pull him toward me and he presses his face to mine and we kiss. We're laughing in between it all, right until I ask him to switch off the camera. He asks if we can keep it on. Seconds later, he scrambles toward the lens and the video shuts off. It ends.

After spending my entire evening hearing what Tyler had to say about me and hearing everything he's remembered over the past two years, even the smallest of details, he's managed to reduce me to tears. They're rolling down my cheeks in warm waves as I stare at the screen. It's gone black again, straight back to the beginning of the video when it's the middle of the night, and I can see my reflection looking back at me. I'm not crying because I'm upset. I'm overwhelmed. My entire body feels numb. To really understand just how deeply Tyler loves me, to really *feel* it . . . I think it's the most comforting yet frightening thing in the world.

I play the video again, this time skipping straight to the two-hour mark. I jump back and forth for a while within a half-hour time frame, searching for a specific moment. It's my favorite one from the entire video, the only time Tyler directly speaks to me rather than the camera as I'm still sleeping. When I find it, I exhale, leaning back against the pillows. Hitting the play button once more, I close my eyes, and I listen.

"I don't know what being in love with someone is supposed to feel like," Tyler admits with a breathy laugh, *"but if being in love means thinking about someone every second of every day . . . If being in love means your entire mood shifts when they're around . . . If being in love means you'd do anything and everything for them,"* he murmurs, *"then I am* endlessly *in love with you."*

27

It's almost ten by the time I shut down Tyler's laptop. I've been lying here for a while. Just thinking. About Tyler and about the video and about him and me. I wonder where all of this is going. When Dean finds out the truth and when we break the news to our parents, what happens then? What's next? Will Tyler and I get together? Are we supposed to wait a few months and let everything cool down first? I don't know. All I know is that I'm growing tired of waiting. It's been two years and we haven't gotten anywhere yet. Two years and I have yet to be able to proudly introduce Tyler to people as my boyfriend. Will I ever get to do that? I can only hope and I can only pray that no one looks back at me with wide eyes and shocked gasps.

I'm still sitting alone in silence, comfortable in the dark, when the door slowly opens with a creak. I glance up expecting to see Emily, but instead I see Tyler. His head is hung low as he lingers at the door, his hand resting on the handle. He appears calm now. Not confused or angry, but not quite relaxed either. Just calm.

"Can we talk?" he asks quietly. There's a nervous undertone to his voice, like he's expecting me to say no. I might not be able to clearly see his face, but I can tell that he doesn't want to look me in the eyes right now. He's staring at the ground.

I don't reply, only nod once and hope that he can see it. I press my palms down on the mattress and shift my body over to the other side of the bed, closest to the window, and I wait for him to join me in the warm space I've just left. That's exactly what he does. In silence, he closes the door behind him with an inaudible click and makes his way over, gently slipping into the bed by my side. He stays on top of the comforter, putting an arm around me as I rest my head against his shoulder. We both breathe softly for a while, and even though he asked if we could talk, neither of us wants to. We both just look ahead of us to the mirrored closet doors opposite the foot of the bed, staring at the reflections of our outlines through the dark.

After a short while, Tyler decides to finally say something, but he doesn't move an inch as he clears his throat. "What happened yesterday?" he asks so quietly that it's almost a whisper. The silence feels too fragile to speak any louder.

I squeeze my eyes shut and try to consider everything that happened today and yesterday. Everything has gone wrong since Tuesday, since the moment Tiffani stepped foot in Manhattan. I'm just relieved now that although I made a mess of it all and that Dean's probably already been told the truth by now, Tiffani didn't get her way. It backfired. The fact that Tyler's here with me right now already proves that he's taking my side, that it's *me* he believes. "Tiffani wanted you back," I admit, my head still against his shoulder. His chest rises and falls. "She thought the only way that would happen was if I wasn't in the way. She said I had to cut things off with you or she'd tell Dean the truth. If we beat her to it and told Dean first, she'd tell our parents." It's a little more complicated than that, but I simplify it all for the sole reason that I don't particularly want to talk about it. I try to glance up at Tyler, but from my angle I can only see his forehead.

"Fuck," he murmurs. I see him run his free hand back through his hair as he exhales a long breath. Slowly, he shakes his head and squeezes my body tighter against his. "I'm sorry for being such an asshole earlier. I was just pissed off at you and I wasn't thinking straight."

"I'm sorry too," I tell him.

He manages to laugh a little, a quiet, breathy laugh, just like the times he laughed during the video. I don't think I'll tell him that I know about it. I think I'll keep that a secret. "Seriously, I thought you'd given up on me," Tyler admits. "Don't ever scare the hell out of me like that again."

I don't think I'll ever give up, especially not now, and I think this exact moment is a better time than any to show Tyler the new addition to my wrist. I don't need to reply to him right now. I think his own words, his own quote is the only reply he needs. Smiling, I hold up my hand and raise my pinky, purposely angling my wrist in Tyler's direction as I say, "I promise I won't."

He's just about to interlock his pinky with mine when he pauses, grasping my wrist instead and bolting upright, then leaning forward. When I glance sideways at him, he's squinting through the dark at the words inked upon my skin. He looks to me with wide eyes. "What's this?"

"You might want to turn on a light," I say, biting down on my lower lip as I grow slightly anxious. I can imagine Tyler's eyebrows shooting up as he unwraps his arm from my body and reaches over me to turn on the lamp on the bedside table, his other hand never letting go of my wrist.

The room immediately brightens up, setting both our faces aglow, and I don't even look to my wrist. I look at Tyler, admiring the way his eyes gloss over and his lips part, his entire face lighting up with surprise in the most adorable of ways as he studies my wrist with great intensity. "No way," he says, blinking at me with an expression full of innocence. It all makes him seem younger in that exact moment, like he's just a kid again.

I laugh and pull my wrist free from his hand, scanning my new tattoo again for myself. It's still rather red and occasionally I can feel a hot sting, but it's all worth it for Tyler's expression alone. "I got it this afternoon," I say, answering the question he hasn't even asked. I know he's wondering about it, though, so I continue to explain. "It was the only thing I could think of that would make sense to only you and me. It's yours. It's what you wrote."

"You were way more thoughtful than me," he says with a sheepish smile as he lifts his left arm up a little, glancing down at his own tattoo, the one on his bicep and the one that's only four letters long. "I wasn't that original. Hey, the '*te*' looks a little squint," he says, pointing to the words on my wrist again.

"That's because *you* wrote it a little squint," I fire back at him, rolling my eyes, and he seems to realize only then that my tattoo is in his very own handwriting, because color rises to his cheeks and he looks away. I roll out of the bed still smiling, dropping to my knees on the carpet and looking back across the bed to Tyler. It's hard to believe that this afternoon everything went wrong and now everything feels right again. "By the way," I say, "Emily knows."

"Knows what?" Tyler asks, his eyes never leaving mine.

"About us," I say slowly. I push myself up from the floor and get to my feet. I look down at Tyler, still in the bed, studying me. "She knows that we're more than just stepsiblings."

"You told her?" Immediately he pushes back the comforter and slides out of the bed, straightening up as panic pools in his eyes.

"She figured it out herself," I tell him. His expression shifts from worry to confusion as he tries to process the fact that Emily knows the truth. "*And*," I say, walking around the bed with a wide grin toying at my lips, "she doesn't even care. She's totally cool with it."

Tyler's eyes are wide again as they follow me across the room. "She is?"

"Yeah." When I reach him, I cup his face in my hands and stretch up to kiss him, pressing my lips to his before pulling away to add, "People knowing the truth isn't that bad after all."

He looks at me hard for a moment, his eyes searching mine. I wonder if he thinks I'm kidding, but I'm most definitely not, so I kiss him again almost as a way to reassure him that everything is okay for once. I can't stop myself. I'm smiling against his lips, squeezing my eyes shut, and I bask in that feeling of acceptance again. It's so overwhelming and so incredible that I don't quite know how to handle it. I'm no longer terrified of people discovering that I'm in love with my stepbrother. We're just two people with a label plastered upon us. That's all it is.

Even though he struggles to tear his lips from mine, Tyler

pulls away, and he drops his hands to my waist and gently pushes me back a step. "Does Snake know?"

"Don't think so," I say, shaking my head once. Slowly, a smile fueled by nervous excitement grows on my lips as I reach for one of Tyler's hands. I remove it from my waist and twist my fingers around his. "Is he back yet? We should tell him. C'mon, can we tell him?"

Tyler lets out a laugh, throwing his head back at the same time as he pulls my body against his. "If only you were this enthusiastic about breaking the news to your dad," he murmurs, smirking as he reaches for the door with his free hand.

He leads me into the living room, and it's the first time I've left his bedroom in almost five hours. I was too caught up in the video Emily showed me. The one that lasts for four hours and twenty-seven minutes.

Speaking of Emily, she's perched on one of the couches in the living room, surrounded by notebooks and odd scraps of paper that decorate the coffee table. The TV is on, but the volume is low, as though it's only on in the first place to serve as background noise. She glances up when she hears us shuffling our way across the carpet, and immediately her lips curve up into a smile. "So I take it you two have sorted everything out?"

Tyler doesn't answer her question, only walks me over to the couch instead. He lifts up our interlocked hands and arches his eyebrows at her. "You know?"

"Yeah."

"And it doesn't freak you out?" he asks, just as confused as I was earlier. For two years straight, both of us predicted reactions that were nothing like hers. Tyler drops our hands back down, letting go.

"Nope," Emily says. She shakes her head and clicks her pen a couple times, expression nonchalant. "Honestly, just do what you guys want to do. Life's way too short not to."

Her words make me smile and I wrap my arms around Tyler's bicep as I squeeze him tight. "*La breve vita*," I murmur, glancing up at him. "Life is short."

Just as he's about to open his mouth to say something back, there's some commotion at the door. Some tapping and some fumbling. All three of us glance over, and at first I think it could be Dean trying to ram the door down so that he can kill both Tyler and me, but I breathe a sigh of relief when I hear a key being inserted into the lock. It's Snake, finally.

The door swings open only moments later and out of habit I let go of Tyler and jump back a step or two. Besides, we haven't told Snake yet.

"That was one hell of a long lunch date," Emily throws at him, leaning forward on the couch so that she can see him past Tyler and me. She bites down on the end of the pen in her hand as she wiggles her eyebrows at him, teasing him a little.

Snake only rolls his gray eyes as he saunters over to the kitchen. It's the first time I've seen him since he left to buy groceries last night and, surprisingly, he's now dressed up rather nice. He's even wearing a shirt, pressed and all. "Yeah, yeah, I took her out for dinner too. Gave her the grand tour of Manhattan."

"Snake," I say, playfully throwing him a stern glance as I fold my arms across my chest, "who told you you could take my best friend out on a date?"

I'm only kidding, of course, but he still spins around and

narrows his eyes at me. "What's she doing back here already?" he asks, directing his eyes to Tyler instead. But he's only being playful too. "Are you guys best buds again?"

"Actually . . ." I cut in, stepping forward and twiddling my thumbs anxiously. I want Snake to know the truth. I want to *tell* him the truth. We've never done that before, and right now I feel brave enough to try it. "We have something we wanna tell you."

I steal a quick glance at Emily, who's now gnawing at her pen on the couch as she watches in anticipation, and then I look over my shoulder to Tyler. He's smoldering his eyes at me as he smirks, but not in a malicious way, more in a let's-do-this kind of way. He takes a step forward so that he's by my side again. Snake studies the two of us with curious eyes.

I don't exactly know what to say or how to phrase the truth, but suddenly I no longer even have to say anything at all, because I'm being spun around by Tyler as he draws me toward him. Out of nowhere, he crashes his lips to mine for what feels like the hundredth time now.

It takes me by surprise. It's the last thing I expected right now, but at the same time I can't pull away. I keep kissing him back, caught up in the familiarity of how his lips feel against mine. I'm most definitely aware that both Snake and Emily are watching us, yet I can't bring myself to care.

Tyler quickly draws away almost as abruptly as he kissed me in the first place, and he flashes his eyes back to Snake. "Give me your opinion," he orders. "Right now."

I look at Snake. He's staring back at us from the kitchen, his posture frozen, and he does nothing but blink at us. He's a little stunned, but that's okay. I expect people to be shocked at first. Slowly, he swallows and exchanges a rather concerned glance with Emily. "What the fuck?" he says. Pulling a face, he breathes an uncomfortable laugh, unsure of what to think and what to say.

"I'm in love with her," Tyler tells him, and his voice is so soft and so honest that I can't help but smile sideways at him. I think I could listen to Tyler say those words over and over again, forever on repeat. I don't think I'll ever get bored of hearing him say it out loud.

"But . . ." Snake tapers off and glances to Emily again, as though he's looking for backup. He must wonder why she's not as shocked as he is and why she's smiling as she watches the scene unfold before her. Snake shakes his head and exhales. "Aren't you guys, like, stepsiblings?"

"Yeah," I say, brave enough to speak up and defend our case. I'm done feeling as though I'm doing something wrong just because I fell for my stepbrother. I know it's okay. "So we're not related by blood," I explain. "We didn't grow up together so we don't view each other as siblings. Get it?" I widen my eyes at him as innocently as I can, praying that he'll understand and that he'll hopefully come to terms with it. Right now, he still looks a little taken aback.

"Uhh . . . So are you guys dating or what?" he asks. He grips the edge of the kitchen worktop with one hand and then scratches his head with the other. "Is this even real right now or are you guys just messing with me?"

"We're not dating," Tyler answers in reply to his first question, his voice firm. "It's complicated. Just tell me what's going through your mind right now."

Snake shrugs. "I mean, it's a little weird," he admits. "My parents are totally religious. I'm pretty sure they'd expect me to report you guys to Jesus." He eases up a little, rolling his eyes, then turning to pull open a cupboard door and searching around inside it. He pulls out a bag of Doritos and opens it up. As he leans back against the farthest worktop, he tosses a couple chips into his mouth and chews loudly while studying Emily. "What do you think about all of this?" he asks her after a minute.

"I already knew," Emily says with a shrug. She shuffles the scraps of paper in her hands. "It doesn't bother me."

Snake munches on several more chips as he thinks, tilting his head a degree to the side. "It's a little weird," he says again, "but I don't have a problem with it." He starts to smile but it quickly transforms into a smirk instead as he raises an eyebrow at Tyler. "So do you guys have kinky family traditions?"

Both Tyler and I let out a laugh at the exact same time, but our moment of relief doesn't last long. There's a knock at the door that draws all of our attention. Not just any old knock, either, but a pounding rap that echoes around the apartment. It's relentless and so forceful that it's blatantly obvious it's fueled by anger. I glance to Tyler as panic sweeps through me. It's late at night. We're all here. There's only one other person who'd turn up at this time and there's only one person who could possibly be livid enough to bang on the door like that. Tyler realizes this too, because his eyes pool with dread as he swallows. We both know it's Dean. Tiffani must have finally told him the truth.

"Don't open the door," Snake blurts out quickly in a low voice, squeezing the bag of Doritos tight in his hand. "Sounds like a cop."

"It's not a cop," I say quietly, but my eyes never leave the door. Dean's still knocking. After a second he yells my name, and the moment I hear the strain in his voice, my heart breaks. He definitely knows. He knows the truth and he found out in the worst way possible. I know I have to open the door. I've got to face him, however much I really don't want to.

Tyler, Snake and Emily watch me in silence as I force my body across the apartment. My legs feel stiff and my stomach feels unsettled, and when I reach the door I slowly unlock it. I pull it open.

Dean's standing before me, breathing heavily as his tightened fist pauses mid-air, ready to keep knocking. His furious eyes meet mine, and my entire body freezes, the blood in my veins thinning as my limbs give way. The expression in his eyes is something I've never, ever seen before. They're so dark, so sharp and so pained. It's so not Dean, and that's what's so frightening. His cheeks are a flaming red as the anger consumes him. "Is it true?" he asks, voice strained.

I grip onto the door even harder than I already am as I keep holding it open, and I feel so sick that I don't think I can possibly speak. I squeeze my eyes shut and hang my head low. I can't bear to look at him. It hurts too much, but my silence tells him everything he needs to know. My silence tells him that it's true, that I've been in love with Tyler this entire time.

Dean blows out a long breath as he processes this, and I can sense him shaking his head for a while, right before he demands, "Who?"

Now I really do have to look up. My eyebrows furrow in confusion as I study him, tears welling in my eyes as I consider the harsh reality of the situation. I knew Dean would get hurt at the end of this. I knew it straight from the moment I arrived in this city, right from the second Tyler made it clear he wasn't over me. It was inevitable. We had no other choice. If we didn't tell him the truth, he'd get hurt. If we did tell him the truth, he'd still get hurt. That we understood. Dean's question, however, I certainly don't understand. "What?"

"Who have you been cheating on me with?" he spits. His voice is seething with contempt as he glares at me in disgust. I can't blame him. I hate myself for all of this too. "At least have the decency to tell me."

My throat tightens. *Of course.* Of course Tiffani didn't mention Tyler. Of course she would want to make me admit it on my own. I don't know if I can, though. I don't know if I can say Tyler's name. That would hurt Dean too much. I could lie. I could refuse to tell him or I could blurt out a fake name, but as I look at him again—really, really look at him—I see his agonized eyes, and I realize that honesty is really the only thing I can give him right now. I can't lie to him anymore.

Forcing myself to keep breathing, I throw a glance over my shoulder. Snake's leaning over the worktop, tossing chips into his mouth as he watches Dean and I with extreme interest, and Emily is still gnawing on her pen as she listens, but she at least makes the effort to appear inconspicuous about the fact that she's watching the fallout, because she angles her face down toward her notebooks all while looking at us out of the corner of her eye, and either Dean hasn't noticed that we have company or he simply doesn't care. Tyler, however, is already on his way over.

He stops directly behind me, placing his hand on the door too, just above mine. Now that he's holding it open instead, I let go and focus on Dean again. He's still waiting for an answer, growing more enraged with each second that passes.

I'm glad that Tyler's come over, though. I'm relieved that I'm not doing this on my own, that he's by my side, and that we're in this together.

I sense Tyler take a deep breath from behind me, and he dares to breathe the words, "She's been cheating on you with me."

Dean flinches, his entire face consumed by disbelief as he steps into the lobby, backing away from us. He shakes his head fast. "What are you talking about?"

"Dean," I whisper, my voice hitching in my throat. I swallow back the nerves, fighting the urge to cry. "I love you. *So* much." It hurts to say it, because it's true, and that's the worst part about this. I do love him. Perhaps all of this would be much easier if I didn't. "It's just that I love Tyler too."

"What do you mean?" Dean now looks more confused than furious. Our words don't seem to be sinking in. Glancing between Tyler and me, he moves his lips as though he's attempting to say something, but the words evade him.

"Look," Tyler starts, stepping forward. He tries to place his hand on Dean's shoulder, but Dean aggressively shrugs it off, backing even further out into the lobby. Tyler continues, spluttering out an explanation as a messy string of words. "I'm the other guy she's been seeing. We didn't set out for it to happen like this. Honestly, we didn't, but we couldn't help it. You think I'd *choose* to fall for my goddamn stepsister? Because I didn't. It's just the way things have turned out and we were . . . we were gonna tell you. Trust me, we've wanted to for a long time, but we didn't know how. I'm sorry, man. I really fucking am, but I—I need her."

Dean stays silent for several long moments, his mind trying to take in the new information he's just been hit with. "The two of you . . ." he starts, struggling to get the words out at first. Curling his hands into fists by his sides, he flashes his glare to me. "How long has this been going on for?"

"Two years," I whisper. I know I'm going to burst into tears any second. I can feel them pressing at my waterlines, fighting to break free. I will them not to. "I fell for Tyler before I fell for you."

"Two years?" Dean echoes, gaping at me in disbelief, his eyes dilating with both disappointment and fury as he discovers that the entire time I've been with him, my heart has been in two different places. He's trying to make sense of it all, and when he finally does he takes a step forward to close the small distance between him and Tyler. He edges his face toward Tyler's, his lips pressed into a bold line as his pained, vicious eyes scour Tyler's expression. Finally, their eyes lock, only inches from one another. "Have you slept with her?" Dean asks slowly. The question shatters him. He doesn't want to hear the answer. He really doesn't. "Have you fucking slept with her?"

"Man, look," Tyler tries, but attempting to muster up an explanation couldn't be more pointless right now. His best friend has already snapped.

"You fucking asshole!" Dean snarls. His knuckles turn white as he raises his fists, and within a split second he spirals his left into the side of Tyler's face, just below his eye.

Tyler stumbles backward into the apartment, his body nudging mine, and I lose my balance. I fall back a step, as does Tyler, and both Snake and Emily gasp from somewhere in the background. I forgot they were still watching. Emily's now on her feet, her jaw hanging open as she struggles to decide whether or not she should get involved. Snake's still ramming more chips into his mouth as he observes the scene with raised eyebrows.

Tyler straightens up again as he regains his balance, narrowing his eyes across the room to Dean as he enters the apartment, fists still tightly curled. "Go for it," he orders firmly with a nod. "Hit me again. I deserve it. C'mon."

Dean doesn't object. Within seconds, he swings at Tyler once more, his knuckles grinding into the center of Tyler's cheek with a dull aching sound. Dean's cheeks are flaring hot with rage and he lifts his fists again, ready to throw another punch.

Slowly, Tyler rubs the side of his face, massaging away the ache as his eyes start to look lethal. They never leave Dean's. "Alright," he says sharply, voice threatening. "Hit me again and I'm hitting you back twice as hard."

I suck in a horrified gasp as Dean spins his fist through the air once more, but Tyler swiftly blocks the hit, their bodies lunging into each other. They spiral backward, tumbling across the apartment as Emily darts out of the way just before they collapse into the back of the couch. Dean finally gets that third punch in, catching Tyler hard right on the bridge of his nose.

Tyler has lost his temper for the first time in years, and he's so riled up by this point that the depths of his eyes are now like storms, fierce and dangerous and unpredictable. He winds back his right arm and slams his fist into Dean's jaw. His biceps are bulging, all his strength being transferred into his hands as he continues to spin his fist at Dean, hitting him so fast and so relentlessly that Dean doesn't even stand a chance at swinging back.

"Tyler, stop it!" I scream, but it comes out as nothing

more than a strangled cry. I rush over, attempting to grab at the back of Tyler's T-shirt to pull him away from Dean, but it's like he doesn't even notice that I'm there, because as he continues to throw punches each second, he ends up almost elbowing me in the face. I stumble backward, pressing my hands to my cheeks. I'm not sure what I'm supposed to do.

Somehow, Dean manages to duck down, ramming his body into Tyler's chest as he shoves him backward, both of them flying into the coffee table in the center of the living room. There's a tremendous crash as the glass shatters beneath them and a sickening thud as Tyler's body hits the floor first, surrounded by tiny shards of glass and all of Emily's scraps of paper. It doesn't stop them, though. There's so much adrenaline running through both their veins right now that they don't feel any pain whatsoever.

"Do something!" I scream at Snake, firing my eyes over to him as he continues to watch from the safety of the kitchen. He's the only one who's strong enough to help, and I don't even realize I'm crying until now.

"Alright, alright," Snake says loudly, tossing the bag of Doritos onto the worktop and quickly rushing around the counter into the living room. Rolling up his sleeves, he edges around the couches and grabs at Dean, wrapping his arms tightly around his torso as he tugs him up off of Tyler. "Fucking cut it out already!" he yells. Roughly, he throws Dean to one side, toward me.

Even Emily rushes in to help, extending her hand to Tyler as she pulls him up from the ground. His jaw is clenched tightly as he glares at Dean from across the room, but then the adrenaline rush seems to fade, because he glances down at himself and his eyes soften up. There's a lot of glass stuck to him and he doesn't hesitate to reach for the hem of his shirt, quickly pulling it off. A series of scratches now decorate the skin on his back, but I'm more focused on his right arm. There's blood gushing from his tricep, flowing straight down past his elbow, dripping onto the carpet. When he finally notices it, all he can do is blink as Emily runs into the kitchen to grab the first-aid kit.

With tears flowing down my cheeks, I glance over to Dean to see if he's okay. He doesn't look too hurt in comparison with Tyler, although his jaw is deeply grazed and his left eye is swollen. Panting heavily, he squeezes that eye half shut as he looks back at me.

"Get outside," he orders, his voice still as harsh as it was when he first turned up at the door. He doesn't wait for me. Storming across the apartment, he stomps out the door and into the lobby.

Feeling sick to the pit of my stomach, I look back to Tyler before I make my move. He's still standing amongst the glass where the coffee table once stood, his expression a little spaced out, as though he's in a daze. Emily's by his side again and Snake is offering his assistance, the two of them tossing bandages around. I want nothing more than to help too. After all, I caused all of this, but I know that right now I need to deal with Dean.

Trembling with nerves, I force myself toward the door, following Dean out into the lobby. The second I get there and stand before him, he slams the door shut behind us. This time it appears he doesn't want an audience, and at this point I feel too broken to speak, so I don't. I just wipe the tears away while I struggle to meet his eyes.

"You've been cheating on me," Dean mutters, like he

needs to say it out loud so that he'll believe it. Cautiously, his narrowed eyes meet mine, and my heart shatters at his expression. Devastated. Destroyed. "I've loved you and the entire time . . . the whole entire time you've had this thing with Tyler. He's my best friend, Eden! He's your brother!"

"I'm sorry!" I cry, my voice cracking. It's far too late for apologies, but it's the only thing I can do. I don't think Dean'll ever forgive me. I can tell by the loathing that has spread over his features. I'm not used to seeing Dean like this. I'm used to seeing his soft eyes and his gentle smile. I don't think I'll ever witness them again. "I don't know what else to say."

"Don't ever talk to me again," he warns. His voice is raspy and coarse. Taking a step back, he increases the distance between us and roughly shoves his hand into the back pocket of his jeans, pulling out his wallet. His grazed cheek has started to bleed and I fight the urge to touch him, to help. "Here," Dean spits after a few seconds. Harshly, he tosses a five-dollar bill at me. It hits my chest and I catch it before it falls to the ground, and when I glance down to look at it, I realize it's *our* five-dollar bill. I look back up, my heart breaking even more than it already is. My lips are quivering as Dean mutters, "Five bucks for both of you to stay the hell out of my life."

Stuffing his wallet back into his pocket, he rubs at his cheek and turns his back on me. Without waiting a second longer, he storms off, marching down the lobby toward the elevator without even so much as a glance over his shoulder. I watch him leave, tears streaming down my cheeks as I stare after him, feeling entirely helpless. I press my back to the door of Tyler's apartment as my knees weaken beneath me and I simply cannot remain standing any longer, so I slide down the door into a seated position. Burying my head in my hands, I sob even harder, and I listen to the sound of Dean leaving.

The one thing I always hoped was that I would never lose him. I always hoped he'd be able to understand and be able to forgive us, even if it took a while. I always hoped Dean would be okay, but I clearly didn't hope long and hard enough, because everything I hoped wouldn't happen is exactly what has.

28

The following morning, there's some tension between us all in the apartment. I sensed it from the moment I woke up a couple hours ago. No one has been talking much, all four of us silently pivoting around one another. I think Snake is still trying to come to terms with the truth about Tyler and me, because every time I come within a two-foot radius of Tyler I notice Snake studying us intensely from afar. Tyler is quieter than usual today. I understand, because I am too. It's hard to be bubbly when I feel so lost and upset over everything that has happened. Tyler and I don't want to talk about what went down last night. We don't want to talk about Dean. Dean, who I haven't heard from since he turned his back on me last night. I'm not surprised. I doubt I'll ever hear from him again, let alone the very next morning. I haven't heard anything from Tiffani either. No texts flaunting her glee at being able to tell Dean the truth. No more sadistic taunts. Just silence. Rachael is the only one who's messaged me, and it was for the sole purpose of demanding an explanation as to what's going on, so I'm meeting her for coffee soon. I'm dreading it.

Exiting the laundry room after miserably shoving mounds of clothes into the dryer for a half-hour, I make my way through to the kitchen and steal a glance at the clock on the wall. It's nearing 11:30. I shift my gaze over to the living room, where Tyler and Snake are musing about the results of some football game. The room seems a little bare without the coffee table. It took us forever to clean up last night, and now we're no longer allowed to walk into the living room barefoot, just in case there are still some pieces of glass hidden in the carpet.

"I'm gonna get going," I say. I've been ready for a while now, but I've kept myself busy while I wait for the right time to leave. I don't want to be there too early, but I don't want to be late, either.

Tyler immediately gets to his feet, his forehead creasing with concern. His entire upper right arm is still wrapped in gauze. The glass cut him up pretty bad. "Are you sure you don't want me to come?"

"I think it's just better if I explain it to her on my own," I say, offering him a smile of appreciation at the offer. Of course I'd love for Tyler to be by my side, but I know it's really only me who Rachael wants to talk to. I have to face her alone. "I shouldn't be too long."

"Eden," Snake says, snapping his fingers once in the air to grab my attention. When I look to him, he grins. "Tell Rachael I'll come by her hotel tonight at eight to pick her up."

I fold my arms across my chest and frown at him, suspicious of his motives. "You *are* aware that she leaves tomorrow, right?"

"Eden," he says again, his tone stern as he shakes his head at me. He straightens up, looking back at me from the couch and pressing both hands to his heart. "Don't you believe in true love? It has no boundaries. Distance ain't nothin' but a number." He tries to keep a straight face, attempting to look sincere, but he can't hold it for long: The words have only just left his lips when he snickers and drops his hands from his chest.

"Give me a break." Rolling my eyes, I laugh and reach for my keys on the worktop before heading for the door. Of course, I do throw a glance over my shoulder to Tyler before I leave. He's still frowning at me. He looks helpless, like he wants to come with me so that I don't have to explain our situation all on my own. I can only shrug and force myself to smile reassuringly back at him, despite how nervous I'm beginning to feel. Without hesitating, I leave the apartment.

I take the stairs rather than the elevator, and as I make my way down all twelve flights of them I fire Rachael a text to let her know that I'm on my way. I'm meeting her at Joe Coffee, just around the block. I've only been there once, with Tyler, but it's the first place I thought of and I remember their coffee being great. Rachael and I figured meeting at the Lowell would be a bad idea, given that Dean never wants to see me again for the rest of his life. So we're staying clear of the hotel.

As I make my exit from the building, that's when the nerves really begin to take over. I'm not entirely sure what to expect from Rachael. She could be understanding. She could be disgusted. She could be furious. I've got a lot of explaining to do, about both Tyler and Dean. Based on the tone of her messages earlier this morning, I get the impression that she's not very impressed with the decisions I've been making.

Breathing deeply as I turn onto Lexington Avenue, I try to remain as calm as I possibly can be right now. Joe Coffee is just ahead, but I halt and press a hand against the window of a clothing store to steady myself. It takes me at least a minute or so to slow down my breathing and for the knots in my stomach to loosen. I just want all of this to be over already. I just want everyone to know the truth and to accept it. I just want to skip this part entirely, the part where we explain ourselves. Frowning, I realize the next people who are going to find out the truth are our parents.

By the time I reach Joe Coffee, it's just after 11:30. I head inside. It's rather small, with only a few tables. I join the line and pull out a five-dollar bill from the back pocket of my jeans. Glancing down at it, I heave a sigh. It's not *that* bill, but still, it's enough to remind me of it. Am I supposed to keep the five-dollar bill I've shared with Dean for the past two years? The bill that he recklessly wrote all over? Am I supposed to just spend it? Throw it in the trash? Donate it to some homeless guy out on the street? I'm sure he wouldn't mind that the bill is a little wrecked.

The line edges forward, and as I continue to wait I end up staring at the jars of cookies lining the counter. I wonder what Dean's doing right now. How he's feeling. If he's okay. I doubt that he is. Last night, he looked destroyed. I could hear the devastation in his voice and I could see it in his eyes. There's no way he's okay.

My throat feels dry by the time the barista gets to me, so I croak out my order. I skip my usual extra shot of caramel. Too fattening. Swallowing hard, I drum the tips of my fingers along the counter as I wait, stepping to the side. I wish I could ignore the thoughts in my head. I don't want to think about Dean. I don't want to think about how despicable I am and how dreadful I feel.

It doesn't take too long for my latte to be served, steaming hot as requested, and I make my way over to the empty table against the front windows. I set down my coffee and pull out a chair, slowly slumping down into it as my eyes scan the avenue outside. Right now, I could be in the Refinery. I could be staring out at Santa Monica Boulevard. I could be back home, back in Santa Monica. At least it feels that way for a moment. But then I remember that I'm not in the Refinery and that I'm not in Santa Monica; I'm still in New York. Part of me feels homesick. Part of me feels glad.

Joe Coffee has a relaxed ambience, yet I feel anything but. My heart feels like it's throbbing against my chest as my gaze rests on the faint reflection of myself in the window. Right now, I'm not proud of myself. For two years, I've been doing everything wrong. I've messed up, and now I'm wondering if it's even worth it.

Without thinking, I wrap my hands so tightly around my mug that I end up scorching my palms, and I recoil, snapping out of the trance I'm in. Feeling slightly empty, I stare down at my hands for a while, studying the creases of my palms.

"Eden." My eyes drift up to discover Rachael. She's frowning down at me, her lips pressed into a firm line as she pulls out the other chair and sits down, placing her purse carefully onto the table.

I watch her as she looks out the window for a while. The tension is clear. Neither of us is willing to speak first, and the silence feels strained. My throat feels tight, yet I know I need to say something, so I pick up my mug and take a long sip of my latte. Placing it back down on the table, I part my lips, but Rachael turns her head to face me at the exact same time and, surprisingly, she talks first.

"I can't believe you," she says through gritted teeth, her voice low and hushed.

"Rachael . . ." I try to think of what to say, how to explain myself, but she cuts me off before I have the chance to muster up another word.

"No, Eden," she snaps. "I cannot believe you cheated on Dean. And with Tyler. *Tyler!*" She scoffs and swallows hard, shaking her head in disgust and angling her body slightly away from me.

"Please just hear me out," I plead, glancing around us to ensure no one has overheard. I'd much rather the other customers aren't made aware that I'm a horrible person.

"Do you know how long it took me to calm Dean down last night? Do you have any idea at all?" Rachael flashes her eyes back to me, her expression irate and her tone sharp. "Because for three hours straight," she continues, "I had to watch one of my best friends cry. Do you know how shitty that was? Watching him cry because *you* thought it was okay to cheat on him?"

"I didn't think it was okay," I murmur. Looking away from her, I prop my elbows up on the table and bury my head in my hands. I exhale deeply against my palms, squeezing my eyes shut. I'm too ashamed to meet her gaze. I can't justify my decisions and my actions, but I can at least try to explain the reasons behind them, so that's exactly what I do. "I was involved with Tyler before I was involved with Dean," I admit, my voice muffled by my hands. A lump grows in my throat. "All of this started two years ago when I first met all of you. Back then, it just wasn't possible for things to go any further between Tyler and me, so I gave up on him. Not because I wanted to, but because I had to." It still feels unusual talking to people about my relationship with Tyler. Being so open about it . . . It feels odd. Keeping all of this a secret has become far too familiar by now. I tilt my head further down, my words still murmured and quiet. "And then I realized I liked Dean too," I admit. "But there was always *something* still there with Tyler. I've ignored it for a year and half, Rachael. I tried so hard to ignore it, honestly, I did." Swallowing the lump in my throat, I run my hands through my hair. Slowly, I lift my head and glance sideways at Rachael. She's listening carefully. "But then I came over here and I . . . I realized that I really do love Tyler. And that I want to be with *him*. We were going to tell Dean today, but Tiffani beat us to it."

Rachael doesn't say anything for a while. She only glances between the window and me, her lips occasionally twitching. "I can't believe you're even saying that."

"Saying what?"

"That you love Tyler." She quite literally shudders as the words leave her lips. "Like, what the hell, Eden?"

I groan under my breath and reach for my latte again, taking a long sip to buy time as I try to piece together a logical explanation. I can imagine it being hard for someone to comprehend unless they've ever been in the same situation under the exact same circumstances. "Let me put it into perspective for you," I say. Leaning forward and shifting to the edge of my chair, I look at her hard as I place my mug back down. "Imagine your parents are divorced. Then imagine your dad got married to, say . . . Stephen's mom."

Rachael tries to suppress the blush that rises to her cheeks, gnawing on her lips as she listens to me. Using Stephen to get through to her is the only thing I can think of. The only thing that'll make sense to her.

"So that means Stephen would then be your stepbrother. But would you *really* view him as your brother? No blood relation," I clarify with great emphasis, and then fold my arms across my chest. "He would literally just be some stranger who you're forced to consider a sibling. You can't help it if you fall for him, can you? What if that person is The One, and the only thing stopping you from being together is some fucking marriage certificate between your parents? Because that's what's happened to Tyler and me," I say, "and it sucks, Rachael. It really sucks." I let out a long breath as I shake my head, saddened by the reality of it all. If my dad and Ella weren't together, being in love with Tyler would be totally fine. But they *are* together, so being in love with Tyler is considered unacceptable. Glancing away from Rachael, I fix my eyes on the sidewalk outside again as I slump back against my chair.

"I've looked at the two of you as siblings for years," Rachael says quietly, "so obviously it's freaking me out. Why didn't you say anything before? I'm your best friend. Why didn't you tell me?"

"I was scared," I admit with a shrug. I still am scared, just not as much as I used to be. The thought of keeping my relationship with Tyler a secret forever is definitely scarier than the thought of telling our parents. "I felt ashamed of it too. I felt like I was doing something wrong, but I'm over that now. I know it's okay to feel the way I feel about him." I glance sideways at her to gauge what she's thinking, and I'm relieved to find that she no longer looks as angry as she did when she first arrived. She just looks overwhelmed by it all, like there are a hundred questions running through her mind that she's dying to ask. And she does.

"Do your dad and Ella know? Your mom?"

"We're telling them when we get home," I say. I try not to dwell on this thought for too long. I might not be quite as nervous or apprehensive about it anymore, but that doesn't mean I'm still not dreading it. If I overthink it too much, I'll end up thinking of everything that could go wrong.

"And then what?" Rachael presses, tilting her head. Our voices have risen from low whispers to relatively normal levels. The churning and the steaming and the clicking of the coffee machines are giving us no choice. "You're gonna get together?"

"I don't know."

Rachael frowns and throws her hands up in frustration. "Then what's the point? What was the point in fucking Dean over like this if you and Tyler aren't even going to get together?" Her chair screeches against the floor as she pushes herself away from the table and gets to her feet. "Honestly, I don't know what you're thinking," she says. Grabbing her purse from the table, she backs a few steps away from me. "Dean loves you. You know that. He's been nothing but good to you since the day you met him, yet you're choosing Tyler over him? What do you even see in Tyler? You know what they say about kids who've been abused," she murmurs, reaching for the door. A couple people from the communal table behind us have glanced up, surprised by the topic of conversation. Rachael doesn't even flinch, just shrugs and pulls open the door as she finishes. "They end up being abusive too when they grow up. Don't come crawling back to Dean when Tyler turns vicious."

I drop my hands to my lap, where Rachael can't notice that they're balled into fists. My teeth grind together as I will myself not to explode. I even bite back the shocked gasp that's rising in my throat. I'm well aware that Rachael has never really liked Tyler, despite the fact that they've always been in the same friendship circle, but that doesn't give her the right to be downright rude and nasty about him. She doesn't know him the way I do. She doesn't understand how hard he's tried to fix things, to be better. Trying to keep calm, I wrap my hands around my latte again, turning to face the window once more. "Have a nice flight home tomorrow," I say stiffly. I refuse to listen to her opinion on Tyler. I don't care what she thinks about him and I don't care if she accepts the two of us together or not. I really, really don't care anymore. I'm over it. "By the way," I say, crossing one leg over the other and reaching for my coffee, "Stephen says be ready for eight."

And with that, a draught breezes over me as the door to Joe Coffee falls shut behind her. Rachael doesn't hang around outside, only disappears out of view within a matter of seconds. Letting out a breath I didn't know I was holding, I drop my gaze to the table and focus instead on the steamy wisps that rise from my latte.

I don't think I could be any more relieved to know that Rachael, Dean, and Tiffani are heading home tomorrow. The past few days have flown by in what feels like a painful blur, and I'm glad I no longer have to face them. At least until next week. Tyler and I are heading home too in just four days' time, on Wednesday evening. Maybe by then Rachael's anger and disbelief will have subsided, and maybe by that point I'll be able to talk to her again. Maybe by then she'll have forgiven me. Likewise, maybe I'll have forgiven her for the remark about Tyler. Maybe, just maybe, she'll finally understand that I didn't mean for any of this to happen.

I hang around at Joe Coffee for a while. It's nice to be alone again. As alone as I can be in New York City. I trace circles on the wood of the table. I head back over to the counter for a second latte without feeling guilty about it. *And* I add a shot of caramel. I study the people walking by the window as they head along Lexington Avenue. I take a few minutes to reply to some texts from my mom and Ella, omitting the fact that I'm no longer dating Dean. Mom loves Dean. So does Ella. Sweetest guy around, they would say.

When I finally glance at my watch, I realize I've been here for almost two hours. It's nearly 1:30. Tyler must be wondering where I am by now, because although our relationship is complicated it certainly doesn't take two hours to explain it.

So I head back to the apartment, my pace slow and out of sync with the rest of the city. I walk as though I don't have a motive, because I don't. I'm just strolling down Lexington Avenue and onto Seventy-fourth Street feeling . . . Well, nothing. That's just it. I don't feel empty or deflated or sad, nor do I feel overjoyed or thrilled. I just feel nothing. I'm numb.

By the time I climb up the twelve flights of stairs to Tyler's apartment, half of me is ready to collapse into bed and sleep for an eternity. The other half? The other half is ready to kiss Tyler endlessly.

And when I unlock the door and push it open, Tyler is the first person to greet me. He's already walking over from the kitchen with a butter knife in his hand, his forehead creased with concern the exact same way it was before I left. I highly doubt he's relaxed since the moment I walked out the door.

"How'd it go?" he asks immediately. He pushes the door shut behind me as I head into the living room, and then he stands still as he waits for an answer.

"Let me put it this way," I murmur, pressing my lips and

frowning. "When we get home, I don't think we're gonna have many friends."

Tyler's eyebrows slowly arch. "I'm guessing it didn't go that great."

Cocking my head to one side and glancing over his shoulder, I run my eyes over Snake and Emily. They're in the kitchen, arguing with plates in their hands while waving cutlery around. In this apartment, making lunch is always a group task, and it never runs smoothly. I look back to Tyler and sigh, saying, "I swear, you better be worth all of this. You better be worth losing Dean and you better be worth arguing with Rachael for."

Almost in slow motion, the corners of Tyler's lips pull up into the smallest of smirks. He takes a step toward me, his eyes smoldering. "I don't know about that," he says quietly, "but I really hope so." His smirk widens into a grin, mirroring my own smile, both our faces aglow. Carefully, he cups my jaw with one hand and leans down to kiss me.

"Hey!" Snake yells from the kitchen. It's so abrupt that Tyler and I immediately pause, flinching away from each other before our lips can even brush. We both flash our eyes over to Snake, only to find that he and Emily are staring back at us from behind the kitchen counter. They're both smiling, their expressions playful. With a plate in his hand, Snake points it toward us. "No immoral kissing in the living room!"

And for once, all four of us laugh.

29

Four days later, I'm struggling to accept that my time in New York has come to an end. For an entire year I counted down the days until I could come to the city, and now the experience I was so excited about is all over. My six weeks are up. Tyler's year here is done. It's time to head back to Santa Monica and the beach and the promenade and the pier. It's time for us to go home.

As I'm rolling my suitcase into the living room, I'm beginning to feel nostalgic. It's true what people say about New York City—it really, really is incredible. I'll miss being woken up by the sound of the traffic outside. I'll miss the constant flow of people on the sidewalks. I'll miss riding the godawful subway. Central Park. The endless buzz of noise. Baseball. The hard accents. I think I'll miss every single thing about this city, and it's clear now why it's so iconic.

"Are you ready?" I hear Tyler ask as he walks up behind me.

I glance over my shoulder to him and wistfully sigh, my smile sad. "I guess so."

He looks younger today, mostly due to the fact that this morning he decided to shave completely. Now there's no stubble whatsoever and his jaw is smooth and bare. It's knocked a few years off him, so he looks nineteen for once.

Walking across the room, he dumps his black duffel bag on the couch and then turns back to face me, eyeing up my suitcase. It's completely overpacked. It could be that I've bought a lot of stuff while I've been in the city or it could be that everything has just been thrown in carelessly, but either way, it looks so huge that I'm starting to worry that my luggage will be over the weight limit. It took me five minutes to zip it up, and even now I can see it threatening to burst open.

"You know, you could have just shipped half your stuff when I did," Tyler says, finally letting out a laugh. When he walks over, he tilts my suitcase onto the floor and crouches down, opening it. I fold my arms across my chest and watch him as he grabs a pile of my things, then moves back across the room to place them into his own luggage. "Try it now," he says.

Rolling my eyes, I attempt to zip up my suitcase once more, and this time it closes much more willingly. I straighten up and smile, and then quickly dart into his bedroom one last time to grab my shoes and my backpack. They're both lying on the floor, but before I scoop them up I run my eyes over the room. It's completely bare. No posters on the walls. Nothing in the closet. The room usually smells like Tyler, of cologne and firewood, but not today. Today the room is empty. Tyler's car and the majority of his belongings were shipped across the country three days ago.

The past few days, we've hardly been in the apartment. We've been too busy trying to fill our final days with as many memories as possible, like revisiting the main tourist attractions once more before we leave and searching for coffee shops that we haven't yet stopped at and playing baseball again at Central Park and spending an entire day traveling between each of the four other boroughs. Last night, Tyler even took me to Pietrasanta again to conclude our summer the exact same way we started it, and it couldn't have been any more perfect.

Slipping on my Converse and carrying my backpack through into the living room, I frown. Tyler's smile fades, his expression questioning. "I don't want to go home," I admit.

Tyler doesn't reply for a while, only looks at me with his head angled a degree to the side, his eyes smoldering. "Aren't you excited to tell your dad that you're so deeply in love with me?" he finally says, trying his hardest to suppress both his laughter and his smirk.

"Oh, I'm sure he'll be thrilled." My voice is dripping with sarcasm, yet I'm smiling. "You know, since you're quite the charmer."

Tyler chuckles as he shakes his head. We both know he and my dad have never really bonded all that well, so out of all the guys I could have fallen in love with, I don't think my dad will be too impressed that it's Tyler. And that's if he can even get over the fact that we're stepsiblings first.

The door to Snake's bedroom swings open and Snake sticks his head around it, leaning against the frame. "You guys are *still* here?"

"You think we'd leave without saying goodbye to you, Stephen Rivera?" Tyler shoots back, narrowing his eyes challengingly as he advances across the room toward his roommate.

"God, I'm so glad I'm getting rid of you," Snake mutters, and he grins as they embrace one another in one of those half-hugs, thumping each other on the back.

It feels just like yesterday morning all over again, when all three of us were saying goodbye to Emily. It was just after

5AM and we were all half asleep, and Emily was getting upset. We promised we'd all stay in touch. Even joked about a yearly reunion. These kinds of goodbyes are the scary goodbyes. The goodbyes where you know the chances of seeing each other again are very slim. Emily will be back in London by now, and by tonight Tyler and I will be in Santa Monica. Snake's the only one left in New York, with his final year of college still to go. Honestly, I don't think I could have asked for two better people to enjoy my trip to New York with, and I still couldn't be more grateful for their acceptance. I'm really going to miss them both.

Tyler and Snake reflect on the past year for a while, laughing and playfully insulting each other before sighing. Snake even draws me into a hug at that point. He tells me that I'm not that bad, and I tell him that he's not that bad either. We smile at each other before he musters up one final Portland joke, and then Tyler and I grab our luggage and we leave the apartment for the very last time.

It's nearing eight back on the West Coast by the time we arrive in LA. We're at LAX, of course, and Tyler and I spend a good twenty minutes lingering by the baggage carousel before our luggage is the last to roll around. It's what we get for being among the first few people to check in back at Newark. And even though Tyler has grown gruff with impatience, he manages to lighten up again by the time we start to make our way across the arrivals level of Terminal 6.

It doesn't take us long to spot Jamie. It's hard to miss him. He comes out of nowhere and makes a beeline straight for us, throwing a hand up into the air to grab our attention. His entire face is dominated by a grin. It's a rather warm feeling seeing Jamie happy to see us, and for a moment coming back home doesn't seem so bad anymore.

"There he is," I say, and when I glance sideways at Tyler, he's barely even listening to me. He's too focused on his brother, his smile reaching his eyes.

Only a few moments later Jamie finally reaches us, and Tyler immediately draws him into a hug. I hang back a step or two, my own smile growing as I watch the two of them. After spending six weeks with Tyler, I've forgotten that the rest of our family hasn't seen him in over a year.

Tyler pulls away after a while, resting his hands on Jamie's shoulders as he studies him with wide eyes. "Man, I hardly even recognize you!" Tyler says with a laugh. "When'd you get this tall? And what'd you do to your hair?"

Jamie shrugs a little sheepishly, awkwardly reaching up to touch his hair. I don't really see that much of a drastic change, mostly because I haven't been gone for so long, but Jamie *has* grown several inches and cut his hair over the past year. It's been cut short for months now and his height is quickly catching up with Tyler's. Both of them are way taller than me.

"Yeah, yeah, whatever," Jamie says, slightly embarrassed. He averts his eyes to me instead. "How was New York?"

"Amazing," I say. I refrain from exchanging a knowing glance with Tyler, and instead I bite my lip and keep my eyes trained on Jamie. "Did you manage to get here alright?"

"Yeah. Eventually," he answers. Reaching into the back pocket of his jeans, he pulls out a set of car keys. "Ended up on the lower level first. Finally found my way up to the parking lots. Mom's directions weren't that clear."

"Hey," Tyler says, lunging forward. He snatches the keys from Jamie's hand and holds them up, scrutinizing them before he shifts his gaze back to his brother. "She gave you the Range Rover? What the hell? Mom never let me drive it when I was your age. Didn't she buy you that BMW? Where's that?"

"Uh, I totaled the front bumper last week," Jamie admits, dropping his eyes to the floor of the terminal as color rises to his cheeks. "I hit a street light. It's at Hugh Carter's garage right now, so you can tell Dean to fix it up real nice for me and then throw in a discount while he's at it," he jokes, but neither Tyler nor I laugh.

We exchange a sideways glance, our smiles faltering. Tyler runs a hand through his hair and sighs just as there's an announcement over the intercom. It allows for us to be silent for a moment without Jamie wondering why we've gone quiet. Perhaps we should mention the fact that Dean no longer wants to deal with Tyler and me and that I don't think Dean or his dad will be offering discounts to our family on our car repairs anytime soon, but it just doesn't feel like the right time.

"Let's get going," Tyler says, shrugging the strap of his duffel bag further along his shoulder as he nudges Jamie forward, nodding toward the exit. "I wanna see these shitty driving skills of yours."

"Better than yours," Jamie mutters, but he's still grinning as he grabs the keys back from Tyler. He dangles them from his index finger and I notice that there's a photo attached amongst the collection of key rings Ella has added over the years. It's only a small photo, one of Tyler, Jamie and Chase when they were much younger. I bet Ella can't wait to see her eldest son. I can picture her already, probably pacing the house as she waits for him to return.

As Tyler and Jamie head off, Tyler's arm slung over his brother's shoulders, I wheel my suitcase along behind them. I slowly exhale, finding myself smiling almost sadly. It's hard to believe that Tyler's been gone for an entire year, and honestly, I'm not quite sure how he's managed to cope with being on his own for so long. Sure, he might have smoked weed again over the past year, but not anymore. It's comforting to know that he's here again. That he's home.

"Hey, have I ever hit a street light?" Tyler shoots back at Jamie, his tone light and playful. "Never, because I'm the better driver."

"Really?" Jamie asks with an air of sarcasm. "Because your car arrived last night and you definitely need some new tires. What the hell did you do to them?"

"You can blame Eden for that," Tyler murmurs, glancing over his shoulder at me. He smirks and I glare back in return, pushing the back of his shoulder.

We head out of the terminal, making our way across the roadways to the Terminal 6 parking structure, following Jamie deep inside the lower level until we spot Ella's car. It's wedged into a tight spot and Tyler immediately clucks his tongue in disapproval as Jamie pops the trunk.

"What?" Jamie demands as he folds his arms across his chest in agitation, lingering by the door to the driver's seat.

"Shit parking skills too," Tyler comments. Throwing his duffel bag into the trunk, he turns around and takes my suitcase from me, still smiling as he places it inside. It still weighs a tonne and I couldn't even pull it off the baggage carousel on my own without his help, let alone lift it, so I say thanks and then slide into the backseat.

Tyler slams the trunk shut again with a thud before both he

and Jamie climb into the car, throwing several more remarks at one another while Jamie starts up the engine and begins the difficult task of navigating his way out of the airport grounds. Kudos to him for offering to pick us up, because if I were him, I'd have definitely said no. Far too many looping roads. Far too easy to end up on the wrong boulevard.

Nonetheless, with Tyler's help, Jamie manages to get us onto Lincoln Boulevard, heading north straight for Santa Monica. It's the easiest route back to the city. I relax in the backseat as he drives, slumped against the leather while I gaze out of the window. It feels strange being able to see what's in the distance. It feels odd not having buildings and skyscrapers towering over us. By now the sun has slowly begun to disappear, the sky a gorgeous orange. The radio is playing quietly in the background as Tyler and Jamie talk softly for the majority of the ride, catching up on a year's worth of conversations and laughing every few minutes. I keep out of the conversation and instead fumble around with the AC in the back so that it's directed straight at my face, and then I cross my legs on the seat and close my eyes, resting my head against the window. So peaceful. So chilled out. So California.

Twenty minutes later, just as we're arriving into Santa Monica, my attention is grabbed when I hear Jamie say, "There's something I need to tell you. But later."

"Why not tell me right now?" Tyler asks. Slowly, I peel open my eyes slightly, not moving an inch as I listen.

"Uh," Jamie says, glancing in the rearview mirror at me. I squeeze my eyes shut again, hoping that I'll pass as being asleep. "Eden's here."

"And?" Tyler fires back. His tone is no longer gentle, but aggravated. "Unless you've knocked up that girlfriend of yours or something, then whatever you gotta tell me you can tell me right now. What is it?"

When I peek through my eyelids again, I notice the way Jamie turns to look directly at the road, both hands gripping the steering wheel. He remains quiet for a while, his posture stiff. Tyler angles his body to face him as he narrows his eyes, waiting. Very slowly, Jamie's shoulders sink as he sighs deeply. "I'm only telling you this because Mom was planning not to, and I just think you should know," he says. He sounds nervous and he pauses again for a long moment. Finally, he glances directly at Tyler, and that's when he says the words I least expect to hear. "Dad's out."

Tyler's lips part. "What?"

"He got out a couple weeks ago," Jamie says, voice feeble. When I glance at the rearview mirror, I can see him frowning. Tyler, however, turns pale as he falls back against the seat, staring blankly out of the windshield as he tries to process the news Jamie has just hit him with. The radio is still playing, the quirky pop song out of place in the tense atmosphere of the car.

I really do open my eyes wide this time, pushing myself up from my slumped position. I'm a little shocked too. I've always known their dad was in prison. I'd only ever imagined him being locked up in a cell. But what I'd never thought about was the fact that one day he'd be getting out, because that's the part you don't think about. You don't think about that person walking the streets again. You don't think about that person having the free will again to do whatever they want. You don't think about that person living a life again. That's the scary part. That's the part that no one wants to think about.

"It's been seven years already?" Tyler asks almost in disbelief as he shoots forward, his body upright. Pressing a hand to the dashboard, he releases his seatbelt and turns directly to face Jamie, eyes fierce, voice angry. "I thought it'd only been six," he snaps. "It's only been fucking six!"

"It's been seven," Jamie mumbles. He glances between Tyler and the road as he tries to focus on his driving, but Tyler's growing fury is making it difficult for him. "Mom's hardly telling me anything," Jamie continues, "but do you remember Wesley Meyer? He came around so often we used to call him Uncle Wes?" Again, he glances quickly at Tyler to gauge his response, but Tyler's only clenching his jaw in return. "Well, Mom thinks Dad's been staying at his place."

"He's in the fucking city?" Tyler hisses, immediately turning off the radio. The car falls silent, the only noise the sound of the engine as we continue through Santa Monica, crossing Pico Boulevard. "He's *here*?"

From the backseat, I feel helpless. There's nothing I can do about the situation, but I do know that Tyler is growing more and more livid with each passing second, so I move forward and place my hand on his shoulder. I squeeze tightly to let him know that I'm here.

"Drive there," Tyler orders out of nowhere, thumping his fist twice against the dashboard as he fixes Jamie with a firm, slightly threatening glare.

"What?"

"Wesley Meyer's place. Right now."

"Tyler . . ." Jamie tapers off and shakes his head. "I'm not driving you over there."

"Alright, then pull over." Angling his body away from Jamie and toward the door instead, he reaches for the handle and glances back at Jamie again over his shoulder, still glaring. Only this time, he's waiting.

"I'm not pulling over," Jamie says. He grips the steering wheel even tighter.

"I'm not kidding, Jay!" Tyler growls, slamming his palm down against the dashboard once again. The abruptness startles Jamie, because he flinches and the car swerves slightly to the right, almost mounting the curb. If Ella's car gets home without a single scratch, then I'm pretty sure that at the very least the dashboard will have some dents in it. "Pull the fuck over."

Groaning, Jamie finally succumbs to the pressure. Pulling up against the sidewalk, he leaves the engine running as he throws open the car door and slides out. "You know this is a stupid idea," he mutters. Kicking at the road, he makes his way around the vehicle.

Tyler's just about to push open his own door, but before he can jump out I hold his shoulder tight against the back of the seat to prevent him from moving. Unbuckling my seatbelt with my free hand, I lean forward over the center console and tilt my head to look at him. "What are you doing, Tyler?"

Now that I can look directly into his eyes, I can tell just how enraged he really is. Part of me can't blame him for being aggravated, but part of me is also wondering what's running through his mind right now. Knowing how irrational Tyler can be, I'm a little concerned. Especially with the way he's looking back at me, his eyes blazing and his jaw tight. Refusing to give me an answer, he shrugs my grip off his shoulder and kicks open the car door, stepping out onto the sidewalk.

"Tyler!" I yell, but he's already out of the car and walking around to the driver's side. Jamie slips into the passenger seat, slamming the door behind him, then folding his arms across his chest in defeat. Even I frown and settle into the backseat again, twiddling my thumbs. I'm unsure of what I'm supposed to do.

Tyler slides into the car behind the wheel, taking a moment or two to adjust to the automatic controls, then he takes off. Ella's car screeches along Ninth Street controlled by Tyler's fury as he continues to head north through the city. I try to catch his eye in the rearview mirror a couple times, but he never seems to be checking it, so he doesn't notice.

"This is why Mom didn't want to tell you," Jamie says, throwing his hands up in exasperation as Tyler runs a stop sign. "She knew you'd flip out."

Tyler doesn't reply to his brother, the same way he didn't reply to me, and I think both Jamie and I have figured out by now that he's done talking. Neither of us attempts to say anything more. We only exchange concerned glances and shrugs as Tyler drives. We also both know exactly where he's heading, yet there's nothing we can do about it. He even taps his index fingers against the steering wheel as the anger continues to build up inside of him.

And in less than ten minutes, the car is crawling eastbound along Alta Avenue as Tyler glances from left to right, his eyes searching. He slams on the brakes at the intersection of Twenty-fifth Street, his glare coming to rest on one specific house. The one before us right now on the corner, with the white bricking and the red roof tiles. It's Wesley Meyer's house, whoever the hell he is, which means that it is also Tyler and Jamie's dad's current place of residence. And of course, that is the sole reason why we're even here. Because of their dad.

Tyler cuts the engine, allowing silence to fall as he stares at the house. That's all he does. Just stares as he breathes heavily, clenching his jaw over and over again. It's like he's mentally fighting with himself over whether or not he should get out of the car.

"So what?" Jamie asks after a minute or so, breaking the tense silence. "You're gonna walk up to that door and tell him you hate him? Throw a punch? Kick his ass?"

Tyler grinds his teeth together and angles his face even more toward the window, as far away from Jamie's stern glare as he can get. "You don't get it," he hisses, and the glass steams up.

"Hey," Jamie says quickly, shaking his head despite the fact that Tyler's not even looking, "you don't think I wanna beat the hell out of him too? For your sake? But c'mon. Think about it. What's the point? It's stupid, and Mom'll only have a breakdown if she knows you went near him."

Jamie's speaking a lot of sense, but it only seems to push Tyler toward the idea of getting out of the car, because that's exactly what he does. He throws open the car door and slides out just as I'm parting my lips to speak, and immediately I jump out too. It's almost like a reflex action to go after Tyler by now, and I run around the vehicle and throw my body in front of his on the middle of the lawn. Pressing my hands hard against his chest, I push him back a step.

"Jamie's right," I say. "You don't want to do this."

"I do." He still has that terrifying look in his eyes that I'm not quite used to anymore. Two years ago, I was. Now? Not so much. It's not him anymore. Tyler lost all that hostility a while ago, and it was replaced by all the positivity that came into his life while using his past as a means to help others.

Yet now it seems like that's all gone again. That aggravation is back. The kid with the hardened expression and the fierce eyes, the kid who spent every second of every day loathing his father is exactly who's standing in front of me right now. "Why the fuck shouldn't I?"

And just like I did back then, I try my best to help to do what's right for him. And right now, the best thing for him is to get away from this house before he does something he'll regret. "Because you've been okay for almost two years now," I whisper. My hands are still pressed to his chest, so I can feel his heart beating hard and fast beneath my palms. "Please don't get wrapped up in all of this mess again. Look what it did to you before, Tyler. Just stay away from him."

"Eden," Tyler says slowly through gritted teeth. Reaching up, he takes both of my hands in his, still holding them against his chest. His heart seems to beat even faster as his eyes soften up for the briefest of moments. "I want him to see me now. I just wanna stand in front of him for the first time in seven years. I need him to know that he messed up, because he doesn't get to be a part of our lives anymore. Not mine, not Jamie's, not Chase's, not Mom's. We're all doing perfectly fucking fine without him now. I want him to know that." Tilting his head down, he sighs and squeezes my hands. After a moment, he glances back up. "*And* maybe swing a fist or two."

"I get it," I say, keeping my voice low. I fear that if we raise our voices any louder, his dad might hear us from inside. That's if he's even here in the first place. "I get that you wanna face up to him. I can't blame you. But Tyler, think about it. What happens if you snap the second you see him again? You're already mad, so just drop it. At least for tonight. You can deal with your dad another time. You need to let all of this sink in first, okay?"

Tyler glances over my shoulder toward the house. He studies it for a while, a range of emotions flickering in his eyes. I can't work out exactly what he's feeling. They change too fast.

Relaxing his jaw, he swallows and looks back to me. "Okay," he whispers. Letting go of my hands, he moves his to my face, gently cupping my cheeks as he tilts my chin up so I can look at him more directly. "Okay." Closing his eyes, he leans in, pressing his lips softly and slowly against mine. It takes me aback for a split second: It's so out of place amidst his rage. I'm not sure what the reason behind it is, whether it's for comfort or for reassurance or both, but I do know that it's clear Tyler has forgotten we're not alone.

As panic sweeps through me, I quickly recoil. Pulling my lips away from Tyler's, I push him away from me and then fire my eyes over to the Range Rover still parked out on the road. Through the windshield, our brother is blinking back at us.

30

Jamie drives in silence. He's back behind the wheel, his lips pressed into a firm line. His eyes don't leave the road, because he doesn't even so much as glance at Tyler or me. I can't figure out if he's stunned or furious or both. Either way, his expression makes it clear that he hasn't taken the news well. Perhaps Tyler could have been less blunt when he told our brother the truth and perhaps I could have made a better attempt at offering an explanation, because now Jamie just looks disgusted. However, the new situation at hand was enough to distract Tyler and get him back into the car and off Wesley Meyer's front lawn.

I'm in the backseat once more, anxiously gnawing on my lower lip and fumbling with my seatbelt while feeling, yet again, rather ashamed. Seeing Jamie appear sickened at the idea of Tyler and me together is giving me absolutely no hope whatsoever for our parents. If our sixteen-year-old brother can't handle it, then I highly doubt Dad and Ella will. Thankfully, we're not heading there right now. We're going to my mom's place. We're breaking the news to her first. Tyler's idea. We were going to wait until tomorrow, but now that Jamie knows, it's best to just tell the rest of our family tonight. Each second, I grow more and more nauseous at the thought of it. The time really is here.

The drive to my mom's place only takes a few minutes. Jamie pulls up behind my car on the sidewalk, leaving the engine running while he remains silent. He doesn't say a single word, nor does he take his hands off the wheel. He just stares out of the windshield with narrowed eyes. Tyler does look at his brother for a long while, trying to catch his eye, but it's useless. Eventually, he just glances over his shoulder to me and shrugs, letting me know that it's time to go.

I release my seatbelt and numbly slip out of the car. There's a frown upon my lips, mostly because I'm feeling incredibly guilty. I can't help it. Tyler and Jamie have always been close, much closer than either of them is with Chase, and they rarely ever argue. But now Jamie just seems pissed off, and I feel like it's all because of me. This tense atmosphere would not be suffocating us right now if I hadn't fallen for Tyler. All I can do now is hope that soon Jamie will come around, the same way I'm hoping Rachael will. But there's absolutely no point in hoping that Dean will ever accept Tyler and me. I'd be deluded if I ever believed that could happen.

Gently closing the car door behind me, I head around to the trunk, where I meet Tyler. He's already hauling my suitcase out onto the sidewalk, expression pained as he tries to offer me a reassuring smile. It doesn't make me feel any better, because there's no genuine reassurance in his features. Tyler's as worried as I am.

Sliding the strap of his duffel bag onto his shoulder, he slams the trunk shut and moves around the vehicle. He stops by the driver's side window and taps his knuckles twice against the glass. Jamie doesn't react to begin with, but when he realizes that Tyler's not going to walk away, he decides to roll the window down. For the first time since we left Wesley Meyer's front lawn, Jamie turns to look at his brother.

"We'll be coming over to the house soon," Tyler murmurs softly, his eyes gentle as he tries to appeal to Jamie's sympathetic side. "So just . . . Just don't say anything. Please. We gotta tell Mom and Dave on our own." Tilting his head down to the ground for a second, he blows out a breath and then glances back up. "Okay?"

Jamie doesn't react, so we can't be sure if he'll rush home and break the news to our parents himself or not. All he does is turn his head away again as he puts the window back up. It forces Tyler to remove his hands from the door and step back, frowning the exact same way that I am. The two of us watch as Jamie drives off, and the Range Rover disappears around the corner only moments later. I don't know about Tyler, but I feel uneasy.

"I guess that could have gone down a whole lot better," Tyler says. As he turns to face me, I notice how his lips have formed a sad smile. Yet it's warm and somehow almost playful, which is enough to make me forget for a second that we're about to walk inside my house and tell my mom the truth.

"Yeah," I say, shrugging my backpack further up my shoulder, "I don't think kissing me in front of him was the best way to break the news."

Slowly, Tyler grins. "My bad."

Rolling my eyes, I pull out the handle of my suitcase and begin to pull it along the path toward the front door. Tyler follows close behind me, so close that I can hear him breathing, and just as he places his hand on the small of my back, the front door swings open. Immediately, his touch disappears.

"You're home!" Mom yells as she hurls herself over the

threshold, rushing toward me. Within a split second I've been drawn into her warm embrace as she wraps her arms tightly around me. She hugs me so tight that I fear I might stop breathing, and just as I'm about to attempt to wriggle my way out of her grip, I hear a familiar loud bark.

Over Mom's shoulder, I can see Gucci bounding out of the house toward me, ears pricked upright, tail wagging fast, tongue out. I squeeze my eyes shut and prepare myself, waiting for the moment that her strong body will knock me to the ground, and that's exactly what happens. She jumps, stretched up on her hind legs, her paws against my chest, and I promptly fall out of Mom's arms. I tumble backward from Gucci's weight, only I don't land on the ground. Tyler catches me before that can happen, my body crashing into his as the two of us fall back a step. Gucci finally drops back down onto all four legs.

"Jeez," I say, brushing myself off as Tyler steadies me. Thankfully, Gucci shifts her attention to him, but as she eagerly circles his legs and loudly sniffs at his boots, her tail repeatedly whacks the back of my knees, so I step away from the two of them and wheel my suitcase back toward my mom.

"She cried for a week straight after you left," Mom says with a laugh, pulling me into another hug. This time, it's only brief, and she stands back to run her eyes twice over me. "But I've definitely missed you way more than she has. I'm so glad you made it home alive."

I roll my eyes, shaking my head at her. "Yep, here I am. Alive. Even after riding the subway and walking around Manhattan on my own and visiting the Bronx," I add, my smile teasing.

Mom looks horrified. "Tyler!"

Tyler glances up from scratching behind Gucci's ears, tilting his face up to look at my mom. "Huh?"

"You took my daughter to the Bronx?" Mom questions, but we all know she's just playing. Sternly, she folds her arms across her chest and taps her foot as she waits for a reply.

"Sorry about that," Tyler apologizes with a smile, patting Gucci's head once more before he straightens up. His eyes, his smile, and his voice are all innocent. "It was for a baseball game. But other than that, I think I took good care of her." His eyes meet mine and his smile widens.

"You convinced me to sit on the edge of the roof of your apartment building," I point out.

He jumps forward quickly, looping his arm around me from behind and pressing his hand gently over my mouth. "Shhh." Shrugging, he nervously laughs and throws my mom another one of his smiles, the type that makes it impossible to be mad at him.

"Oh, Tyler," Mom says with a laugh. Shaking her head, she exhales and studies him with a warm glow to her face. "Welcome home. I bet it feels weird being back. But hey, both of you come on inside and tell us all about New York." Clapping her hands together, she whistles once and calls, "Gucci! Inside!" to which our hyperactive dog responds by leaping back into the house. Mom follows.

Neither Tyler nor I budge an inch, and once Mom disappears, I turn to him and take a deep breath. "So we're really doing this?" I ask, my voice low.

"We sure are," Tyler says without hesitation. Throwing an arm over my shoulders, he pulls me in close and presses his lips to my temple. "I hope your mom isn't looking out the window," he whispers.

I glance sideways at him, only to find that he's smirking. Laughing, I shrug his arm off me and push him away as I reach for my suitcase instead, dragging it toward the open front door. I'm glad that Tyler still has the ability to muster up some humor right now, because it's making this all seem much less daunting, and I'm glad that he's no longer thinking about his dad. I'm happy that right now everything seems okay. Ten minutes from now, I don't know if it still will be.

Tyler follows me into the house, closing the door behind us, and immediately I can smell cinnamon. My forehead creases with worry at the thought of Mom attempting to bake, and I ditch my suitcase by the door and pad my way over to the kitchen, studying the worktops for any catastrophic, deformed scones. Before I can find anything, Mom comes along from the hall with Jack by her side and I instantly stop fumbling around by the cupboards. I can see Tyler rolling his eyes at me.

"So, Eden," Jack urges as he smiles at me with his sparkling white teeth. At the same time, he's fiddling with the watch on his wrist as he adjusts the clasp on it, and I figure from his ruffled, damp hair that he might have just got out the shower. "How was New York?"

"Amazing," I say, but my eyes have wandered to my mom's hands. I study them with great intensity just in case anything major might have taken place while I've been gone. But nope. Still no ring. *Sigh.*

Mom turns to him and rests her hand on his arm, her smile warm. "They look a little tired. How about some coffee?" She throws a pointed glance at both Tyler and me. "You look like you could both do with some good old caffeine," she tells us.

"I'm on it," Jack says, rubbing her shoulder before he brushes past me, heading for the coffee machine.

"That's okay," I say quickly. I fire Tyler a glance and nod once at him, right before I look back to my mom. "We're not staying long. We haven't seen Dad or Ella yet, so we gotta drop by their place too. Actually, Mom, could you just sit down for a sec? You too, Jack."

I think the shaky tone of my voice makes it pretty damn clear that the two of them should be worried, because the moment the words leave my lips, that's exactly how they both suddenly look. Their smiles fade and their eyebrows arch in suspicion. They exchange a cautious glance and then follow me over to the living room.

"Oh God," Mom groans, pressing her hands to her temples as she walks over. Even Gucci comes bouncing back through from the other side of the house as though to hear the news, brushing up against Mom's legs as she sits down. Jack joins her. "What happened in New York? What did you do, Eden?"

When I glance at Tyler, he offers me a small smile of reassurance, and this time it's sincere. He slides his bag off his shoulder, letting it drop to the floor, and then he walks over to me. Pressing a hand to the small of my back, he directs me toward the opposite couch, and we both sit down. When I look up to see my mom and Jack facing back at me with wary gazes, that's when it hits me that we're really doing this. We're really about to confess the truth. We've done it before. We've told Snake the truth—or rather, we've shown him the truth—but telling our parents is different. Ella and my dad are the ones who really matter, because they're *our* parents, but telling my mom is still a big step too.

"Eden?" Mom presses. Anxiously, she tucks stray strands of hair back into her once-neat pin-up. "What is it? You're scaring the hell out of me."

I know that if I stay silent for any longer, Mom will most likely jump to conclusions. She'll think I committed murder in New York. She'll think I robbed a bank. She'll think I broke every single law ever known to mankind, so I know I need to start talking pretty soon. Tyler seems to sense my apprehension, because he leans forward slightly, placing his hand on my knee and squeezing to get my attention. My eyes flicker sideways to meet his, and he looks back at me from beneath his eyelashes, parting his lips as though he's about to speak for me. But thankfully, he doesn't. He only nods. We both know I have to be the one to tell my mom the truth, and I'm hoping that Tyler will do all the talking when it comes to telling Dad and Ella.

I shift my eyes to Gucci. She's sprawled out on the floor by Jack's feet now, breathing heavily. Swallowing the lump in my throat, I let out the breath I've been holding. "What we need to tell you is really important," I begin, still staring at the dog. Tyler's hand has yet to leave my knee. "So please keep an open mind."

"Eden," Mom says. "What's going on?"

I glance up. She's folded her arms across her chest now, her expression growing more stern than worried. Even Jack looks a little exasperated, as though my slow unraveling of the truth is torturing the pair of them. I can't help it. It's hard to force the words out. Tyler squeezes my knee even harder. "Okay," I say, mostly as an attempt to convince myself that I can do this. My stomach twists as I try to meet Mom's eyes, but it's hard. I'm afraid that in a few moments from now they'll pool with disgust and disappointment. "Okay," I say again. Breathing deeply, I rest my eyes on Mom's shoulder, and I force myself to bluntly utter the words I've always dreaded having to say.

Only three words. So simple, and most definitely the easiest way to phrase the truth. And so I murmur, "I love Tyler."

Silence ensues after that. Mom and Jack only stare at me. I want them to say something. Anything. Growing frustrated with the lack of reaction I'm getting, I glance at Tyler for help, but he's too busy furrowing his eyebrows to even attempt to offer me a suggestion. I turn back to my mom, and as though to emphasize my words, I place my hand on top of Tyler's on my knee and shift my body closer to his on the couch. Still no reaction. "Like, *in love* with him," I clarify. She doesn't even blink. "Like, this Tyler. Him," I add, jabbing my finger toward Tyler in a final attempt at making myself clear. "You know, my stepbrother?"

Finally, Mom slowly parts her lips. She and Jack exchange a look. I'm waiting for her to explode, to demand an explanation for my irrational feelings, but instead, she playfully pushes Jack's shoulder. "You owe me seventy bucks!"

Jack groans, but he's laughing as Mom's lips curve into a smile, and all I can do is rapidly blink back at them. Now I'm the one waiting for an answer. Even Tyler rubs his jaw from beside me, attempting to understand why the people sitting across from us are laughing. *Laughing*. Perhaps Mom thinks I'm kidding. Maybe she thinks this is all a joke.

I remove my hand from Tyler's, shaking my head in confusion. "Mom?"

Her gaze shifts from Jack back to me, and her small laugh subsides, but her smile remains. As she sighs, her shoulders relax. "We made a bet," she admits. "Fifty bucks that there was something going on between you guys," she continues, nodding to Tyler and me, "and another twenty bucks if you told us about it."

"What?" I breathe in disbelief. Even Tyler laughs now, but I still don't understand. I'm not sure what's going on. I don't get why I'm not being yelled at.

"Eden, please," Mom says, rolling her eyes as she leans down to scratch behind Gucci's ears. "I'm your mother. I notice everything about you, especially the way you look at him," she murmurs, glancing up from the dog for a second to grin at Tyler. "I always thought it was similar to the way you look at Dean." Immediately, she pauses and sits back up. Her smile falters and once again her forehead creases with concern as a new thought occurs to her. "Eden . . . What about Dean?"

My chest tightens at the mere mention of his name. I'm still drowning in guilt. I've been trying not to think about Dean too much, but it's difficult. It's hard to ignore the fact that I hurt him. Bile rises in my throat, but I swallow hard and blow out some air. "He knows," I murmur quietly, unable to meet my mom's eyes. "It's over. He hates us."

"Oh, Eden," Mom says, her lips pursing in sympathy. She must see the way my expression shifts and she must surely notice the way Tyler rubs my thigh as though to make me feel slightly better, because she frowns at the two of us before she says, "I'm sorry about Dean. He was a nice kid." Her words only make me want to burst into tears, and she must notice, because she quickly attempts to lighten the mood by asking, "So from now on whenever I see Liz at the grocery store, do I have to give her the my-kid-broke-your-kid's-heart smile? Or would you rather I kept my head down and kept walking?"

"Mom," I say sternly. "Be serious right now. You really don't care?" Just to be clear again, I motion between Tyler and me.

"Of course, it's not ideal," Mom admits, "but know that if you go ahead with this, I doubt it'll be easy. You're going to get people who won't like it. You're going to get people who won't support you. But when it comes to me, I don't mind. Who can blame you?" She throws a dazzling grin in Tyler's direction, her eyes sparkling as she gives me an understanding nod. It's almost horrifying, in fact, given that she's, like, forty.

"Mom!" I gasp, mortified. When I look at Tyler, he's blushing a little sheepishly as he laughs under his breath. And as though to validate my mother's point, I notice that his eyes have begun to smolder. It wouldn't even surprise me if he's doing it on purpose. That's just Tyler.

Jack pats Mom's thigh quickly and gets to his feet, playfully shaking his head in disapproval. "I don't know about you guys, but I definitely need some coffee. And Karen? Stay away from the teenagers." Winking at her, he moves around the couch and heads over to the kitchen. Gucci gets up and follows.

Mom rolls her eyes at Jack and then leans back against the couch, crossing one leg over the other. "So I take it you haven't told your father and Ella?"

"Not yet," Tyler answers for me, shifting his body to the edge of the couch and leaning forward slightly. He clears his throat after having been silent for a long while. "That's what we're doing next."

"You guys are brave," Mom says as the coffee machine churns to life in the background. "Good luck."

"We'll need it," I say, smiling. Pushing Tyler's hand off my leg, I get to my feet and reach for my mom's hands, pulling her up from the couch and drawing her tightly into my arms. Acceptance. Again. I don't think I'll ever be able to get over how great it feels. "Thanks, Mom. Honestly. Thank you," I whisper, burying my face into her shoulder as I hug her close against me.

"Hey, I'm okay with anything you decide as long as it makes you happy," she tells me. As she pulls away from me and steps back, I think she's just about to smile, but then her expression falters. She grasps my wrist, examining the scabbing words on my skin. "What the hell is this?"

I smile wide and pull my wrist away from her. Quickly, I spin around and reach for Tyler, sliding my hand into his and yanking him up from the couch. I think I almost dislocate his shoulder in the process. "Sorry, Mom, gotta go!" I call, pulling Tyler toward the front door. I let go of him, rushing into the kitchen to grab my car keys from the key holder on the wall, almost tripping over Gucci at the exact same time. Jack raises his eyebrows at me, but I shrug and dash back over to Tyler, who's grabbing his bag from the floor.

"Eden!" Mom yells, but I'm already over the threshold.

"Your kid is way too reckless!" Tyler calls back into the house, wholeheartedly laughing as he pulls the front door shut behind us. He's still laughing as he jogs to catch up with me, his lips moist and his eyes soft. Neither of us expected the past five minutes to go down the way they just did. Neither of us expected it to be so easy.

"Next up," I say, my voice mocking that of a TV commentator, "we have the ultimate showdown." Unlocking my car, I run around to the driver's side and slip inside, starting up the engine. It feels a little odd being behind the wheel of my car again.

Tyler throws his bag onto the backseat before he jumps into the passenger seat, a lopsided smile playing on his lips.

"Just think," he says as he pulls the door shut behind him, "this is the final time we ever have to do this."

"That's why I can't wait," I tell him, because he's exactly right. After we tell our parents, we're done with having to tell the truth. Everyone that matters will know. No more secrets. Even the thought of this is enough to make me grin as I maneuver my way into the road, beginning the short ride to our parents' house. "By the way," I add, "this time all the talking is on you."

Tyler laughs again, leaning back in the seat as he places his hand on my thigh. I think he does it without even thinking about it, but on my end it's awfully distracting. "No problem," he says. "It's your dad I'm worried about most. He hates me enough as it is. Wait until he hears I've been sleeping with his daughter." Scoffing, he squeezes my thigh tighter, and I quite literally almost crash into a parked car.

"Yeah, do me a favor and don't mention that to him," I murmur, throwing Tyler a sideways warning glance as I regain control of the vehicle. He's smirking, though, and so am I. We both know my dad would kill him if he were to find out. Dad was never happy with the fact that sometimes I'd spend the night at Dean's, and he *liked* Dean.

"So how'd you like me to word it?" Tyler asks, angling his body to face me as I drive. He's got a stupid expression on his face, almost giddy in a way, and he dramatically clears his throat and uses his free hand to sync movements to his words. "*Mr. Munro, may I take a second out of your holy time to inform you that I totally have the hots for your one and only daughter, who, by the way, is no longer a minor and can make her own decisions,*" he says, his voice mockingly solemn as he adopts a sophisticated tone. "*Also, David Munro, your stubborn and persistent and intelligent and gorgeous daughter has an incredible ass."*

I pull around the corner onto Deidre Avenue, rolling my eyes at Tyler. He's on the verge of bursting into laughter, but he's biting it back. "Well?" he urges. "You think he'd like that?"

"Let's not take that route either," I say. Tyler finally gives up on the joke, letting out the laugh he's been suppressing, and I can't help but think about how nice this feels. The two of us laughing right now, of all times. I like that we can make the situation seem humorous, even when it's far from it, and I like that we're only minutes from the house, yet I don't feel nervous at all.

Only seconds later, we pass Dean's house. It's impossible to ignore the way the atmosphere in the car immediately thickens. Both Tyler and I glance over at the house at the exact same time, our eyes never leaving it as we drive past. Dean's car is parked on the drive. So is his dad's truck. The one Dean and I once wrecked the tires of. As though Tyler feels guilty, he takes his hand off my thigh.

"You think he's in there right now?" he asks, voice quiet.

"I don't know," I say.

Swallowing hard, I shift my eyes back to the avenue ahead and keep driving, pressing my foot down on the accelerator even harder so that I can get away from Dean's house faster. I refrain from looking back in my rearview mirror. I only keep on driving. From now on, I'll start tracing a different route between my mom's place and my dad's place. A route that bypasses Dean's house entirely.

It's after nine by now and the sky is continuing to darken, but our house is well lit as I pull up behind Tyler's car out on the sidewalk. Dad's Lexus and Ella's Range Rover occupy the drive, the same way they always do, forcing us kids to use the road. Jamie's car is missing, of course, because of that dented bumper he mentioned.

"I'm guessing they're home?" I joke, nodding through the windshield toward the house. Every single light possible must be switched on, and the entire place looks like a giant light bulb. Even the light in the room I sleep in when I stay over is on, which stresses me out for a split second as I wonder why the hell that is.

"Hey, I'm just glad my baby got here in one piece," Tyler says. He points to his Audi, smiling with satisfaction as he pushes open my car door and steps out. Grabbing his bag from the backseat, he heads off without me to circle his vehicle, probably searching for any suspicious scratches that might have resulted from lousy handling as it was shipped from one coast to the other.

Sighing, I cut the engine and slide out of my car, which looks like a piece of junk next to Tyler's, and then glance between the house and my stepbrother. Now I'm starting to feel a little nervous. "So are you coming?"

"Uh-huh," Tyler says, a little spaced out. Sliding the strap of his duffel bag over his shoulder for what feels like the hundredth time today, he pats the hood of his beloved car and then walks over to join me on the lawn. Slowly, his lips quirk up into a small smile, and at the exact same time, we both turn to face the house.

Side by side, we're about to face our biggest fear after two years. It's been a long ride, one that's been rough from the moment it began, but it's a relief to know that it's finally all about to be over. Our parents always needed to find out eventually. It's taken us two years to accept the truth and build up the courage to admit it to those who matter most, and now that the final hurdle is right in front of us, it's impossible to back out now.

Exhaling from beside me, Tyler's hand finds mine and tightly he interlocks our fingers. We exchange a sideways glance. Both of us are smiling.

"Let's do this," he says.

31

As always, the house smells like lavender. It's Ella's trademark. When you've been gone for a while, it always seems to be more noticeable when you return. As Tyler and I edge into the hall, we linger by the bottom of the staircase. We glance into the living room, but there's no one there despite the fact that the TV is on.

Tyler drops his bag onto the stairs, relaxing his shoulders before he clears his throat and yells, "We're home!"

For a few seconds, we wait. There's some commotion as Ella comes rushing through from the kitchen at the exact same time as we hear footsteps upstairs, but Ella is the first to reach us. She's in tears before she's even said a word, a huge smile on her face as she grasps Tyler in her arms and pulls him against her. He's much taller than her, but she rests her hands on his hair as he hugs her back. I watch them with a small smile on my lips, a smile that's both sad and content. Ella and Tyler have always had a close bond, and I know first-hand just how much she's missed her son over the past year. All the time, she would talk about him. Mention how proud she was. Ask if calling him five times in one day was too much. Dad would often roll his eyes and leave the room. I'd always stay. I'd always tell her that I missed Tyler too.

Ella takes a step back, cupping Tyler's jaw in her hands as she gazes up at him with undying love and affection. "You're really here!" Almost bubbling with joy as the tears continue to escape her eyes, she smothers his face in kisses.

"Mom, c'mon." Tyler says as he turns his head to the side. Reaching for her wrists, he moves her hands from his face and lets out a laugh. "Gross."

Ella sniffs, her smile sheepish as she wipes away her tears with her thumb. She's just about to part her lips to say something else at the exact same time as Chase comes through from the kitchen, but Tyler doesn't even get a single second to acknowledge his brother, because suddenly our attention is drawn to the pounding on the staircase.

Dad is definitely not thrilled to see us. He comes storming down the stairs, his eyes narrowed and his cheeks a flaming red. Before he even reaches the bottom, he's already growling, "Is it true?" He's not looking at Ella. He's not looking at Chase. He's looking at Tyler and he's looking at me.

It's perfectly clear what my dad is referring to. We both know it. My entire body deflates; my heart sinks in my chest. I can't bring myself to answer, and neither can Tyler. We're too taken aback by Dad's question to even react.

"Dave . . ." Ella murmurs, stepping forward and turning to face her husband. Her expression is perplexed, her eyebrows knitting together. "What are you talking about?"

A figure moves at the top of the staircase, which immediately catches my eye. I glance up, looking past Dad, to find Jamie. He's hovering on the landing with his lips pressed into a firm line and his arms folded across his chest as he watches the scene unfold. It's not difficult to make sense of the situation, to know that Jamie simply couldn't keep quiet until we got here, even when Tyler made it clear that we wanted to tell our parents on our own. Telling them ourselves would have been the right thing to do. Jamie being the one to break the news to Dad is quite literally the worst thing that could have happened. It makes it seem like we weren't planning on telling him and Ella the truth in the first place.

Tyler must notice Jamie too, because he lunges toward the stairs with his hands balled into fists, muttering something under his breath that I don't quite catch. Without a second of hesitation, however, Dad blocks him from going any further by grabbing his shirt and pushing him back across the hall. He slams Tyler against the wall, pressing his arm firmly across his chest as he holds him there. Ella sucks in a horrified gasp at the exact same time as she jumps forward, attempting to shove Dad off Tyler by pushing at his shoulder, but he's too strong for her and doesn't even budge.

"Is it true?" Dad yells again, his face only inches from Tyler's as he leans harder against his chest. There's suddenly a waft of booze in the air too, and I squint at my dad suspiciously when I realize it's coming from him.

Ella takes a cautious step toward him and Tyler. Her eyes slowly widen as she quietly asks, "Is what true?"

"The two of them!" Dad almost chokes on his words, so wrapped up in fury and disbelief that he can hardly string his sentences together. His voice is still loud and coarse, though, and he manages to give a clipped nod in my direction. "Him and Eden! God, I—I don't even know what to think!"

Tyler finally pushes Dad away from him with one firm shove, immediately straightening up. The veins in his neck stand out as he mutters, "Let us fucking explain."

Ella still doesn't understand what's going on. She glances

around Dad, Tyler and me for a few moments as though she's searching our expressions for answers. Dad's breathing heavily, both hands pressed to his temples as he shakes his head at the floor, trying to comprehend this new information. And so she turns to Tyler instead, her features twisting with worry the same way my mom's did. I can only imagine what's running through her mind right now. "Explain what, Tyler?"

Tyler runs a hand back through his hair as he looks at her, taking a second to think of the right words to say. Dad's glanced up again to glare at him as he waits to hear what the explanation will be, and his breathing is so loud that the only sound we can all hear right now is that and the TV. But Tyler doesn't even look at my dad. He only keeps on looking straight at Ella and occasionally at Chase, who doesn't really know what's going on but is listening anyway. And after a while, Tyler finally drops his eyes to the floor and exhales, ready to talk for us both. "None of this was supposed to happen," he says quietly, never looking up, "but all of it did. I can't feel bad about it and I can't feel sorry about it, because I'm not. It's just the way things have turned out, and honestly, it's not our fault. If it's anyone's, it's yours." He tilts his face up now, glancing between Ella and my dad. He swallows hard. "It's your fault for putting us together in the first place."

Dad immediately scoffs, placing his hands on his hips as he turns to face the opposite direction, still shaking his head. Ella, however, only blinks. She looks more perplexed than she did a few seconds ago.

"What are you talking about?" she asks.

"I'm talking about Eden," Tyler says without a moment's pause. He glances over his shoulder at me, locking his eyes with mine. They soften briefly, and he nods, so I edge forward, joining him by his side. I'm so thankful that he's doing all the talking. I can hardly even look Dad and Ella in the eye, let alone come clean to them. Tyler, on the other hand, keeps on going now that he's gotten started. "I'm talking about the fact that I'm in love with her. Have been for two years. So sure, Dave, it's true."

Ella's jaw falls open slightly and she barely manages to whisper, "What?" as she blinks fast and rapidly.

"This is disgraceful! You're making a mockery out of this family! Is that what you want to do? Make us all look like fools? God, can you imagine the laughter if this ever gets out!" Dad spits, turning back around to face us all. The wrinkles around his eyes seem even more noticeable right now, perhaps with how narrowed his glower has become. And as though he can no longer bear the sight of us, he begins to walk away, muttering, "You disgust me." It's to me, of course, and as he storms by, he shoulders me out of the way.

Suddenly Tyler jolts from beside me, taking a step forward and hurling his clenched fist through the air. It hits the exact center of my dad's cheek with a sickening thud. Dad instantly spirals to one side, his body falling against the stairs as he lands in a sprawling heap.

"Tyler!" Ella yells, jumping forward. She doesn't go to her son, though. She goes to Dad, bending down to check if he's okay, rubbing softly at his face.

At the exact same time, I turn to Tyler. I throw my hands up in exasperation at him, wondering what the hell he's playing at. His chest is rising and falling rapidly as he breathes and his eyes are still set on my dad, so as a precaution I grab his fist. Just in case.

Jamie has descended a few steps toward Dad while trying

his best not to make eye contact with Tyler and me. His cheeks are rather flushed by now and maybe he's feeling too guilty to get involved, because he just lingers in the background, observing but not helping. Even Chase decides to stay out of the situation. He backs slowly away toward the kitchen, watching from afar.

"Hey, Eden," Dad mutters in contempt, drawing my attention to him as he rises to his feet again, his eyes fierce, "even if Tyler wasn't your damn stepbrother . . . is this the kinda guy you wanna be with, huh?" He points to his cheek and then nods toward Tyler. "Some out-of-control kid who's gonna end up in a cell just like his father?"

"David!" Ella gasps.

Dad's words are so cruel that I momentarily feel sick at the fact that he thought it was okay to say such a thing, no matter how furious he is. It's enough to cause me to become enraged myself, and I grind my teeth together so hard that I fear my entire mouth might just shatter. When I force myself to glance sideways at Tyler, I can see the pain and devastation in his eyes, and he reacts to Dad's words the only way he knows how: with anger and violence, the way he was raised. The muscle in his jaw is twitching and his fist is clenching even harder beneath my hand, so I let go. Dad deserves it.

Tyler throws another punch without hesitation. Of course he does. This time, I can't blame him. In fact, I even feel rather satisfied when his fist catches Dad's nose. Dad only falls back a step or two this time, managing to keep his balance as he reaches up to touch his face, checking for blood. There is none, but he still raises his eyebrows and manages to smile in disbelief.

"Look at this!" Dad bellows. "Assaulted twice within a minute! God, Eden, your life choices are fantastic! First you choose some bullshit school halfway across the country and now you choose this asshole! Your stepbrother!" He starts to laugh, his entire demeanor vicious as he leans against the wall.

Tyler steps toward him again, ready to throw another punch. "Look who's talking."

Honestly, I think I could swing at Dad too by now. Ever since he walked out on Mom and me, my relationship with him has been strained. Maybe it's the fact I didn't see him for three years. Maybe it's the fact he didn't *want* to see me for three years. Something changed when he left, and ever since then it's been hard, but it's been stable for a while. We've been trying to get along and it's been working, until now. He's never been so nasty before, never so harsh. I'm trying my best to keep my temper cool, but it's hard not to explode. There are a million things I could yell back at him, but before either Tyler or I can do anything stupid, Ella comes running through from the kitchen. I didn't even notice her disappear, but she's suddenly in front of us again, pushing both Tyler and I backward and away from Dad.

"Look, get out of here," she says quickly in a low voice, forcing Tyler's car keys into his palm and squeezing his hand closed around them. "I don't know what to think right now and I'm sorry about him." She throws a glance over her shoulder toward Dad. He's still laughing, but now Jamie is attempting to shut him up, and when Ella turns back to face us, she's frowning. "He's got the rest of the week off work, so he's had a few drinks and . . . Look, you two, I'm really sorry. We need to really talk about what's going on between you both, but right now you need to leave."

"Don't be mad at us," I whisper, swallowing hard. "Please don't."

Ella releases a heavy sigh, glancing back to check on Dad again. Her frown deepens. "Just let me think about it. Now go." Gently, she pats Tyler's cheek. "And fix up that hand."

Both Tyler and I glance down at the exact same time. I don't think he's even noticed until now, but he's busted open two knuckles on his right hand, and he's bleeding. He sighs, shaking his hand and glancing back up. I try to meet his eyes, but he refuses to look at me. Instead, he reaches for his bag, which has been knocked onto the floor, at the same time as Ella returns to Dad, helping Jamie to calm him down. Chase is still hiding in the kitchen.

Tyler doesn't say a word as he turns back around for the door, only brushes his shoulder against mine as he walks past me, heading straight outside. I immediately spin around and follow close on his heels, jogging to keep up with his strides as he marches across the lawn toward his car.

"Tyler," I say. No reply. Just silence. "Tyler," I say again, reaching for his elbow. When he senses my touch, he finally stops walking and turns around to look at me.

"What the hell do we do now?" he asks, eyes dark. All the color in his face has completely drained and his expression is blank.

"You can stay at my mom's place," I say immediately. Mom won't mind. Mom likes Tyler, and given the circumstances, I'm sure she'll let him spend the night. "C'mon, follow me over."

"Okay," is all he says. He turns and walks the final few feet to his car as I study him, wondering if it's safe to let him drive. He looks slightly numb and spaced out, like he might just pass out any second, but he slides into his car nonetheless and starts the engine.

I drive my own car back to my mom's house, with Tyler trailing along behind me, and the entire time I wonder why I don't feel anything. I don't feel upset. Not angry. Not anymore, at least. Not frustrated. Not anything. In a way, the outcome is almost like I always expected it to be. Dad was never going to take the news well, sober or not, and Ella . . . I don't know about Ella. I can't quite figure out if she's repulsed or just shocked. Dad, however, is just an asshole, the same way he always has been. I'm used to it by now. Sometimes he's alright. Sometimes he's the guy he is tonight.

I don't know what's going to happen now. I don't know if by tomorrow everything will have calmed down again. All we need is a chance to explain ourselves, to make them understand, and that can only happen if Dad and Ella give us the time to do so. Tonight, they certainly didn't. Maybe once the initial anger and confusion and shock wears off, they'll hear us out. They have to. They don't have another choice. What else can they do? Kick us out of the family forever? Forbid us from being together?

I bypass Dean's house on the way home, tapping my fingers impatiently on the wheel as I drive in silence. I keep glancing in my rearview mirror to check that Tyler's still there. He is, of course, tailgating me to the point where I firmly believe that any second now he might just rear-end me. Both our cars make it back to my mom's place without a scratch, however, and I waste no time clambering out of my vehicle.

It's after ten by now, and I walk around to Tyler's car door and wait for him as he steps out. He still looks as pale as he did when he first got in and his hand seems to have gotten worse.

"I'd say sorry for hitting your dad," he says quietly as he reaches back into the car for his bag, "but I'm not." Slamming the door shut, he turns and advances along the footpath toward the front door. Again, he doesn't wait for me, and I'm starting to get the feeling that he's mad at me.

"Did I do something wrong?" I ask once I catch up to him again. I fall into place directly opposite him as we pause by the door for a second before heading inside.

"No," he says. As he glances out onto the street, he sighs and presses a hand to his forehead before his eyes meet mine again. "I'm sorry. Tonight has been a mess. I'm thinking about my dad and I'm thinking about Jamie and I'm thinking about my mom and I'm thinking about your dad and I'm thinking about you," he murmurs. Slowly, his lips pull up into a half-smile. "But mostly just you." He drops his gaze to his watch, and when he glances back up, he shrugs. "You know, it's after 1AM in New York. I don't know about you, but I'm exhausted."

I wasn't tired, but now that Tyler has brought it up, I suddenly feel my body sinking with fatigue. It feels like New York was forever ago, but the truth is we were still there this afternoon. So much has happened since then, with a six-hour flight in the middle of it all, and with the time difference thrown in too, I really do want nothing more right now than to just head straight to bed. So I say, "How about we deal with this in the morning?" to which Tyler nods, and we head inside.

Mom and Jack are watching some Lifetime movie on TV when we walk in, both of them sprawled out on the couch, wrapped up in each other's arms. Gucci's asleep on the floor, and although she does open her eyes to the sound of our entrance, she doesn't bother to get up and greet us. Mom and Jack, however, immediately pause the TV and pull themselves up into a seated position.

"You guys don't look all that relieved," Mom comments, furrowing her eyebrows. She's draped in her gown by this point, so she holds it closed with one hand as she gets to her feet. "Tyler, what are you doing back here?"

"It didn't go great," I admit, glancing sideways at Tyler as I shrug. He still seems quiet. "Dad was drunk, so he was a jerk and Ella told us to leave."

A huff of disapproval leaves Mom's lips as she shakes her head in rebuke, most likely at Dad, and she floats across the living room toward us. Quickly, she becomes sympathetic, smiling softly at us both. "I'm sure everything will be okay," she reassures us, her tone soothing. "Just give them some time to come to terms with it."

My head feels heavy, and I frown. "What if they don't?"

Mom thinks about my question for a short while, even glancing at Jack for help, but all he does is shrug, so all she can do is pull a face and shrug too. "I don't know what to tell you, Eden," she says.

"Can you clean up Tyler's hand?" I ask quickly, changing the subject. I'm kind of done with Dad and Ella right now. I'm too tired to deal with them, and Tyler's hand is still busted up, so I focus on that instead. Gently, I reach for his hand and hold it up for Mom to examine.

"God, what the hell did you do?" she blurts as her eyes flash up to meet Tyler's. Now he looks embarrassed.

"He hit Dad," I answer for him. "Twice."

"That's too bad for Dave," Mom murmurs, but she's suppressing a smile. "Tyler, come on over to the sink."

Mom only takes a few minutes to fix up Tyler's hand. In those minutes, however, Jack manages to offer Tyler a beer and I manage to awkwardly ask if Tyler can spend the night, and

Mom agrees. According to her, anyone who can throw a punch at Dad is more than welcome to stay. Tyler's thankful for the hospitality, although he does decline the beer. He's too tired.

"We're gonna get some sleep," I tell Mom as she tidies up in the kitchen while Tyler tightens and relaxes his hand repeatedly, as though the exercise will make the cuts disappear. "It's late in New York."

"Well, I hope you both feel a little better about everything in the morning," Mom says, angling her body to face me as she pulls me into a brief hug, and then both she and Jack wish us goodnight as they return to their movie.

I reach for Tyler's hand, interlocking our fingers as I pull him toward the hall. My room is the very first door, yet I've barely even touched the handle when I hear Mom clear her throat from behind us. I quickly let go of Tyler and turn around.

"I know I'm a super-cool mom and all, but I'm not *that* cool," she says, giving Tyler a pointed glance, her expression stern. "Tyler gets the guest room."

"No problem," Tyler says.

Rolling my eyes, I turn back and head straight down the hall. The guest room is the last room on the left and it's the one room in the house that's hardly ever used, so I lead Tyler over and then halt by the door. The lights in the hall are off too, so when I turn to face him, I end up looking at him through the faint darkness. I keep quiet for a moment while I allow my eyes to adjust, and when they do, I realize that Tyler's staring at the floor.

"Are you sure you're okay?" I ask, now growing more concerned than anything else. I try to force his gaze to meet mine, but it doesn't.

Instead, Tyler reaches for the door and pushes it open, walking past me and into the guest room without even glancing up. "I'll talk to you later," he says quietly.

"Hey," I say sharply, folding my arms across my chest as I follow him into the room and flick on the light. I stand and wait, pressing my lips into a firm line. "I asked you if you were okay."

Tyler sighs as he tilts his face down, his back still turned to me. He throws his bag onto the center of the bed and runs his hand through his hair, softly tugging on the ends before he turns his body to face mine. "I'm not gonna lie and tell you that I'm okay when I'm not," he finally says.

"Then talk to me." I take a few steps toward him, closing the distance between us, and I press a hand to his chest. I look up at him from beneath my eyelashes, feeling his heart beating slow and hard beneath my palm.

But Tyler clearly doesn't want to talk about it, because he carefully reaches for my wrist and moves my hand away as he takes a step back from me. "I said I'll talk to you later," he says with a firm edge to his voice, like he really means it and doesn't want me to push the matter any further. Spinning back around, he sits down on the edge of the bed and bends forward, interlocking his hands. "Can you shut the door on the way out?" he asks, his voice so low and so quiet that it's almost a whisper.

I'm not entirely sure what's up with Tyler right now, but he's making it pretty clear that he wants some space, so I bite my lip and force myself to leave, despite how much I'd rather stay. When I reach the door, I press my hand to the frame and glance back over my shoulder at him. He's sitting still, hardly blinking, just breathing.

"If you want, you can sneak over to my room any time after midnight," I whisper, but he doesn't even react, let alone respond, so I shut the door and leave him alone.

I don't know what time it is when I flinch awake and I don't know how long Tyler's been nudging me for, but I do know that it startles the hell out of me. I almost roll completely off my bed, so surprised by the intruder in my room that I suffer heart palpitations. Pushing back my comforter, I push my body up and lean over to my bedside table, fumbling around with the light switch in the darkness. Finally, I find it, and the corner of my room brightens up with a warm glow.

"Jesus Christ, Tyler," I mutter, exhaling as I tilt my head forward, pressing my hand across my forehead. I know I told him to try sneak across the hall, but I seem to have fallen into such a deep slumber that I totally forgot. I'm not used to being in my own room again and I'm certainly not used to having Tyler staying over. "Way to scare the hell out of me."

Tyler's standing by the side of my bed, but not too close, and as his sheer height towers over me his face is illuminated by the lamplight. It allows me to see the tightness in his jaw, the nervousness in his eyes and the lump in his throat. "I need to talk to you now," he tells me quietly.

"Really? You need to talk to me *now*?" Holding my comforter tight against my chest, I reach for my phone on my bedside table with my free hand and check the time. It's just after 4AM, so I groan and lean back against my pillows, rolling my eyes in irritation. That's when I realize that Tyler's still fully dressed, only now he's pulled on a jacket. I get the feeling he's not here to slip into bed alongside me, so I quickly sit forward again. "Tyler?"

Tyler chews on his lower lip rather anxiously as he rubs at the back of his neck. At the exact same time, he retreats away from me even further, moving toward the door. The light from the lamp on my bedside table doesn't quite stretch that far, so there's a shadow cast over his face that prevents me from seeing his expression as he says, "I need to get out of this city."

At first, I don't understand. His words don't make sense and they come so out of nowhere that I don't reply to begin with. I listen to the silence of the house instead, blinking at Tyler's silhouette by the door. "What do you mean?" I finally bring myself to ask.

"I mean that I'm gonna leave for a while," Tyler says.

My stomach twists, suddenly knotted. Now I'm wide awake and Tyler has my full attention. A shiver even surges down my spine as every inch of my body tells me that none of this is good. "Why?"

Tyler releases a slow, deep sigh. He walks back around to the side of my bed, back into the light, and his shadow flits across the walls. "There's too much going on right now," he admits, "and I need to figure things out." Leaning back against my wall, he pauses for a second to string together his next few sentences, deeply thinking about the right words to say and the right things to tell me. The entire time, my body is growing stiff.

"You know, I don't want to be anywhere near my dad. I can't cope with it, and I don't think I can handle your dad, either, because I might just end up beating the hell out of both of them." Another pause. Now my body is starting to feel cold, even though I'm under the comforter. Worry crosses Tyler's face and his voice drops to a whisper as he asks, "What if your dad's right? What if I do end up like mine?"

"You're nothing like your dad, Tyler."

"But I am," he argues, his jaw tightening. "My temper snaps just as fast as his used to, and that's what scares the hell out of me. I want out of this city and as far away from him as I can get."

"Come to Chicago with me," I blurt immediately. It's the first thought that hits me, and it's not a bad idea. I'm leaving in the fall, packing up and heading halfway across the country to settle down in the Windy City. And I realize then that I haven't once thought about what would happen in September when I left. I never considered the fact that Tyler and I would be separated by distance again, so suddenly the idea of Tyler coming with me to Illinois is the only thing I'm rooting for. Kind of like running away together. Kind of.

But my new plan for us both is quickly shot down, because Tyler simply says, "No."

"Why?" I ask, both dismayed and confused. My moment of excitement comes to an end. So much for Chicago.

Tyler closes his eyes for a second and tilts his face down to my carpet, leaning against the wall. He still looks tired, and I'm starting to wonder if he's even slept at all. The longer he takes to reply to me, the more nervous I grow, and it turns out I have every right to be anxious, because when he glances back up at me, his expression has contorted, twisting with hurt as he whispers, "Because I don't really want to be near you either."

I want to have misheard. I *need* to have misheard, because the moment the final word escapes his lips, Tyler's lips, everything inside of me shifts. My stomach tightens even more than it already has and my voice catches in my throat, taken aback by his words. "What are you talking about?" I force myself to ask, my voice feeble.

"Maybe you were right before," he says without hesitation, talking fast as he shakes his head. "Maybe we shouldn't be together."

"Where the hell is this coming from?" I demand, anger rushing through every single inch of my being as I push back my comforter and swing out of my bed, straightening up on my feet. I'm really praying that I'm dreaming right now. I have to be. Tyler would never say that.

Tyler quickly flinches away from me as I approach, pivoting around me and walking back toward the door again. As his back is turned to me, his rasping voice dares to tell me, "I don't know if I want to do this anymore."

And right then, everything inside of me shatters. My heart stands still. My lungs collapse. My blood thins. My throat hurts. Everything, absolutely everything, suddenly hurts. From the way my head suddenly feels way too heavy to the way my knees slowly buckle beneath me, I have to press a hand to the wall to stabilize myself. My breathing has quickened, and I'm almost hyperventilating as I try to understand what's going on. "You didn't just say that," I croak.

"I'm sorry," Tyler blurts quickly, spinning around to look at me. His eyes are dull, far from furious, looking more damaged than anything else, yet his apology doesn't sound sincere at all. He doesn't sound sorry. "Look, I gotta go." He pulls out his car keys from the pocket of his jeans and reaches for the door.

Although I feel paralyzed, I force my legs to move and I rush over to him, sliding my body between his and the door. I press my back against the wood, pushing it closed as I block his only exit. "No! You don't get to just walk out like this!" I yell, exasperated with the abruptness of the situation and the reasoning behind it. At the moment, Tyler hasn't given me a reason for his sudden change of mind, and it's making this all hurt even more than it would if he was just honest with me. "What happened to this, huh?" Pushing Tyler a step back from me, I throw up my arm and force my wrist toward his face, my hand clenched so tight that my veins are visible beneath my tattoo. "You said as long as I didn't give up, you wouldn't either!" I don't care if I wake Mom and Jack. Right now, they're the last thing on my mind. "And I haven't given up, so why the hell have you?"

Tyler pinches the bridge of his nose with his thumb and his forefinger, closing his eyes and refusing to look at his very own words, the words that are etched upon my skin. It's clear now that he no longer believes in them, and it's even clearer that I'm an idiot for believing that he did. As I drop my hand back down, my chest heaves, and I think I might just hurl, so I clasp a hand over my mouth. I shouldn't, though, because Tyler sees it as a prime opportunity to grasp my shoulders and quickly move me to the side. That's exactly what he does, finally throwing open the door and making his lame departure.

But we appear to have woken Gucci, because she's sitting out in the hall on the other side of my door, her eyes glistening, and Tyler promptly trips straight over her as though he hasn't even noticed that she's there. Gucci lets out a sharp cry, darting away.

"Tyler!"

"Fuck," Tyler mutters, steadying himself. He pauses in the darkness of the hall, frowning, and then heads toward the living room. Of course, I rush after him, racking my mind for something, anything, I could say to him that might make him stay or at least reconsider what he's doing. As he grabs his bag from the couch, I say the only words I can think of.

"Please, please, please," I beg, my throat so dry that it's starting to hurt when I talk. I step in front of him again, but it's hard to get him to meet my eyes, and so I press my hands to his chest instead. "Please don't. You're just upset about everything that's happened, so you're being irrational. That's all this is, Tyler," I whisper as tears threaten to fall, my voice cracking. "You don't even have a real reason for why you're leaving like this. If you really want to get out of Santa Monica, then just come to Chicago with me. And don't repeat yourself by saying you don't want to be with me anymore, because I don't believe you. How can everything be going great—I mean, we finally *told* everyone, Tyler! The hard part is over!—and then you suddenly decide *this*?"

Tyler has closed his eyes again, because it seems to be the easiest way for him to avoid looking at me. I don't think he's been able to look me straight in the eye since the moment he woke me up. Parting his lips, he exhales. And then he slowly shakes his head. That's all. No reply. No further explanation. Just the weak shake of his head that makes it clear that no matter what I say, he's still going to leave.

Reaching for my hands on his chest, he squeezes them tight and lowers them back to my sides, and I'm trying so hard not to cry that I can't even bring myself to attempt to stop him. That's why when he turns and walks through the dark living room toward the front door, I don't do anything. I don't go after him. I don't even turn around. I only stare at the wall, my lips trembling as the tears break free anyway. I touch my throat and swallow hard, fighting back the urge to sniff. I don't want Tyler to hear me crying, but when I hear him unlock the front door, one final wave of anger washes over me, so I'm forced to turn around.

"So we pissed off our parents for *nothing*? We hurt Dean for *nothing*?" I yell, grinding my teeth together as my cheeks dampen. Tyler pauses to listen. "All because you're wimping out at the last second?"

"I'm not," Tyler objects, finally deciding to talk again. He glances over his shoulder at me, his eyes pooling with an emotion I can't quite figure out. "I just need space for a while. I'll come back when I'm ready."

"But I love you," I whisper, not because I think it'll change his mind, but because I want him to remember that when he walks out the door.

"And I need *you*," Tyler breathes. It takes me by surprise, given the circumstances. It contradicts the fact that he's claiming he doesn't want to do this anymore, that he's giving up. "And that's the problem, Eden. The only reason I didn't kick my dad's ass earlier was because of you. Not because I knew the right thing to do was to walk away. And you know, when I was trying to get off coke, I was doing it for you and not because I had to do it to get on the tour. It's like I need you in order to be okay, and I can't live my life depending on you like that. I need to be able to *want* to do the right thing, to do it for myself and not for you, so I need some space without you for a while. I need to know that I won't be like my dad, and as soon as I know that, I'll come back." His eyes are swollen, like he's fighting back tears, and the only thing he can finish with is a pained whisper of, "I promise."

Without explaining himself any further, he rests his head on the door frame, takes a deep breath, and then leaves. Just like that. He opens up my front door, throws me a gut-wrenching final glance, and walks out. He lets the door fall shut on its own behind him, and when I hear that awful click, it hits me even harder at that exact moment that Tyler just gave up. And I still don't really know why.

The house is dark and silent and even slightly cold, and numbly I remain in my spot in the middle of the living room. Through the cracks in the blinds, I see Tyler's car light up as his figure nears it. He slides into the driver's seat, and I hear the thud of his door as he slams it shut. Then his engine. My throat tightens when I hear it growl to life. *He's really leaving*, I think, *and there's nothing I can do to stop him.* His car pulls out onto the quiet road. And he drives away. He leaves.

My throat releases a pained whimper through my sobs as the car headlights race across the walls of the living room and then disappear. I feel so weak that I can no longer stand, so I reach around for the furniture to give myself a crutch as I move to the couch. I drop my body down onto it, pulling my legs up and holding them to my chest as I try to control my excessive trembling. I don't know what to think.

How long is Tyler going to take to find his own willpower and strength? How long is it going to take for him to control them both? A few days? Weeks? Months? What am I supposed to do in the meantime? Put my life on pause and wait for him? Unfortunately, that can't happen. Now I've got to face Dad and Ella on my own. I've got to deal with Dean on my own. I've got to handle Rachael and Tiffani on my own. Tyler has left me to deal with *our* mess all by myself. It was supposed to be us against the world, Tyler and me versus everyone else. Now it's just me.

Out of nowhere, I hear Gucci's paws on the hardwood flooring as she quietly pads over to me, still weeping a little from the pain Tyler accidentally inflicted upon her. She jumps up onto the couch, nudging my knee with her nose as though she's concerned. It only sends a new batch of tears cascading down my cheeks. Reaching for her body, I pull her close and wrap my arms around her, burying my face into her fur. *Don't worry,* I think, *he hurt me too.*

Acknowledgements

Thank you to my readers who've been with me since the start and watched this book grow. Thank you for making the writing process so enjoyable, and thank you for sticking with me for so long. Thanks to everyone at Black & White Publishing for believing in this book as much as I do. I'm forever grateful to Janne, for wishing to take over the world; Karyn, for all your comments and your expertise; and Laura, for always looking after me. Thanks to my family for their endless support and encouragement, especially my mum, Fenella, for always taking me to the library when I was younger so that I could fall in love with books; my dad, Stuart, for always encouraging me to be a writer; and finally my grandad, George West, for believing in me from day one. Thank you Heather Allen and Shannon Kinnear for listening to my ideas and allowing me to ramble on about this book, without ever telling me to be quiet, despite however much my excitement most likely drove you both insane. Thank you Neil Drysdale for helping me get to where I am. Thank you, thank you, thank you. And finally, thank you to Danica Proe, my teacher back when I was eleven, for being the first person to tell me that I wrote like a real author, and for making me realise that an author was exactly what I wanted to be.

